W9-BPK-204

DISCARDED

Cary Area Public Library
1606 Three Oaks Road
Cary, IL 60013

PRAISE FOR CHRIS FABRY

Under a Cloudless Sky

"*Under a Cloudless Sky* captivated me from page one. I cared immediately what happened to Ruby and Bean, and the stakes kept rising as tidbits of history were revealed, unraveling the mystery that held Ruby captive. A terrific reading experience!"

FRANCINE RIVERS, *NEW YORK TIMES* BESTSELLING AUTHOR

The Promise of Jesse Woods

"[In this] soul-searching novel of faith, friendship, and promises, Chris Fabry invigorates the small-town lives of three teens in 1970s West Virginia with his exquisite, lyrical writing. . . . A literary delight . . . this novel is worthy of a standing ovation."

SHELF AWARENESS

"This riveting, no-punches-pulled coming-of-age tale is reminiscent of Richard Bachman's (Stephen King) short story, 'The Body,' which was made into the movie *Stand by Me*."

BOOKLIST

Dogwood

"[*Dogwood*] is difficult to put down, what with Fabry's surprising plot resolution and themes of forgiveness, sacrificial love, and suffering."

PUBLISHERS WEEKLY

"Ultimately a story of love and forgiveness, [*Dogwood*] should appeal to a wide audience."

CBA RETAILERS+RESOURCES

"Solidly literary fiction with deep, flawed characters and beautiful prose, *Dogwood* also contains a mystery within the story that adds tension and a deepening plot."

NOVEL REVIEWS

June Bug

"[*June Bug*] is a stunning success, and readers will find themselves responding with enthusiastic inner applause."

PUBLISHERS WEEKLY

"An involving novel with enough plot twists and dramatic tension to keep readers turning the pages."

BOOKLIST

"I haven't read anything so riveting and unforgettable since *Redeeming Love* by Francine Rivers. . . . A remarkable love story, one that's filled with sacrifice, hope, and forgiveness!"

NOVEL REVIEWS

"Precise details of places and experiences immediately set you in the story, and the complex, likable characters give *June Bug* the enduring quality of a classic."

TITLETRAKK.COM

Almost Heaven

"[A] mesmerizing tale . . . [*Almost Heaven*] will surprise readers in the best possible way; plot twists unfold and unexpected character transformations occur throughout this tender story."

PUBLISHERS WEEKLY

"Fabry has a true gift for prose, and [*Almost Heaven*] is amazing. . . . You'll most definitely want to move this to the top of your 'to buy' list."

ROMANTIC TIMES, 4½-STAR TOP PICK REVIEW

"Fabry is a talented writer with a lilting flow to his words."

CROSSWALK.COM

Not in the Heart

"A story of hope, redemption, and sacrifice. . . . It's hard to imagine inspirational fiction done better than this."

WORLD MAGAZINE

"Christy Award–winning Fabry has written a nail-biter with plenty of twists and turns to keep readers riveted. Fans of Jerry B. Jenkins and Jodi Picoult might want to try this title."

LIBRARY JOURNAL

"A fine piece of storytelling. . . . Down to its final pages, *Not in the Heart* is a gripping read. While the mystery at its core is compelling, it's Wiley's inner conflict that's truly engrossing."

CROSSWALK.COM

"This absorbing novel should further boost Fabry's reputation as one of the most talented authors in Christian fiction."

CBA RETAILERS+RESOURCES

Borders of the Heart

"A thoroughly enjoyable read. . . . Chris Fabry is a masterful storyteller."

CBA RETAILERS+RESOURCES

"In this edge-of-your-seat romantic suspense, all of the characters ring true. . . ."

BOOKLIST, STARRED REVIEW

"Ups the ante for fans of Fabry's high-charged, emotionally driven fiction by adding a strong suspense thread."

TITLETRAKK.COM

Every Waking Moment

"Writing in his trademark lyrical style, Fabry spins a poignant tale about our society's invisible seniors and the woman and man who see their potential."

BOOKLIST

"Christy Award–winning novelist Fabry crafts a character-driven tale of dignity and compassion for those who seem to have lost importance to society and, for some, even to their own families. This thought-provoking read challenges the prevailing cultural calculations of the value of a person's life."

PUBLISHERS WEEKLY

"The skillfully woven plot twists, intermingled with humor, angst, and questions of faith, make *Every Waking Moment* a true page-turner."

HOMECOMING MAGAZINE

"*Every Waking Moment* has depth and beauty. I really don't think I could say enough good things about this novel. It's thrilling. It's poignant. It's touching. It's deep. It's beautiful. And it should be read."

JOSH OLDS, LIFE IS STORY

UNDER A CLOUDLESS SKY

Under a Cloudless Sky

CHRIS FABRY

Tyndale House Publishers, Inc.
Carol Stream, Illinois

DISCARDED

Cary Area Public Library
1606 Three Oaks Road
Cary, IL 60013

Visit Tyndale online at www.tyndale.com.

Visit Chris Fabry's website at www.chrisfabry.com.

TYNDALE and Tyndale's quill logo are registered trademarks of Tyndale House Publishers, Inc.

Under a Cloudless Sky

Copyright © 2017 by Chris Fabry. All rights reserved.

Cover photograph of church copyright © by Allison/Adobe Stock. All rights reserved.

Cover photograph of mountains copyright © by aheflin/Adobe Stock. All rights reserved.

Cover photograph of girl copyright © by Ratiu Bia/Unsplash.com. All rights reserved.

Author photograph by Cynthia Howe Photos, copyright © 2016. All rights reserved.

Designed by Jennifer Ghionzoli

Edited by Sarah Mason Rische

All Scripture quotations, unless otherwise indicated, are taken from the Holy Bible, *New International Version,*® *NIV.*® Copyright © 1973, 1978, 1984, 2011 by Biblica, Inc.® Used by permission. All rights reserved worldwide.

Scripture quotations in chapter 22 are taken from the *Holy Bible*, King James Version.

Under a Cloudless Sky is a work of fiction. Where real people, events, establishments, organizations, or locales appear, they are used fictitiously. All other elements of the novel are drawn from the author's imagination.

For information about special discounts for bulk purchases, please contact Tyndale House Publishers at csresponse@tyndale.com, or call 1-800-323-9400.

Library of Congress Cataloging-in-Publication Data

Names: Fabry, Chris, date- author.
Title: Under a cloudless sky / Chris Fabry.
Description: Carol Stream, Illinois : Tyndale House Publishers, Inc., [2017]
Identifiers: LCCN 2017030264| ISBN 9781496428288 (hardcover) | ISBN 9781414387789 (softcover)
Subjects: LCSH: Life change events—Fiction. | City and town life—Fiction. | Homecoming—Fiction. | GSAFD: Christian fiction.
Classification: LCC PS3556.A26 U53 2017 | DDC 813/.54—dc23 LC record available at https://lccn.loc.gov/2017030264

Printed in the United States of America

23   22   21   20   19   18   17
7   6   5   4   3   2   1

To my grandparents,

John & Elizabeth Muchy Fabry

— and —

Homer & Allie Runion Spurlock

I lift up my eyes to the mountains—

where does my help come from?

PSALM 121:1

Part 1

Ruby and Bean met in the summer of 1933 in a town called Beulah Mountain, in the southwestern coalfields of West Virginia, shortly before the massacre that has become a footnote in some history books. When people speak of that time, they talk of red and black. Blood was the price paid and coal was the prize. Miners' families were collateral damage in a war against the earth itself, a battle fought with pick and TNT.

There are a thousand places to begin the story. Ruby and Bean's first meeting . . . Bean's big regret . . . where her name came from . . . the shock when they discovered what was happening on the third floor of the company store. But there is another memory that floats to the surface and sits on the water like a katydid on a lily pad. The memory is wrapped in music and preaching and two friends tripping through the underbrush, hand in hand, giggling, and for a moment without a care in the world, the hurt and pain of life dismissed.

Ruby held on to Bean like a tight-eyed, newborn kitten, more afraid to let go than to hang on. She didn't know the hills like her friend, and the speed Bean gathered frightened Ruby. It is a grace to be able to hold on to someone who runs at life when you can only imagine walking.

"Slow down," Ruby said without a drawl, with a hint of northern refinement. To those in Beulah Mountain, Ruby sounded uppity, like she was putting on airs, and there were some in the congregation who questioned whether this daughter of a mine owner belonged in their church. Some thought she might be spying and trying to get information about the union rumors.

Ruby wore the dress her mother had picked from a catalog, a dress she only wore on Sundays and late at night when she couldn't sleep. This dress, other than the pictures and jewelry and sweet-smelling memorabilia she kept in a box on her dresser, was the last connection with her mother. The woman's voice was fading from memory, which troubled Ruby, though the fine contours of her mother's face and the rich brown hair and long eyelashes were still there when she closed her eyes.

Ruby's fingernails were finely trimmed and her hair shone in the sunlight as it bounced and wiggled in curls down her back. She wore pink ribbons that Mrs. Grigsby had positioned for her. Mrs. Grigsby, the wife of the company store proprietor, had been hired to watch Ruby and keep her from children who lived on the other side of the tracks, a task Mrs. Grigsby had failed at miserably. Like water and coal slurry, children will find their own worthy level and pool.

It is a fine thing to see two hearts beat as one. And the hearts of Ruby and Bean did that. Their friendship raised eyebrows at the beginning, of course, but in the summer of 1933, as the church bell rang, Bean pulled Ruby a little harder and their shoes slid down the bank through the ferns and rhododendrons and saplings and onto the path that led toward the white church with the people streaming in from all sides of the mountain.

"I swear," Bean said, "this church is the most excitement I have all week. It's the only reason to stay in this town."

"You'll be here until the day you die, Bean, and you know it," Ruby said.

"Will not," Bean said. "I'm going to see the world. And take my mama with me. These hills can't hold me."

"Slow down!"

Bean's shoes were held together with sea-grass string and prayer. Her fingernails were bit to the quick and dirty from gathering coal for the cookstove and plucking chickens and digging worms for fishing. Bean—given name Beatrice—was lean and tall for a twelve-year-old, and she had seen more than her share of pain. She had helped bury two brothers and a sister who had never given so much as a single cry. She had held her mother's hand and comforted her when her father wasn't around.

"Don't never run for the doctor again," her mother had said after the last stillborn child. "You've got to promise me."

"Why, Mama?"

"That man don't care a whit for people like us," she said. "He just makes it harder. Next time I'm sick, don't you get him. You hear?"

Bean had promised but didn't understand the ramifications of such a thing and the turmoil it might bring.

Ruby was older than Bean, but not much. Bean was a lot stronger and tougher and her exterior was as rough as a cob (she ran barefoot most days). There could not be two girls on the planet who were from more different families, and yet, here they were.

"Hold up," Bean said when they reached the edge of the woods.

Ruby was out of breath and welcomed the pause. "What is it?"

"Look there."

Ruby saw movement and peered through the underbrush at an animal. Elegant. Stately. When its head passed a wide tree, she saw it was a deer.

"Ain't it beautiful?" Bean said.

"Will he hurt us?" Ruby whispered.

"It's a she and she probably has young ones. I'm glad my daddy isn't here or he'd shoot her quick as look at her. We'd have venison for dinner but the view here wouldn't be half as pretty."

The deer stopped and looked straight at Ruby and Bean.

"Stay real still," Bean whispered. "Deer know things people don't."

"What do you mean?" Ruby said. When she turned her head, the deer jumped and ran quickly into the brush.

Bean sighed. "They see things you and I can't. If I could have been born as anything else, I'd have chosen a deer."

Music from the old piano in the church lifted over the valley and Bean picked up her pace again. The heat and humidity of summer made the piano keys stick, but she recognized the introduction to her favorite hymn.

"Come on, we're going to miss 'Beulah,'" she said.

Though the church tried to keep the piano in tune, summer was hard on the instrument and winter was worse. Those occupying the pews sang louder each week to overcome the weathering effects on the Franklin upright. The piano's story was rich—Bean's father said it had been rescued and redeemed from a saloon in Matewan a few years prior, and before that it was used in a Chicago brothel that Al Capone had frequented and the bullet holes in the right side had been made by Bugs Moran. All of these stories seemed too wild for anyone but Ruby and Bean to believe, though neither knew what a "brothel" was. That a piano could be rescued and redeemed in a church felt like something God would do.

Benches creaked and snapped as the congregation stood, and nasal voices rose in unison as the girls neared the wooden steps. Bean let go of her friend's hand, grabbed the iron railing, and catapulted to the top and through the door where an older man with only a few teeth looked down. Sopranos strained to overcome the off-key male voices.

"Far away the noise of strife upon my ear is falling;
Then I know the sins of earth beset on every hand;
Doubt and fear and things of earth in vain to me are calling;
None of these shall move me from Beulah Land."

Bean rushed past women waving fans and men who had freshly shaved and washed away as much coal dust as they could. She found her mother in her usual spot and the woman drew her in with one arm as Ruby joined them, out of breath but smiling.

"I'm living on the mountain, underneath a cloudless sky,
I'm drinking at the fountain that never shall run dry;
Oh, yes! I'm feasting on the manna from a bountiful supply,
For I am dwelling in Beulah Land."

Not every church service began with this hymn, but at some point on either Sunday morning or Sunday evening, the congregation raised its voice in praise to the God who allowed them to live in Beulah Mountain and long for their heavenly home.

Ruby had never heard such singing before moving to Beulah Mountain. She had taken piano lessons early and could read music on the page, a feat that amazed Bean. But what happened when these people sang was more than just humans hitting notes. The music seemed to come from somewhere deep inside and when their voices united, it felt like goose bumps on the soul. Something like joy bubbled up from inside her and leaked through her eyes.

When they had sung the requisite number of choruses and verses, the pews creaked again from the weight of slight men and women and their children. There were soft coughs that would be termed *silicosis* in the years ahead, but for now it was simply a "coughing spell." Ruby burrowed herself under Bean's mother's arm and Bean did the same on the other side. Though it was hot and muggy, and the pregnant woman between them would have been more comfortable being left alone, she spread her wings like a mother hen.

The pastor was a thick man with thin hair slicked back. He looked like a miner who had moved toward ministry, but he talked with a wheeze and Ruby sat enraptured by his words and the readings from the King James Bible that lay open on the pulpit in front of him. His name was printed on the bulletin at the bottom, H. G. Brace, and Ruby thought it humble of him that his name was so low on the page.

The text this day was from the book of Exodus, about the plight of the Israelites enslaved by cruel Pharaoh and the Egyptians who used the Israelites for their own devices, having forgotten all that Joseph had done. Joseph had interpreted the dream of Pharaoh and had saved the Egyptians, but a new leader had arisen who either didn't know the story or didn't care. Pastor Brace reminded them that Joseph's brothers had meant to do him evil, but God brought good from it and could do the same in their lives.

There was a smattering of *amen*s in the room, followed by more crusty coughing. As the pastor continued, Ruby leaned forward and noticed a commotion coming through the open windows. There was noise down the railroad tracks. The pastor continued until they heard the audible voices of miners shouting for help.

Hollis Beasley grabbed his truck keys and headed for his F-150, which sat waiting outside like a faithful horse.

"Where you goin'?" Juniper said from the bedroom.

He paused, keys clinking. "To see if it's true. I want to hear it from Curtis."

"They got this thing called a phone. You just dial some numbers and you talk to the people on the other end. It saves gas and brake pads."

He wanted to say something snippy, but he thought better of it. He'd spend the whole day and half the week apologizing and the rest of his life regretting. Best to keep the trap shut.

"You need anything from the store?" he said.

"I thought you was going to see Curtis."

"I am. But if you need something, I'll go into town." There was an edge to his voice and he was sorry for it.

"I don't need anything. But you ought to leave that family alone. It's none of your business what they do."

"We had an agreement."

"You and me had an agreement a long time ago you didn't live up to." Juniper coughed and it sounded awful.

She said things like this when she was in pain and it hurt him, but it hurt more to bite back at her, so he bit his tongue—literally put it between his teeth and put pressure on it—and counted to ten like the preacher had said when they went to their one counseling session before they were married. Sometimes love looks like a bloody tongue, he guessed.

"I'll be back directly."

She muttered something as he grabbed the doorknob and he waited a minute to see if she'd mention cough drops or the little mints she liked. The kind in the green foil that came in a box. It was funny how her face could light up from a chocolate mint that cost next to nothing or a bag of those corn chips with the chili powder. When she didn't say more, he pulled the door closed but it didn't click. He needed to fix that, but he'd probably have to replace the whole doorjamb because the wood was old and couldn't hold a screw. And what good is a new door if you can't stay on the land under the house?

At the truck Hollis paused again to glance up the hill at the cemetery and the green vista beyond. In his mind he could lift himself straight off that mountain and look down on God's creation and let it take his breath away. Especially this time of year when every plant and tree turned from green to the brightest colors, preparing for winter. Preparing for death.

The view here was changing and even though he couldn't see the machinery, he could hear it across the ridge. And he could see the white scar in the earth a mile from there. A scar is supposed to heal and get smaller, but this one expanded and moved closer to Beulah Mountain and he wasn't sure there was any stopping it.

Years ago he would have prayed. He would have asked God for

wisdom or at least the restraint to not wring Curtis's neck. Now he just got in the truck and pushed the clutch and let it roll down the hill before he turned the key.

The dirt-and-gravel road wound around the mountain like red on a candy cane. There was hardly room in places for one vehicle, and Juniper complained that they were going to slide off the edge one day during a rainstorm. Maybe she was right. Maybe she'd be better off if he slid over the hill.

At the bottom of the driveway a rusty farm gate stood open. The gate and latch were attached to telephone poles sunk deep on either side. Hollis had sawn the fallen pole in two and used the pieces to flank the entrance, like a castle gate. Posted and Keep Out signs were nailed to the poles. Underneath were Keep Out and Trespassers Will Be Prosecuted signs.

Hollis hit the blacktop and the bumpy ride smoothed a bit until he came to the crumbling asphalt. With the onslaught of the new mining came a bevy of overweight trucks that tore up the roads. There is always a cost to progress.

He wound down the mountain toward the town and slowed when he saw the black mailbox with *Williams* painted in white. It leaned out toward the road like it was looking to pull into traffic. Hollis parked behind an El Camino that had been there since the Iranians took hostages. Grass grew over the back fender. He remembered when Curtis bought it and how proud he was to have the first half car–half truck in the county. It seemed like a good idea at the time, but then many things do.

The Williams house sat on the cusp of a hill that flooded each year in heavy rain. Hollis had grown up with Curtis. Rode the same school bus. They had loved the same girl in high school and both of their hearts had broken when she left the hollow. Her name was like a song heard in childhood, a tune you remembered but words you couldn't recall. Hollis hadn't heard from her again and he doubted he ever would. Just thinking of her smile made him feel guilty because it would hurt Juniper to know he was thinking of another woman, even if she was only a memory.

He rang the bell and heard whispers and creaking linoleum, then his name on the lips of Curtis's wife, Ruthanne. He knocked and called for Curtis and they finally opened the door.

"Hey, Hollis, how you doin'?" Curtis said, smiling at him through the screen. All three of them knew why Hollis was there, but there was a moment of silence, like the anticipation of a test that lay facedown on a desk.

"I got a phone call," Hollis said.

"So your phone still works up there?"

Hollis didn't smile. "Is it true?"

"Is what true?" Curtis said.

"The company made you an offer? That little . . ." Hollis didn't say the word he was thinking. "Buddy offered to buy you out?"

"Hollis, it ain't none of your business. I don't need your permission—"

"You're right. You don't need my permission to talk with anybody. But we had an agreement. That is my business."

Ruthanne appeared behind Curtis with arms folded. "We need the money. We can't pay the taxes. I'm surprised you can, with Juniper and all the doctor bills."

"You know why the taxes were raised. You know how CCE is in with the county. What they say goes. And Buddy wants to—"

"It don't make no difference why they was raised," Curtis said, looking at the floor. "We can't pay it. Nobody can. It only makes sense to sell while somebody's offering a fair price. If we don't take it, they'll get the land dirt cheap. Come on, Hollis, surely you can see that."

"This is exactly what he wants. He's worked his way up and now he's proving to the company he ought to be running the show. And you're helping him."

"He already runs the show. It's only a matter of time until he gets your part of Beulah Mountain."

"Maybe so, but they can't take the cemetery," Hollis said. "The government won't let him. They care more about the dead than the living. And I'm ready to put up a fight he'll never forget."

"I swear, Hollis, you'd still be bailing out the *Titanic* if you was on it," Ruthanne said.

Hollis stared hard at her, then at Curtis, and he saw it clearly. The conversations in the dead of night, pillow to pillow. The fear somebody like that pip-squeak Buddy Coleman could put in a man. The desire of a wife for stability. It was in a man to fight and it was in a woman to nest, and those desires competed and wore both down until they became one flesh.

He turned and saw the tire swing hanging limp from the L-shaped oak tree by the creek. A memory flashed of him and Curtis playing, back before the house was built. He saw his son playing with Curtis and Ruthanne's daughter right there at that same tree. The cookouts and laughter. The floods and all the people moving to higher ground. And the coal dust that settled on the leaves and windowpanes and in lungs.

"At some point you have to admit you're licked. Use the money. You could move Juniper into a nice place in Charleston, closer to the medical center."

Hollis took off his baseball cap and scratched the back of his head. "You know they'll level your house and doze the mountain and push it down here so it covers the creek and that old tree. Then they'll scrape out everything that's worth a dollar and load it up and throw out grass seed and call it good. Head to the next mountain."

Ruthanne turned and walked into the kitchen. Curtis stepped onto the porch and closed the screen door behind him, and Hollis felt like he could breathe, felt like he could just talk to his friend without the pressure of another.

"I'm sorry, Hollis. I didn't want to go back on my word. I had to make the hard choice. We have to at least salvage something." He shoved his hands in his pockets. "This is like the big flood. The water comes up and at some point you get to high ground and take what means most. Let the rest go."

Hollis drew a deep breath, remembering his own father's labored breathing from his years in the mines. That he could draw his lungs full and not cough was a blessing he didn't take for granted. "I know you got obligations. But I thought we agreed."

"We did. Until it got clear we ain't never keeping this land. And even if we did, there's nothing left here."

Hollis leaned against the porch railing. "I seen this man on TV the other day talking about how people give up too quick. It was one of them PBS things where they ask for money. He was saying that most people who really want something give up just before they're about to get it. Happens in politics and war and careers. Said it's when you're close to getting what you want that things get the hardest. You have to choose early on whether you're going to fight or give in because if you wait until things get hard, you'll give up."

"That's what he said?"

Hollis nodded.

"Sounds like that feller never run up against Buddy Coleman."

"I expect he never did." Hollis pulled his cap down and held out a hand. Curtis shook it. "Have you signed the papers?"

"They'll be ready in a day or two."

"You heard about the meeting Wednesday. Would you come and listen?"

Curtis winced. "I'm sorry, Hollis. There's more people ready to sell. I admire you for taking a stand. I got no quarrel with your heart."

"Thank you for opening the door."

"Tell Juniper we said hey."

Hollis walked toward his truck and stopped. He stared at the tire swing again and then closed his eyes and could almost hear the voices from the past echo through the valley.

3

Ruby Handley Freeman sat at her kitchen table with the overhead fan circling lazily above, just fast enough to make her wispy white hair wave. She strung half-runners and snapped them and dropped them in a pot of cold water, the white beans squeezing out every now and then. She'd bought them at the FoodFair, along with some sugar and other ingredients for baking, which was Ruby's love language. The few people she interacted with received care in dialects of cakes and brownies and treats that came from the cookbook in her head. No one who tried Ruby's carrot cake ever complained of her scrimping on ingredients, particularly sugar.

Her fingers were bent and gnarled from arthritis, but she had enough dexterity to grab the string on either end and pull, then snap the beans. When she had enough for a mess, she swirled her hand inside the pot, held down the beans and dumped the water, then ran more in until it was half-full. She put the pot on the burner and retrieved bacon from the refrigerator and put it in to boil along with the beans. She never cooked a pot of beans or ate them without at some point thinking about her friend from Beulah Mountain. Strange how those memories returned as the beans grew limp in the pot and the steam rose around the covering lid and the smell of those gifts of God permeated the room.

The volume on the radio in the corner was turned to earsplitting levels, but it was just right for Ruby. She listened to the Christian station on the left side of the FM dial and never saw a reason to change it. The teaching was encouraging, the Southern gospel uplifting, and she got all the news and information she needed, which wasn't much at her age. In fact, the less she knew about the goings-on in the world, the better, as far as she was concerned. Wars and rumors of them filled the papers, and she could feel the rancor rising with Bush and Kerry going at each other. Her husband had been more political than her and that he wasn't around to see this election was a small comfort after the loss of her lifetime companion. He had listened to baseball games on this radio in his shop, and when she found it after he died, just turning the knob made her feel a little less lonely.

Ruby lived for the afternoon broadcast—replayed again at 11 p.m.—of Reverend Franklin Brown, an old-time preacher turned radio man who made her feel like he was right there in the kitchen or in the living room if she wanted to put her feet up in the recliner by the TV. The man had a gentle way of speaking the truth without banging people over the head and was more encourager than prophet. He announced birthdays and mentioned those who supported him, and of course, she always smiled when she heard him say, "And a big thank-you to Queen Ruby from Biding, Kentucky—who lived for a time in my old stomping grounds, Beulah Mountain, West Virginia. These days the queen lives far away from the noise of strife, which reminds me, we should play 'Dwelling in Beulah Land' before we end today. I'll try to work it in before the clock on the wall says it's time to leave."

The daily program was just beginning when she heard a sound at the door and saw a shadow in the three small windows that ran alongside it. She turned down the heat under the beans and did the same for the radio volume and waltzed to the door, though to any objective observer it might've looked more like shuffling.

A sheriff stood there. At least he wore a uniform of a sheriff. Ruby had promised her son and daughter she wouldn't open the door to any strangers after the last incident, and she wondered if maybe this man was an impostor.

Ruby wiped her hands on her apron. "What do you want?"

"Can you open the door, ma'am? It's the sheriff."

"How do I know you're really a sheriff?"

He pushed his hat back and turned, and through the window she saw the lights on his squad car swirling. Maybe some escaped convict was in the area. Or the convict had overpowered the sheriff and was dressed in his clothes. Now she was thinking like Frances, picking out the worst thing that could happen and treating it like reality.

He held up a card to the window and the picture looked like him, so she unlatched the rickety lock and struggled to pull the door open.

"How can I help you, Officer?"

It was a deputy, with a closely shaved haircut and burly arms like tree trunks. He had kind eyes and a boyish face.

"Ma'am, we got a 911 call from this location. Did you make it?"

She pulled her head back like a turtle into its shell and furrowed her brow. "What in the world would I do that for?"

"We got a call from this residence and we're required to check it out. Do you mind if I come inside?"

She shrugged. "Sure, come on in. Can I get you a slice of coconut cake?"

The man smiled and took off his hat. "No, ma'am. I'm fine." He followed her into the kitchen, scanning the room and glancing at the pantry that served as a hallway to her bedroom. He noticed the phone on the kitchen table. "Have you made any calls lately? To friends or family? Maybe you misdialed?"

Ruby put a hand on her hip and stared at the phone as if looking at the thing would bring back the past. "The only thing I did was call to check on something I ordered. I put in the tracking number, but it didn't work. Then I called the cable company. The bill was ten dollars more this month and it's already sky-high. Do you have cable?"

"I have satellite TV and they charge like a mad bull."

Ruby tipped her head back and laughed, grabbing a kitchen chair for stability. "Sounds like your satellite company and my cable company are in cahoots."

"Do you mind if I look at the numbers you dialed?"

"How do you do that?"

"Here on the phone. You just press this button right here and it brings up the last number you dialed."

"Is that right? Well, go ahead and push it."

The man pressed the button three times and leaned down to get a better look. "Yeah, here it is. See this long string of numbers?"

"Let me get my glasses," she said, and by the time she found them and returned, the man had to punch the button again.

"The number you dialed started with 911."

Ruby's mouth dropped open and she stared up at the man with bewilderment. Then her eyes got big and she pointed a gnarled finger at him. "You know what? Now you wait right here."

She moved to the living room, where another phone sat on a stand by twin recliners. She picked up a blue page and handed it to him. "Right there it is. It does start with 911."

"You dialed the tracking number. You have to call this number down here and then you punch those numbers in. When you dialed

911, it didn't matter how many numbers you dialed after that, it came straight to us."

"And you came all the way out here because I did that?"

"It's all right, ma'am. It happens all the time. Little kids play with their phones and think it's a toy or somebody your age misdials . . ." He saw the look on her face and quickly said, "I'm just glad you're okay."

"Right. It was an honest mistake, wasn't it?"

"It sure was, ma'am. Now you have yourself a—"

Ruby put up a hand. "You don't have to report this, do you?"

"Well, I need to let them know everything's okay, if that's what you mean."

Ruby rubbed her hands together. "I have a son and a daughter who don't think I should be living here. They want to move me into a home or some place where they fix all your meals and tell you when to take your medicine—and I don't need that."

"You like your independence."

"I've earned the right to live where I want, don't you think?"

"I wouldn't argue with you, ma'am."

"I keep telling them that I can take care of myself. And they say, 'Well, if you fall and break your hip'—I'm not going to fall. They'll say, 'What will happen if you fall going to get the mail or the paper?' I'm not going to fall walking down the driveway. Walking keeps me spry."

"My mother says the same thing, ma'am. She doesn't want anybody telling her what she can and can't do."

"That's exactly right. 'Don't drive to the store—we'll take you.' That's what they say. Do you know how far away my daughter lives? She's an accountant for this outfit down in Nashville. And my son's ten miles away and he comes to mow my yard every week or so. I can't wait a week to go to the store, and I'm not going to bother him to do something I can do myself."

"Your daughter visits often?"

"No, I hardly ever see her. When she calls, she talks like she's double-parked."

The deputy smiled. "Well, I'd better be going, ma'am."

"I feel bad about this. I apologize for the mix-up. I won't do it again. But you don't have to tell them, right? My son and daughter? They'd have a fit."

"It'll be our secret, ma'am."

"Let me get you something. Wait here a minute."

Ruby hurried back to the kitchen and it took five minutes, but she returned with three pieces of cake on a sturdy paper plate wrapped in plastic. "This is my coconut cake that Leslie loved—that's my husband. He passed away. He said if he ever went into a coma, he wanted this fed to him intravenously."

The deputy laughed out loud and took the plate, thanking her. "I'll share this with the boys at the station."

"You do that, and you come back for more when you're ready. I'm so sorry I made you come all the way out here for nothing."

"It's not a problem, ma'am. Thank you for the cake."

Ruby watched the deputy walk to his car and get in and put the cake on the seat beside him. She closed the door and slid the lock in place. Back in the kitchen, she turned up the radio and heard the song "Dust on Mother's Bible," stirring the beans as she hummed along. The man on the radio followed with the song "Gone Home," and it was all Ruby could do to hold back the memories of all the people she'd known who were no longer alive.

The doorbell rang again and she thought it was like Grand Central Station today.

"Here's your mail, ma'am. I tend to agree with your kids. That's a long driveway and it's uneven in places. Rocky. If you fall, there's nobody around who would see you."

She took the mail. "But you're not going to tell them about the phone call, are you?"

"No, ma'am. That's between us." He smiled and touched his hat. "Have a good day, ma'am."

Ruby locked the door and sat at the kitchen table with the mail still in her hand. She knew exactly where they'd put her. Sunnyside. It was a long brick building with little apartments on one side and a convalescent center on the other. Across the street was a storage unit behind iron bars, and she thought both were places you put things you didn't have room for anymore.

Franklin Brown came back on the radio after another song. He always had a devotional or some kind of teaching he gave in the middle of the songs. Once a pastor, always a pastor.

"Forgiveness is a wonderful thing, isn't it?" he said. "Now, there's plenty of people who can believe that God forgives, as a theological proposition. God forgives sinners. God doesn't hold bad things against us when we're in Christ. That's a concept we can grasp. But until forgiveness has *grasped you*, it doesn't do you much good.

"Let me explain. It's one thing to believe God can forgive you. It's another to believe it so deeply that you accept that forgiveness."

The man paused for effect, but he didn't need to. Ruby was right there with him.

"There's probably somebody listening now who has held on to guilt and shame for years. Or you're holding a grudge against someone from the past and it's eating you up inside. I'm here to tell you today, God doesn't want you to live in the shadow of that mistake or that grudge any longer. You can be forgiven. You can forgive. You can live again. Bring that thing into the light. Don't let it isolate you. God wants to set you free from whatever is holding you back."

Ruby stared at the radio, thinking there was no way that man could know what was going on in her soul, and yet here he was saying words that cut to the marrow. She was glad when he played another song. It enabled her to focus on something other than the past or the phone call that brought the sheriff.

She studied the mail. The electric bill was on top. Followed by coupons from FoodFair for flour and sugar and other things she bought every week. How did they know? There was a receipt from another ministry she supported and a political flyer. At the bottom of the stack was an envelope with her name written in calligraphy. She stared at the return address, then flipped the envelope over and saw an image in a wax stamp that took her breath away.

Ruby put the envelope in the top drawer of her dresser, next to the other invitation that had come a month before, and closed the drawer. She sat and spooned beans into a bowl and put a pat of butter on top and watched it melt. Then she shook salt and pepper over the beans and when she took a bite, it was like tasting her childhood. Finally she retrieved the envelope from the dresser and read the card inside.

4

Charlotte Beasley pulled her 1988 Toyota Camry over at a rest stop on I-64 a few miles east of Louisville and studied the MapQuest directions she had printed. Her grandfather had bought her this car so she could drive from her apartment to Marshall University and not have to take the bus. If she had a car, he reasoned, she could drive home to Beulah Mountain on weekends or holidays or whenever she needed a break from the "city." She had taken one look at the repainted Toyota and said, "Papaw, it's almost old enough to vote."

"It's just getting broken in," he had said. "That engine will probably outlive me."

Charlotte shook her head, but she loved him. She teased him for his frugal ways, but down deep she knew he wanted the best for her, even if the title to the car read "restored salvage." Maybe that was why he had bought the car in the first place; their lives felt like "restored salvage." She had named the car Black Betty, and with the excellent gas mileage she saw the gift not as a slap in the face but as a gentle hug.

Charlotte had walked across the stage in May to receive her diploma and she'd heard her grandfather's familiar hoot owl call from the back of the arena. Now with a degree in journalism and all the hope in the world, she was ready to use her education to change that world, though she was more unsure now than ever about how that was going to happen.

She got back on the interstate, accelerating through the curve of the on-ramp, and heard the slight knocking in the left front near the wheel. A friend had said it was probably a strut issue, though Charlotte wasn't sure what that meant. She turned up the radio when she heard "Meant to Live" by Switchfoot and sang along.

"We want more than the wars of our fathers."

She stopped singing at that line, the words bringing up something she wanted to forget. A face that hadn't been there at graduation.

A half hour later she pulled up the long driveway of Ruby Handley Freeman's house. At least, she hoped it was the woman's house. There was no name on the mailbox, just a street address, and a car sat in the graveled parking area. The house was up on a little knoll and the view seemed fitting for a rich old woman, though the house was far from a mansion.

Someone had constructed a ramp to the door over the front steps. Charlotte assumed this was to prevent a fall. She parked and stared at the house, waiting for someone to open the front door or pull back the curtains.

After a few minutes she walked up the Astroturf-covered plywood and took a deep breath. She listened closely and heard a resonant voice inside that vibrated the windowpanes. She pushed the doorbell and waited. When nothing happened, she pushed it again and held on. The voice stopped and the windowpanes rested. Footsteps inside now. Then white hair and two beady eyes looking out the window beside the door.

"Mrs. Freeman?" Charlotte said with a pleasant tone, loud enough to be heard through the wood door.

"Whatever you got, I don't want any."

It was an aged voice but there was strength to it. There was a twinge of mountain in the accent but only a twinge. And something that sounded like fear. But maybe that was Charlotte's own emotion.

"I'm not selling anything, Mrs. Freeman. I just want to talk."

"I don't talk to strangers. Now get back in your car and move on down the road before I call the sheriff. He's already been here once today."

Charlotte smiled and moved to her left so the old woman could see her face better. She wasn't blessed with height. Charlotte stood five feet four inches and that was with heels. But everyone always said Charlotte had the nicest smile and dimples, so she turned on the charm.

"Mrs. Freeman, my name's Charlotte Beasley. I've been calling your phone for several weeks. I've tried to leave messages and the historical society sent you two invitations. But we haven't heard a thing."

"And you're not going to hear anything. I don't pick up the phone unless I recognize the number. And I don't talk to people I don't know through the door. That's the rule. Good-bye."

Charlotte batted her eyelashes now like a little girl who wanted a different-flavor lollipop for trick or treat and wasn't afraid to ask. "Mrs. Freeman, if you'll give me a minute, I've driven an awful long way. I don't mean any harm."

No response from inside but Charlotte still saw the wisps of white hair in the window, so she forged ahead.

"I'm from Beulah Mountain. I think you know where that is

because, as I understand it, you lived there for a while. Way back in the 1930s? Is that right?"

Silence from inside.

"I was hoping to ask you a few questions for the local paper, the *Beulah Mountain Breeze*. That's why I wrote and called. I was hoping since I've driven several hours to get here that you would at least talk to me."

Nothing.

"My granddaddy is Hollis Beasley. He owns a good part of Beulah Mountain that was passed down to him. The family was probably living there when you were young. I think it was 1933 that you moved there with your daddy? Anyway, my papaw owns that land, at least for a while longer. And my daddy, his son, worked in the mines and . . . well, you don't need to know everything about me, do you?"

Charlotte laughed nervously, trying to gauge whether her monologue was having any effect. It was a lot like writing for the newspaper—you had to go on faith that someone actually read your words.

"I also work for the Company Store Museum. I was told by Mrs. Grigsby-Mollie they sent you an invitation to the grand opening. Is that right? Did you get it?"

No response.

"Mrs. Grigsby-Mollie is head of the historical society. It's going to be something, Mrs. Freeman. Everybody's excited about it and all the history it represents, and people are going to come from all over. I've been writing these articles about the way life was and what the store looked like and I've come up dry on some things."

"What things?"

Charlotte's heart quickened. "Well, one of them is the Esau scrip. I was hoping you knew about that."

The white hair moved away from the window and Charlotte peered in but couldn't see much.

"I know your daddy was one of the mine owners, so I thought you could give me some recollections. They've rebuilt everything—even your old room over the store. The people at the museum said you don't talk with anybody but I thought it was worth trying. They gave me the job because of the paper I wrote in school about . . . well, the history of that area. I was interested because of my family and all."

Charlotte wondered if any of this was getting through the thick door between them. She liked to think she had tenacity, that she wouldn't give up with a single no. She had worked at a call center for a semester and hated it, but the dictum that you had to make people tell you no three times was something she never forgot. Her inclination as a polite person was to take the first no and walk away, but sometimes if you really wanted something, you had to keep asking. To Charlotte, journalism was a lot like digging coal, just not as hard on the back or the lungs.

"Mrs. Freeman, you still in there?"

"I'm here. I'm just waiting for you to leave. Now I'm going to call the sheriff. Is that what you want?"

"No, ma'am, it's not. Could you at least tell me if you got the invitations?"

"I did."

"And you know that the big ceremony is this Saturday. Will you be able to attend?"

"Don't set a place for me," the woman said.

Charlotte wanted to open the door and walk inside. She could probably have crawled through a window, but you had to draw a line somewhere. They had talked about this in an ethics class, how far you could push the boundaries of propriety. Charlotte had walked away from the class confused. In the end she thought if you treated people like they were family, you couldn't go wrong. Be kind and as thoughtful as you could and let the chips fall.

"Well, we'd sure love to have you join us. You see, I graduated from college in May and I've been looking for a full-time job. I'm doing more historical research than news right now. I'm trying to let people on the outside know we're not a bunch of hillbillies. A lot of classmates made fun of how I talk, but the way I look at it, they're the poor ones. They don't know what I know about my people. And this museum is going to change that."

She expected the door to open any second. The way she pictured it, the woman would invite her in and they'd become best friends and Mrs. Freeman would ask Charlotte to write her life story instead of it being a big mystery. Or she'd write an article and send it to the *New York Times* and just like Rick Bragg she'd be famous.

"I also write for the *Beulah Mountain Breeze*, but it's not exactly my dream. My papaw says just bloom where you're planted. You know, 'Whatever your hand finds to do, do it with all your might.' That's what he keeps quoting me."

With each peek into her life, Charlotte felt she was making headway. If the old woman was moved, she might open that door and they'd drink sweet tea and Mrs. Freeman would reveal what she knew about the massacre and the Esau scrip and the third-floor rumors.

"If you want to check out my credentials, I can slide them under the door. All I have is my driver's license, or you can call my editor at the *Breeze*."

She opened her purse and pulled out her wallet. There was her driver's license and in the window next to it was a round, worn medallion with the number 736 on it. She touched it and smiled.

"If you won't listen to reason, you'll just have to talk with the sheriff," Ruby said.

Charlotte heard the dial tone from a speakerphone inside and then three beeps. She was calling 911.

"All right, I won't bother you," Charlotte said. "You don't have to call the sheriff."

She closed her wallet and put it back in her purse and hopped in Black Betty. This was going to be harder than she thought.

5

RUBY MEETS BEAN'S FATHER
BEULAH MOUNTAIN, WEST VIRGINIA
JUNE 1933

The commotion outside the church that Sunday morning in 1933 was not a mine cave-in or explosion, though there had been plenty of those in the town's memory. No, what sent the congregants to the windows and the children spilling out the front door were shouts of warning that trouble was coming. And then there was the gunfire.

"What's going on?" Ruby said to Bean as she tried to see what was happening up the road.

"It's my daddy," Bean said. "I can tell by his voice. And he's got him a gun."

Bean's father, Judson Dingess, had survived so many accidents in the mine that many wondered if he hadn't caused them himself or pretended to be part of them after the fact. Injured miners received help from the company. When her daddy was hurt, he couldn't crawl into the mine but he found the energy to crawl up the hills where they made the good whiskey, not the stuff closer to town that was watered down. The most recent accident concerning her father was a collapse of timbers that rolled off a wagon and knocked him unconscious, and no one had accused him of manufacturing that event because there was too much blood. Plus, he had been disoriented when he finally woke up. He thrashed around like a freshly caught channel bass, thinking he was back in the trenches of France, until Bean and her mother calmed him.

While life in the mines had sent Bean's father running toward drink, Bean's mother ran toward the church and the stability that a tight hold on God would bring. This was the push-pull of their marriage and Bean was caught between. She adored her mother and the rock-ribbed belief she had that God was there and cared about hard-living people. But she also loved her father in ways she couldn't explain. She had seen him being kind and gentle, and he loved to laugh and played the fiddle like nobody's business. There was music inside him that came spilling out and echoed off the hills. Except he had lost that fiddle in a card game when he was trying to win money for another drink, so the house had gone silent.

"Bean, you get back inside," her mother said from the church door.

Bean looked back but didn't obey. She loved her mother more than life itself but she knew only she could coax her father away from what the devil was trying to do. She had awakened early each day with the first light coming over the ridge and walked with her father to the train, carrying his dinner bucket. She'd squeeze his hand tight before he left and then watch him join the miners climbing onto the cars as those returning home spilled out so black and dirty you couldn't tell they were human.

Ruby stopped at the bottom of the steps and watched Bean run toward the road.

"Ruby, come back here and stay with me," Bean's mother said.

Ruby wanted to go with her friend, but she was gone, running toward her father, toward the shouts and name-calling. Bean flew like the wind, her feet barely touching the ground, it seemed. Just dust flying up from the shoes that were falling apart at the seams and her hair trailing behind her until she disappeared around the dense foliage that was taking over the road.

A shot rang out and Ruby ran up the stairs as Pastor Brace herded the women inside. Several men followed Bean. One went the opposite direction, saying he would get the sheriff. The pastor closed the doors behind him and said, "It's time to pray."

Ruby retreated with the other women as they knelt at the altar and the pastor raised his voice in supplication. Ruby closed her eyes and listened to the words prayed aloud and the groaning and moaning of the women. They rocked in pews, the wood creaking beneath them, as if their movement might tip the hand of God in their favor.

"What's wrong with him?" Ruby said. "Bean's daddy."

"Judd's got problems on the inside."

"What kind of problems?" Ruby said, lowering her voice to match the woman's whisper.

"The kind that don't have answers outside of the Lord's work in his heart. That's what I've been praying about."

"Has he always been like this?"

Bean's mother shook her head and her eyes pooled. "Stay here where it's safe, okay?" She stood, with some effort, and walked toward the door, reaching for a pew to steady herself. She closed the door behind her and Ruby turned back to the kneeling women.

"Please, God," Ruby whispered, "don't let Bean get hurt. Don't let anything bad happen to her mother. Do something for her daddy. Don't let him hurt anybody. Please, God."

It was a sincere prayer and the words tasted sweet to Ruby. Ruby's father was not religious and the death of her own mother had hardened him further to the thought of a deity who allowed such things.

If Bean's daddy had run toward drink to soothe and salve his life, or at least allow him to numb it enough to be tolerable, her own father had run toward building his empire, as if the things of earth could fill such a hole of hurt. It didn't make him yell in the roadway and fire a pistol, but the effects were the same. There was distance in his eyes and a hunger no one could assuage.

Another shot rang out and there was more shouting. Ruby finally had enough and hurried outside. Praying was fine when there wasn't anything left to do, but it seemed like spectating would be better than sitting and just *thinking*. Was that all praying was?

The putt-putt of a motorcar came from down the ridge and Ruby figured it was the sheriff. He and her father owned two of the only cars in town and most of the time they had trouble navigating the muddy, washed-out roads. She caught up with Bean's mother and grabbed her hand. The woman was having a hard time catching her breath in the heavy mountain air.

They came around the corner and saw several men standing cross-armed a stone's throw away from Bean and her father. Bean was close enough to spit on him and she was pleading, holding out both hands. "Daddy, just give me the gun. Please. Nobody needs to get hurt."

The man swayed in the sunlight and tried to focus on her face, but he kept glancing at the men and holding the pistol out toward them at an odd angle.

"Bean, come away from him," her mother shouted.

Bean's father looked down the road at his wife and opened his mouth but nothing came out. Bean took another step closer and reached out to him.

"I swear, that girl has more sand than any man in this town," someone said behind Ruby.

Pastor Brace joined them and spoke to Bean's mother. "Cora Jean, the sheriff is almost here and he's not going to like being drug out of bed at this time on a Sunday morning."

"I was on my way to church, Pastor," Judd shouted, his words barely intelligible. "You got room for sinners in that church of yours?"

"Put the gun down, Judd," Pastor Brace yelled.

"Play 'Beulah Land'! Can you sing that one?"

The sheriff's car chugged up the hill behind them, laboring.

"We'll sing anything you want. Just put down the gun."

Everything seemed to move in slow motion and Ruby wondered if, in years to come, she would be able to recall this scene. Bean reached to grab the gun. Bean's father was staring at his wife and saying something about being sorry. He made a pitiful sound like some animal caught in a trap.

Bean had the gun now, and she dropped it behind her. One of the men came up quickly and retrieved it as she led her father toward the church.

The car stopped behind them and Ruby relaxed. But Sheriff Kirby Banning set the brake and got out, clearly unhappy.

"I ain't got no beef with you, Banning," Judd called. He was leaning all his weight on Bean as he stumbled over rocks and tree limbs by the road. "I'm just on my way to church."

The sheriff cursed under his breath, then glanced at Bean's mother. He spit something black into the dirt and cinched up his pants.

Bean's father began singing alternate words to their beloved hymn. "'I'm working in the mountain; I can't see the cloudy sky. I'm drinking from a fountain I hope never does run dry.'" He laughed and stumbled and fell, Bean tumbling after him.

"All right, that's enough," Sheriff Banning said, glancing at the men from church. "Get him into the car."

"Where we going, Sheriff? A little religion won't hurt you."

Pastor Brace stepped forward. "We can take care of him. We'll get him sobered up."

Sheriff Banning shook his head.

"Oh, come on, Kirby," Judd said, struggling to make it to his knees. "I ain't got no problem with you. It's Coleman and Handley I want to use for target practice."

Sheriff Banning waved a hand at the men and they put Judd in the car. Bean's mother pleaded with the sheriff, "He's had a hard time since the accident. Please, let us take him."

"He can sleep it off in jail. Plus, he just made a threat. That'll have to be dealt with."

"Who's making threats?" Judd said as they closed the door. "I didn't make no threats."

Bean dusted off her clothes and stood by Ruby. As the car turned around in a wide place in the road and drove past them, Ruby heard someone singing "Beulah Land" and laughing.

Hollis Beasley walked out of the Family Dollar carrying a case of water bottles and a box of green mints. It nearly killed him to buy water in plastic bottles because he had grown up drinking out of the streams and wells that dotted the hills. Water was something you took for granted and buying it made as much sense as paying for air. Now he bought it from companies that hauled it in hot trailers pulled by diesel trucks. He had tried a filtering system at home, but when he turned on the faucet, you could smell the sulfur and he knew Juniper's health had taken a turn because of the water quality and the chalky air.

He was putting the water in the back of his truck and the mints in the passenger seat when someone called his name. Crossing the street, from the Company Store Museum, came Randall Mullen, a man who had grown up in Beulah Mountain and had escaped the mines by doing odd jobs and woodwork and, for a time, built covered-wagon table lamps that he sold at an antique store in Lexington. To turn them on, you pushed down on the brake, and it had fascinated Hollis's son, Daniel, when he brought one home. It was a miniature work of art, but other people started making them for less and Randall had moved to fishing lures and cribs and rocking chairs for toddlers.

In need of more steady work, Randall found a home builder an hour's drive away in an area that was growing faster than autumn olives by a creek. A chemical plant had opened a new division along one of the tributaries that ran into the Ohio River and people needed cheap housing, so Randall had invested in a set of knee pads and installed carpet until his back screamed every morning and his knees turned to jelly. Now he walked stooped, though he was twenty years younger than Hollis.

"I seen that ad you put in the paper," Randall said.

"It wasn't an ad. It was an announcement."

"You still having the meeting?"

"Of course I am. Why wouldn't I?"

Randall put a hand on the truck and steadied himself, stretching his left leg like some nerve was acting up that made it too painful to stand. "I don't know. Just don't think it's a good idea."

"And why is that?"

"Hollis, you've known me since I was coming up. I don't want this place to change any more than you. But there's things you and I can't stop. CCE is giving people jobs. Randy Jr. is running a dragline now. That's good money."

"It ought to be good money. He's taking the place of a hundred miners with that machine."

"That ain't his fault."

"I'm not saying it is."

"It's how things are done now. You want us to go back to the horse and buggy?"

"Never said I did."

"Well, it seems like it. You're stirring people up. Fighting CCE tooth and nail. My son's got a family to feed and you want to take away the only good-paying job he's ever had. I swear, Hollis, there's people here that don't understand you anymore."

Hollis paused, then said, "I found out a long time ago that it ain't my business to make people understand me."

"So what's Randy supposed to do? You want him to build a windmill in his front yard?"

"He can start by not being party to blowing up half of creation."

"There you go again."

Hollis turned and leaned on the truck. "Nobody is against getting the coal. It's how you get it that makes a difference. You've seen what the explosions and dumping do to the streams. Possum Creek doesn't even run anymore. It trickles, red as blood. Like some plague in Egypt."

"You can't have it both ways, Hollis. You can't say you're for getting the coal out and then go over with the tree huggers."

"I'm a lot of things, but I'm not a tree hugger and you know it."

"You're acting like one. Calling a meeting like you were organizing a new union. Just let it be. You used to be one of those turn-the-other-cheek kind of people."

Hollis groaned. "There comes a point when a man has to decide whether he's going to move out of the way or stand up. I've turned my cheek so many times it gave me vertigo."

"Then stand alone and stop dragging the rest of us with you."

"I'm not forcing you to do anything, Randall. Do what you want with your land. Randy can do the same."

"Well, there's people who think you ought to sell. For your sake and Juniper's, too. You're dragging her down to her grave. Now I'm sorry to say that. I don't mean to be unkind. But this thing you're doing is all about you and none about her or the rest of us."

Hollis looked hard at the man. "I'm sure it would be a lot easier if I backed off. I should keep quiet and let them level this place all the way to that museum Buddy Coleman shelled out for. You ever ask yourself why he wanted to restore that place?"

"The historical society wanted—"

"The historical society, my eye. Don't you see, Randall? This is not about coal. This is our heritage. My people didn't hand this place down so I would sell it to somebody who would blast the top six hundred feet off of it. I made a promise."

"To your parents?"

"To them and to Daniel."

Randall took off his hat and wiped his forehead. He looked back at the museum as a mail carrier pulled up to the box outside.

"What did they hire you to do over there?" Hollis said, changing the subject.

"Fixing some stairs that curve up to the third floor. They're worried people could fall and don't want a lawsuit. Tightening the railings. That kind of thing."

"I'm sure you're doing fine work."

"Beats laying carpet, I'll tell you that. You been inside?"

Hollis shook his head.

"You should peek in there before the grand opening. There's some pictures I never seen before. And Charlotte has been writing her tail off and putting up facts and stories of the different people. You oughta be proud of that granddaughter of yours."

"I am. But I don't need to go inside to remember." He tapped the side of his head. "I got it right here. And a lot of it isn't pretty."

"I hear you." Randall took in the view of the shrinking town like he was Cecil B. DeMille. "Someday they oughta make a movie about this place, don't you think? Maybe that's how they'll bring back some jobs."

"Hollywood ain't interested in our story, Randall. And if we're not careful, this will all be gone." He snapped his fingers.

Randall cursed. "There you go again."

Randall asked about Juniper and told about his latest fishing expedition. By the time Hollis got back in the truck, the mints were soft.

Ruby parked her Town Car at the FoodFair toward the middle of the lot where there were four empty spaces. Ingress and egress were paramount to her visits. She preferred going to Walmart where the prices were lower, but navigating that stretch of road and the busy parking lot made her nervous. And the place was so big she needed a nap by the time she checked out.

Getting out of the car was as hard as driving or shopping. She had to position her purse by the door, grab her cane from the passenger side, and use it to push the heavy door open. Then she swiveled her feet onto the pavement and used the cane and the door to catapult herself to a standing position. Every time the Olympics rolled around, Ruby thought there ought to be an exiting-the-car competition for octogenarians. They could have it in summer and winter and include divisions for those with previously broken hips.

She grabbed her purse and found an errant cart and used it to support herself. The only problem was the ramp leading up to the automatic doors. If she didn't get enough momentum, she would wobble and fall. Coming down the ramp was also difficult, particularly if she had heavy bags of sugar that made her pick up speed. Once, a few weeks earlier, the cart had gotten away from her. She'd scraped up her hands a bit on the asphalt but the real damage was the truck the cart hit. It made a long scratch in the bright-red paint on the side and Ruby felt terrible. She stood in the hot sun for fifteen minutes, waiting for the truck's owner, then finally sat inside her car and turned on the air-conditioning. She had cooled off somewhat when a burly, round-bellied, bearded man exited the store and headed for the truck. Ruby got her door open and had swung her feet out, but the man was in and gone in a flash. That experience had made her skittish about pushing the cart to her car, so after that she had asked one of the baggers to help and slipped him a dollar.

Ruby needed some extra sugar this trip and the five-pound bags were right at the top end of her weight limit. The kind she liked was shelved low, which she could never understand, so she settled for the bags at eye level, which were thirty cents more. She didn't want to throw her back out.

"Can I help you with that, ma'am?" someone said behind her.

Ruby turned to see a young woman about her height who looked to be in her twenties, but just barely. Maybe one of the store workers, but she wasn't wearing the red shirt with the FoodFair insignia. She had on jeans and tennis shoes and a collared top. She also had a twinkle in her eyes and a voice that sounded vaguely familiar.

"How many of those do you need?" the young woman said.

"Well, I was just going to get one, but if I have help, I could use three."

"Three it is."

"If you don't mind bending, I like those down there."

The young woman knelt and picked up two of the bags and put them in Ruby's cart. How anybody got down that far and got up so fast was beyond Ruby, but such was the nimbleness of youth.

"Can you put them up here on the seat?" Ruby said. "I can't unload the heavy stuff when I check out if it's in the front."

"Be glad to," she said, placing the sugar by Ruby's purse.

"And leave a little space between because it's hard for my fingers to get in there and pick them up."

The young woman retrieved one more bag and positioned them with a little space between, just like Ruby had asked.

"Well, I thank you for your kindness."

"It's no trouble, ma'am. Would you like help with anything else?"

"I'm sure you've got better things to do than follow after an old codger like me."

"Oh, it would be my pleasure. I used to shop with my mamaw when I was little. She would let me ride in the cart and pick out the cereal and bread and whatnot. Made me feel special. I don't get to do that with her anymore."

"Did she pass?"

"No, ma'am. She's still living, but she doesn't get out. Her health has gone downhill. I miss those trips to the store, so this brings back good memories."

Ruby smiled. "Well, this is about the only reason I go out anymore. I go to the FoodFair and back. And my children don't like it much."

"Why not?"

"They think I'm some kind of invalid. Tell me I'm going to kill somebody. I keep telling them I'm no different than I've always been. I may be a little slow, but I'm not decrepit."

The girl laughed. "No, ma'am, you're certainly not. What else is on your list? It looks like you're baking for an army."

"Not an army. I just bake for the fun of it. Give people in the community the fruit of my labor. Cakes are my specialty. I was going to make a German chocolate one for the mailman. He brings packages to the house and rings the bell, and I like to give him something every now and then."

"So you probably need flour, right? And baking soda?"

Ruby pointed out what she needed from the baking aisle, then led the way to the dairy section for milk and eggs. She forgot the coconut flakes, so they retreated to the baking aisle and made sure they didn't get the shredded coconut but the flakes.

"Aren't you getting anything?" Ruby said when she was through.

"I just came in for a cold bottle of pop," the girl said.

"Well, let me treat you!" Ruby said. "They have a cooler up front by the cashier."

"You don't have to do that, ma'am."

"I want to. And after all the hard work you've done, you at least deserve a cool drink. Now I just need to get a mess of green beans and then we can go to the front. You can help me lug this to my car, if you don't mind."

When they arrived at the front, the cashier smiled and said, "How are you doing today, Miss Ruby?"

"Not bad for being over the hill and up the other side."

The cashier laughed. "Looks like you got yourself a helper. Is this your granddaughter?"

"Why no, this . . . We met in the baking aisle and have been friends ever since. What did you say your name was, honey?"

"Charlotte," the girl said.

"Charlotte. Right. She was a big help. I was only going to get enough to get me to the weekend, but I told her to load up the cart."

"Looks like you're going to do a lot of baking," the cashier said.

Ruby told the cashier exactly what she was planning to bake and who she was baking for and two customers pulled in behind her before she got the hint that she needed to pay and move along. She made sure Charlotte got her soda and gave the cashier her credit card. When everything was loaded in the cart, the bagger offered to accompany Ruby.

"I'll help you, Mrs. Freeman," Charlotte said.

As Ruby took her cane from the cart, something clicked. Charlotte pushed the cart down the ramp and straight to Ruby's car.

Ruby finally caught up with the young woman. "How did you know this was my car?"

Charlotte turned, red-faced.

"I never told you my last name, did I?"

"No, ma'am. I'm sorry—"

"You were at my door earlier, weren't you?"

Charlotte dipped her head. "Yes, ma'am. But I don't mean you any harm. I thought if you met me face-to-face, we could talk. And you'd come to trust me. I think you'd want to help."

"I told you at the house: I don't talk to strangers."

"And we're not now. I helped get your groceries. I don't want a thing from you but your story. I'd be glad to drive you over to Beulah Mountain to see the museum. If you come for the grand opening, you'll be the guest of honor."

Ruby unlocked the car and opened the back door. She grabbed one of the heavy bags but couldn't lift it.

"Let me do that for you, Mrs. Freeman."

"You leave it alone. I'll do it myself."

"Ma'am, these are too heavy."

Ruby pointed the cane at Charlotte and narrowed her gaze. "I said I'd do it myself. I've got people all around me telling me what I can't do. I don't need any more on the list." Her voice rose in intensity and emotion. "I have family who tell me not to drive when I'm fully capable of doing everything they do and then some. I'm tired of it. And I don't talk to strangers. Now go on home."

Ruby grunted and groaned and managed to get the five-pound bags of sugar in the backseat, then the rest of the groceries. When the cart was empty, Charlotte reached for it to return it to the corral.

"I said I'd do it myself," Ruby said.

Ruby passed her and focused on getting the cart situated. When she came back, Charlotte was still there.

"I apologize for intruding, ma'am. I came up here with good intentions—"

"Good intentions, my eye. You came up here to scam me."

"No, I came to talk. To find out what really happened. Because there's things being told that I don't think are true. But I won't trouble you anymore. I thank you for the pop."

Ruby opened the front door and began the long process of putting her purse into the passenger seat with her cane, then turning to wedge herself in behind the steering wheel.

"You're lucky I haven't called the police," Ruby said, reaching her cane out to close the door.

"I suppose I should be grateful for that kindness, ma'am. Where I'm from, people open the door and hear others out. But then you're not from Beulah Mountain."

Ruby squinted at her and was about to say something, but Charlotte walked toward her little black car. When she got inside, Ruby could swear the girl was crying. But that was no doubt an act.

Ruby started her car and pulled away, wondering how in the world she would get all those groceries into the house.

8

RUBY LEARNS WHY HER FRIEND IS CALLED BEAN
BEULAH MOUNTAIN, WEST VIRGINIA
AUGUST 1933

"Why do they call you Bean?" Ruby said as they sat in her room above the company store leafing through a Sears catalog. "Did they shorten 'Beatrice' to 'Bea' and just add an *n* to the end?"

"No, there's more to it than that."

"Then what is it?"

Bean hovered over the catalog like she'd found hidden gold, her mouth open wide. "Look how pretty this material is. My mama would die just looking at it."

"Does she make your clothes?" Ruby said, hoping this question might be answered fully.

"She tries to." Bean pulled the sleeve of her dress and put it between her thumb and index finger. "But she don't have much to work with. Hand-me-downs from people we don't know that gave some dresses to the church."

"Can't she buy some at the store?"

"I reckon she could if my daddy didn't spend his scrip on other things." She flipped some pages. "Now here's a coat I'd like to see my daddy wear. He gets awful cold in the wintertime."

Ruby couldn't understand why Bean would care about her father if he did things like spend all their money. She moved toward safer territory. "But why did your parents name you Bean?"

Bean sat back and slumped her shoulders with a sigh. "Well, you might think it was because I'm long and skinny, like a beanpole, but she named me before I had my growth spurt. We was living over at Rossmore by Island Creek. My daddy was working a different mine. My mama had just lost a baby to stillbirth. And the midwife said because of all she'd gone through, she shouldn't have any more children. That meant I would be the only one in the family, which vexed my mama to no end. She wanted lots of kids. I was something like four when I took sick. They didn't know what was wrong and the mine doctor gave me medicine I threw back up every time. It tasted like cod liver oil and smelled worse. You ever take cod liver oil?"

Ruby shook her head.

"Count yourself lucky. That's what Mama gave for everything. I can still taste it to this day."

Ruby leaned forward, waiting. Finally she said, "But why did she name you Bean?"

"You don't have to get snippy. Mama says when I tell a story, I take the roundabout, like a horse and buggy will go the long way when you could just walk over the hill? I got to follow my own trail."

Ruby stifled a smile and put her hands in her lap to listen.

"I wouldn't eat nothing they put in front of me. I plumb lost my appetite. I lost weight. I was skin and bones. Like a skeleton walking around with my cheeks sunk in. My daddy would come back from the mine with food from somebody's lunch box. Corn bread and buttermilk? Nothing doing. Biscuits and gravy? Nope. Don't want it. I got to where anything I put down my gullet would just come back up. So I didn't want that awful feeling and I give up on eating. And my stomach hurt like the dickens."

Ruby waited, becoming accustomed to this wild-natured girl with her tall tales.

"One day these people on a farm brought us a poke filled with green beans. Half-runners. Mama didn't grow those in the little garden out back, so it was a treat. She cooked them up with some fatback in a pot on the stove—"

"What's fatback?" Ruby said.

Bean rolled her eyes. "It's what it sounds like. It's the fat from the back of the pig. Don't you know anything? It looks like bacon but it's just white—there's no meat to it at all. Kinda like lard. They sell fatback in the company store. It's over by the—"

"Okay, go on. So you liked it?"

"Would you let me tell the story?" Bean turned another page in the catalog and sat transfixed by the shoes. "Can you imagine me wearing a pair of these in the mud and the muck by our house? I'd sink to my waist and they'd never come out. But they sure are pretty, aren't they? One day I'm going to live in a house with a paved road right to the front door so I don't ever have to set foot in the mud. Wouldn't that be something?"

"I know where there are some pretty shoes," Ruby said.

Bean waved a hand. "All you got downstairs is work boots for men and oxfords for women."

"You haven't seen the ones I'm talking about," Ruby said. "These are special."

She flipped the catalog closed. "Show me."

Ruby hesitated. "Finish your story."

"All right. Where was I?"

"The beans were in a pot on the stove."

"Right. For some reason the smell of those beans drew me like a fly to honey. I stood there watching the pot bubbling and boiling with the top on—my mama told me this later, I don't remember it. Evidently the smell of those beans made me interested. You wouldn't think a little kid would like vegetables, and to this day I don't know why they drew me, but when Mama ladled out a bowl full of those beans with the fatback in the middle and a pat of cow butter melting on top and a pinch of salt all around, I'll tell you what, I went to town. I inhaled that whole bowl and asked for another. Just shoveled them in. And Mama stood at the stove and cried and I asked her what was the matter and she said they were happy tears. She was glad I was hungry for something."

"You didn't throw it up?"

Bean shook her head. "No. It all stayed down until I tried something else the next day."

"Why didn't she name you 'fatback'?" Ruby said.

Bean laughed. "There weren't no fat to me. The beans did the trick, though. Saved my life. My daddy walked clear over to that family to buy some more from them, and when they heard the story, they just handed him a poke and said to pick all he needed."

"And they called you Bean from then on?"

"It kindly stuck. Now show me the shoes."

Ruby took the catalog and put it on the coffee table. "I don't think I should. My father would be upset."

"Why?"

"Because of where they are."

"Where are they, on top of the store?"

"No, they're in a room he told me not to go in."

"And how would you know what's in there if you didn't go in?"

Ruby frowned. "I peeked."

"So let's peek again," Bean said. "I won't tell nobody."

"All right, but we have to be quiet. I'm not supposed to even have you in our apartment, let alone take you up there."

"I'll be as quiet as a mouse."

Ruby led Bean to the front room of the apartment and listened at the door. The store was closed on Sundays and her father was having lunch with the other owner of the mine, a man named Thaddeus Coleman that Ruby disliked the moment she met him. Ruby's father had laid out the plans for the mining community, designing and building the homes that dotted the valley. The company store was his creation as well, designed to accommodate miners and their families for everything from canned goods to tools to clothing. Blueprints were drawn to include an apartment on the second floor with an exterior entrance as well as a "hidden" back stairway.

Ruby waved Bean through the door and led them up the smaller set of stairs that curved, the steps getting closer together, until they reached the third-floor landing.

"You have to promise not to tell anyone what I'm about to show you," Ruby said.

"I promise."

She tried to open the door but it was locked.

"Don't you have a key?" Bean said.

Ruby shook her head. "But there's another way. Come on."

They retreated to the apartment and Ruby took Bean through the kitchen area to what looked like a large cabinet built into the wall. She opened the door and inside was an empty box big enough for one of them to fit inside.

"Get in," Ruby said.

"I'm not crawling in there."

"Silly, it's a dumbwaiter. It won't hurt you."

"I'm not dumb enough to crawl in."

"You know the kitchen they have downstairs?"

"You mean the restaurant?"

"It's not really—well, right. They put food in here for us and send it up. Or to the third floor."

Bean's mouth dropped open. "It's like a supper elevator?"

Ruby giggled. She'd never thought of it that way.

"You go first," Bean said.

"Okay, I'll send it back down to you and bring you up."

Ruby crawled inside and sat with her legs crossed. She showed Bean the button to push. The gears engaged and soon Ruby rose out of sight. Bean leaned into the opening and watched the chains swaying from Ruby's weight. Light flashed inside the shaft and Bean saw Ruby step out, then the dumbwaiter descended and stopped. She took a deep breath, crawled inside, and the machine took her up.

The first thing she noticed when she stepped into the room was the darkness. There were big windows that looked down on the town and toward the mine, but heavy curtains covered them and only a single shaft of light peeked through. There was also a heavy smell of cigar smoke that seemed baked into the walls. When her eyes adjusted, she noticed a maple table and chairs in one corner and what looked like a half-open chifforobe, but instead of clothes hanging, there were bottles of amber liquid and glasses stacked on top of each other. In the other corner was a stuffed chair and a couch that Bean wondered how they ever lugged up to the third floor. The hardwood floor had two thick throw rugs that felt like velvet beneath her feet. She'd never seen such exquisite colors and patterns.

"Look here," Ruby said.

Ruby opened the curtain as Bean turned to see a shelving unit attached to the wall. The shelves were lined with women's shoes. Some were just like in the catalog with elegant straps. Others had laces that tied. Most had heels. Bean's mouth dropped. It was the most beautiful display she had ever seen, the quality much better than the shoes downstairs. She picked up a pair and closed her eyes as she smelled the leather.

"They're so soft. They must cost a fortune. But there's no price tag."

"I'm not sure how much they are," Ruby said. "I've never been able to figure out why they put them up here. But sometimes I'll hear noises in this room."

"What kind of noises?"

"Men's voices. The company men have meetings here, I think. Mr. Coleman has some of the bosses over and they're here late at night. And sometimes . . ."

"Sometimes what?"

"I hear women's voices, too. Sometimes they're laughing. And sometimes they cry."

There was a noise downstairs—perhaps a door closing. Ruby held a finger to her lips. Bean's heart beat wildly and Ruby's eyes flashed what looked like fear.

Ruby led Bean the back way and unlatched a window. "Go down the fire escape. And come see me tomorrow, okay?"

"Are you going to get in trouble?"

Ruby shook her head. "Just go."

Bean stepped onto the steep stairwell and climbed down backward. The feeling she'd had in the room was a mixture of awe and dread. She loved looking at the shoes and finely upholstered furniture. But something was off in there. Something dark clouded the room. What was it?

When she got to the ground, she looked up. Ruby was at the window waving and smiling. Below her, on the second floor, was a figure looking out another window straight at her.

9

RUBY GETS ANOTHER UNWANTED VISIT
BIDING, KENTUCKY
TUESDAY, SEPTEMBER 28, 2004

Ruby was putting her third cake of the day in the oven, singing jauntily with the radio, when sunlight glinted through the window and flashed on the ceiling. The radio was up loud and she didn't touch the volume. She walked to the front door and peered through the window. A car sat in the driveway.

It was that girl again, probably, back for another round of questions. Painful questions that had brought about a sleepless night. But if she hadn't lost sleep, she wouldn't have heard the repeated message by Pastor Franklin Brown. There was something about listening the second time that burned the message about forgiveness into her soul.

Upon closer examination she realized the car was not the girl's from Beulah Mountain, but her daughter's. And there was Frances, with her nut-brown hair shaking as she talked. It had been recently cut to her shoulders. She had her father's nose and a long face that had bothered her as a teenager. How that girl had worried about her looks and her grades and just about everything.

There was someone else with Frances. Maybe she'd heard about the sheriff. Maybe someone from the FoodFair had alerted Frances about the scene in the parking lot. Frances worried too much. She always had. She saw the glass half-empty and suspected the water in the bottom was contaminated.

Ruby rubbed her hands together. Had she paid her property taxes? Maybe somebody from the county was with Frances, and she was right now pleading with them for leniency.

The man leaned forward and Ruby saw the face of her son. Jerry was lean and tall with dark hair but no worry gene. In fact, she wished he had inherited a little worry because it would have kept him from some of the building projects he'd gotten into that had failed.

If Frances and Jerry were talking, the situation had to be bad. They never talked, at least about anything of import. Had somebody died? Ruby didn't have any living relatives. And there were no close friends. Her closest friend—her husband, Leslie—had died ten years earlier. The best friend she'd had died seventy years ago at Beulah Mountain.

What in the world could they be talking about? And why didn't they come inside? She wiped her hands on her apron and reached for the doorknob, then thought better of it. She'd let them make the first move. She'd go on about her business and keep singing.

Maybe they were just visiting. Maybe Frances was moving to Kentucky. Perhaps it was about Julia, Ruby's granddaughter.

Ruby was singing "Midnight Cry" when the two of them walked through the front door and into the kitchen. Immediately her son frowned and his tone was crisp.

"Mama, I thought we told you to lock this door. Anybody could walk in and conk you on the head."

"I unlocked it when I saw you two sitting out there jawing. And there's nobody around here who wants to conk me on the head."

Jerry glanced at Frances but kept quiet.

"If you're going to come in here and tell me everything I need to do, I might turn things around and tell you a thing or two, Jerry."

He stared at her, slack-jawed.

"Hi, Mama," Frances said gently, giving her mother a hug.

"Hi, honey," Ruby said, staring daggers at her son until he leaned in and patted her on the back.

"What are you baking?" he said. "Smells good."

Ruby didn't answer, just waved her hand at the table behind her and the cakes that stood as testament to her culinary powers. Ruby turned down the radio, which galled her—she wanted to listen to the music. Her children made small talk about the state of the yard and whether the back steps needed a ramp.

"Now you two didn't come all the way over here to talk about the yard. Frances, why didn't you call and tell me you were coming?"

"Are you upset to see me?" Frances said.

"Tell me why you're here and I'll answer."

"You're right, Mama. Jerry and I wanted to have a talk."

"Well, you've already had one in the driveway."

"We have something we want to discuss with you," Jerry said.

"Why didn't you call?" Ruby said. "Does this have anything to do with the sheriff?"

Her kids looked at each other like she had spoken to them in Mandarin.

"Should we ask about the sheriff?" Frances said. "What happened? And where are you going?"

"I'm locking the door, like you said." Ruby put the chain on and sat in the large chair facing the couch in the living room. She didn't want to sit at the table and feel flanked. Jerry and Frances followed and sat on the couch together.

"All right. Let her rip. What do you want to talk about?"

Frances put her hands together and sat forward. "Mama, we're concerned."

"About what?"

"Your driving."

Ruby stared at her.

"We don't think you should take the car out anymore," Jerry said.

Ruby measured her words. "You came here to criticize my driving?"

"Mr. Clawson told us you took out his mailbox last week," Jerry said. "There's a dent in your fender."

Ruby shook her head. "First of all, Clive's mailbox was never set right. When it rains, the ground softens and now it's leaning further than the Tower of Pisa. I brushed against it slightly and because the termites have been at it, the post fell over. I'll pay for a new one if he wants, but I'm not . . ." She paused, then her voice rose with passion. "Are you two serious? You came here because of a mailbox?"

"We came here because next time it's not going to be a mailbox, Mama," Frances said.

"Yeah," Jerry said. "Next time you're going to get distracted and hit a kid on a bike. You want that?"

Ruby couldn't believe what she was hearing. "I'm a better driver than either of you. How many tickets for speeding have you two gotten in the last year?"

"That's not the point, Mama, and you know it," Frances said.

"It *is* the point. I'm careful. I'm in control. And I don't need you two looking over my shoulder every time I want to go to town."

Frances fiddled with her hair. "We've talked with a deacon at your church and he said they can arrange rides."

"I don't want somebody wasting their time taking me to the store when I can drive myself. What sense does that make?"

"Let's talk about where you need to go, Mama, so we can get a strategy together for—"

"I don't need a strategy. I need you to leave me alone. I have a car and my faculties. When I need your help, you'll hear about it."

"You go to the store and to church," Jerry said. "It's not going to be a bother. They want to help. Especially if it'll keep the neighbor kids alive."

"There are trucks that go up and down the road, Mama. You hit one of those like you did the mailbox and it's all over."

Ruby struggled to stand, her shoulders bent, her face on fire. When she was in full control of her balance, she pointed a bony finger. "I'm not going to sit here and listen to this. I've got work to do. And when I want to go to Eula's to get my hair done, I'll drive. If I want to mail something or buy stamps, I'll go to the post office. And maybe stop at Dairy Queen. And FoodFair, to boot."

"Who in the world do you bake for?" Jerry said. "Nobody needs all those cakes."

"I give them to people who appreciate them. I gave a slab of a coconut cake to the deputy who stopped by . . . when was it? Yesterday? I think it was yesterday. And he thanked me for it."

"Why did the deputy stop, Mama?" Frances said.

She regretted mentioning it. "That's none of your business."

"It is our business because we care about you. We want you to be safe. And for others—"

"I am safe," Ruby howled. "I don't talk on the phone to anybody anymore whose number I don't recognize. I keep the door locked. I don't let strangers in. Though I probably should have locked the door on you two. I'm careful on the road. I only go out when there's no traffic."

Jerry rolled his eyes and Frances put a hand on his shoulder.

"You two are worrywarts. Frances, this sounds like your idea."

"It was both of us, Mama," Jerry said.

"You're worried about nothing. We've had this conversation. I'm not having it again."

Ruby walked to the kitchen and Frances followed. "Mama, why won't you listen to reason? You don't want to see anybody get hurt, but that's going to happen. It's not a question of if but when. You're going to hit somebody's car or someone's child that you don't see."

"Nothing bad is going to happen."

"That's what you said about the front steps until you fell and snapped your wrist," Jerry said from the living room. "You're lucky it wasn't your hip."

Frances ignored her brother. "You could move closer to me. There's a little house for sale just down from me—it's on a flat patch of ground. It has all the space you'd need and I would feel so much better. There's a flower garden and woods behind it where you can throw out your scraps and feed the animals."

"I saw the house online," Jerry said, stepping into the kitchen.

"I sent Jerry a link," Frances said. "I do taxes for a Realtor and she brought it up to me."

"Of course I've been wanting to build you something for a long time," Jerry said. "But you'd be really happy in that area."

Ruby looked from one to the other, incredulous at their words. "You listen to me. I've earned the right to live and die where I want. I'm leaving here feetfirst just like your father. Do you understand?"

The two looked away but she wasn't finished.

"I took care of your father in that back bedroom because this was where he wanted to spend his last days. He didn't want to move to some retirement home or a facility. He wanted to be here. I gave that to him."

"And we helped you," Jerry said. "Remember?"

Ruby ignored him and kept her eyes on Frances. "You two think you know what's best. Seems to me you've both made decisions you'd like to have over again."

Frances tensed but didn't look at Ruby.

"This is not about me being safe or kids in the neighborhood. This is about what you want. You don't care what I want."

"That's not true," Frances said. "If we didn't care, we wouldn't be here. But there are things you can't see. You're getting older, and we don't want to lose you."

"You're not going to lose me. You know exactly where I am. You gave me that cell phone so I could call if I fall."

"And where is it, Mama?" Jerry said.

She looked around the kitchen. "It's here somewhere."

"See? That's what we're talking about. If you fell—"

"I'm not going to fall. I'm careful."

"—it would be days before anybody would find you."

"Well, they'd be days I'd like a lot better than being shut up in some home. Or dragged to Nashville to a house with a flower patch."

Jerry turned and shook his head. "There's no talking to her. I told you it would be this way."

"Mama, put yourself in our place. We love you. We don't want anything to happen."

"Nothing's going to happen!" Ruby yelled.

"And we can't let you keep driving," Jerry said. "Isn't that right, Frances?"

Frances got a grim look on her face. "Here's what we think, Mama. We need you to agree that you won't drive or we'll have to take some steps . . . We want you to live where you want. But we can't keep going like we're going."

Ruby looked at the oven timer. She got her mitts off the table and opened the door. Jerry moved to help and she glared at him like a lion standing over a fresh kill. He took a step back and watched. Ruby took the cake from the middle rack and placed it shakily on the table. She put the mitts down and wiped her forehead with the back of her arm.

She hadn't slept well and that put her on edge. She regretted snapping at her children, but they had crossed a boundary. She had a No Trespassing sign up on her freedom and they had transgressed it.

"So you didn't come here to talk. You came here to take my keys. Is that it?"

Frances spoke softly. "We came here to see if we could reach a compromise. We know you want to stay, for this to be where you finish your race. We want to give that to you."

"It's not yours to give," Ruby muttered.

Tears came to Frances's eyes. "We also want to love you well, Mama. But we don't know how. And you're not making it easy."

"It's not my job to make it easy. This is my life. I've got plans. I've got things I want to do. Do you think about that?"

And then the emotion came. Ruby walked to the sink and ripped off a paper towel, then sat at the table and dabbed at her eyes. Frances put a hand on her shoulder and Ruby pulled away.

"I can't believe you would treat me this way," Ruby said through tears.

"We've never done this with you before," Frances said. "Remember when Daddy's eyes got bad and he couldn't drive?"

"He had me to drive him," Ruby said, crying.

"I know," Frances said. "This is hard for us. We don't want to take your freedom."

Ruby retreated behind the paper towel and, like a child caught with a hand in the cookie jar, began to consider her options. How could she get her kids from the house so she could think? She worked up the tears and added a few weeping moans for effect until she got up the energy to stand. In her younger days, Ruby would have stomped out of the room quick as a whip. Now, she struggled to her feet and reached for the counter as the room began to spin. She made it up the two stairs and through the little pantry to her bedroom.

"Take the keys," she said to no one in particular.

"Mama, now don't be this way," Jerry said.

Ruby closed the bedroom door behind her and locked it, waiting for them to leave.

10

BUDDY COLEMAN SURPRISES HOLLIS
BEULAH MOUNTAIN, WEST VIRGINIA
TUESDAY, SEPTEMBER 28, 2004

Hollis heard the Jeep engine laboring up the winding driveway but it wasn't until he saw the *CCE* on the side of the vehicle that he believed it was really the man he hated. The Jeep was shiny black all over except for the mud splatters. That the man would have the audacity to show up here made Hollis's stomach turn. He thought about retrieving a rifle from inside the front door, the one he kept handy for the groundhog that was eating his strawberries, then thought better of it.

Hollis stepped off the porch and his dog came barking from a cool spot under the house. Cooper's voice was the only thing Hollis heard as the Jeep's engine quit and he didn't try to quiet the dog.

Buddy Coleman stepped out of the vehicle wearing a red polo shirt and crisp, tight-fitting jeans that came down over his leather boots. His Coleman Coal and Energy baseball cap was pulled down to eyebrow level. Hollis had seen this look in his dreams—a man in the same outfit speaking at a press conference, stoic and sorrowful. The only thing the company was sorry about was decreased coal production after an accident.

Buddy Coleman was the new face of the company, clean-shaven and boyish. Hollis wondered if he even had to shave. He wanted to say that Buddy wasn't half the man his grandfather was, but you can't halve a zero. He had seen Buddy on the news, but he hadn't expected him to be so small. His boots looked taller than he was.

Buddy got as far as the edge of the Jeep and stopped, glancing at the barking dog, who didn't give ground. Buddy looked at Hollis, then back at Cooper, and knelt, his jeans tightening as he reached eye level with the black Labrador. He held out the back of his hand and Cooper moved closer and sniffed.

"Good girl," Buddy said with a soothing voice. "Just had a corn dog from the Company Store. Would've saved some if I'd known I was going to meet a pretty thing like you."

He stood and Cooper retreated, swishing his tail and sitting beside Hollis.

Buddy scanned the horizon. "No wonder you don't want to give this up, Mr. Beasley."

"Am I supposed to thank you for saying that?"

"No, I'm just empathizing with how hard it would be to let it go. This is some view."

"Why don't you empathize from the main road? This is not your property."

Buddy leaned on his Jeep and crossed his arms. "You're right. It's not. But both of us know what's going to eventually happen."

The man's face was like a basset hound's. Sad eyes for such a young man.

"Both of us don't know anything of the sort," Hollis said.

Buddy frowned. "You're smarter than that, Mr. Beasley. I know you are. The only real question about this land is what you're going to get out of it. If you leave sooner, you'll do well for yourself and your family. Leave later and it won't go so well."

"I got a camera inside that records everything that happens out here," Hollis said, lying.

Two hands in the air and a big smile. "Knock yourself out. Record all you want. I didn't come up here with any agenda but friendship." Buddy turned to look toward the top of the hill. "We'll take care of them. You know that."

"I don't trust you with the living. Why would I trust you with the dead?"

"Now be reasonable, Mr. Beasley." He paused dramatically. "You heard the Adkinses are selling."

Hollis stared at him.

"They made the sensible choice. And we're taking good care of them. Giving a fair price. They've got a future and a hope now. They're out from under the taxes. They can make a new start. And with the amount of acreage you have here, you'd walk away with a pretty penny."

"I don't need a pretty penny. I don't need your friendship, either."

Buddy took a deep breath like he was about to go underwater. "Let's say you keep this strip of the mountain. Let's say you manage to stay. The view's going to change. The blasting will give you a headache. The machines will run up and down all day. That won't be good for Mrs. Beasley. I hear she needs medical attention."

"Leave her out of this."

"The price for this mountain would provide what you'd need to move somewhere nice. Out West, maybe, where the air's dry. Or near the ocean. You could retire comfortably."

"I'm retiring here. That's my choice. And you've made yours. You and the company won't be happy until you've made Beulah Mountain a ghost town like the others up and down the ridge."

"That's not true. Have you seen the museum? I hear your grand-daughter works there. It's a new day in Beulah Mountain. We're bringing jobs back. Safe jobs."

That last phrase made Hollis flinch.

Buddy pursed his lips and continued. "I came here in good faith to make you an offer. I know the pull you have with people. They respect you. I'm authorized to offer a bonus for everybody who follows your lead. All you have to do is sign the papers."

"I got a question," Hollis said, taking a step forward. "You mentioned the museum. I hear you gave a bunch of money to it. From your inheritance. Why? Especially with the history of that place."

Buddy smiled. "I don't know what history you're talking about. The people who worked those mines and made this hollow their home should be celebrated. People like your father. My grandfather. Outsiders will come here and walk back in time."

"I'd be careful walking too far back, especially when it comes to your grandfather."

"Look, Mr. Beasley, I'm not the evil person you may think I am."

Hollis took another step forward. "I know what you're trying to do. I got a friend who tells me things."

"What kind of things would that be?"

"How you worked yourself into the company. How impressed leadership is with the way you get things done. The board meeting is coming up Saturday where they're going to vote on you becoming president. Same day as the Company Store grand opening. All the stars are aligning, aren't they?"

Buddy rubbed the back of his neck, his face turning red. "I don't know where you get your information."

"It would be the feather in the cap you're looking for to get the rest of Beulah Mountain, wouldn't it? Be honest."

"Hollis, I'm trying to do the kind thing. I'm trying to treat you how I'd want to be treated. And the truth is, you're going to lose this mountain."

"I've lost more than you can ever replace."

"Now that was before my time. But from what I heard, the company was fair. Got your granddaughter an education. That doesn't make up for your loss, of course. I'm sorry about your son."

Hollis spit on the ground.

Buddy leaned against the Jeep again and crossed his legs in front of him. "Let me put it to you square. How much are the taxes on this property?"

"Too much. I'm sure you know the figure."

"I heard the county raised the assessment. That means the property value is going up. That's good news for you."

"Not if I want to stay, it's not. I know you have people in the assessor's office in your back pocket."

Buddy frowned. "Here's the deal. If you stay and everybody around you sells, your property's not worth dog manure. If you get behind on the taxes, the government will take the land. Either way you lose. It doesn't have to end that way. I'm here as a friend. You and I are from the same stock. I know what you're going through."

"You and I aren't even from the same herd. Or species."

"I'm sorry you feel that way."

Hollis shook his head. "I can't figure out whether you want this land for the coal or the view. Maybe you want to move our kin from their graves and build a big castle, like your daddy did before he lost his shirt."

Buddy took a step toward Hollis. When Cooper stood and gave a low growl, Buddy stopped and put his hands in his pockets. "I didn't figure you'd listen, but I had to try. I'm not your enemy. I'm the good guy here. Think about it. There's more than a dozen families we've made an offer to. I'll give you $10,000 per family that follows you if you'll sign."

"Hollis?" Juniper said from the doorway.

"Afternoon, ma'am," Buddy said, tipping his baseball hat.

"Hollis, that's a lot of money," Juniper said through the screen.

"You're right about that, ma'am," Buddy said.

Hollis had taken Juniper with him to buy a truck from a dealer in Charleston and told her to keep quiet while he negotiated. It was the last time he ever took her with him while he dickered and he got the same feeling now.

"I'll tell you what," Buddy said, putting his chest out like he was about to toss hundred-dollar bills from the top of the Company Store. "I'll give you an extra $50,000 right now. On top of the asking price and the ten grand apiece. I got the papers in the glove compartment."

For a minute Hollis tried to calculate the money Coleman was tossing his way. It was a large sum in addition to the offer he'd already been given. The extra money would solve some of Hollis's problems and relieve a lot of headaches. Pay bills that were stacked on the kitchen counter. It would give him and Juniper a fresh start.

"You ought to take it, Hollis," Juniper said, her voice gentle as a summer breeze.

Buddy turned and opened the door of the Jeep.

"Don't bother with the contract," Hollis said.

"Hollis," Juniper said, but he threw a hand in the air. She slammed the door and Hollis wondered how she got the strength to do it.

Buddy turned, a cloud passing over his face. "So you're going to do this the hard way? You ought to listen to your wife."

Hollis pointed at the Jeep. "Get in your shiny car and leave."

Buddy started the engine and it purred as he backed up in the gravel and headed down the hill. He stopped and rolled down his window. "Talk it over with her. She deserves better."

Hollis wanted to say something snippy. Wanted to give him a comeback that would put him in his place. Instead he kept quiet and wondered how he would get the resolve needed to keep his land.

_11_

Ruby stewed the rest of the morning about her children. When she was sure they had gone, she went to the front room and saw they had taken her car key but left the fob that opened the doors and the trunk and had the panic button she was told to use if anybody broke in the house.

Frances had left a note under the fob that said, _We love you, Mama._ _Call me. I'll be at Jerry and Laurie's._

The key-taking incident sent her into a tailspin that made her pack up her baking materials and put them in the pantry. Ruby was a believer that everything in life had a purpose and that the hurdles you encountered were there to make you stronger, but at eighty-four she'd stopped jumping hurdles and had crawled under them more often than not. Now, she felt like lying down in front of this one and giving up.

She couldn't do that, of course. Not just because of the spunk she still had but because of the bitter resolve she'd felt after listening to Franklin Brown on the radio. After hearing his program twice in the same day, she had known what she'd been putting off and what she needed to do. She had no idea how to do it.

She'd hoped everything would remain under the rug, but somehow God had taken that rug and hung it on heaven's clothesline and was whacking it with Gabriel's horn. The dust filtered down on her and convicted her—a conviction she bore alone because nobody else knew what she knew, except for God. And he seemed to be telling her that it was time.

She made her supper, some roast turkey she had bought at FoodFair that was a day from expiring and some cheese and lettuce on toasted wheat bread. She gave thanks, remembering how she and Leslie would take turns thanking God together.

She'd never told her husband the secret. It wasn't that she didn't think he would understand or forgive. She just didn't want to dredge up the past. Nothing good could come from it. So she kept the memories like the locked trunk in the basement. And her children knew nothing. How could she trust kids who would take her keys?

She had taken her first bite of the sandwich when she heard a tapping at the door. Ruby shook her head and thought about "girding up her loins," laughing aloud. Her husband would have beaten her to the King James reference and the laugh.

She expected to see Frances or Jerry, but instead it was a neighbor she barely knew. She struggled to think of his name.

"Hi, Miss Ruby, it's Drew from down the road. Drew Fetty. I know your son, Jerry."

"Hello," she said, keeping the screen door closed. "How is everybody at your house?"

"Fine, ma'am. Enjoying the fall weather. How are you doing?"

"I'm well, considering my advanced age. What can I do for you?"

"Well, I was hoping I could take it for a drive, if that would be all right."

"Excuse me?"

"The car. Maybe Jerry didn't tell you, but I'm interested in buying it. My daughter's got her a job in town and she needs something reliable."

"I don't understand."

"Jerry said you were selling it. That you're not driving anymore. I know how hard that can be because we had to about tear the keys from my daddy's hands. He passed not long after that."

The man would keep rattling like a lawnmower if she didn't interrupt. "Is that what my son said? That I was selling the car?"

"Yes, ma'am. I talked with him yesterday. I was interested right off because I know you take good care of it. And it's probably got low miles. We're looking for something dependable. She'll be tickled with whatever I find for her, but this one . . ." He turned and looked at it. "She'll be over the moon, I think. She's expecting me to get her some old beater, you know? Something with the fender hanging down. How many miles do you have on it?"

Ruby ignored the question and grabbed the doorknob behind her. "You're going to have to come back, Drew."

"Is there a problem, ma'am?"

"I can't sell it to you. My kids took my keys this morning. You go home and dicker with Jerry later on, all right?"

"I'm sorry if I jumped the gun. Now that you mention it, Jerry said not to contact you, but I was so excited for my daughter. I apologize."

She almost had the door closed when he said, "They didn't tell you, Miss Ruby? That they were selling your car?"

"You go on home, Drew."

"I didn't mean to cause trouble, ma'am. I can come back tomorrow. Would that be better?"

"Talk with Jerry. This is his deal. But wait until tomorrow. Now, I'm not feeling well. I need to go."

"Yes, ma'am. I'm real sorry."

She shut the door while he muttered something. She couldn't believe it. They had not only taken her keys, they were selling the car. How long had they been planning this?

"Think," Ruby whispered to herself. "You need to think."

She tossed her uneaten sandwich out back for the critters and gathered some clothes from her dresser and toiletries from the bathroom. Then she found the cell phone Jerry had given her and placed it in the side pouch of her purse. That would come in handy if she got into a bind. In the pantry she found the lockbox that never locked and retrieved cash in the amount of $1,765. Her kids would have a fit if they knew she had that much cash.

She counted the money twice and computed how much she'd need for the trip. This amount would be enough and if she needed more . . . She would try not to use her credit card. They could track her with that. She'd seen that on TV, how a man who escaped from prison had stolen a credit card and the authorities tracked him down to a hotel in Florida. Her kids mustn't know where she was going, and she'd be back before they missed her. Or gone just long enough to scare them for a day or two.

The more she thought and planned, the more excited she became. It would be like stepping into a time machine and going back to her childhood. But would she have the strength and the will to return? And what memories might stir inside?

As the sun went down, Ruby stepped onto the porch and watched the orange ball sink lazily into the trees.

When you rise in the morning, old friend, I'll meet you on the road.

Part 2

12

Frances Freeman's heart fell when she saw no car in her mother's driveway. Through the years her mother would say, "Don't get your bowels into an uproar." It meant don't make a fuss. Don't think of the worst. But when she opened the unlocked front door and walked inside, she knew something was amiss. She stood in the entryway, her mind racing.

"Mama?" she called.

The house was silent except for the sound of Frances's wildly beating heart.

An intruder. Someone could have broken in. They could still be here now, waiting. Frances had seen enough movies like that to make her swallow hard. But where was the car? She checked the front door. No broken chain or doorjamb. Jerry had taken the keys. On the drive home he had said they should let their mother stew, that she would get used to the idea of living without a car. A person driving her would give her someone to talk to instead of living alone with her baking and the radio. There'd been comical references to hiring Morgan Freeman and changing her name to Miss Daisy, but Frances couldn't put out of her mind the way her mother had stomped into her bedroom.

Frances and Jerry had talked about this eventuality. It had been a Herculean task to care for their father, but the family had survived and Ruby had accomplished her mission of letting him die at home. The way she grieved for him afterward made Frances think that her mother would want to move, would choose to be closer to Frances and transition to a new stage of life.

"Mama? Are you home?" Frances called loudly.

Dishes sat in the drying rack in the kitchen. Two cakes stood like coconut candles on the table, saran-wrapped. Strange, she thought.

Frances checked the bedroom, knocking softly as she entered. The curtains were pulled and the room dark. She opened them and saw the bed had been hastily made. A shelf on the wall held knickknacks. Ruby had gone through a period when she collected wooden, pewter, glass, and metal owls. A large owl had occupied the space above the mailbox at the end of the driveway but now only its talons remained after a drive-by baseball bat attack.

Next she checked the bathrooms and back bedrooms. She returned to the pantry and opened her mother's cash box. It was empty.

She picked up the phone and dialed her brother.

"I'll be right there," Jerry said. "Don't panic. I'm sure there's an explanation."

Telling Frances not to panic, which was her brother's answer for everything, caused the opposite reaction. She had carried most of the emotion in the family her whole life.

If someone had broken in, they could have thrown Mama down

into the musty basement and stolen her money, then hot-wired her car. But nothing else of value was gone. Why would they leave jewelry and electronics?

Unwilling to wait—how could she live with herself if her mother was alive downstairs?— Frances turned on the light to the stairwell and inched down the rickety steps. Her father's old flight jacket hung on a nail and for a moment she could see him in it, walking the property or riding on his lawn mower. The jacket brought back warm memories, but she continued, holding tightly to the rail.

She found two old refrigerators, a disconnected washer and dryer, an aging hot-water heater leaking around the seal, and two rooms of dusty furniture Goodwill would reject. There was no sign of Ruby.

"Someone took her," Frances said when Jerry arrived.

He rolled his eyes. "Don't jump to conclusions. She's making us pay for taking her keys. She's probably hiding in a closet waiting to jump out and scare us."

He made a sweep through the house and joined Frances on the front porch. "You're right. Not a hide nor hair of her."

"You took both sets of keys, right?"

He nodded, biting his cheek. "But maybe she had another one." He snapped his fingers. "Remember when she locked her keys in the car? When she was at the beauty shop?"

"Daddy walked all the way into town."

"Yeah, but didn't she have another set made? She put them in her purse to make sure it never happened again. Remember?"

Frances stared at him. "She let you take those keys knowing she had a backup. Unless someone stole it last night."

"Nobody would steal her car. She's joyriding to make us miserable."

"Her money is gone from the lockbox."

"What?" Jerry went pale. "All of it?"

"There's not a dollar left. Do you know how much she had?"

"I never counted it, but there had to be more than a thousand in there. Maybe even a couple."

"Two thousand dollars? What was she using it for?"

"She said she needed it to pay the kid who mows her yard. And the lady who comes to clean every two weeks."

Frances sighed. Two more leads in the Ruby mystery.

"I never let on that I saw her stash, but I did tell her not to keep money lying around the way things are these days," Jerry said. "Went in one ear and out the other."

Frances turned to go inside. "I'm calling the police. Something's not right."

"Hold on. Don't get the police involved yet."

"Why not? Somebody could have conked her in the head like you said yesterday and put her in the trunk."

"I'm thinking of her," Jerry said. "If she took off, which you know she probably did, calling the police and sending the posse out would embarrass her to no end. They'd plaster her face all over the news and she'd never live it down."

"Let's say she took the car and drove into some unfamiliar neighborhood. She might be out there right now trying to get home but can't find her way. Or she could have had a spell and gotten disoriented. She might be in a ditch."

"You know Mama. If she drove into a river, she'd probably keep pushing the gas pedal to get to the other side. And she'd make it."

Something about his reaction concerned Frances. Jerry rarely had an opinion about what to do. He followed others like a hungry puppy. She was surprised he didn't have somebody prompt him to say, "I do," at his wedding to Laurie. Now he was asserting himself. But she couldn't argue with his claim that it would be embarrassing for Ruby if the police were called into the search.

Jerry pulled out his phone and scrolled through his contacts and punched a button. He frowned when the call went to voice mail.

"I bought her that cell phone so she'd always be able to communicate, and I doubt it's ever been charged."

"If we don't call the police, what do we do?"

"Let me drive to the store and do a sweep through town. She's probably buying up all the flour and sugar at Walmart. She might have rented a U-Haul to get a bigger load. Though I doubt that. She wouldn't spend the money on the rental." He said it with disgust.

Jerry had always had a problem with the way their mother lived. She could have bought a large estate and hired several servants on her inheritance, but she had insisted on living simply and only off her husband's income and now his retirement.

"And what am I supposed to do?" Frances said.

"Stay here. If she comes back, pry the keys out of her hand."

They locked eyes. There was nothing that could prepare a son or daughter for the loss of a parent. There was also nothing that could prepare a grown child for the possibility that the same parent had been abducted or, perhaps worse, had run away from home. In that moment, something akin to fear and tenderness passed between them, a sense of knowing each other at the core, even if it was only for a moment.

Frances retreated inside and sat at the kitchen table. She needed to think positively, not about her mother becoming disoriented while driving and winding up in a cornfield. Not about the reports of heroin addicts looking for things to steal. Not about news reporters doing live shots in front of her mother's house and a young female reporter saying, "Many in this community don't understand how her children would leave an old woman alone to begin with. An heiress to a coal fortune lived in this house behind me. She was reportedly worth millions, but now she's vanished and her children are answering some hard questions."

Frances spread out a hand to smooth the tablecloth and imagined herself looking into a camera lens and saying, "If you're holding her, please let her go. Please don't hurt my mother." And then all the tabloids and social commentators would weigh in about the believability of Frances and her brother and how much they'd be getting from the inheritance and what they might have done with the body.

So much for thinking positively.

That line of thought led Frances back to Jerry's quick response about the police. Was it really because he wanted to save his mother embarrassment or did he need time to cover his tracks? The thought made her shiver—and wag a finger at herself. There was no way Jerry would ever harm their mother. And yet, what did friends and family say about serial killers when they were interviewed? As investigators lugged away body bags, neighbors always said, "He was the last person I would ever suspect."

Jerry was a contractor and had invested in several dubious parcels of land through the years. Some of them were successful, others weren't, and Frances always wondered how he was able to make ends meet. Jerry was not the most fiscally responsible in the family. And his wife, Laurie, was known to go overboard shopping for their two children and herself.

Someone pecked at the front door and Frances jumped. She hoped she would see her mother wearing that impish grin of hers. Instead, a man stood alone, looking at Frances's car in the driveway.

"Hello," Frances said, opening the door.

"Hi there, ma'am. I'm from down the road. Drew Fetty." He handed her a rolled-up newspaper from the end of the driveway. "I tried to call Jerry and apologize, but I couldn't reach him last night. I left a message but thought—"

"Apologize for what?"

He shoved his hands in his pockets. "Well, I came over here yesterday . . ." He paused. "You're the daughter, aren't you?"

Frances nodded and invited him inside.

"No, ma'am, I just wanted to apologize for upsetting her. I didn't mean to but I can see now that it was bad timing."

"You mean you upset my mother?"

"Yes, ma'am. I came over about the car. It's the perfect thing for my daughter. She thinks I'm going to get her some old beater. I've been talking that up and kidding her about finding a rusty truck. Your mama has taken really good care of her car and it'd be perfect for driving to work. Evidently I jumped the gun. Miss Ruby didn't know you were selling it."

"Oh, dear."

"Yeah, I feel bad. I left a message for Jerry, like I said, but I wanted to make sure she's all right and to say I didn't mean to upset her."

"It was a misunderstanding," Frances said, wondering what Jerry had been thinking.

"That's exactly what it was, a misunderstanding. If I had it to do over, I would hold my horses. Can you tell her that? Is she here?"

"No, she's not. But I'll tell her when she gets back. I'm sure it will all work out."

"I sure hope so."

"It was sweet of you to come by. Thank you."

He gave a gap-toothed smile and turned to leave, then looked back. "Fred over at the shop said he'd give it a once-over this afternoon. You know, just to check it out. I'm not worried about the engine compression."

"I think we should wait on that for now, Mr. Fetty."

"Of course. Hold the horses. You have Jerry call me."

She closed the door and watched him through the small windows as he walked to the road and disappeared behind a willow. Had his conversation with Ruby the day before sent her mother reeling? It made sense.

There was something strange about the man returning this morning, though. Frances wanted to do a background check on Drew and see if he had any priors. He could have come here to mention his conversation to make things sound plausible later.

She shook the thought away and straightened the kitchen, though everything was neatly piled around the room. Aged cookbooks sat on a dusty shelf underneath the phone mounted to the wall. Newspapers from the previous six days were stacked on a dresser that had been moved into the kitchen corner to store papers and display her mother's cake creations. Frances removed the rubber band from around the fresh newspaper and unfolded it on top of the pile. She noticed a headline about Iraq. Another headline said, "Wreck Snarls Traffic on I-64."

She glanced at the photo, then turned the paper over. She didn't want to think of all the things that might happen to her mother in traffic. It was one thing to take out a mailbox or sideswipe a car in a parking lot, but what happened if her mother went the wrong way on the interstate and hit a semi?

She had to think of something uplifting. Something positive. Maybe her mother just had a doctor's appointment she hadn't told them about. Maybe she was there now because she didn't want Frances to worry. She'd kept the cancer diagnosis a secret and was going for early morning chemo.

Frances stared at the cakes on the table. There had been three yesterday and now only two remained. Perhaps Ruby had remembered the extra set of keys and was taking a cake to someone who wasn't feeling well. Her mother used food as medicine and as a gift for the soul—it was her one way of connecting with others.

Beside the newspapers were two stacks of mail. The phone bill and the electric bill needed to be paid and there were already stamps on both return envelopes. A yellow sticky note with her mother's scrawled handwriting showed when to mail the payment. Beside the bills was another stack, every envelope torn open haphazardly with arthritic fingers. There was an unopened *Our Daily Bread* and an update on a ministry based in Colorado that had somehow gotten her mother's address.

At the bottom of the stack was a card sent from Asheville, North Carolina, the return address headed by the name *Rev. Franklin Brown*. Frances opened the card and read.

Dear Queen Ruby,

Just wanted you to know we received your generous gift and the tapes. There were a few songs I have never heard and I'm working on putting them in our rotation. Thank you, as always. Very thoughtful.

My humble thanks for helping us keep the ministry going in your neck of the woods. If it weren't for people like you, this music and this old radio voice would be silenced. So I am in your debt.

I'm praying you are doing well and that you'll be encouraged in some way by what you hear today. Remembering Leslie fondly as I write this. I miss him with you.

Sincerely in the love of Christ,
Franklin Brown

Frances recognized the name as someone her mother listened to on the radio. That she had a personal relationship with him surprised Frances. She put the card back in the envelope and straightened the pile. If her mother caught her going through her things, she would bristle.

Oh, that her mother would return and bristle, Frances thought.

She went to the phone in the living room, the one with the big numbers and the giant caller ID she had bought for her mother after the phone incident no one brought up anymore. The time her mother had been scammed. Scrolling backward through the incoming calls, she recognized the last names of two church members. There were calls from telemarketers or pollsters that had gone unanswered, which pleased Frances. One number from the 304 area code was listed several times, also unanswered. There was a call from Julia, Frances's daughter, who was at college. Frances smiled at this, knowing how much it meant to her mother to hear from Julia. There was also a caller listed as unavailable.

She scrolled through the outgoing calls and noticed one to Eula's Salon the day before. Two days earlier her mother had dialed a number in the 704 area code. She wrote that one down and stuffed the paper in her pocket. She had also dialed Julia the same day.

Glancing out the front window and seeing no sign of her brother or mother, Frances wandered into her mother's bedroom. For some reason the closet drew her and she slid the door from the left and looked at her mother's clothes. Ruby had a hard time letting go of any outfit she might wear again, which seemed to be everything she'd ever owned. At the bottom of the closet was a shelf for shoes. She slid the door from right to left and noticed a box that brought back memories.

Frances had found the box in her mother's closet when she was five years old and had removed the stylish boots that laced to the top. The box could hold all the dolls Frances owned if she stacked them on top of each other.

Frances remembered the gasp behind her and the look on her mother's face, one of pure horror. "Don't you ever let me catch you in here with those again, you hear me?" her mother said as she swatted Frances's behind.

Later that night as Frances was tucked into bed, her mother apologized. "It's just that some things are personal. You'll understand when you get a little older."

"Mama, why do you keep shoes you never wear?"

Ruby had looked at her with a sadness Frances recalled but still could not comprehend. "I need you to leave my things alone. Do you understand?"

Frances stared at the box now and wasn't sure she ever understood. And she realized she'd never asked.

She heard the front door open and hurried to the living room.

Jerry stood at the kitchen table, his hand on the back of the ladder-back chair. Frances would have described her brother as a blank slate or a hard read. His face rarely betrayed what was happening behind the curtain, if, in fact, there was any activity there. But now the consternation he felt inside was written on him like some childhood memory verse.

"I drove to every place I could think of and didn't see a trace. Beauty salon, church, the FoodFair, even Walmart."

"What about the doctor's office? Do you think maybe she could have made an appointment we didn't know about?"

"She lets me or Laurie drive her because she doesn't like driving in town." He opened the top drawer of the dresser in the corner and pulled out an inspirational calendar with pictures of sunsets and flowers. The day's date was blank except for the tiny note, *Take medicine* that was written on every day. "She writes down the doctor's appointments. There's nothing here."

Frances took the calendar and flipped back a month and forward and nothing stood out to her. Just reminders about birthdays and anniversaries. There was a question mark scrawled on Saturday's date but nothing else. "What do you think that means?"

"Who knows?" Jerry said.

Frances put the calendar away. "What about the cemetery? Maybe she wanted to visit Dad's grave by herself."

"Can a person spend that long at a cemetery? I hadn't thought of that, but she ought to have been back by now if that's where she went. That road is winding and narrow and it has drop-offs."

Frances looked up. "There was a man who stopped by. Fetty. Do you know him?"

"Drew?"

She nodded. "He came to apologize about talking with Mom about her car."

"Oh, for crying out loud. I told him not to say anything."

Frances tried not to show her frustration, but she didn't do a very good job.

"I saw him in town and he mentioned the car and his daughter," Jerry said. "I told him we *might* be looking to sell it."

"You should have made it clear."

"All right, next time we take the keys from our mother, I'll remember that."

"Jerry, we need to call the police. Something is not right."

He pursed his lips and looked back at the table. "Weren't there three of those here last night?" he said, nodding toward the cakes.

"I think so."

His eyes darted. "Maybe that's where she is. Off with a fresh cake for somebody."

"I don't know. It's a possibility, but I think it's time—"

"Give it twenty-four hours. She'll call us. We'll find her. We can figure this out and save her and us a lot of trouble."

Frances stared at the cakes, sitting like twin towers. "If we haven't found her by this time tomorrow, I'm calling."

"Deal. I'll head to the cemetery."

Though Ruby's father was not a religious man himself, he allowed her to attend church with Bean and her mother. If that was what she wanted to do on Sunday mornings, it was her decision. After church, Ruby ate dinner at Bean's house.

Her father had become less averse to Ruby and Bean's friendship because, Ruby assumed, he must have seen the comfort such a friend gave a girl who felt alone in the world without her mother. That Ruby enjoyed the company of Bean's mother was natural, though the man tried to have the lady at the company store take that role. Ruby wasn't having it because Mrs. Grigsby was a thin, droll woman who seemed to want to keep her from ever smiling again. Bean did a spot-on impression of the woman, curling her lips and furrowing her brow, and Ruby laughed every time she saw Mrs. Grigsby because Bean's impersonation was so good.

There was still a cloud over Ruby's father, however. He would get into a funk over work and the conflicts with his partner, Thaddeus Coleman, or perhaps over the memories of his wife. He tried to mix with the workers, but that was difficult because of his station. He was the co-owner, and there was a chasm between the upper crust and the common, though her father envisioned something different.

Occasionally he took Ruby to dinner in a neighboring town or they would travel overnight by train on short trips to hotels. Once they went to Parkersburg for dinner and a moving picture show. The next Sunday, Ruby filled Bean in as they walked home after church.

"Tell me what the train's like," Bean said. "I want to know every little thing. And the hotel. What movie did you see?"

The film was *King Kong* and Ruby described the innocent but beautiful look of Fay Wray and how the film reminded her of the story *Beauty and the Beast*.

Bean closed her eyes and said she was trying to conjure up the giant ape crawling to the top of the Empire State Building. "What does the Empire State Building look like?" she asked as they walked into her house.

Ruby tried to describe it. "King Kong swatted at the airplanes flying around with one hand and he held on to Fay Wray with the other."

"How did he keep from squishing her?" Bean said.

Bean's mother laughed as she brought food to the table. A simple meal of potatoes and green beans and some kind of meat Ruby couldn't identify and didn't ask about.

"What was the theater like? And what did you eat?"

Ruby smiled and told her about the tall, block building with the white columns in front and the marquee outside.

"What's a marquee?" Bean said.

"It's the lighted sign out front that you walk under. Bean, you have to go with me. The carpet is as thick as moss by a tree stump. You sink in all the way to your ankles. And the popcorn and cotton candy are so heavy in the air you feel like you're eating it with each breath."

Bean took a deep breath.

"It's impossible not to eat something while you're there," Ruby said. "But there are so many choices. They have chocolate-covered peanuts and hot cashews and jujubes and red and black licorice, just like we have at the store."

Bean took a bite of green beans. "I can almost taste it. What did you get?"

"Popcorn and cashews. The sweet stuff hurts my stomach."

"I'd have had all of it. One of everything."

"And then we went inside the theater. Mirrors on the walls and glass chandeliers hanging from the ceiling. Posters of movies that are coming and chairs so soft you sink down deep."

"It sounds like a dream," Bean said.

Mrs. Dingess listened to the description as closely as Bean did as they ate Sunday supper. "The way you describe it, it's almost like being there, Ruby."

When they finished, the girls cleared the table and Bean pumped water to do the dishes. The two laughed as they cleaned the plates and let Bean's mother rest. The baby was growing and moving and sapping the woman's strength.

"Mama thinks this one's going to take," Bean whispered as they cleaned the plates and forks. "But all the other babies have died before they came out, so I have my doubts that this one is gonna be fully baked."

Ruby held up a fork and looked at the intricate design, then handed it to Bean to dry. "How come you have such nice silverware?"

"You mean, why do we not own nothing else of value and still have this?"

"I didn't mean anything by it," Ruby said.

"It's all right. Mama's family gave her this set when she and Daddy got married. They gave her lots of plates and teacups, too, but most of that got smashed. You can't smash silver. You can lose it or people can steal it or trade it."

"Has some of it been stolen?" Ruby said.

Bean glanced at her mother fanning herself in a rocking chair. "My daddy traded most of it for corn mash. People up on the mountain have a still. He's got a taste for the silly sauce."

"Is that where he is now?" Ruby said.

"Mama says he's out chasin' the devil, whatever that means. And when he's not doing that, he's drumming up people for the union. I don't know where he is."

"So your daddy's a union man?"

"You bet he is. There's a lot of people who are."

"My father said the miners are a lot better off without a union here," Ruby said.

Bean gave a smirk. "It figures your daddy would say that. He doesn't have to crawl into a mine. He gets to stay aboveground and make rules. The union's comin' whether your daddy thinks it's good or not. From what I hear, just about all mines have a union. Protects the workers."

Ruby dipped the meat plate in the dirty water and scrubbed at the grease. "My father said unions sometimes take as much from the miners as the bosses. But if there are good bosses who are fair—"

Bean leaned toward Ruby. "If my daddy ever shows up, don't let him hear you talking that way."

Ruby nodded. "I'll admit I don't know a whole lot about it."

In the silence that followed, Ruby heard a creaking behind her and turned to see Bean's mother uncover something on the wooden counter by the window.

"Made you something, Bean," Mrs. Dingess said. "Who wants cake for dessert?"

Bean's mouth dropped open and she squealed. "Mama makes the best cakes in the county."

"Now don't promise something I can't deliver," her mother said, chuckling. "I didn't have enough sugar for frosting, but the cake will be good."

"I'll spread some apple butter on top," Bean said. "Or just cow butter if it's warm enough."

"I can get you sugar," Ruby said. "It won't be any trouble. We have lots at the store."

"No, we can't afford it," Mrs. Dingess said.

"And Mama's not big on credit."

"It would be a gift," Ruby said.

"She ain't big on gifts, either, because it feels like credit."

"I only want a sliver," Ruby said.

"What's wrong? You don't like cake?"

"I told you I don't do well with sweets."

There was a peck at the screen door and Ruby saw her father. She ran and opened it, and he stepped inside and took off his black fedora. "I came to take Ruby off your hands." His voice was high-pitched but warm and kind.

"Oh, we love having her," Bean's mother said.

He reached out a hand and took hers. "I'm Jacob Handley."

"Cora Jean," she said, smiling. "Why don't you have some cake with us?"

"I'm not eating mine," Ruby said. "You can have it."

Her father hesitated and finally put his hat on the table and sat. He tasted the cake and raised his eyebrows. "This is wonderful."

"They didn't have sugar for the frosting and I said we could get some from the store."

"Of course," her father said.

Mrs. Dingess ignored the offer. "Ruby was telling us stories of the movie theater and concessions."

"You never told us about the hotel," Bean said. "Or the train trip. Or what the town was like. I have a million questions."

"Ruby is quite the storyteller," her father said, brushing crumbs from his mustache. "She's dramatic enough to be in the movies, I think. Maybe one day you'll see her up there on the silver screen, Bean."

The front door squealed on its hinges and Bean's father walked inside. Swayed was more like it. He was teetering from one side to the other, squinting at the man sitting at his kitchen table like he was trying to focus.

"Well, we need to get home," Mr. Handley said. "Get your Bible and your things, Ruby."

"What's your hurry?" Judd Dingess said, his words slurred. He steadied himself with a hand on the wall. "Stay awhile. You built this palace, didn't you?" He banged his palm and left a dent in the plaster. "Not as nice as where you live or where Coleman lays his head, but then we're just common folks."

Jacob Handley looked at Mrs. Dingess and tried to smile. "The cake was wonderful, ma'am. Thank you for your hospitality. Ruby, let's go."

Ruby was out the door carrying her Bible, but Bean's father stepped in front of the door, blocking her father. "Fraternizing with the chattel is frowned on in most coal camps, cap'n. You have your side of the tracks, we have our'n." He cocked his head. "Unless you're interested in something else we got other than coal." He glanced at his wife.

"Judd, stop it," Cora Jean said. "Leave them alone."

Bean's father threw his hands up. "Hey, far be it from me to hold a man back." Then he leaned close. "You'd never hold a man back from what he needed, would you, Handley? You'd never stop a man from doing what he really needed to do?"

"Daddy, please," Bean said.

Judd laughed and gave a crusty cough. Ruby's father pushed past him and down the step, and Judd pushed the screen door open and spit phlegm into the yard.

"Go on back to your store! Go on back to your fine life and moving pictures while the rest of us die in a dark hole."

Ruby felt a hand on her shoulder as they quickly walked away.

"I think it might be best for you to stay away from their house."

"Why? This is the first I've seen Mr. Dingess there."

"Well, he showed up today, didn't he?"

"They're nice, Dad. Bean's mom is so kind. And Bean's the best friend I've ever had."

"I know. I'm not saying you can't be friends. But I think you need to stop going over there. The talk in the town . . ."

"What talk? You mean about the union?"

He stopped and stared at her. "What have you heard?"

Ruby saw his concern and considered her response. "Bean mentioned something. But I heard Mrs. Grigsby talking about it in the store, too. I don't understand. Why do the men want a union if you're treating them well?"

He took a deep breath and resumed his walk. "It's complicated. The workers want us to be fair. That was my goal when I agreed to invest in this. I didn't come here to just make money. I wanted this mine to be different. There's so much greed, Ruby. So much disparity between rich and poor. I wanted to help create an atmosphere where those working in the mine and those who ran it shared success. The houses we built—I wanted them to be better than anything people like Bean's family could afford."

"Her house isn't that nice."

"That's because my plans weren't followed. And your mother's illness prevented me from being more involved. Since we've come here, I've tried to change things."

"And Mr. Coleman doesn't like that."

Her father's gait slowed and he clasped his hands behind him. "He has a different agenda I didn't see. I should have. I should have known by the men he's hired to run things. Other mines have had skirmishes.

South of here—Matewan, Blair Mountain. It's been brutal. The working conditions, living conditions—awful. Men have lost their lives and it doesn't have to be that way. But Coleman doesn't share my vision. We've been at odds since we arrived."

"What can you do?"

"He's offered to buy me out. He wants me to sell my half and leave. That would be the easiest."

Ruby stopped. "Are you going to?"

"Don't be upset. Of course not. Bean and her mother deserve better. The other families, too. If someone doesn't stand up . . . I have power to help change things."

"Why don't you buy Mr. Coleman's half?"

"I've offered. But these hills are gold to him." He leaned down, his hands on his knees. "Things may get worse before they get better. I've been thinking that this is no place for a girl. And I don't see myself leaving right now."

"I'm not going anywhere, Dad. I'm going to school in October with Bean. She explained why they don't start until then here in the mountains. It's going to be so much fun—"

"Yes, about school." His face turned grave. "I promised your mother something before she died."

Ruby couldn't breathe. She knew what was coming. "No. You can't, Dad!"

A miner passed with a bamboo pole on his shoulder and a stringer of fish. Her father smiled and waved, then put a hand on Ruby's shoulder and they walked toward town. "We'll talk about it at home."

14

Frances sat in front of Eula's Beauty Salon watching women coming and going. Jerry called and told her there was no sign of Ruby at the cemetery or in any of the surrounding gullies. The caretaker wasn't around but he left a note and asked him to call.

Frances put her phone in her purse. She had considered calling Eula but wanted to see her face-to-face and gauge her reaction to her questions. Sometimes the face betrays the heart. Frances had learned this the hard way. She had also learned there were times when the face told you nothing about the betrayal.

Eula's salon was the front of her house—she had added a different living area on the back when business took off. She hired younger stylists who then started their own shops in other towns, so Eula's was known as a launching pad. A nicely dressed young woman greeted her and Frances explained she didn't have an appointment but wanted to speak with Eula.

"Eula is taking a break," the young woman said. "But I'll see if she'll talk with you. Wait here."

After a few moments Frances was ushered to the back of the shop and through a sliding door that separated the old from the new. Eula was somewhere in her sixties with hair she had refused to let go gray. She didn't look much different than when Frances had met her when her parents had planted in the little town.

Eula offered tea. Frances could tell it was a polite accommodation but said yes anyway.

"Sit, sit," Eula said. "How's your mother? I haven't seen her in a couple of weeks."

"That's why I'm here. I wanted to see if you've noticed anything different lately. I don't want to infringe on stylist-client privilege." Frances smiled.

Eula put the hot water down and squinted. "Why do you ask?"

"Jerry and I have been concerned about her driving. We talked with her about it and—"

"It didn't go well."

"That's an understatement."

Eula poured hot water over a chamomile tea bag and pushed the sugar bowl toward Frances. "Why don't you ask Ruby what's wrong?"

"I was hoping to get another perspective."

"Mm-hmm." Eula sat back and folded her hands. "That mother of yours has so much life in her. Every time she sits in the chair, she talks about you. She wonders how long it's going to be before you two lock her up in a home."

"We've worked hard at allowing her to be independent."

"That's noble of you," Eula said with a tinge of sarcasm.

"We just want Mom to be safe. And to not do anything she'd

regret. Like hit a child on a bike. It would kill her if she did that, but we can't get her to see something bad is going to happen."

Eula narrowed her gaze. "It kills her you're so far away, that she's another box on the list for you and your brother to check off. Call Mom—check."

Frances tried to take the words as well-intended venom. "Is that what she talks about when she's here? Jerry and me?"

"She talks about a lot of things. Politics. The election. Jesus. What's going on over at the church—I don't think she's ever been in here and not invited me to a service."

"And you've never come, have you?"

"That's between your mother and me. She's tried to get me to listen to that fellow on the radio, too. The one she's gaga about. Mentions her name on the program. Calls her Queen Ruby. I've told her she ought to drive down there and take him to lunch. His wife passed six months ago."

Frances's mouth dropped open. "Mom is interested in someone romantically?"

"The way she talks about him makes me think so, but she denies it. Said your father was the only man for her. But I half expect her to hop in that Town Car one day and point it south."

"Where does he live?"

"North Carolina. He's in her age range, from what she says. Grew up on a ridge close to where her father owned the mine. Before all of the ugly happened."

"She doesn't talk about that with me. She never has."

"She doesn't talk much about it with me either," Eula said.

Frances looked away through the large back window with the flower garden and a swarm of hummingbirds fighting over a feeder.

Eula leaned forward. "I know you love her. But she thinks she's an inconvenience. You're off doing your important things, crunching other people's numbers. Making a good living."

"Trying to," Frances said.

"I can't understand why you don't spend more time getting to know her. You're missing out, Frances."

Frances knew a little of Eula's life and family, and she wondered whether the words Eula spoke were really for her or if she was projecting what she felt about her own children.

"I didn't mean to step on your toes," Eula said. "I get a little exercised about this—and I've been storing it for a while. Waiting to have this conversation."

"I want to hear what you have to say."

Eula stared out the window and it seemed to Frances that she was looking beyond, to something she could only see with her heart. "There's things people tell you while you're washing their hair or coloring it that they won't tell anybody else in the world. Things come spilling out. I don't know why—maybe it's how relaxed people get when you wash their hair. Think about it. How many people have touched your hair in your lifetime? Your mother did when she combed it. Maybe your father, putting his hand on your head?"

Frances could think of only one other person who had ever touched her hair, and she pushed the memory away.

"Well, one day Ruby was leaned back in the sink and I was shampooing her scalp, massaging it, getting her to relax. The most peaceful look came over her. She said her mother used to wash her hair. Said it made her feel loved and cherished. I could see her going back in her memory, all those years melting away because I was washing her hair like her mother."

"Did she talk about her mother?"

"Not much. She'd go down the trail talking about her and then turn around. There's part of remembering the past that's a comfort and part that's a burden, and there just seemed to be some rooms she wanted to keep closed."

"You know her father was killed," Frances said.

Eula nodded. "The Beulah Mountain Massacre. I've heard about it. Ruby said they're making a museum."

"I didn't hear about that."

"She had a newspaper with her the last time she was in and it had a picture of what they were making."

"She lived there for a while with her father, after her mother died," Frances said.

A doorbell rang and Eula stood, pushing off the chair with a grunt. "That's my cue. Need to get back. It was nice talking with you, Frances."

"You've given me a lot to think about."

"I sympathize with your situation. I don't want her hitting anyone with that car. But maybe there's a way to give your mother freedom and still keep her safe."

"How?" Frances said.

"The three of you are going to have to figure that out. I wish you well."

Frances drove by the FoodFair and the post office, hoping to spot Ruby's car. She had wanted to flat-out ask Eula where she thought her mother had gone, but decided to accede to Jerry's wishes and keep quiet. As she drove, she heard Eula's words rattle in her soul like a bad muffler.

Sitting in the drugstore parking lot, watching cars head toward the interstate, Frances turned on the radio and tried to find the station her mother liked. When a man read a Bible verse, she knew she had discovered the right one.

"I hope you're having a good day and that you woke up like I do every morning and put one foot down and then the other. I stretch my hands toward heaven to say, 'Good morning, Lord. This is the day you have made. I will rejoice and be glad in it.' If that's not how you started your day, do that now. Come on, stretch out and give God thanks."

There was something to the man's voice that made Frances feel warm, even though the style felt hokey, a little too down-home. The man's voice was a soothing, rich baritone. He spoke in Christian platitudes and well-rehearsed lines he had given a thousand times, but there was nothing that didn't seem genuine. He really believed what he was saying.

"I'm Franklin Brown and I'll be with you for the next hour as we comb through some of the stacks of records and tapes and CDs I have of the best Southern gospel. I hope it will blow the dust from your soul and that something we play or say or pray will draw you closer to the One who loved you enough to die for you.

"And speaking of a love that can change your heart and destiny, that's a good place to start. Does your burdened soul need liberty? It's available right now, whatever you're going through."

He played "At Calvary," and Frances drank in the words as she drove back toward her mother's house. After another song, Reverend Brown returned with his folksy, conversational tone. He mentioned two listeners who were having birthdays and invited people to e-mail him with anniversaries and announcements they wanted others to know. A listener in Rainelle, West Virginia, was having a "spiritual birthday" and the man gave thanks to God for the person's life.

"And I would be remiss if I didn't mention my friend in Kentucky, Queen Ruby. What a generous soul. You know, if it weren't for people like Ruby investing in what we do, well, we wouldn't be doing what we do, would we? It takes funds from people like you to help us continue and if you can help us, I'll give our address in a minute. You can get a pen and paper and write it down. But back to Ruby—I got a nice note from her the other day, and she included some music sent in memory of her late husband, Leslie. What a fine man who served our country well and served the Lord well, too. Let me play this for Queen Ruby today up there in Kentucky."

Frances pulled into the driveway and there was no sign of her mother's car. Her heart fell. She sat in the car until the next song ended, then went inside and dialed the 704 number she had found on caller ID. A machine picked up. It was the same voice she'd heard on the radio and she left a brief message.

As she turned on the radio in the kitchen, the front door opened and her heart leapt. She ran to look and saw Jerry.

"No luck?" she said.

He shook his head. "She's AWOL. Can't find a trace. I talked with her pastor. I talked with the lady who runs the FoodFair. Stood in line at the post office."

"Did you ask if they'd seen her?"

"Of course. But I couched it in how they think Mom's doing with her driving. If they've noticed what we have."

"People are going to figure out she's gone, Jerry. We need to call the police."

He put up a hand. "Not yet. We're going to find her and when we do, I swear, I'm going to chain her to her La-Z-Boy."

Frances told him about her conversation with Eula and brought up the idea of a possible romance with the reverend on the radio.

Jerry was stunned. "You don't think she drove to North Carolina, do you?"

"At this point, anything is possible. And every hour that goes by is another one we've lost getting help. She could have been abducted by some crazed loonies high on drugs for all we know."

Jerry snapped his fingers. "Her credit card. We can track her credit card. I've got the information at home. She made me a copy of everything and I keep it, along with the will. I'm listed on the account, so I can call and get them to tell us where it was used last."

Frances didn't feel any better about the prospect of seeing where her mother had used her credit card—or where thieves might have used it, but at least it was something. "I'll stay here. Maybe she'll show up by dark."

She said the words but knew her mother wouldn't return. Something deep inside said nothing would be the same again.

Frances was picking at a sandwich when the ringing phone made her jump. She made a mental note to switch it away from the "wake the dead" setting.

"Frances, this is Franklin Brown in Shelby, North Carolina."

It was like listening to her own personal radio, hearing him on the phone. "Thank you so much for returning my call, Reverend."

"I'm glad to do it. Please, call me Franklin. How's Queen Ruby?"

Frances had hoped the man might say her mother had made it to North Carolina and he was about to take her out for dinner. "Your number came up on her phone as someone she dialed recently. I was hoping you could tell me what you talked about."

A pause. "Well, Frances, couldn't you ask Ruby that?"

His voice sounded off. Like he knew he was being accused of something.

"She's not here right now."

"What do you mean?"

His voice was so soothing, so pastoral, that she let her defenses down. "Rev—Franklin, we had a disagreement about her driving. It's been difficult—with her getting older and unable to see well. She's made some bad decisions, trusting people she shouldn't. My brother and I felt it best to take her keys."

A sigh. "That is so hard. I sympathize with what you're going through. I'm sorry for you and for Ruby. That had to be jarring for her."

"Franklin . . . Reverend, I'll be honest. I think my mother may have become infatuated."

"With what?"

"With you."

He laughed long and hard and that turned into a coughing fit. When he caught his breath, he said, "That's funny. Frances, I can assure you there's nothing going on . . ." He took a pause to laugh again. "Ruby and I are from different sides of the tracks, if you know what I mean. I grew up along a creek bank, up a hollow off Ten Mile. That doesn't mean anything to you, but it does to Ruby and me. I was born so far up the hollow they had to pipe in the sunshine."

"So she didn't contact you again? You don't think she's headed your way?"

"I would highly doubt it. And if what you say is true, I did nothing to encourage this. You have to believe that."

"Well, mentioning her on the radio . . ."

"I do that for all of my supporters. Ruby has been quite respectful of my own loss. My wife passed six months ago and it's been terribly difficult. But I have no designs on your mother, if that's what you're asking."

"You know her financial situation, though."

"What situation is that?"

"My mother has considerable resources. And we have to protect her from . . . Well, you understand."

His voice grew low and even, taking on a tone she hadn't heard on the radio. "Yes, I do. And while I applaud you caring for your mother, I have to wonder if you care more about her 'considerable resources,' as you call them, than you do Ruby. She's mentioned the tension in the family to me."

Frances shook the accusation away. "Reverend, my mother's gone. She left after all of this happened. And I'm worked up and just trying to figure out where she might be."

"I'm sorry. How long has she been gone?"

"We spoke with her yesterday, and when I got here this morning, she had left."

"No note? No explanation?"

"Nothing."

"Have you contacted the authorities?"

"Not yet. We were hoping we'd find her and save her the embarrassment of a big to-do. I think she'd hate that."

"I see. But something bad could have happened. And from what I read about cases like this, the first twenty-four hours are critical."

Her heart raced at the statement she knew was true. Still, something about how in control the man seemed unnerved her. "We're going to call them soon. But let me ask, was this the first time my mother called you?"

"Yes, I was surprised to hear her voice. I'd never spoken by phone, just by letter. Her handwriting is still impeccable, you know."

"Did she talk about something specific?"

"Yes. She had heard a program that concerned her."

"Concerned her?"

"I did an hour on forgiveness. The music, the Bible reading—all of it was centered around how we're told by God to forgive others."

Frances couldn't think of anyone her mother needed to forgive, except for the person who had scammed her, and perhaps her children. "Did she say who she might need to forgive?"

"We didn't get into specifics, but she was distraught, there's no doubt. This is just my guess, but I had the impression she's been carrying this for a long time."

"I don't know a lot about her early life. I know she lived in a boarding school for a few years after her father was killed. And after that she went into the service . . . Anyway, I thank you for calling back. If you hear from her, would you let me know?"

He took Frances's cell phone number and promised he'd call if he heard from Ruby. When she hung up, there were more unanswered questions than before their conversation. But Franklin Brown sounded believable and she had no real reason to distrust him other than the reputation of shady preachers who were in it for the money.

She couldn't sit, so she went through the house looking for any missed clues to her mother's whereabouts or her state of mind. She pulled out the calendar in the top dresser drawer in the kitchen. Why wasn't it tacked on the wall? Her mother probably had a reason. The only things on the wall in the kitchen were a dry-erase board and a picture of a bearded old man praying over his bowl of soup and loaf of bread.

Frances leafed through the calendar and saw doctor's and hair appointments. She stared at the question mark on Saturday, October 2. Strange.

She put the calendar aside and rummaged through the drawer, finding loose coins and hairpins, paper clips, an unopened box of staples, and articles cut from the newspaper. She set the articles aside and kept digging.

In the next drawer were bank statements and investment documents. There was a copy of Ruby's will here, plus Frances knew she kept one in the strongbox on a shelf in the closet. Ruby had sent duplicates to Jerry and Frances after their father died to make sure everyone had a copy.

Then came the drawer of greeting cards her mother had stowed. Sympathy cards from church friends with written prayers inside. She came upon a plain card with not much written on it and recognized her ex-husband's writing. She quickly closed the drawer.

Frances found her mother's checkbook and registers going back decades. She flipped through a recent one, feeling a sense of dread. On one line she noticed Jerry's name. When she saw the amount, her mouth dropped.

The crickets and frogs were in full voice when Jerry walked inside. Dusk had fallen and night encroached quickly.

"Anything?" Frances said.

He shook his head. "Still no sign. But I went over to the sheriff's."

Frances felt a flood of relief. "I'm so glad they know."

"They don't. Not yet. I wanted to find out what happened the day the sheriff came to the house."

"Why didn't you tell them she's missing? She's been gone all day, Jerry, and it's getting dark. She can't see well enough to drive in the dark."

"Now don't get all worked up."

"Don't tell me what to get worked up about. We should have called the police immediately. Now they're going to think we had something to do with it."

"Why would they think that?" Jerry said, an incredulous look on his face. "I'm trying to protect her."

Frances handed him the checkbook and Jerry stared at it. When he didn't respond, she said, "You want to explain that?"

"Not particularly."

"It's none of my business what goes on between you and Mom financially. She can give you as much as she wants. But that amount of money raises questions."

"What questions?"

"Questions about why you needed it. Questions from the police about who's going to inherit Mom's estate. And that you're the executor."

His shoulders slumped. "You think I'd hurt her?"

"I'm not saying that. I'm saying . . . I don't know what I'm saying. I'm scared. And this doesn't look good."

"You do whatever you want, Frances," Jerry said, tossing the checkbook at her. It fluttered to the ground as he walked out the front door.

15

Hollis Beasley held his tongue, but just barely. He had gathered the group inside the Beulah Mountain Baptist Church by hook or by crook and phone calls and a few flyers and an announcement in the *Breeze*. His granddaughter, Charlotte, sat in the back with a notepad and pen and scribbled furiously as residents stood and spoke, but Hollis wasn't sure he wanted the ink in the *Breeze* with the way things were going. Juniper had come to town with him but decided she couldn't take the elevated blood pressure levels the arguing was sure to produce, so she visited a friend near the church.

It had been years since Hollis had been inside the building and walking in gave him the yips. Lots of memories flooded, many of them good. He pushed the nostalgia away and began by saying Buddy Coleman had driven his shiny Jeep to his house and offered extra money if he would sign and lead others away from Beulah Mountain. Hollis conjectured about the board meeting and how Buddy was angling for CEO. This came as no shock to anyone.

Shorty Hutchins grabbed the pew in front of him and pulled himself to a standing position. His wife, Thelma, was a pillar of the congregation and, as Hollis remembered, always raised a hand for an unspoken request. Hollis wondered if getting Shorty to attend church was the reason for the hand in the air.

"Hollis, if I was you, I'd have taken that offer," Shorty said with a nasal twang. "Everybody here knows CCE is going to take this land. They're going to doze it flat and get all the coal they can. This mountain is only worth what's underneath it and if we don't sell, we'll get nothing."

Heads nodded and another hand shot up, this one from Pearl Reynolds, the widow of a miner who had succumbed to black lung. "Every one of us sympathizes with what you and your family have been through, Hollis. I've walked the same road you have, in a lot of ways. But there comes a time, like in the book of Daniel, when you see the writing on the wall. The hand of God writes the truth up there and you have to live with it."

"If God writes something on the wall, I'll read it," Jared Stover said. He spoke without standing because of his weight. His jowls bounced as he talked and he held a cane between his legs that reached the underside of his chin. "But if the devil writes something, I say pay no attention. Buddy Coleman's the devil incarnate. That pip-squeak is offering us poisoned fruit. I say we don't eat it."

"He ain't the devil, Jared," Curtis Williams said.

"He grew up not far from here," someone else said. "My kids went to school with him."

"I don't know why we're so afraid. He's no bigger than a gnat."

"What's the devil do?" Jared said. "He kills, steals, and destroys. What's Buddy want to do? Same exact thing. His daddy before him was crooked as Possum Creek. His granddaddy was worse. If we don't stand up, who's going to?"

Just then Juniper walked in the back and sat beside Charlotte. The girl hugged her grandmother and scooted over, though Juniper didn't need much room. She was nothing but skin and bones.

Curtis stood. "Look, folks, I got no horse in this race. I've signed the papers. It hurt like the dickens and I didn't want to let Hollis down. But once they start blasting, we won't be able to breathe. Let's say I refuse to sell. We band together. Will that stop them? Of course not. Beulah Mountain is the bull's-eye of Buddy Coleman's target. He's showing the company he can get things done. I hate to leave this hollow. I got kin buried on your property, Hollis. You think I want to leave them?"

There was real emotion in Curtis's voice now and the room got quiet with people looking at the floor.

"I look at it this way. This land we love has provided a way out. We can thank our parents and their parents for their hard work. I can either hang on to the past or look to the future. I'm choosing the future."

Curtis sat and Ruthanne drew closer. Several others spoke, all saying selling was the only choice. Virginia Davis said a ridge a few miles away had been mined and now looked fine. "I don't see what the big deal is. There's grass all over and trees sprouting up and they've built a soccer field."

"Soccer fields?" Jared Stover said. "Who's going to play soccer when they've blasted the land flat? Don't you get it? There ain't nobody going to be living here to play soccer."

It was starting to feel like a union meeting gone bad over a wage hike. The church hadn't seen this much drama since it had hosted a gospel sing-off with competing traveling groups. When the Family Buford sang "Wayfarin' Stranger," a song the Roleys had recorded and had actually been played on the radio, Ben Roley shut off the circuit breaker, which took out the microphones and bass guitar. When the Family Buford kept singing and the lady playing the piano didn't stop, Ben put his foot through the bass drum and knocked over the hi-hat cymbals while yelling, "You knowed that was our song!" Hollis had been there that night and the memory made him smile.

He waved for quiet. When things settled, he spoke.

"A lot of you don't agree with me. I can handle that. All I asked was to be heard. I thank you. I got one more thing."

Hollis looked at Juniper in the back row and Charlotte still scribbling in her notebook. He saw the pain on Juniper's face and the hope on Charlotte's, the starkest difference he thought he'd ever seen. It was unbridled youth up against seasoned experience.

"I grew up on this mountain. It's all I've ever known. It fed my mother and father and me. We shot game, we planted corn, and in the end I planted them on the hill. And my time's coming. There's a lot more water over the dam of my life than in the reservoir. But I want to ask a question.

"What's so precious to you, deep in your heart, that you can't put a price tag on it? I would hope your children are part of that. You'd never sell one of your kids. You'd fight anybody who tried to hurt them.

"For me, my spot on Beulah Mountain is the same. It's the one thing in my life I'd die fighting for and not feel like it was a waste. To me, this mountain is worth more than the coal under it. It's worth more than Buddy Coleman will ever pay. He says it's valuable because of the coal. I say it's valuable because God gave it to us. If we won't defend it, who will?

"Is there anything in this life that would make you draw a line in the sand and say, 'You can come this far but you can't come no farther'? That's how I feel. And I can't make you stand with me. Curtis and Ruthanne are friends, and they'll be friends even though we've got this between us. But I'll be standing here when they drive the trucks in filled with dynamite."

The room was still now except for the creaking of one pew in the back. He looked up and saw Juniper rocking her thin frame back and forth and finally standing and heading for the door.

"There's fear in here as thick as apple butter," Hollis said. "You're afraid of what you might lose. I say there's a bigger fear. What if this is not about losing money or land? What if the next generation is looking at us and asking how they ought to live?"

He stared at the top of Charlotte's head. She wrote furiously.

"We've bought the lie that Coleman sets the price. He doesn't own this town. We have more power than we know. We have something valuable. We can sell our birthright, like old Esau, or we can do something daring. We can say no. We're the ones who can do that."

Hollis had heard many sermons in this old church. Some were fire and brimstone. Others were filled with grace and mercy. Most were a little of both. He'd never been so convinced of what he was saying.

"It's been a while since I've heard from the Lord. I've been asking him to raise up people to stand with me. The other night I heard him clear as a bell. *You won't stand alone, Hollis.* And I believe it. So I'm asking that we choose faith over fear.

"It's going to take backbone to say no. But if we stand together, we're giving somebody on the next ridge that same chance. It lets them know it's an option. It opens the door to letting people think differently. And we need some different kind of thinking."

Thelma Hutchins spoke. "Hollis, you made good points. You know we respect you and nobody here wants to give up their land. But you got to know when to hold and when to fold, and you don't have the face cards, and Coleman is the dealer."

Her words were like a dagger in the back. "That's where you've got it wrong, Thelma. Coleman is not the dealer. He pretends he is. The real dealer is the Almighty, and he's looking for one or two of us to stand up. I've made my decision. This is the thing I'll die fighting for. I'm not backing down."

Juniper had stood at the door. She finally leaned against it and pushed her way through. Hollis excused himself and nodded at Charlotte as he passed.

"Nice speech," she whispered.

Hollis found Juniper navigating the concrete steps to the parking lot. The laws about the disabled hadn't reached Beulah Mountain.

"Where you going?" Hollis said, taking one hand as she held on to the iron railing with the other.

"Sit in the truck."

"I thought you were visiting with Debbie."

"I was. And then I got to wondering what was happening in there."

"Why don't you stay? Why don't you speak up?"

She looked at him. "If you'll die for that mountain, you'll die alone. There's been enough dying in this family. That granddaughter of yours don't need you dying. She needs you living."

She swayed in the gentle breeze, then reached out both hands and grabbed on to the rail. "I ain't telling you to back away from what the Lord says. But I'm not climbing onto the bandwagon. There's things worth more than a mountain, Hollis. It hurts me to hear you say it's the most important thing."

"Look, you know what I meant."

He opened the truck door for her and she climbed in and sat there, winded. He thought of Job's wife. Juniper hadn't told him to curse God and die, but it felt the same. How could two people who had gone through so much together be at odds over something so fundamental?

"You know I'd do anything for you," he said.

"Are you sure?" She reached out and closed the door.

As he walked into the church, he noticed Charlotte scribbling. "What did they say while I was gone?"

She whispered, "They all sympathize. They think you're right. But they're still going to sell."

He sat beside her. "What do you think?"

Charlotte stared at her notepad. "This is like *It's a Wonderful Life*, Papaw. Old Man Potter and his bank want to own everything in town, and the only thing standing in his way is the Building and Loan. I don't know if George Bailey has enough friends this time."

Hollis put his arm around her.

"Hollis, we've come to a decision," Shorty Hutchins said. "There ain't one person in here that wants to hurt you or see you lose your slice of that mountain. Every one of us will help in whatever way we can."

"That's right," people said around the room.

"Nobody wants Buddy to win. But we don't see no other way. I worked these hills. Saw the union come in. Went on strike and had to dig ginseng to sell. I've eaten my share of squirrel and possum. It's been hard. And it'll get harder if we try to outlast the company. I'm sorry, Hollis."

Thelma looked at him with pupils as wide as pinholes. "You ought to think of Juniper."

The bile rose and he nearly said something he regretted. He glanced at Jared Stover, who was curiously studying the floor. Either that or he was having an episode. Maybe his wife had gotten to him.

It felt like someone should pray or sing a final hymn. Instead, one by one, people rose and left. Hollis turned off the lights and locked the door. Charlotte stood with him on the steps.

"You going to write about this?"

"Yeah. What you said in there, all of it was true. But it didn't sway anybody."

"Didn't think it would. I still had to try."

"Well, you still have me, Papaw."

"Yes, I do. That'll have to be enough."

"I've been doing research. I've found out some things about the history of the mine . . . probably won't change anything."

"What kind of things?"

"You ever heard of a woman named Ruby Handley? She married a Freeman, so her name—"

"I heard of her," he said, interrupting. "I wouldn't pee on her foot if it was on fire."

"That's terrible, Papaw. You don't even know her."

"I know enough. She and her daddy were part of the problem, coming in here from the outside and taking what they wanted."

"She was just a child, though."

"My parents didn't have much good to say about any of the owners. I expect she has their DNA."

Charlotte turned to him but he couldn't help staring at Juniper in the front seat of the truck. She'd looked sick for a long time but he'd never seen her this defeated.

"Did the Lord really say that to you?" Charlotte said.

"Excuse me?"

"What you said in the meeting. Did God speak to you and say you wouldn't stand alone?"

Hollis looked away. "I've not heard from him in a while. I'm not sure I'd recognize his voice. But if he had spoken to me, that's what I would have wanted him to say."

Charlotte gave him a hug. "Good night, Papaw."

16

FRANCES MAKES A HARD PHONE CALL
BIDING, KENTUCKY
WEDNESDAY, SEPTEMBER 29, 2004

Darkness enveloped the house and it took on a ghostly feel. Every creak of the floor and scratch of the wind-driven rosebushes against the siding made Frances uneasy, as if she were being watched. She looked out a front window, searching for headlights, and said a silent prayer for her mother.

She had put her mother through this, of course, in her teenage years. She'd gone off with friends several times when her mother wanted her home. The roads were too slick or it was the weekend and there were drunks out. Each time Frances had returned after curfew and found her mother waiting in the darkened living room. She gave no warnings or shame, simply put a hand on Frances's shoulder and said, "Good night."

As a teenager, Frances wished her mother had yelled. It was more unnerving to see her walk silently to her room and leave her wondering. But this was her mother's way.

Frances went to the kitchen and turned on the light, memories swirling like the aroma of her mother's cooking. She collected the news clippings from the dresser and sat at the table. Some clippings were yellowing and brittle. They were mostly from a newspaper called the *Beulah Mountain Breeze*. A few fresh copies were in the stack to be recycled. It was clear from the address label and the postage stamped on the front that Ruby had the paper mailed each week. Frances took the top paper from the stack and flipped through it.

The *Breeze* was a glorified grocery store flyer, but the pictures of the small town and the stories about the people were quaint. There was something sad about the pages and pictures, though. Each story had subtext of the struggle in the hills where industry and progress had moved away—and with it the people.

She replaced the paper and turned back to the clippings her mother had saved. Some were stories of residents pictured at kitchen tables or on front stoops in rocking chairs. Most were obituaries with forgotten histories and genealogies.

One obituary from 1974 had a star next to it. Beside the star in her mother's flowing handwriting were the words *The man who led me to Jesus*. The man, Haddon Gander Brace, had been the pastor of Beulah Mountain Baptist Church since 1931. Frances studied his face. He had a bulbous nose and thick glasses. Very little hair. His expression looked almost mischievous as if he'd just kicked a skunk into the baptistery.

The obituary detailed the man's life, how he had survived a mine war in Matewan and how he was called to the ministry. That call came when he was trapped inside a mine in Waldorf, West Virginia. Brace made a promise to serve God if he survived and was good to his word. He had traveled to Chicago and studied at a Bible school and then returned to the hills and became the pastor of Beulah Mountain Baptist, and stayed there most of his life.

Frances smiled at the man's picture and wished she could ask her mother about him. From the sketchy history Frances knew, her mother had been in Beulah Mountain only a short time. That this man had made an impact on her spiritually warmed Frances. She wondered if there were more pictures or documents saved that detailed Ruby's life. Frankly, she hadn't been interested enough to ask, but now she wished she had. She remembered an old steamer trunk her mother had kept covered with a tablecloth at the foot of her bed. Where had she put that?

She riffled through a few more articles and obituaries and put them aside, then walked through the pantry, noticing the bags of flour and sugar stacked at eye level. How had her mother moved all of that?

The old trunk wasn't in her mother's bedroom or in any room on the main floor. Perhaps she had gotten rid of it. No, she wouldn't have done that. She would have stored it. Frances opened the basement door and turned on the light, but the musty smell and the darkness were too much.

She sat on the couch and tried to still her heart.

What would Ruby do?

That made her smile, thinking of the *WWRD* bracelet she could make and sell. If their roles were reversed, her mother wouldn't stop looking. Ruby would keep going until she found Frances, until she figured out what was going on inside her that had caused her to leave. Was it spite? Anger? Was Ruby holed up in a Holiday Inn a few miles away, happy she was making them worry?

She dialed her brother's house and her sister-in-law answered after the third ring.

"No, we haven't heard anything," Laurie said abruptly. "I don't know why you would upset her like this."

"Why *I* would upset her?" Frances said.

"Jerry told me what you did and how much it hurt Ruby. And then for you to accuse him of doing something? It's beyond me, Frances."

"Laurie, I didn't accuse him. I simply asked—"

"You stuck your nose in where you had no business. If you ask me, she's probably waiting for you to leave so she can come home. You always blow things up bigger than they are."

Laurie's vitriol took Frances's breath away. She could only imagine how Jerry had described their conversations. Through the years Laurie had been polite, but there was always something beneath the surface of their interactions. Call it anger or distrust or frustration—it was bobbing now in an ugly way.

"May I speak with Jerry?" Frances said, her voice trembling.

A noise on the phone like Laurie had covered the mouthpiece. After a moment she said, "He's in bed. He said he'd call you in the morning."

"Well, could you tell me if he found out anything about her credit card? He said he was going to call the card company—"

"He said he'd call you in the morning. Good night, Frances."

The line went dead. Frances took a deep breath and hung up. More mind swirling. What if Laurie was right? What if Frances had caused her mother to leave?

She turned off the kitchen light but left the small one on above the stove and wandered to the living room. Her mother had either the radio or the TV on at all times of the day and Frances had to fight the urge to do the same. It was easier to turn something on that drowned out the pain and questions. She sat back in the easy chair and let the events of the day flow through her mind. The stream felt toxic, tainted by anger and the hurt of the past, but she had learned some things.

Her mother had called Franklin Brown after a message on forgiveness. Who did Ruby need to forgive? What had dredged up the past infraction? Did it have something to do with Jerry?

No matter how Frances turned and twisted the possibilities, she couldn't come up with any explanation other than the worst: her mother had met with tragedy. There were stories every day about disoriented older people driving into lakes and rivers. Or stories of older people found in the trunks of burned-out cars, the perpetrators never caught.

She closed her eyes and tried not to think of her mother banging on the inside of her car trunk with her cane. Or floating in water at the bottom of a reservoir. Or going through a guardrail and careening down a mountainside. The possibilities were endless and Frances knew it was going to be a long night.

What if this wasn't about the car? What if Ruby had found evidence her husband had been unfaithful? What if Frances's father had a child by another woman? Ruby could be traveling to see the woman or the child. What if the unavailable number was the child making contact or wanting an inheritance? Or someone who was scamming her at that very moment?

Frances had let her thoughts betray her father. He was a one-woman kind of man and had loved her mother dearly. She needed to calm herself and stop *thinking*. All her life, if she could put the x's and y's together with the right combination of theoretic equations, she could move forward. Her job was numbers. Addition and subtraction and everything balancing from top to bottom.

Frances picked up the phone and scrolled through the call list again. She had seen the calls to and from her daughter and assumed they were chatting. There had been a falling-out between Frances and Julia. Her daughter had asked for space. It was a hard conversation but Frances hoped they could reconcile and things would return to normal. They had always been close.

But what if Julia was in trouble? Did it have something to do with her boyfriend? He wasn't good for her. From what Frances knew, he seemed a lot like . . . Well, she didn't want to go there.

What if Julia had called Ruby to ask for help? What if Julia had avoided calling her own mother? What if Julia had sworn Ruby to secrecy about something?

Frances sat up straight, a lightbulb going on in her head.

What if Ruby, at that very moment, was in the college town with Julia, sleeping in some hotel near campus, preparing to drive her granddaughter to the pro-life clinic? Or what if the forgiveness she was seeking had something to do with her granddaughter and an abortion? What if the frantic call to the radio preacher was about forgiveness Julia needed?

Frances dialed Julia's cell number but it went to her voice mail. She hung up and dialed the apartment.

"Hello?" someone said on the other end.

"Is this Melanie?" Frances said.

"Yes, who's this?"

"It's Julia's mother. I apologize for calling so late. I'm trying to reach her."

"Hello, Mrs. Freeman. She's not here. You can try her cell."

"I did. There was no answer."

"Oh, it's here. She's charging it. She said something about having trouble with it."

Frances looked at the clock. "Do you know where she went?"

"She just said she was meeting somebody."

"And you don't know who?"

"We don't talk a whole lot these days. She's been in a funk since . . ."

"Since what? Is something wrong?"

"Since the breakup. Did she tell you?"

"No. I had no idea." *Finally some good news,* Frances thought. "I didn't think . . . well, it doesn't matter what I thought."

"I hope I didn't overstep," Melanie said.

"You didn't. I won't mention anything about it when I talk with Julia. Melanie, has she said anything about her grandmother?"

"No. But she's kind of in her own world with studying and everything that's going on."

"And you have no idea who she's meeting tonight?"

"I heard her on the phone with someone but I try not to listen. Do you want me to give her a message?"

Frances tried to think quickly but there were so many competing thoughts. "Just ask her to call me. Say it's important. A family matter."

"I'll do that, Mrs. Freeman."

"Thank you, Melanie."

Frances held the phone in one hand like it was a loaded weapon without a safety and she was so caught up she didn't notice the fast beeping. She placed it on the cradle.

Julia's school was six hours away. But the way Ruby drove, it could be eight hours or more. Or a two-day trip. Could Ruby be caught between a promise made to her granddaughter and the concern of her own children about her driving?

She had her hand on the phone when the most terrifying thought came. Her mouth dropped and the air went out of her lungs.

No. She didn't go there. That can't be where she went.

She closed her eyes, surveying her life, her choices, her own need of forgiveness. The pain and abandonment that had brought her life to a screeching halt years earlier. What if Ruby had gone down *that* road of forgiveness? If she had, could Frances follow?

She found the number on her phone, took a deep breath, and dialed.

"Hello?"

The voice sounded groggy and annoyed on the other end, but it brought back pain and sweetness to Frances. The man she had known and trusted and divorced. She had awakened him and she regretted it, but her fear about her mother had trumped all other concerns, even reaching out to her ex.

"Wallace, it's Frances. I'm sorry to wake you."

"Frances . . ."

He said the word like it was a noose he had forgotten was there. She was noose and trapdoor, even after all these years.

"What time is it?" he said.

"Close to midnight. But I wouldn't call if this weren't important."

"Is it Julia?" he said, sounding like he was sitting up.

"Why? Do you know something about her?"

"Frances, I don't even know who I am right now. I was in the middle of some dream . . ." He let that thought go. "Why did you call?"

"I don't think it's about Julia, but I'm not sure. I thought you might be able to help."

"Okay." He was waking now, gaining his faculties. Wallace had always been a hard sleeper, able to drift off without any help. Just put his head against the window on the passenger side or the end of the couch and roll through sleep's silent gate. It was sweet at first and then she resented his ability to drift on that sea while she stayed onshore holding all the towlines.

"Has my mother made contact with you?" she said.

"Ruby? No, why would she?"

"It's a hunch. It's either you or Julia. And I was hoping it was you."

"What in the world are you talking about?"

"I think my mother needs to forgive someone. But I'm not sure."

"It sounds like you've worked yourself up about something that has nothing to do with me."

"Wallace, I need your help. My mother is gone."

His tone changed. "What do you mean?"

She told him the story in one long stream of consciousness and included her fears about Jerry, Julia, the deputy at the door, the pastor on the radio, the man down the street, and Ruby's inability to keep her car between the lines. She told him about the missing cash but left out the part about taking Ruby's keys. When she surfaced from her monologue to take a breath, Wallace jumped in.

"I don't suppose you've called the police."

"Jerry didn't want us to."

"Why not?"

"He said we should be sensitive to her and not make a fuss. And then I found a check she had written to him."

"Frances . . ."

"Wallace, I think Jerry is in some kind of financial trouble. I don't know. I feel like we have to consider all the possibilities."

"Jerry wouldn't hurt your mother. You know that."

"You know how much she's worth. If Jerry is in debt . . ."

"You've been watching too many crime shows on TV."

"Maybe so. Maybe there's a better explanation. Another theory is that Julia's in some kind of trouble and Mom went down there."

"What do you base that on?"

"They've been talking on the phone."

"Frances . . ."

"I'm not making things up. I called her but she hasn't called back."

"It's understandable you're upset about your mother. All these theories are not helping."

"Don't dismiss this. It took a lot for me to realize I needed help. I'm swallowing my pride. Just hear me out."

A heavy sigh. "I haven't hung up, have I?"

"No," she said, her voice whimpering. "What do you think? Doesn't this sound like foul play?"

He paused. "What happened between you and Ruby?"

"Jerry and I took her car keys."

"Oh, for crying out loud, Frances."

"She's going to kill somebody, Wallace."

"Taking that woman's car keys is like taking a microphone away from Rush Limbaugh. She's making you pay."

The way he said it made her think it was less about Ruby and more about her. He was saying, *It's in the blood. You and your mother make everyone pay for their mistakes.*

"I'd guess she's within fifteen miles of you, holed up in some hotel, sleeping like a baby."

"Jerry was going to follow up on her credit card, but he won't speak to me."

Wallace didn't respond.

The thought that her mother might be in a nearby hotel encouraged Frances, particularly coming from Wallace, who had spent years in law enforcement. He had worked his way up the ladder and been close to achieving his dream of detective when the dream crashed. It was a split-second decision in a darkened stairwell. His action was deemed a "bad shoot" and his career was over. Wallace's life spiraled and their marriage followed. He numbed the pain with alcohol and didn't contest the divorce.

"I know this is a lot to ask, but do you think you could come up here?"

"Frances . . ."

He said her name without anger as if he were looking for something he had misplaced. Lost keys in the couch. For the first time since she had called, she wondered if he had hit bottom yet or was still in that long death spiral a plane takes when it loses both engines.

"I haven't asked about you," Frances said.

"I'm fine. But I can't come up there right now. New job."

"I understand. It's a lot to ask."

"She'll probably call in the morning. Apologize for making you worry. You should try to get some sleep."

Frances slept on the couch, if you could call it sleep, staring at the ceiling and listening to the clock tick and chime. She pulled the living room phone with the fifty-foot cord to the coffee table. Before dawn she got in her car and drove through the parking lots of five hotels.

Daylight came and she returned to the house and made coffee and stared out the front window. Just before eight, Jerry pulled up the driveway and got out alone and sauntered inside. Eyes looking at the floor.

"Credit card company said the system's down," he said.

"Wallace thinks she's punishing us."

"You called him?"

"I was desperate."

He looked at her. "I'm surprised he would talk to you."

Frances glanced at him but let it go. No sense stirring things up that had been settled in a courtroom.

"Did he say anything else?"

"Just that he thought she'd call and apologize for worrying us by this morning."

Jerry chewed on the inside of his cheek. "Doesn't look like that's going to happen."

"He asked if we'd called the police."

"That's the only thing left to do."

She held back saying she had been right, that it was the first thing they should have done. She leaned against the wall. "I feel like there's something we're missing, but I can't put my finger on it."

"Yeah, we're missing Mama."

"I'll call them," she said.

Frances picked up the phone just as a car pulled up outside in the gravel. Jerry looked out a window. "I don't believe it."

Her heart skipped a beat and she looked outside but instead of her mother, her ex-husband got out of his car. She didn't know whether to laugh or cry. She remembered him in the courtroom, looking hungover, defeated.

Wallace walked in the door and shook hands with Jerry. His hair was cut short and a little more gray around the edges than she remembered. He'd lost weight but not in a bad way. From the day's worth of stubble she figured he had gotten up before sunrise and made the trek without shaving. He wore jeans and a tucked-in polo shirt that fit snugly and showed off his muscular arms.

"I thought you had to work," Frances said.

He looked at her with those deep-set brown eyes. If she had seen more of his eyes, maybe all the problems they'd had would have gone away. Eyes are the window to the soul and Wallace had kept the curtains drawn their whole marriage.

"I told them it was important." He shoved his hands in his pockets and wandered back to the kitchen, looking around. "Just like I remember it. We had some good talks at this table."

"And some hard ones," Frances said.

"For sure. I thought about coming back when your father passed. Just didn't happen."

"My mother kept the card you sent," Frances said. "It must have meant a lot."

Wallace looked at the pile of clippings on the dresser. "Looks like she kept a lot of things."

She smiled. "You look good, Wallace. I mean, you look healthy. Like you're taking care of yourself."

"Been going to AA. That's helped keep me on the straight and narrow. It's surprising what you can accomplish when you're not drunk every other day. Or not having to be drunk in order to face the day." He pointed at the mound of clippings and the calendar. "Is this how you found everything?"

Frances showed him around the house, pointing out the empty spot where her mother kept her cash. She was like a kid showing her house to a new friend, letting him in on the secret things no one else ever saw. He scrolled through caller ID, then walked around the bedroom and inspected the front and back doors and all the windows.

He went downstairs and walked out to the garage and around the perimeter of the house and stood on the ramp leading to the front door, with the green Astroturf that curled up at the edges.

"Did Julia ever call?" Wallace said.

Frances shook her head.

"I'll reach out to her." To Jerry he said, "When did you talk with the credit card company?"

"I called last night and before I came over. The system was down."

"Can you try again?"

"Sure," Jerry said, heading into the house.

"What do you think?" Frances said.

"Nothing makes me think there was any kind of forced entry. Her bed was made. She took her cane."

"How do you know she uses a cane?"

"Her age. Marks on the linoleum. A picture Julia showed me of the three of you."

Frances let that hang there. It was something she would have to think about—her ex-husband looking at a picture of her mother, daughter, and her so closely he noticed the cane. Maybe all men did that. Or all ex-police officers. But something about it sent a shiver through her and she wasn't sure whether that was bad or good.

"Is there anybody who comes in and checks on her other than you two?"

"She's pretty independent. Has a cleaning lady every couple of weeks."

He rubbed his cheek. "This is Thursday. Julia has a nine o'clock, I think." He got out his cell phone.

"You know her class schedule?"

He glanced at her sheepishly and tapped the side of his head. "You know me. Hard to get stuff out of there once it gets in."

Frances checked her watch. "If she's headed to school, you don't want to distract her driving."

Wallace cocked his head. "She walks. From the new apartment."

"Oh? When did that happen?"

He turned away and put the phone to an ear. "Hey, it's me. You headed to class?"

Frances heard her daughter's voice but couldn't make out any of the words because of the wind and the birds.

"Good. I don't want to bother you, but I'm here at your grandmother's house. She—" He pushed the phone a little closer to his ear. "Yeah, she is. It sounds like Ruby left yesterday morning. We were wondering if you'd heard anything from her. Has she called in the last few days?"

Julia replied and it was all Frances could do to hold back from ripping the phone out of her ex-husband's hand. She waited, watching the back of his head. He was built like a cinder block, stocky with broad shoulders. He listened to Julia intently without making the sounds she did, the *mm-hmms* and gasps of a mother paying attention.

"But nothing other than that?" he said.

Frances wanted to ask if Julia was having an abortion. Or if she was seeing that ne'er-do-well boyfriend again. She wanted to tap Wallace on the shoulder and give him a list of questions, but right then Jerry bounded outside.

"The system's back up at the card company," Jerry said, out of breath.

Frances looked at Jerry's handwriting and tried to make out what he'd scribbled. When Wallace ended the call with Julia, he joined them.

"The card was used Monday, the twenty-seventh, at the FoodFair."

"Maybe she took her cash to avoid using the card," Wallace said.

"Is that good news or bad?" Frances said.

"It just decreases our chances of finding her."

"I knew we should have called the police."

"Thinking that way is not going to help," Jerry said.

"I knew from the moment this happened something was wrong. She could be lying in a ditch somewhere right now. Lying out there all night in a pool of blood."

Wallace went inside the house as they argued. He returned a few minutes later. "I called the sheriff. They're on the way."

Frances put her face in her hands. "I knew it. We pushed her too hard."

She felt a hand on her arm and looked up to see Wallace. "Your mother is a strong woman. Maybe she stopped at a hotel on her way to . . . wherever. The pastor you mentioned."

"Pastor?" Jerry said.

Frances waved a hand as if she'd explain later. "I didn't tell her I loved her. I should have seen what it would do to her. And now she's gone."

"Stay with me, okay?" Wallace said. "Whatever happens, you were trying to love her. Nobody can fault you for that. You waited a long time. Even in the waiting, you were caring."

Frances nodded and turned away. She went inside for a box of tissues and didn't go back out until the sheriff arrived.

17

RUBY GIVES BEAN A ROOT BEER FLOAT
BEULAH MOUNTAIN, WEST VIRGINIA
SEPTEMBER 1933

Ruby hadn't seen Bean for a few days, which was uncharacteristic, and she wondered if something was wrong. Late on a Saturday afternoon Ruby spotted something moving through the honeysuckle behind the company store. She opened the window and waved Bean up the fire escape. The two sat on her bed, Bean taking off her shoes, Ruby staring at the holes in her friend's socks. Bean had turned the socks around and around to get all the wear out of them, but even so, the cotton was as thin as hosiery on the bottom.

"Where have you been?" Ruby said. "You were supposed to come over two days ago."

"My mama took sick. I've been caring for her. The company doctor's not too good with miners—let alone their pregnant wives."

"Is she going to be okay? And the baby?"

"I think she's turned the corner. She was up at the stove when I left."

Ruby's face beamed. "I have good news. Mrs. Grigsby showed me how to make root beer floats."

"Really?"

"There's not much to it, just root beer over ice cream. When the store closes, I'll take you down and make you one. Would you like that?"

"Boy, would I!" Bean said. "But are you sure it's all right?"

"They lock the place tight but we can go down the dumbwaiter. Nobody will know."

Bean rubbed her hands in delight.

The two talked and looked through a new catalog Ruby's father had received. As they studied the pages, Ruby opened her heart to her friend.

"There's something I don't get," she said as she flipped another page. A man in a three-piece suit with perfect hair stared at her. "Why do some have it good and some have it bad?"

"You mean, why do a few have it good and the rest of us don't?" Bean said.

"Maybe."

Bean stared at the page. "Some say it's the luck of the draw. Some call it God's will. I think it's somewhere in the middle. You got to take the good with the bad. Now for you, you have lots of nice things and your daddy is well off and you probably won't want for anything the rest of your life. But you don't have a mama. That's a load to bear. Me, on the other hand, I'll be scratching and clawing till kingdom come. But you know what? I'll still have my mama. And she's always going to love me." She picked up the pearl-handled brush on Ruby's nightstand. "I wouldn't trade with you. No offense."

"None taken." Ruby stretched out on the bed, hands behind her head, and looked across the room at the picture of her mother she saw each morning and night.

"Would you trade fathers with me?" she said.

Bean sighed. "I guess that's another story, ain't it? Some things in life are good and some are bad and they all get thrown into the stew and you try to eat around the gristle. God doesn't give us the option of a Sunday potluck where you pick what you want and leave the rest. He gives the whole kit and caboodle and we have to deal with what we get."

"Why don't you hate me for what I have?"

"Who says I don't?" Bean said. Then she smiled and both of them laughed.

Bean pointed at the open steamer trunk in the corner. "Where'd you get that?"

"My dad gave it to me."

"What's it for?"

Ruby rolled onto her side. "He's sending me away."

Bean furrowed her brow. "What are you talking about?"

"He promised my mother. There's a school in Pennsylvania where she went as a girl. She told him before she died that she wanted me to go there. At least that's what he said."

"You don't believe him?"

Ruby shrugged. "Maybe she said it. But I think he doesn't want me here with all the problems he's having with the mine and the workers and Coleman."

"And he doesn't want you being friends with me."

Ruby waved a hand. "You're the least of his worries. Now, your father, that's another story. But I think my father likes you."

"Do you want to go?"

Ruby hung her head.

"Can't you talk him out of it? I was all-fired ready to have you in our school."

"And I was all-fired ready to go." Ruby smiled.

"Tell him that. He seems like the kind who will listen."

"He's already sent the money. They're letting me start late. He gave me that trunk to pack up all my stuff. Clothes, shoes, my birth certificate and pictures and everything I need. He's sending it ahead and then I'll take the train."

"Your whole life in a trunk," Bean said. "Doesn't seem fair. How long will you be there?"

"Till college, I guess. My father will probably move back to Pittsburgh and live there after he settles things here."

"Sounds lonely."

"The only thing that would make it tolerable was if you were going with me."

Bean's eyes grew big. "Wouldn't that be something? You and me sharing a room at some fancy school? Learning things and eating dinner together and talking till all hours of the night. And you helping me with my schoolwork."

"I doubt you'd be the one needing help, Bean. You'd probably be the one to help me."

"Pshaw. You're a lot smarter than me. I just got survival instincts."

"If you went, you wouldn't have to worry about food or being snakebit or getting cold at night."

Bean got a far-off look. "Yeah, but we could never afford it."

"My father has enough money to send us both a thousand times. I told him it would be good for me to have a friend instead of going alone."

"You asked him to pay my way?"

Ruby nodded.

"What did he say?"

Ruby sighed. "He said even if he agreed, your family wouldn't."

"He's right about that. But you know what? If I went with you, I wouldn't have to have a trunk. I could get all my things in a pillowcase."

Ruby laughed. "I swear, Bean, you're the funniest thing. Would you go if you had the chance?"

Bean shrugged. "I'd go in a heartbeat if it wasn't for Mama. It would be hard to leave her and the new baby. She's going to need help. My daddy won't be much good."

A door slammed downstairs and a lock clicked. Ruby held up a hand. "They're closing. Let's go!"

Ruby rode the dumbwaiter downstairs and sent it back, and Bean appeared a few moments later. She looked around the darkened store. "It's so exciting I have to pee!"

"The bathroom's in the back and around the corner," Ruby said. "I'll make your root beer float."

Ruby scanned the counter and set out two glasses. She would need to leave things the way she had found them. She put ice cream in one glass and poured root beer over it. In the other she put only root beer.

Bean returned and sat on the stool in front of the counter.

"You should have seen all the foam that came up when I put the soda on the ice cream," Ruby said. "What were you doing back there?"

"Doing what everybody does in the bathroom. Don't get so nosy."

"When we go to school, we'll be in dorms and share a bathroom."

"I'll just be glad I don't have to run outside every time I get the urge."

Bean took a sip of the concoction and closed her eyes. Her face was beatific as if she had been transported to some higher plane of heaven. "I declare, that's about the best thing I ever tasted. It's all bubbly and sweet." Ruby handed her a spoon and Bean scooped out some vanilla ice cream and moaned with pleasure. "I've never had ice cream."

"Are you serious?"

"There was some kind of family reunion on my daddy's side that was supposed to have it all churned up in a bucket with ice and salt,

I think, but he took off the day before and we never went. Mama said I cried all day wanting something I'd never tasted."

"Well, you're going to have all the ice cream you can eat at the boarding school."

"Ruby, you know that's another dream I'll never wake up to. Besides, I don't belong in a place like—"

Bean stopped talking as footsteps sounded on the wooden porch. Keys jangled and the door opened. Ruby ducked her head behind the counter.

Bean sat, transfixed by the opening door, the spoon in her mouth.

Mrs. Grigsby toddled inside and closed the door and flipped the light. When she saw Bean, she gave a hop and dropped her keys.

"How did you get in here?" the woman said. "And what are you drinking?"

Bean looked at the empty counter, then back at Mrs. Grigsby. "I've never had a root beer float and thought I'd try one, ma'am."

The woman pointed a finger. "You stay here. Do you understand?"

"Yes, ma'am."

Mrs. Grigsby retreated to the front door.

"Go get in the dumbwaiter," Ruby whispered.

Before Bean could react, Mrs. Grigsby stepped back inside followed by Ruby's father.

"And I found her right there at the counter. Now the door was locked, so there's no question who let her in."

Ruby's father put his thumbs in his vest pockets and nodded. "Hello, Bean."

"I didn't mean nothing bad, Mr. Handley. I'll pay you back for the root beer float."

He ignored her words. "Ruby? Come on out. I know you're here."

When Ruby stood, Mrs. Grigsby gave a flustered sigh. When she was done with her harangue, Ruby's father held up a hand.

"Bean, did you enjoy it?"

"Boy, did I. I've never had ice cream. I've seen it in the cooler and watched other people eat it, and I've always wondered what it tasted like."

"Just because you've never had it doesn't mean you can steal it," Mrs. Grigsby said.

"She didn't steal it. I gave it to her," Ruby said.

"That's enough," Ruby's father said, a smirk on his face. "But how did you get in here? The doors are locked—no, on second thought, don't tell me. I don't want to know. I just don't want you doing this again. Is that understood?"

"Yes, sir," Bean said.

Before Ruby could speak, the front door opened and Thaddeus Coleman walked inside with three other men. Ruby took a step backward and knocked a glass to the floor, shattering it.

"Oh, now see what you've done," Mrs. Grigsby said, scurrying to the other side of the counter.

"Looks like you've got a couple of stowaways," Coleman said. "You forget to lock the door?"

"I can handle this, Thaddeus," Ruby's father said.

"This is exactly the kind of thing you can handle." The man smiled at Ruby's father. "Come on, boys."

The four headed to the stairwell, mud and gravel clicking on the hardwood. Ruby noticed the pistols the men carried in holsters.

When they disappeared upstairs, Ruby's father said, "Ruby, pour Bean another glass and I'll walk her home."

"That's all right, Mr. Handley. I'm done," Bean said. "I can walk myself, thank you." She looked back when she got to the door. "Bye, Ruby."

"Can I go with you?" Ruby said.

"Not on your life," Mrs. Grigsby said. "You'll clean up this mess and go right upstairs."

Bean hurried through the front door but Ruby's father followed.

"Bean, wait."

He caught up to her and knelt, looking her in the eyes. "What do you have in your back pocket?"

"Sir?"

"It's better to tell me now."

Bean's face fell and she reached in her back pocket and pulled out a cardboard box. The man studied it. "It's for Mama's stomach. She chews on sassafras and makes tea but it still hurts."

"Why doesn't she see the company doctor?"

"She don't like him. And I don't blame her. I thought this might do her some good."

The man pursed his lips. He pointed at a rocking chair on the porch. "Sit."

Bean felt like running. Ruby's father had caught her stealing—something she never intended to do, but when she saw the medicine section in the store and what it said on the outside of the box, she couldn't help herself. Her love for her mother trumped her conscience. If there had been any question whether she would go with Ruby to the boarding school, this was the nail in the coffin. The sheriff would arrest her and call her a chip off the old block.

Mr. Handley returned to the porch and held out a brown bottle. "This will be better for her stomach. Take it."

"I can't, sir."

"You could steal the other and refuse a gift?" He sat beside her and tipped his hat back. "Your mother is a fine woman. She doesn't . . . She deserves to be treated better."

Bean stared at the bottle.

"You're probably wondering how you can give her this," he said.

"She don't take charity."

He took the bottle from her, opened it, held it over the railing, and poured some on the ground. He tore some of the label and smudged the writing with his thumb. "We were talking tonight at the store about her stomach problems and I suggested she take this. I'd hate to see it go to waste."

He handed Bean the bottle. Above them, through the open window, came the laughter of men and the tinkling of glass.

"Is Ruby going to be in trouble?"

"Don't worry about Ruby. Seems you have enough worries, Bean."

"I won't sleep a wink tonight if she's going to be in trouble."

The man smiled. "We'll work it out. I'm not the hard man your father is."

"He's a good man when he's not drinking and carousing."

"I'm sure he is."

Bean thanked him and he walked with her into the moonlight. Looking back, she saw the rocking chairs moving and a light on in the window above.

18

FRANCES MEETS WITH THE SHERIFF
BIDING, KENTUCKY
THURSDAY, SEPTEMBER 30, 2004

The sheriff was a tall man with a shaved head. Muscular and barrel-chested, he had kind eyes that seemed to want to comfort and search out the truth. Frances answered his questions and showed him the house, the empty cash box, and everything else. She couldn't bring herself to mention her concerns about Jerry, however. She had enough worries of her own without bringing him into it. If the sheriff asked, she would tell him.

Wallace hung back as if he didn't want to intrude. Jerry milled around outside. These things always fell to the women, Frances thought. The hard things of life, the injuries, blood and broken bones and tears were always put at the feet of women and she didn't know why. Once, just once, she wondered what would happen if there wasn't a woman to deal with the muck of life. The men would probably run to find one.

The sheriff took note of everything she showed him, and the wheels of justice began to spin quickly, but not fast enough for Frances's racing heart.

"She lives here alone?" the man said.

It might have been just a question to confirm her status, but Frances couldn't help but hear suspicion in the man's voice. Behind the question was *Why would you let a woman this age live alone? Why wouldn't you help your aged mother?*

"Yes, she lives alone by her own choice. She says this is where she wants to die. Which makes her disappearance even more disconcerting."

He nodded the way men of the law did on TV, a tight-lipped assent to the response.

Jerry's wife, Laurie, pulled up with their two kids, adding one more car to the parked search party. The children went out back to the swing set Frances's father had installed ages ago. Laurie sat with Jerry, who had settled in front of the TV. She didn't say a word to Frances.

The first step for the police was to put out a multistate alert with Ruby's car and license plate number along with her description. It turned Frances's stomach to think that there would be people judging her mother as some senile granny who had escaped an old folks' home. Her mother wasn't like that—she had all her faculties. She explained this to the sheriff, but there was nothing she could do about what others thought.

"Ma'am, I have to say I wish you would have called us yesterday when you found her gone," the sheriff said in a low voice. "It would have made things a lot easier." He wasn't being unkind. He said it as if he were telling her this for the next time it happened.

"We wanted to think the best instead of the worst," Frances said. "If I had it to do over again . . ."

The man nodded but the look on his face was more than grim. "Is there anyone who might want to harm your mother?"

"My mother's the most likable person on the planet. She's never had an enemy."

"No one comes to mind?"

Frances took a deep breath. "There's something you need to know. You couldn't tell it from the house or her car, but she's wealthy. My brother and I don't actually know exactly how much she's worth, but it's a considerable sum."

The man looked at Wallace. "Is he part of the family?"

"He's my ex. Former police officer. Long story. I called and asked for his help."

"So you have a good relationship?"

"We don't have any relationship. But from the moment I told him, he suggested we call the police."

"I see."

"Have you ever seen anything like this before?" Frances heard the pleading in her question. "I mean, have you ever seen a parent leave because they're upset and make it back safely?"

"I've seen a lot of things, ma'am. Most of the time things turn out fine. The parent gets mad and drives off in a huff and then they get lost or turned around. We usually find them."

"Usually?"

"I've seen some ugly things, especially when drugs are involved. I've seen grandchildren hurt their grandparents. The hardest ones are where everything seems fine but you uncover a family secret and the skeletons tumble. I don't say that to upset you. I say it as a comfort because this looks different."

Frances pondered the words and wondered if she should tell the officer about Jerry and what she'd found in her mother's checkbook and the suspicions she held.

"I have a good feeling about this," the sheriff said. "I think we're going to find her."

"Why do you say that?"

He shrugged. "It's just a feeling." His radio squawked and he retreated to his car.

Wallace joined Frances, holding an aged photo album. "Where'd you get that?" she said.

"There's a trunk downstairs. Have you seen it?"

"I was looking for it yesterday. Did you find the key to it? Mom always kept it locked."

He gave a sheepish look. "Well, it's open now. Some interesting stuff in there—stuff she had at boarding school, it looks like."

Frances took the photo album. On the opening page was Ruby as a girl, sitting on her father's lap with her mother right beside her. Frances put a finger on the photo and traced the faces.

"Her birth certificate is in there, too. A journal. Clothes. You should see it."

The mailman chugged along the street in a gray Ford Bronco with a muffler that rattled from mailbox to mailbox. Frances wandered toward the road and stopped in the shade of the willow, Wallace following.

"We shouldn't have taken her keys. It was the wrong thing to do."

"Don't blame yourself."

"Who else is there? I'm the one who made the decision. Jerry went along with it. I should have left things alone."

Wallace didn't speak for a moment as if mulling over his options. Finally he said, "Okay, let's say you were standing here today because Ruby had gotten into an accident. Let's say she plowed into some kids waiting at a bus stop. Who would you blame for that?"

Frances didn't answer.

"I'll tell you who. You'd blame yourself because you didn't take her keys. You'd think, *If only.* Either way, you'd take responsibility."

"Somebody has to," Frances said.

Wallace faced her. "Frances, life happens. People make decisions. It's not your fault your mother left. You tried to do the responsible thing. You tried to protect her. You love her. But everybody has an extra set of keys, and you don't control whether they use them."

She looked at him and wondered if he was talking about her mother or himself. The mailman rattled up to the driveway and stopped.

"I should have seen that she'd do something like this. It's my job to crunch the information. Anticipate things. To get out in front of them."

Wallace looked away. "So you're responsible for the present and the future? That's a pretty heavy load. What do you do with the past?"

She ignored the question and waved at the mail carrier. He pulled a few feet ahead of the box and stopped. "Is there something going on with Miss Ruby?"

Frances didn't feel like a long conversation, but she could tell the man cared. She explained her mother was missing, that she'd left the previous day.

The mailman winced. "I was afraid it was something like that. My own mother's the same way. Independent as all get-out. One day she drove to the store and there was a horsefly on the dashboard. She swatted at it and didn't see the curve and went over the hill."

Frances stared at him, unable to speak.

"I'm sorry. I don't mean to burden you more than you already are," the mailman said, handing the mail to Frances.

"What happened to your mother?" Wallace said.

Frances gave him a look.

"Her car went into a pond at the bottom of the hill. There were two kids fishing on the other side and they ran around and jumped in and pulled her out. She's fine. Keeps her windows rolled up tight to keep the flies away."

"So she made it okay?" Wallace said, glancing at Frances.

"She's a tough old bird." The man smiled. "I'll be praying you find Miss Ruby real soon. And that she's all right."

"Thank you," Frances said.

The man chugged down the road and Frances leafed through the letters and bills, looking for some new idea about where her mother had gone, but there were no tea leaves to read among the coupons or flyers.

She walked toward the house and Wallace followed. "You need to get your mind off it."

Frances glanced at him.

"No, I'm serious. Staying here and worrying is not going to do any good. I'm assuming you didn't sleep much."

"What do you want me to do, Wallace? Go to a ball game? Take a nap and act like nothing's happened?"

He chewed at a fingernail, something she couldn't stand. His teeth clicking while they drove or watched TV.

"There's a principle in the Twelve Steps that says you're powerless over your addiction. You're not strong enough to conquer it alone. That held me back because I wanted to be strong. I thought I should be able to conquer it. But when I saw it was okay to need help, it was a first step to getting out of the hole I had dug."

It sounded like an accusation to Frances. That Wallace was comparing his addictions to her situation with her mother. But the more she thought, the more she realized he was confessing. He was opening himself up to her in a way he hadn't.

"Are you out of the hole?" she said.

"I don't know that I'll ever completely be out because the hole is in here." He tapped his head, then his heart. "But things aren't as dark. I don't feel like I'm climbing stairs that lead to a locked door."

"In the meetings, did they tell you to just get your mind off of things? Is that how it works?"

He shook his head. "No, I don't remember them saying that. I guess I want to help and I don't know how. I thought maybe going into town for lunch might be good. You haven't eaten. You'll need to keep your strength up."

"What do you mean?"

"When we find her. She's going to need you."

His words moved her. "You really think we're going to find her alive?"

"Frances, we're talking about Ruby. Come on. She's one of those who walk through the fire without getting burned. I'll never forget the time . . . Well, you don't need to hear that."

"No, please. What were you going to say?"

"She got me alone. Thanksgiving, I think. You and I weren't doing well. I wasn't doing well. She was washing dishes and I was drying. You and your dad were watching football. She had Southern gospel on the radio. Singing along. And she said, without looking at me, just like she was talking to herself or the wall, 'You're not doing well, are you, Wallace?' I said I was doing okay. And she said, 'No, you're not. And if you don't get help, you're going to lose what you care about the most.' She just kept washing the turkey grease off the dishes and handing them to me."

"What year was this?"

"Before the department let me go."

"Wow."

"Yeah. It was the best job of drying dishes I've ever done. I was rubbing so hard, trying not to say anything. When we were done, she dried her hands and looked at me. She said, 'Don't hurt my daughter and my granddaughter by hurting yourself. Get some help.'"

Frances stared at her ex-husband, trying to recall the holiday scene or any clue that her mother had confronted him. Neither he nor she had let on about the conversation.

"I thought about that later, after the end of us and the spiral I went through. I always wanted to thank her. I never did."

"Maybe you'll have the chance to," Frances said, and she smiled and felt something warm inside that she hadn't felt in a long time. It felt like hope and it wasn't just about her mother.

As often happens in life, when you think the sun is peeking over the horizon and life has taken a turn, some dark cloud will sneak up from behind. The front door opened and Jerry bounded out.

"The guy at the cemetery called. He saw her yesterday."

Frances couldn't help thinking of the mailman's story as Wallace drove toward Ridgeview Cemetery. It hadn't been easy, but she had convinced Jerry to remain at the house and wait. His presence with them would only complicate things.

Ridgeview sat atop the hill, next to Ridgeview Baptist Church, an old building with a fresh coat of white paint. A man in coveralls stood by the fence, waiting. His name was Earl Clagg and he was the kind of man who seemed fit for looking after the dead.

"I seen her yesterday morning," the man said after he shook hands with both of them. "Standing right over there leaning on the tombstone. Talking to herself, it looked like."

"Was she alone?" Wallace said.

"I didn't see anybody with her."

"Was she upset?" Frances said.

"Didn't appear to be. She told me it was her husband she'd come to see. Said there was a lot of traffic on the road."

"Did she say where she was going?"

The man looked over his glasses at her. "It wasn't what I would call an in-depth conversation. I just went over to make sure everything was all right with the grave and such. She said her name was

Ruby and told me some about her husband and his military service. Then she started back to her car and I helped steady her. She was all stiff in the joints, you know? And I told her to drive careful and she said she would."

"Is that it?" Frances said.

"Well, she made me take a cake she had in the backseat, all wrapped up. Said the Lord had told her I should have it. Your mama's a good cook."

Frances smiled. "She didn't say where she was going?"

He rubbed the stubble on his chin. "Not that I recall. She just thanked me for the job I did on her husband's grave and told me to have a nice day."

"Which direction?" Wallace said.

The man removed his ball cap and scratched his head. "I don't remember seeing. She came from the main road, so I assume she went back that way."

"Where does this road go?" Wallace said.

"Keeps going a few miles. Turns to dirt right back there. You wouldn't want to go that way without four-wheel drive."

In the car, Frances gave Wallace a worried look. "You don't think she made a wrong turn, do you?"

Wallace set his jaw. "Sometimes people get turned around."

She wondered if that was how he would describe his own life. He took a road he didn't know and wound up on dirt. Somehow he had gotten back on the blacktop.

Wallace turned left and they drove the ridge, looking left and right. There were no guardrails and the hill was so steep it took her breath away. When she saw something white flash in the sunlight, she told him to stop.

They both got out and walked to the edge of the road. Wallace was the first to see the car and he plunged down the hill. "You wait there."

Frances remembered a day she had begged Wallace not to leave the house, worried what he might do to himself, the cloud of his actions on the police force swirling around him. It was the beginning of the end of them. Actually, the end had started long before that, but it was a defining moment. And now she saw his back again, running toward bad news, and something rose up inside. She took off after him down the hill. She couldn't breathe.

PleaseGodpleaseGodpleaseGod.

The bumper was in the air and the rear wheels were off the ground. Frances pulled out her phone. They were probably thirty minutes from the nearest hospital.

"911. What's your emergency?" a woman said.

"It's my mother," Frances said as she neared the car. "We're on a road by Ridgeview Cemetery. I can't remember—"

"It's not her," Wallace said.

"What?" Frances said.

"This isn't Ruby's car. It's been here for years. There's nobody inside."

"Ma'am, what's wrong with your mother?" the woman said.

"I'm sorry," Frances said, putting the phone to her ear. "I thought we'd found her car and that she was hurt. It was a false alarm. I'm so sorry."

"Is your mother missing?" the woman said.

"Yes. The sheriff knows. I'm sorry to bother you. I need to go." She closed the phone and stared at the Oldsmobile. "Why would anyone leave a car here?"

"Come on," Wallace said, holding her arm and helping her up the hill. Dirty bottles and smashed cans littered the hillside.

"You got down the hill pretty fast for someone of your advanced age," Frances said.

"Gravity has a way of doing that. Pulls you down the hill faster than you want."

"I was already writing her obituary. I imagined her final moments, Mom screaming as she plunged over the edge."

"I doubt your mother, even on a bad day, would take a wrong turn at the cemetery. She's been here too many times."

Wallace guided her back to the car. Her phone buzzed and she nearly dropped it from fright. She opened it without looking at the number, expecting to hear the 911 operator. Instead a female voice on the other end said, "Mrs. Freeman? I'm calling about your mother."

Frances sat up straight. "Who is this? Do you know where she is?"

19

CHARLOTTE FOLLOWS LEADS ABOUT BEULAH MOUNTAIN'S HISTORY
BEULAH MOUNTAIN, WEST VIRGINIA
THURSDAY, SEPTEMBER 30, 2004

Charlotte parked in the visitors' lot at CCE headquarters, pushing down the butterflies in her stomach.

Rummaging around in the attic at the store had led her to ask questions of some of the older residents of Beulah Mountain, but many, like her grandfather, could not remember details. So Charlotte had made a savvy journalistic move, which could also be termed "sneaky." She went to the head of the historical society, Marilyn Grigsby-Mollie, a woman who was determined to squelch anything that might taint the vision of the Company Store or the coal company. Marilyn was committed to a vision of the past that was idyllic and sweet. Charlotte affectionately referred to her as Mollieanna.

Marilyn had agreed to make the request of CCE, and now Charlotte was shown to a conference room where several boxes were stacked in a corner. The room was surrounded by windows, so anyone passing by could see her. A security guard sat behind a desk across the hall. This gave Charlotte a sinking feeling that at some point Buddy Coleman might barge in and handcuff her and inspect what she'd found. She decided it was worth the risk.

Many documents and pictures were duplicates of things she had already seen. Others were interesting but not worth copying. She was looking for confirmation of something she had discovered in the archives of the Morrow Library special collections while a student at Marshall University. That crumb led her on a series of discoveries, to the chagrin of her history adviser, about the Beulah Mountain mine. She'd gone round and round with him on the veracity of her research and finally tucked the information away for another time.

The dust from the documents made Charlotte sneeze so much she needed a fresh box of tissues. As she dug into the last box, she found a stack of photos taken inside the company store. The first pictures were of the store manager in front of a soda fountain and candy display. Others showed clothing, tools, and canned goods. But at the bottom of the box she found personal items that looked out of place. A pearl-handled brush and comb. Clothing that looked like it belonged to a younger woman or girl. And when Charlotte pulled out a square, black box, she at first thought it might hold jewelry. She tried to open it, then spied a lens on the front and realized she'd found a vintage camera from the 1930s. She turned it and spied the initials *RH* crudely engraved on the metal edging.

Charlotte felt a presence behind her and turned.

"Find anything useful for the museum?" Buddy Coleman said.

He was a short man, just a bit taller than Charlotte, with dark eyebrows and a face that crinkled when he smiled. Rumor had it Buddy was moving up in the company, and the final vote at the next board meeting was only a formality—that would come Saturday, the same day as the opening of the Company Store.

Charlotte's heart beat double-time and she tried to smile back. "Yes, sir, and thank you for allowing me access. I think these are personal items from the Handley apartment, aren't they?"

Buddy nodded, peering inside. "Sure looks like it. We had a bunch of boxes in storage from the old company store. Gave them to the historical society. Must have missed this one."

"I found these," Charlotte said, handing him a folder of pictures and documents.

"You're Hollis's granddaughter, right?"

"Yes, sir."

"Heard you finished school and made Beulah Mountain proud." He opened the folder and leafed through the pictures.

"I worked hard, sir. And the CCE scholarship helped."

"What do you have there?" he said, pointing to the camera.

"I found it at the bottom. I was thinking we could put it in the Company Store Museum."

Buddy reached for the camera and Charlotte reluctantly handed it to him.

"My daddy had one of these. You open it by pushing a button somewhere." He turned it over and over and finally looked at her. "I've been talking with your grandfather about his property."

"Yes, sir."

"I hear the meeting last night didn't go well."

"Not for him. It appears he has an uphill battle."

"Mm-hmm." He handed the camera back to her along with the folder. "Is this all you found?"

"Yes, sir," Charlotte said. "Is it all right if I take it with me?"

He nodded. "And tell Hollis I'm still hoping he'll come see me."

Buddy walked out, his boots clicking on the tile floor of the entrance, and Charlotte hurried from the building. She wasn't sure why, but she had a strange feeling she had uncovered something important.

On the way back to the office, Charlotte wanted more than ever to talk with Ruby and ask about the camera. She dialed Ruby's house and a woman answered. Charlotte's heart jumped.

"I'm sorry. Ruby isn't here."

"I'd like to speak with her as soon as possible," Charlotte said.

"We'd all like that."

"What do you mean?" Charlotte said.

"Nothing," the woman said. "I can't say any more."

"Wait, don't hang up. If I can't talk with Ruby, maybe you can help me."

"Let me give you a phone number for Frances."

"Who's Frances?"

"Frances Freeman, her daughter."

Charlotte pulled over and scribbled down the number and dialed it as soon as the other woman hung up.

"Mrs. Freeman? I'm calling about your mother," Charlotte said when the woman answered.

"Who is this? Do you know where she is?"

Charlotte paused. "She's missing, isn't she?"

"Tell me who this is or I'm hanging up."

Charlotte told Frances her name and where she was calling from. "If your mother isn't there, I think I might know where she's headed."

"Where?"

Charlotte briefly explained her interest in Ruby's story and how she had tried to speak with her. "I even drove up there to talk with her face-to-face, but she seemed agitated and told me to go away."

Silence on the other end.

"I think your mother is headed to West Virginia. To Beulah Mountain."

"Why?"

Charlotte told her about the Company Store dedication on Saturday. "We sent two invitations and never heard from her. Did she say anything about wanting to come down here?"

"Not a word," Frances said. "But there was a question mark on her calendar for Saturday. You think it's the dedication she's interested in?"

"Yes. I hope she makes it because I found something of hers today I think she'll want to see."

"You found what?" Frances said.

"Perhaps if you came here, I could show you," Charlotte said. "You could see where your mother lived. As soon as I hang up, I'll call the local hotel to see if she might have checked in. Or she could have stayed overnight somewhere between here and there. Maybe I can help you find her."

When Charlotte hung up, she dialed the Beulah Mountain Inn but Ruby had not checked in. She drove to the *Breeze* office and rushed into the newsroom with her find.

Charlotte's editor, Willie "Corky" McCorkle, was a crusty man who still kept a spittoon in the corner of his office for decoration (though Charlotte wondered if he used it occasionally). He was an old-school newspaperman who allowed Charlotte to bring a digital camera to work but preferred older cameras with film, which he developed himself in a small darkroom—a long closet by his office. Still, when Charlotte held out the camera, Corky stared at it like it was a dead fish.

"What's this?" he said.

"You know what it is. I've seen all those old cameras in your collection."

He took the camera and turned it over, inspecting it. "I mean, where did you get it? I haven't seen one of these in a long time."

"Look right there. See those initials? Those are Ruby Handley's. This was her camera."

"You don't know that. Did you find this at CCE?"

She nodded. "There were personal items from their apartment in one of the boxes. I think this was hers."

He handed it back. "Well, good for you. You've got something new for the museum. Now if you don't mind, I'm busy with the special edition—"

"Corky, if Ruby had a camera, she probably took a bunch of pictures," Charlotte said, interrupting. "Those would be gold if we could find them."

"I thought you went through everything in the Company Store archives."

"I did. But there's a couple other places I can think of to look . . . And if we can find Ruby, we can ask her about them. Maybe there's corroboration of—"

"What do you mean, 'if we can find Ruby'? She's up in Kentucky, isn't she?"

Corky gave Charlotte a pained look when she explained what she'd learned from Frances. Then he took the camera back. "Leave this with me and get back to work. And stop chasing whatever you're trying to corroborate. I don't pay you to corroborate. I pay you to report."

She couldn't help smiling at the old curmudgeon. "Anything I can help with on your special edition?"

20

Frances stared out the windshield, mesmerized by the cadence of the wiper blades. A light rain now fell and the blades scraped and stuck on the partially wet glass.

"I don't think you ought to go," Wallace said without looking at her as they returned to Ruby's house.

"I don't think you have much say."

"Maybe not, but it feels like a wild-goose chase."

Frances turned toward him. "Charlotte may know some things about the wild goose. Maybe she's down there wandering around."

Wallace ran a hand through his thinning hair. "What if she's somewhere else? What if she's headed to the coast?"

"I'll buy a swimsuit."

He shook his head. "If they find her here, you'll be a long way off."

"Jerry is here." She said it as a hopeful thing, but it felt more like resignation.

They pulled into the driveway, and as if on cue, there was Jerry sitting like a stone on the front porch under the eaves in one of Ruby's metal lawn chairs. The rain was coming down harder and darker clouds made the overcast sky look like a blanket.

"I called the credit card company again," Jerry said when they took cover on the front porch. "Still hasn't been used."

Frances opened the door and walked to the kitchen with Wallace and Jerry following. She opened the dresser and pulled out the calendar.

"Right here." She pointed at the question mark on Saturday's date.

"We saw that before," Jerry said.

"But Charlotte just told me the dedication of the Company Store Museum in Beulah Mountain is Saturday."

"Who in the world is Charlotte?"

Frances ignored him. "They wanted her there as part of the celebration. But we took her keys."

"Why wouldn't she say anything about wanting to go?" Wallace said.

"I would have driven her down there," Jerry said. "And who's Charlotte?"

Frances stared at the calendar. "Maybe there's someone she wanted to meet. Or something in the past she doesn't want us to know."

Wallace said he would phone the sheriff and let them know what Frances believed. "They can ask the authorities near Beulah Mountain to be on the lookout."

"I know Mom drives slow, but even she would have to have been there by now," Jerry said.

Frances's phone rang and she answered, afraid it was the police informing her of a body. Instead it was her daughter.

"Have you heard anything?" Julia said.

"No, honey. We found a car but it wasn't hers. And she hasn't used her credit card."

Julia cursed. "You must be freaking out."

"I'm close to it. But your dad has been a big help."

"He's still there?"

"Yes. I don't know what I would have done if he hadn't driven up."

There was an awkward silence.

"Has he talked to you? About . . . ?"

"About what?"

"Never mind," Julia said. "Melanie said you called."

"Yes, I'm sorry. I had a harebrained idea that your grandmother might be trying to help you. Might have driven down there—"

"Help me with what?"

"I don't know. You know how I get when things don't go as planned. My mind goes to . . . bad places."

"Melanie told me you sounded upset."

"I'm trying to figure out where she is. I saw your number on her phone."

"You promised you wouldn't call."

Frances let the comment go. "Look, you go back to your studies. You don't need to worry about this."

"Don't tell me what to do, Mom."

"No, I meant that to help. I don't want you to worry."

"She's my grandmother. How can you say that? You can't tell me how to feel."

Frances closed her eyes and took a breath. She wanted a relationship with her daughter more than anything, but every time they had a conversation, things wound up this way. What she said in kindness was twisted.

"Call me when you find out anything, okay?" Julia said quickly.

"I will," Frances said. The line clicked dead on the other end.

"I'm going home," Jerry said, lumbering toward the front door. "I can take a phone call there as well as I can here."

Frances and Wallace watched him leave and they were alone. There was a soft pitter-pat of rain on the roof.

"Look at that," Wallace said, pointing out the back door.

"That must be the cat she told me about. Mom doesn't have pets anymore but she said there's a feral cat who comes around and she tosses it scraps. She said it lets her pet it."

"That cat doesn't look like you would want to get within ten feet of it."

Frances found the can of scraps in the corner. She took the half-eaten ham sandwich outside and threw the contents of the can toward the middle of the backyard. The cat bounded away, then returned gingerly and crouched, eating. Its rib cage showed through the yellow-and-white fur.

"Why doesn't she have a dog?" Wallace said.

"She fell over the last one. I told her if she was going to break a hip, it ought to be for something other than a Chihuahua."

"It's a shame. She was always good with animals."

"They came to her. I think they sensed something about her. How gentle she was."

"Maybe they knew how much money she had."

The thought made Frances chuckle. Nobody knew how much money Ruby had—you couldn't tell it by her car, her clothes, or her house. This was the thing that galled Jerry—he wanted to live first-class on coach income. His mother was the opposite.

"I don't suppose there's anything I can say that will keep you from driving down there," Wallace said.

"No. Even if I don't find her, I'll learn more about her."

Wallace nodded. "Makes sense."

"Do you want something to eat?"

"I'm not hungry, Frances."

The way he said her name, the way it came from his lips, made her heart think there was something behind the words. She held the door open and he brushed her arm as he passed and something electric ran through her. It was like the old days, when they were dating, when his touch could make her come alive.

"You'd better get going if you hope to get there tonight," he said. "The roads will be slick."

Frances stopped at the kitchen table and turned. It reminded her of moments in their past when he found a reason to slip away. When life got hard, Wallace got moving and usually in the other direction. But here he was, standing with her, looking her in the eyes. And that fact gave her hope.

"Is there any part of you that wants to go with me?" she said softly.

He smiled sadly. "Yeah, there is. The part that feels sorry about everything I've put you through."

"We don't have to go over that. I hope you can let it go. I have."

"I'm glad to hear it. Part of why I came was . . . Well, I need to make up for what I did."

"You've been a big help." She put a hand on the back of a chair to steady herself for the next question. "If I asked you to drive me, would you? If I told you I needed you?"

"I'd like to, Frances. With the new job, I'm on thin ice."

"I understand."

There was something about his face that felt like he was searching, and Frances wondered if they were having the same feelings. "Wallace, I've been thinking that there's a purpose behind things that happen."

"You're sounding like Ruby."

She smiled. "Maybe this happened because of you and me. Has that entered your mind?"

He scratched his temple, right at the hairline that was creeping upward. It was a habit when he was nervous or when he wasn't sure what to say or when he was scared of the truth. "Yeah, I've thought about it."

"I used to long for you to have a relationship with Julia. I prayed she wouldn't grow up in a single-parent home. Now you're so involved in her life."

"And you're not sure how to feel about that."

"I'm grateful she has access to us both. I'm glad you're close. When I spoke with her, she asked if you had talked with me. It sounded like she knew something I didn't."

When he glanced up, Frances was sure it was something she didn't want to know.

"Is there something you need to say?" she said.

"This is not the time, Frances."

"No, I think it is."

Wallace studied the floor, then the wall that had the dry-erase board with phone numbers and instructions for her father's medication. After he had died, Ruby had asked that the board be kept as it was. The writing had faded but the record of the past was there in red and green and blue.

Wallace cleared his throat. "I've met someone."

Three-word sentences of the past wound through Frances's mind. *I love you. I hate you. I despise you. I adore you.*

I've met someone.

Her knuckles turned white on the back of the chair and she was glad Jerry had left. He would have asked the woman's name and shoe size and what to get her for Christmas. Or smacked him on the back and said, *Good for you, Wallace.*

She'd heard somewhere that it took more muscles in the face to frown than to smile, though at that moment she didn't believe it. But she tried. She couldn't offer words of congratulation. A smile was all she could give.

"I met her at the group," he said. "Carolyn and I went down to see Julia last weekend. To tell her what was going on."

"Oh?"

"Yeah. Julia seemed to take it well."

"I wonder if that's why she called my mother," Frances said. "To talk things through." She hit rewind on the day. "So when I called and asked for help, was this part of why you came? You wanted to tell me this?"

He took a deep breath. "I heard the fear in your voice. I wanted to help. But I've also had this news. I wanted it to come up naturally."

"So you told Julia first. And you thought she'd break the news to me?"

"No, I told her not to mention it."

Frances laughed derisively, though she tried to hold back. "You asked her to keep your secret."

"It wasn't like that. Don't twist this. I'm trying to do the right thing. I'm trying to get my life together."

"And why couldn't you have tried ten years ago?"

"Maybe I should go."

"Yeah, maybe you should," she said. When he got to the door, she said, "This is what you always did: you walked away."

"You just told me I should go."

"I've waited for you." As soon as Frances spoke, the emotion came and she hated it. "I waited for you to turn around. I waited for you to see what you were doing to us. You never did. I waited for you to hit bottom and every time you did, you bounced. And you fell on me and Julia."

He stood at the door with his hand on the knob.

"Now you came here at my lowest point to tell me you've met *Carolyn*," she said with a catch in her throat. "I really felt like you cared. I thought you were here because you were concerned."

"I do care," he said to the door. "That's why I drove up."

"You drove up to ease your conscience. You took your girlfriend to see our daughter. It must be serious. You must be talking about marriage."

He didn't deny it.

"She's probably telling you it's time to tell me. Answer me truthfully. When did you tell Carolyn about our get-together here? When did you call her?"

Wallace took a few steps back toward Frances. "You called me. It sounded bad. I called my boss and explained I had an emergency. When I hit the road this morning, when I knew she'd be up, I called Carolyn. I told her I felt like I needed to be here."

"And what did the magnanimous Carolyn have to say?" She held up a hand. "You know what? Don't tell me. I don't want to know. This is your life, Wallace. We were over a long time ago and I should have seen that."

"She agreed with me. She thought I should be here."

"I told you not to tell me."

"I know what you told me. I want you to know."

Frances turned her back, then closed her eyes.

"Carolyn's marriage and family fell apart, too. She lost her kids. Made some bad choices just like me. She said if it were her and she had the chance, she would do the same thing."

"What a wonderful person," Frances said quickly.

"I can't make up for what I did. I can't repay you for the wrong. All I can do is tell you how sorry I am. If I could go back and change things, I would."

Frances thought if there were a time machine available, she'd push him inside and lock the door. She kept her back to him and gritted her teeth. She didn't want him to see her weak.

"I probably should have told you about Carolyn before I told Julia. I can see that now. I don't know how all of this works, Frances. I didn't do it well. But I never intended to hurt you again."

"Right. Got it. Thank you."

He gave a deep sigh. She turned quickly and saw a tenderness in his face she hadn't expected.

"Go home, Wallace. Go back to work. I misread things. I have a tendency to see life different than it is."

"I'll drive down there with you if you still want me."

Frances shook her head. "No. This is something I have to do alone."

He lingered, then closed the door behind himself and walked through the rain. Frances turned off the lights and watched him drive away.

"Guess it's time to chase a wild goose," she whispered to herself.

Part 3

21

WE REWIND TO THE DAY RUBY HEADED FOR BEULAH MOUNTAIN
BIDING, KENTUCKY
WEDNESDAY, SEPTEMBER 29, 2004

Ruby woke from a restful sleep at daylight and felt energy she hadn't experienced since Leslie had slept beside her. This was the first day of the rest of her life. She felt like one of the magi following a star.

She saw a swath of light shining through the almost-closed draperies and a song came to mind—an old hymn she remembered from the church in Beulah Mountain.

> *How beautiful to walk in the steps of the Savior,*
> *Stepping in the light, stepping in the light;*
> *How beautiful to walk in the steps of the Savior,*
>   *led in paths of light.*

She walked gingerly at first, gaining balance and momentum, then literally stepped into the sunshine and pulled back the closet door, revealing the clothes she had chosen. Ruby clasped her hands as she noticed sunlight had fallen on the shoe box at the bottom of the closet as if it were a sign, a confirmation. She put the boots on and laced them and walked around the bedroom. They felt snug but strangely comforting.

With her cash safely stashed in the locked glove box and a small cooler with lemonade and sandwiches in the back, next to a fresh cake covered in saran wrap, she adjusted the Rand McNally map beside her, put on her seat belt, started the car, and said a prayer.

"Lord, I believe you've put this in my mind and I'll follow you, even though it scares me. Guide me. Protect me. Into your hands I place my spirit and this Town Car. Amen."

She smiled at the prayer and eased out of the driveway, looking both ways for oncoming traffic. She nearly drove into the FoodFair parking lot because of how many times she had made that trip, but she corrected herself and rolled to a stop at the intersection by the gas station. Jerry had filled the car up two weeks earlier and the gauge was still just below the full mark.

A horn blew behind her and she looked in the crooked rearview mirror. That was the one thing about this car. The mirror was wobbly and Jerry had tried but said it couldn't be tightened. Ruby had put on some duct tape and called it good, but that meant she had to adjust the mirror after hitting bumps and potholes. The truth was, she didn't use the rearview mirror. It made her anxious to look back. The driver of the car behind waved an arm at her and then hit the gas, pulled around her, and ran through the stop sign.

Ruby waved. "Go ahead, it's your funeral."

She pulled onto the county road and got up to a speed she felt comfortable with, her heart beating wildly because of the impatient driver. People were in a hurry to get where they needed to go, she guessed.

She took a deep breath and spoke comforting words. "You're all right, Ruby. You and the Lord are going to get there."

Five miles later, she glanced in the crooked rearview mirror again. A line of cars and trucks stretched as far as she could see. The next turn took her toward the cemetery and though she hadn't planned to go there because of the winding road, she felt like she could breathe again, the cars and trucks passing as she gingerly drove up the hill.

She prayed all the way up and into the gravel lot by the white church. Such a peaceful place. She got out and used her cane to travel the uneven ground to the gate and toward her husband's stone. When she made it, she leaned against it and rested, looking at the trees and the sun shining through them.

"Leslie, there were some things I never told you. I'm sorry. I carried things alone. And it pains me you never knew. But I'm going to deal with it the best I can."

Back on the road, minus the cake she gave to the caretaker, Ruby merged onto the interstate, where semis passed at ungodly speeds. The limit here was sixty-five, but people treated that as a suggestion. Car after car passed her and she looked straight ahead, a death grip on the wheel.

"Go on and gawk," she said under her breath. "You people never see a white-haired woman drive?"

When she got comfortable at forty-five, she accelerated to fifty and the steering wheel began to shake.

"Leslie, I think the car has Parkinson's." She remembered his laugh and it brought tears to her eyes. She was talking to the Lord and her husband and she felt they were smiling as she escaped her overbearing children and headed toward a land fairer by far.

She had gone ten miles when she remembered the car had a radio.

She picked her spot when nobody was passing to reach out and turn the knob. The speakers filled with Southern gospel music and her heart lifted.

Unfortunately she lost the signal about twenty miles farther as it mixed with another station that broke in with some crooning country singer. He sang, "And I gave forgiveness I've been denying . . ." The station went out and Ruby slowed and it came back. ". . . To live like you were dyin'."

She turned off the radio and thought about that. What would it be like to live like you were dying?

A horn to her left brought her back to her senses. Faces as mad as hornets. People late to work, trying to get by. Then she thought of Frances. Frances would dial the house and let it ring a million times. Worry was her middle name. All her life her heart had been prone to wander through all the permutations of the bad that might happen instead of the good. Frances was living on worry. It was fuel for her tank. Jerry didn't seem to worry about anything. He was pretty much oblivious. Just took what was put in front of him at the kitchen table. Frances analyzed the meal and looked for bacteria.

After she got to the house, Frances would find the car gone. Ruby wished she could be there when Frances and Jerry put the pieces together that she had flown the coop. Maybe she should have left a note.

The guilt came like a radio station interfering. She didn't want to worry her children. But they could handle it for a day or two after all they had put her through.

Frances and Jerry had both married people who weren't good for them. It was something Ruby saw, but she couldn't force them to see. Laurie, Jerry's wife, was aloof and distant. She tried being polite but it always came off as indifference. At worst she was a wedge between Ruby and the heart of her son. Wallace had been . . . Well, Wallace was another story entirely, and she didn't want to drive and think of him at the same time because she'd run into the guardrail.

The trees on the hills were still as green as emeralds and the sight brought back her childhood. She thought of the little town, the blackened faces of miners passing the company store, and the lonesome whistle of the train. The steering wheel began to shimmy again and she let off the accelerator, a pain shooting up her right leg. Her muscles cramped and she thought about using the cruise control, but she'd done that long ago and had run up on a slowed school bus and she vowed never to use it again. Cruise control was too dangerous.

Near the West Virginia state line she saw a sign for a rest area. She took the exit and parked. There was one other car there and several semis in the truck lot. She took her keys and cane, locked the doors, and got on the sidewalk and stretched. Since she was there, she figured she should use the restroom, so she did, being careful to look behind her for anyone suspicious.

When she'd washed and dried her hands, she walked outside and noticed a woman by a picnic table with a little Yorkie on a leash, a bow in its hair.

"What a cute dog," Ruby said. "What is his name?"

"It's a her," the woman said without looking up. "Rosie Cotton. We have another one—had, I should say. We named him Samwise. It's from Lord of the Rings."

"Oh," Ruby said as if she understood.

"Hurry up, Rosie," the woman said, tugging the leash.

"Are you on a trip?" Ruby said.

"We were supposed to be at the beach this week, but my mother-in-law fell. We're headed to Tennessee. She's in rehab."

Just the word *rehab* made Ruby wince. "Sorry to hear that." The woman concentrated on the dog as if staring at the brown ball of fur would move its bladder. "I'm headed to a place I haven't been since I was a girl. Down in the coalfields."

"Really?" The woman looked up and studied Ruby's face. "All by yourself?"

Do I look like I need somebody to cart me? Instead of saying that, she laughed. "Yes, all by myself. But I only drive during daylight. Once it gets dark, the lights make it hard to see. I'm real careful."

"Well, you're amazing," the woman said. "I hope I'm driving by myself when I get to be seventy."

"Eighty-four," Ruby said.

The woman laughed and jerked on the leash again, and finally the dog squatted and a yellow stream stained the grass.

Frances and Jerry chided Ruby about telling people more than they needed to hear. They'd be in line at the FoodFair or the Family Dollar getting paper towels or toilet tissue and Ruby would introduce Frances or Jerry to the cashier. This was a person Ruby saw each week, so it made sense to her that the girl behind the register would want to know her children, but Frances and Jerry both said the cashier didn't need to know everything about everybody who came through the line.

"Can you imagine how long it would take people to check out if everybody talked to the cashier the way you do?" Jerry said.

This ran through Ruby's brain as the woman said something to her husband and the man smiled at Ruby and waved. Ruby toddled back to her car and climbed inside, energized by the human contact. A little farther and she spotted the sign over the interstate: Welcome to Wild, Wonderful West Virginia. She made a fist and shook it. There was something defiant about what she was doing, something noble, and she felt it down to her toes.

What she also felt down to her toes was fatigue. And she knew that the easiest part of the drive was now behind her. Soon she would need to leave the safety of these two lanes with traffic headed in the same direction and navigate the winding double-yellow roads into the hills.

She took an exit and began the circuitous route south. The gas gauge dipped below the halfway point and she passed three gas stations before she found one that looked like it would be easy to enter and exit. She remembered the days when young men in coveralls would pump gas and check your oil and clean your windshield. She longed for those days because everything was newfangled now and they wanted you to use your credit card and read the little screen on the pump and her eyes weren't what they used to be. She wanted a human, not a machine.

She eased up to the pump, making sure it was on the same side as the gas tank on her car. Opening the glove compartment, she pulled two twenty-dollar bills from her stash and locked the glove box and the car, then went inside.

Ruby stood in line until she could ask the man behind the counter to turn on her pump number. He took her forty dollars and told her it was ready.

"I'm sure I won't need all forty, so I'll come back for my change."

"All right, ma'am," the cashier said.

Ruby picked up the pump with one hand and reached for the gas cap with the other but it wouldn't budge. She put the pump back in its holder and used both hands but couldn't loosen the cap. She had told Jerry not to screw it on too tight because she had a hard time getting it off. She rubbed her hands together to take away the sting of the arthritis and leaned forward to get a better look.

"Excuse me, ma'am, is there something wrong?" a young woman said.

Ruby turned to see a girl in her twenties by the trash can. She had long, dirty blonde hair and wore tight jeans and a ragged T-shirt. She looked to be about the same age as Ruby's granddaughter, Julia.

"No thank you. I can manage," Ruby said. "It's just this gas cap is on too tight. Jerry was the last one to put it on. That's my son."

"Let me take a look at it," the girl said. "Sometimes it gets put on there whopper-jawed and it's hard to get off."

Ruby took a step back. "My hands aren't what they used to be. With the arthritis and all."

"My mamaw has the same thing," the girl said. She turned and took Ruby's hand gently in her own. "I'm Liz."

"It's nice to meet you, Liz. I'm Ruby. It's kind of you to help. You don't see that too often these days."

"Well, I figure it's the Golden Rule. You do unto others what you'd want them to do for you. Or for your grandmother."

Ruby laughed and Liz smiled, but she covered her mouth when she did and then looked back at the gas cap. "Sure seems stuck. Let me see if my boyfriend can help. Kelly? Come here a minute."

Kelly's hair was as long as Liz's and he had dirty hands like he'd just changed a tire. Tattoos ran up and down both arms.

"This lady's gas cap is stuck. And she . . . What did you say your name was, ma'am?"

"It's Ruby. Ruby Freeman. I'm from Kentucky now, but I'm driving to a town where I lived as a girl. Beulah Mountain. Have you heard of it?"

"Oh yes, ma'am. Everybody's heard of Beulah Mountain. That's quite a ways, isn't it?"

"I suppose it is. I told myself if the gas dips below half a tank, I'll stop. And here I am."

Ruby kept explaining what had happened as she wrung her hands. Kelly worked on the gas cap and glanced back, smiling and nodding, making eye contact, which Ruby thought was good. Most people their age didn't do that and even though their clothes were unkempt, Ruby felt like she'd made two friends.

"Tell you what," Kelly said. "I've got some Channellocks in the truck. Wait here."

"He's good with tools," Liz said. "His daddy has a garage full. Said he's going to give them to Kelly one of these days when we get married. Then he can open his own shop."

"You're thinking about getting married?"

"Oh yeah, it's just a matter of time and us saving some money. Kelly lost his job at the car-parts place and he's been looking. Mostly pizza delivery is all that's available right now and he's got his sights set for something bigger. He does car repair here and there."

Kelly brought what looked like oversize pliers to the car and grasped the cap and turned it. It popped off and Ruby and Liz gave a whoop. But with every victory comes a defeat, and Kelly picked up the cracked cap.

"You're going to have to get a new one," Kelly said. "Can't drive it this way."

Ruby's mouth went dry. "Well, my son can get one when I get home."

"No, Miss Ruby, you need a new one. It could be dangerous, couldn't it, Kelly?"

"Yeah, with the gas fumes and all. The check engine light's going to come on. Probably should get a new one right away."

"Oh, dear," Ruby said.

"Put the gas in there for her," Kelly said to Liz. "Let me check something."

Liz put the pump in the gas tank but it wouldn't start.

"That's funny," Ruby said. "I gave the man inside forty dollars. I'll go tell him."

"What about your credit card?" Liz said. "We can get the cash back."

"I don't use the credit card because I can't see the little screen."

"Let me do it for you. It's easy."

"No, I don't want to use it," Ruby said.

"Well, let me at least show you how. I won't run it through."

Ruby opened her purse and handed her the card.

"It's easy as pie. See this here? The strip on the back goes on this side. You just make sure you put it in this direction and swipe it down." She handed the card back to Ruby.

"I don't know if I can remember that."

Liz put a hand to her forehead. "I forgot to lift the handle." She lifted up a silver lever and began pumping the gas. "You can do it. And now that you know how, if you have to stop for gas, you don't have to pay inside. There's scary people inside gas stations at night, believe me."

"Oh, I don't drive at night," Ruby said. "The lights hurt my eyes."

Liz finished filling the tank and went inside and returned with twenty-two dollars in change. "Let me put this in your pocketbook."

Ruby handed her the purse. "I don't know what I would have done without you two being here to help me."

"Don't think nothing of it, Miss Ruby."

Kelly returned with the cracked cap. "I called the parts place. They have a universal. I can run over there and get it for you."

"You don't have to do that," Ruby said.

"I don't mind, ma'am. Plus, you really shouldn't drive without the cap. The fumes can get out. Tank could explode."

"Oh, dear," Ruby said. "I don't want that."

"Just pull it over to the side there. I won't be long."

"I'll stay with you," Liz said.

"I don't want to be any trouble."

"It's no trouble," Kelly said, and he was off in his rusted truck with the booming stereo.

Liz got in the passenger side and Ruby pulled to a shady spot beside the gas station.

"I can smell the gas from here, can't you?" Liz said.

"I don't smell anything, but my sniffer isn't as good as it used to be. I'm glad it won't be dangerous to drive."

"And now that you know how to use that credit card, you can go anywhere. Some gas stations don't have people inside at night."

"I don't drive at night," Ruby said. "And I don't think I'd be able to use that credit card thing if I didn't have help."

"Well, you should watch yourself. There's people out here meaner than snakes."

"You sound like my son. He builds houses and he's all the time cautioning me about trusting people I shouldn't."

"Well, he sounds like he cares. You didn't raise a dummy."

Ruby laughed and shook her head. "Now why are you out here at the gas station? Don't you have something better to do?"

"Kelly and I were just getting some smokes." Liz glanced at Ruby, then looked at the floorboard. "I'm going to quit and so's he, but right now life is kind of stressful. We agreed it's not time to start something new, if you know what I mean. I saw you were struggling with the gas cap and Kelly said I ought to help."

"Kelly suggested it?"

"He's got a kind heart. I know he don't look like it on the outside."

"Do you have a job?"

"Not right now. I was going to beauty school but the money ran out. One day I'm going to have my own shop. Cut hair all day."

"You should come work for Eula," Ruby said. "That's where I get my hair done. She's helped a lot of young women get started."

"Really? Well, I need to find me a Eula around here. Or move to your neck of the woods."

Kelly rumbled up in his truck and held up a cardboard box. By the time Ruby got out and joined him at the gas tank, he had put the new one on.

"There you go, good as new. You shouldn't have any problems with it."

"Let me see if I can unscrew it," Ruby said. She planted both feet and put her hands on the cap and turned. When it unscrewed easily, she looked up at Kelly with a wide smile. "It came right off!"

"Yeah, I don't know who put your cap on last, but it was crooked. You should be fine now, ma'am."

"Now don't you two go anywhere. I have something for you."

"No need for that. Come on, Liz."

Liz came around from the other side of the car and gave Ruby a hug. "I feel like I've just visited my mamaw again, Miss Ruby. Sure was fun talking to you."

Ruby grabbed her hand. "Now you wait right here. I want to give you something."

"Ma'am, we don't need any payment."

"I don't want to pay you, but I have a gift. Something to help you save up for your wedding."

"Liz, get in the truck."

Ruby held on to Liz's hand and reached for her purse. She looked in her wallet for the change but it wasn't there. Liz must have put it somewhere else. The truck rumbled to life.

"Miss Ruby, I have to go. You have a good day, now."

"No, I want to give you something. Wait a minute."

Ruby let go of Liz and hurried to the passenger side and sat in front of the glove compartment. There was something strange about the lock and the door was crooked. She pulled it down and saw the insurance card and registration, but the money she'd placed there was gone.

The driver's door closed and Ruby saw a tattooed arm next to her. "You wouldn't listen, would you? You wouldn't just get back in the car and leave, would you?"

Ruby stared at Kelly, her jaw slack. Through the window she saw Liz at the steering wheel of the truck, frowning.

Kelly started the car and backed up fast. He hit the brake, then sped forward, and Ruby's door closed on its own.

22

RUBY IS IMMERSED
BEULAH MOUNTAIN, WEST VIRGINIA
SEPTEMBER 1933

In church the day after the root beer floats, Ruby sat with Bean and her mother as usual. The woman hugged Ruby and thanked her for the medicine. Ruby had no idea what she was talking about but she leaned forward and glanced at Bean, who winked as if she would explain later.

All Ruby's questions about life's inequities and struggles seemed to melt into love that morning. The dark question marks about the loss of her mother, the disparity between rich and poor, her fears about leaving for school and going to a place where she didn't know a living soul and what might happen to her friend all seemed to slip through the hardwood of her heart.

The pastor's message, the story he read from the Bible and the verses that spoke of Jesus, made her long for his kind of love.

Everything that had happened up to that point felt like a tilling of the soil of her soul, a preparation for the planting of seeds that sprouted so quickly she couldn't begin to understand. And yet, here she was, the light through the window taking a different hue. The mountains were greener, the faces of those around her more focused, the air cleaner, and the birds singing outside sounded like an orchestra of kindness from God himself.

The hymns took on new meaning as well, and when they came to "Dwelling in Beulah Land," the hymn they sang each week, the words jumped off the page as if they had been written for her.

Viewing here the works of God, I sink in contemplation;
Hearing now His blessed voice, I see the way He planned;
Dwelling in the Spirit, here I learn of full salvation;
Gladly I will tarry in Beulah Land.

Beulah Land was not a spot on a map—it was the holy ground of her heart. And if she yielded land and title to God, he would guide her and make her paths straight. Her coming here was not happenstance. And no matter how far she traveled, she would never forget these people and this day.

There was an altar at the front where Ruby had seen people kneel. It seemed humiliating, people prostrating themselves. Now, she felt pulled there by an unseen hand. Without invitation or chiding, Ruby made her way forward. She put her head on the wooden railing and opened her heart like a flood. She apologized for her selfish ways. She asked God to give her a new heart. As she prayed, Ruby felt that her mother would have been proud.

She felt a warm hand on her shoulder and looked up. Through tears she saw Pastor Brace with his bushy mustache and wrinkled face, the sun-drenched stained-glass windows framing him.

"Welcome home, child," he said softly in her ear.

She smiled, then laughed—which seemed out of place at church, but she couldn't hold it in. When the last refrain was sung, everyone sat and Pastor Brace told them Ruby wanted to be baptized. A murmur rushed through the room, overtaken by several hallelujahs. Pastor Brace ushered her into the back and Talitha Beasley helped her into a baptismal gown.

The baptistery consisted of a hole in the wall behind the pulpit. Narrow wooden stairs led down on either side to a metal trough filled with water. Algae grew there. The pastor helped steady Ruby as she stepped into the chest-deep, chilly water. When she found her footing, she looked out over the congregation and saw Bean with both hands over her mouth.

"The ground is level at the foot of the cross. It doesn't matter where you come from, how much you have or don't have—we all are in need of the forgiveness of God."

"Amen," an older man said in the front, and a woman raised a hand and said, "Hallelujah."

"There is no saving work that happens at baptism. That happens in the heart. But you see here an outward work of God's Spirit on the inner part of this child. Ruby has seen her need of a Savior. She knows there's nothing she can do to earn God's love . . ."

The man's voice trailed off and Ruby studied his face. It seemed he had either come to a fork in the road of his theology or he had seen something startling. Ruby looked at the congregation again and saw her father. He removed his hat, taking a seat on the back row.

"Today Ruby has exchanged her sin for the righteousness of God's only Son. She is now clothed in that righteousness and she's trusting in him fully and completely." Pastor Brace looked down at her. "Is that right, Ruby?"

"Yes, sir," she said, her voice just a smidgen above a mouse squeak. Her hands shook from the temperature of the water.

The pastor asked a few questions about her decision and she

answered them, glancing at the congregation and seeing her father crane his neck.

"In Romans we read, 'If thou shalt confess with thy mouth the Lord Jesus, and shalt believe in thine heart that God hath raised him from the dead, thou shalt be saved.' So because of your confession today, Ruby, it is my honor to baptize you in the name of the Father, the Son, and the Holy Ghost."

The last words were engulfed in the sound of water in her ears and she plunged down only a moment, but it felt like an eternity. When she came up, she gasped for a breath, then wiped water and algae away and embraced the pastor.

Her father met her after the service. He spoke briefly with the pastor and tipped his hat as he passed Bean and her mother. Ruby hugged Bean. "We'll talk later," she whispered.

Ruby's father was the first to speak on the walk home. "You've gotten baptized. Care to explain?"

"I can't. I just finally understood what they were talking about. It was like a window opened and light came in."

"Do you think religion will help you make sense of things? Losing your mother?"

"I'm not looking for religion. I know now that Jesus loves me and gave himself for me. He wants me as part of his family. Mother talked about this when I was little but I didn't understand."

He nodded. "Your mother liked religion—Jesus, as you say."

"Dad, I want you to be baptized. I want you to feel what I feel."

"Which is what?"

"Forgiven."

Her father smiled. "And what do you have to be forgiven for, Ruby? What egregious thing have you done?"

"Terrible things. Terrible thoughts about Mrs. Grigsby and Mr. Coleman. I've disobeyed you a thousand times."

"All perfectly innocent. Compared with the things I've done, you don't hold a candle."

"Exactly. It doesn't matter how bad you've sinned because God is holy. And you and I can't be good enough to make up for our badness. God knew we needed Jesus to take our place on the cross and come live in us. That's what I want for you."

Her father nodded. "I'm happy for you, Ruby." He pulled her close as they walked toward the company store. "I've ordered something for you that I thought would take away some of the sting of leaving Bean behind, and now it seems a gift is even more appropriate. It should be here before you leave."

23

RUBY FEELS GUILTY FOR TRUSTING TWO STRANGERS
SOMEWHERE IN THE HILLS OF WEST VIRGINIA
WEDNESDAY, SEPTEMBER 29, 2004

Ruby stared at the broken glove box as Kelly drove. Had Liz done that? How did she know to look for money in there? He flipped on the radio and tuned to a station playing a song about werewolves and a little old lady getting mutilated. It turned her stomach. The curvy roads didn't help. She wanted the whole episode to be over. She wanted to go home. But how would she face her daughter and son after this lapse of judgment? How could she have trusted these two?

She tried to think of the words to "Dwelling in Beulah Land" but couldn't because of the radio, so she put her hands over her ears like a child. Kelly turned onto another road and Ruby wondered how she'd ever find her way back.

"If you'd have listened to us, you wouldn't be in this fix," Kelly said, taking a draw on a cigarette.

Ruby stared at him. "You're in a fix because . . ." She reached over and hit the Power button on the radio. "You're in a fix because you're a thief. One day the law is going to catch up with you and put you in your place."

Ruby felt better having said it, but the look on Kelly's face made her wish she hadn't.

"If I was you, I'd shut up," he said, slapping the Power button and turning the music up louder.

They drove farther into the woods and uphill, the road narrowing and the trees closing in. Clouds blocked the sunlight. Ruby's stomach growled and she realized she hadn't eaten and her head was light. She reached into the backseat for the cooler she had packed with sandwiches, but Kelly smacked her arm hard.

Ruby whimpered, covering her face. The road beneath them became gravel, then dirt and ruts and bumps, and she felt the arthritis in her hip.

They stopped with a jerk on an uphill grade and Kelly pulled the emergency brake and took the keys. A big dog barked. Ruby didn't like big dogs. She opened her eyes. They were near a trailer at the side of a dirt path that continued into the hills. She felt like she had reached the ends of the earth.

Liz pulled up in the truck and got out as Kelly yelled and gestured with the cigarette. Ruby turned and pulled the soft-packed cooler to herself, unzipping the top. She took out a sandwich and chewed it, watching the two like they were some TV show.

Liz ran a hand through her hair, which wasn't easy because it was a tangled, matted mess. Ruby couldn't believe she had put any stock in what the girl had said. Liz spoke, Kelly shouted and took the envelope of cash and opened it. He dropped his cigarette as he leafed through the bills.

Kelly walked back to the car and opened Ruby's door. "Get out."

Ruby pleaded with him to let her go. She said she wouldn't tell anyone what they had done, and tried to stay in the car, but Kelly grabbed her by the wrist and hauled her out and Ruby felt something pop when he jerked her. It was the same wrist she had injured in her fall on the front steps of her house. She whimpered in pain and held her wrist with the other hand as she fell onto their couch, if you could call it that. It looked like something someone tossed to the side of the road that the two had scavenged. There was a smell of something burning inside the trailer—like a pan had been left on the stove too long. Glass bottles and jars were scattered throughout the kitchen and living room, some with tubes coming out of them. Prescription bottles were stacked on a small table, most of them empty. There were boxes of clothes and pots and pans and a large-screen TV that looked like it was about to topple off its rickety stand. Ruby had never seen such a mess.

"I'll tell you what," Liz said to Kelly, "if she's got that much cash on her, there's more where that came from."

Ruby muttered, "I don't know what you're going to do with the money, but you might want to think about hiring a maid."

Liz ignored her. "You can tell she's loaded. Not by the car or how she's dressed, but I can smell the money. Sometimes that's the dead giveaway—rich people try to look like they're not."

"You don't know what you're talking about," Ruby said.

Kelly opened the screen door and flicked his cigarette out and lit another. "This gets us into a whole different level, Liz. It's one thing to . . ." He waved his hand around the room. "But it's another to kidnap somebody."

"We didn't kidnap anybody. We helped an old woman."

"You stole my money," Ruby said.

"Shut up!" Liz said, and Ruby could tell she meant it. "The police aren't going to bother with some old woman lost in the woods. Besides, nobody saw us."

"I think somebody's going to come looking for her."

"And how are they going to know where she is?"

Ruby sat up straight. "That fellow at the gas station will remember me."

"I've had enough," Liz said, grabbing a roll of duct tape and unraveling a long strip. "Hold out your hands."

Ruby held her arms out, her right wrist shaking. It was turning black-and-blue and was twisted slightly to the side. "My arm's hurt. I need a doctor."

Liz wrapped the tape around her arms tightly, then ripped off another strip.

"I need a drink of water," Ruby said.

"Only water you're going to get is when we toss you into the bottom of a well. Now shut up." She stuck the tape over Ruby's mouth.

Ruby tried to talk but the tape was on too tight. It was hard to breathe, too, and she tried to say that but all they heard were her mumbling groans.

"I say we take her out back and hit her in the head with a shovel," Liz said. "That'll keep her quiet."

Ruby's eyes grew wide and she wondered if they had done that kind of thing before.

"She's right about the gas station," Kelly said. "They might have cameras. All it takes is one by the cash register. Or outside at the pumps."

"Did you see a camera?"

"No, but I wasn't looking for one. If they were there, somebody will see us. I'm telling you, this is bad news."

"We helped her with her gas cap."

Ruby mumbled.

"I did what you told me when she went inside. Screwed it on too tight, remember? The camera catches that and it shows we set her up. This is not good."

"It's a fine time for you to grow a conscience."

The dog barked viciously and Kelly kicked the screen door open and walked outside. He came back with Ruby's purse.

"What was he barking at?" Liz said.

"Squirrel, I reckon."

Kelly tossed the purse to Liz and she dumped the contents on the end of the couch. "Look what we have here. A cell phone." She flipped it open. "Too bad there's no service." Liz scrolled through the contact list. "Lady, either you got no friends in the world or you never use this thing." She opened the back of the phone and removed the battery and tossed it back in the purse. "No matter what, we can't let her talk. That's clear as day."

Kelly pulled the hair away from his face. "What do you mean?"

"Well, if you're so scared, we can get Carl. He owes us. He'll take care of her and give us something for the car. Then we'd be free and clear."

Kelly looked at her like she had two heads. "Carl? You want to give her to Carl? And you think when they find her and then trace her back to Carl, he's going to be quiet? He's not going to say how he found her?"

Liz rubbed the back of her hand across her nose. "I can't believe you're talking like this. We got a gold mine sitting right here. We got cash and a credit card. And if I'm right, there's probably somebody in Kentucky who'd pay a pretty penny to get their mama back." She looked at Ruby. "Ain't that right, old woman?"

Ruby scowled.

Liz sidled up to Kelly and put her arms on his shoulders. "You and me could take a vacation. Find someplace nice to stay. Maybe turn the cash we got into more. Know what I mean?"

Kelly smiled. "I could go for a vacation. But what about her?"

Liz rolled her eyes and kicked at the screen door. She turned to Ruby and pointed a bony finger. "Stay there. You try to get up and I'll duct-tape your legs."

The two went through Ruby's car. What unnerved Ruby the most wasn't the yelling. It was when they got quiet and Liz talked to Kelly sweetly that made her think there was more trouble ahead.

Ruby's lips were parched and her tongue swollen, she guessed from all the fluids rushing to her broken wrist. The dryness and arm pain were only eclipsed by the feeling she got listening to the music Kelly and Liz played. Every drumbeat and pluck of the bass guitar was a thump to her already-taxed aorta. Theirs was music you didn't just hear, you felt down to the joints and marrow. The songs shook the walls and the metal roof of the trailer. She liked her Southern gospel loud, of course, but this was not "I'll Fly Away" or "Mansion over the Hilltop."

When the two came back to the trailer after going through her car, Ruby looked into their eyes. She had always believed the eyes were the windows to the soul, but if that were true, theirs needed a bucket of Windex. Both were dirty brown and cloudy. There was a hint that Kelly had convinced Liz not to harm Ruby more because Kelly called her "ma'am" when he spoke again. Ruby grunted loud enough for Kelly to pull the duct tape off her mouth. She told them her lips were as parched as the Sahara and when they didn't give her anything to drink, Ruby became agitated. She demanded they let her go because she didn't like driving in the dark. That's when Liz turned on her and ordered Kelly to put her in the bedroom.

Kelly helped Ruby to her feet and stared at her wrist.

"I think it's broke," he said to Liz. "It's puffed up and black-and-blue."

"Put her in the bedroom," Liz said again with a flick of the hand as though Ruby were no more than a stick of furniture that needed to be hauled away. Something they should've done with the furniture in their trailer—it all needed to be burnt, Ruby thought.

Kelly led her to a bare twin mattress that rested on a piece of plywood on top of cinder blocks. The mattress was stained with something brown at the bottom and she didn't want to think of the last person who had fallen asleep here or where they might be buried. She sat, her arms still secured with the duct tape, on the opposite end from the stain. Ruby wondered what kind of mark the tape would leave when it was taken off. But maybe no one would ever see it anyway. The rain would make digging a hole in the wet ground much easier.

"You stay right here," Kelly said.

"Can you take this off?" Ruby said softly, nodding at the duct tape on her wrists.

"No, just lay back. Try to rest."

"Have you ever tried to rest with your arms in this position? I'm an old woman. I've got a cramp."

Kelly frowned, then pulled out a pocketknife and cut the tape. Ruby yelped when he ripped the piece off her bad wrist. He leaned down and whispered, "Now you'll stop complaining if you know what's good for you."

What was good for her now was a lot different than she'd thought twenty-four hours earlier. What was good then was a clandestine trip, without the constraints of her children's knowledge, to see the place she had seen in her dreams for more than seventy years. What seemed good was to finally tell herself the truth about what had happened, even though she could not tell another living soul that truth.

Kelly closed the door and Ruby stayed seated out of defiance. If she lay back, she might fall asleep because she was exhausted and her wrist ached. She wanted to elevate it, but there wasn't a pillow and she didn't dare ask for anything. She let her eyes adjust to the room's darkness, lit only by the security light that shone through the window. In the corner was a guitar with a broken neck, held together by rusted strings. She pondered the circumstances of that musical mishap until something gray with a long tail moved beside the guitar. Then she closed her eyes and picked up her feet, putting them on the mattress.

She stared at the window, calculating its height and width and how far the fall would be if she got it open. She would have to climb onto the mattress and lean forward to get her arms out and then let gravity do the rest. Perhaps the rat in the corner would jump at her and that would give her the extra oomph to get over the sill.

Just as she thought she would die of thirst, the door opened and Liz walked in with a mug. She held it out without making eye contact. "You said you was thirsty. Drink this."

"What is it?"

"What does it matter?" Liz said, not seeming to notice or care that the duct tape that had been removed. "Take it."

Ruby took the mug and held it to her lips, sniffing. She could sense a slight tinge of sassafras root in the brown liquid.

"My mama taught me it's not polite to smell what people give them to eat or drink," Liz said.

"I doubt your mama was ever duct-taped and threatened with a shovel," Ruby said. Then she wondered if that was true.

"Your choice: the drink or the shovel."

Ruby thought of Jesus in the garden of Gethsemane drinking the cup of gall. He drank it for her and all of mankind who would acknowledge him. And here was one of the people he died for, standing in the doorway with droopy eyelids and a love for loud music with lyrics screamed at incomprehensible levels. Ruby had wanted to help Liz and Kelly and repay them for their kindness. Their betrayal, and her gullibility, had fueled a growing rage. Now, seeing Liz in the doorway without a stitch of hope for anything but a blazing eternity, Ruby's heart softened.

"Is your mama still living?"

"Why do you want to know about my mama?"

"Because I'll bet she's been praying for you," Ruby said as softly as she could to be heard over the music.

Liz cursed. "I told my mama a long time ago not to waste her prayers on me. I'm too far gone for Jesus."

"As long as you have breath, there's hope. Nobody's too far gone."

"Then you don't know me."

"Maybe not. But I know Jesus. And that's why I think there's a chance."

Liz shook her head. "I'm telling you, old lady, you don't know what you're dealing with."

"I do because I grew up dealing with the likes of you and Kelly. I grew up with people hooked on booze. Hooked deeper than a striped bass on a june bug. There's nobody outside the realm of deliverance if you'll give God a chance."

Liz turned her head toward the kitchen and yelled. "Just our luck to kidnap a preacher. And this one's not drinking the Kool-Aid."

When Liz turned back, Ruby thought she saw a slight opening in her face. "You ought to listen to reason. I know you're caught up in something you can't stop. Something that has hold of you and won't let go. But there's got to be a shred of goodness in you. You don't have to live this way. You don't have to keep running from your troubles with whatever it is you're doing."

"No wonder your kids don't want anything to do with you." Liz walked forward into the dark of the room. "Drink this or I get the shovel."

Ruby looked at her face and believed her. She tipped the mug back and drank, then handed it back. The liquid burned on the way down but she felt like she had a listening ear and she kept talking, kept hoping something would get through.

"I hope you'll consider what I've said. There's a man on the radio I listen to. His name is Franklin Brown. I send him money every now and again and he says that nobody is outside the reach of God's love." She kept on, telling Liz about the message she had heard about forgiveness and how good she felt hearing it. "I've been living under a weight of guilt, you see. I've been sorry for something my whole life. That's why I'm going back to Beulah Mountain. To make things right."

Liz stepped back into a shaft of light from the kitchen. There was no life in her eyes at all. "Better lay down, Grandma. This stuff works fast."

The room began to spin almost as soon as Liz closed the door. No wonder Liz didn't care that Ruby's hands had been freed. Ruby was no longer worried about the rat or the drop from the window. She could only think of letting her head hit the mattress. She closed her eyes, a sick feeling in her stomach that could've been physical or emotional. The music in the next room seemed to recede, the thumping moving into some other dimension. She looked at the water running down the window and the droplets seemed to move in slow motion, like tears falling down a young girl's face.

And then, like lightning, the images and sounds flashed in her mind. The shoes. The third floor. The game the girls played. Root beer floats and a woman's screams. Men smoking cigars and laughing. The flash of gunfire. Blood on hardwood.

Ruby put a hand to her head to stop the memories, the hand with the wrist as big as a pumpkin, but she didn't feel pain any longer. She didn't feel parched or tired or any muscle cramps—just a feeling like she was floating. She opened her eyes, sure this was what it felt like to die. Her heart slowed. She could feel it inside her own chest. The spinning intensified and she looked at the window as lightning flashed. A scared, grief-stricken face looked at her. A face she never thought she would see again, but there it was.

She was looking inside the train.

She was looking at herself.

And then the silver cord broke and there was blackness and she surrendered.

24

RUBY SHOWS BEAN HER PRESENT
BEULAH MOUNTAIN, WEST VIRGINIA
OCTOBER 1, 1933

Ruby dragged Bean up the stairs after church on the first Sunday in October, smiling in anticipation.

"What's got you so all-fired happy?" Bean said. "I thought you were sad about being shipped off to school tomorrow."

Ruby grabbed Bean's hand and pulled her inside the apartment. "You have to see what my father bought. It's to help me remember you and everything here in Beulah Mountain."

On a table sat a black box and Bean studied it. "What's inside?"

"It's a camera, silly," Ruby said. "My dad said I could take pictures and he's going to develop them and send them to me."

Bean picked up the box and turned it, finding the lens. "Reckon he'd let me have one so's I could remember you?"

Ruby nodded and pointed the camera at Bean. "Hold real still and don't move."

Bean primped her hair. "Should I smile or just act natural?"

Ruby shook her head. "I swear, Bean, I don't know what I'm going to do without you around to make me laugh."

"Hey, when the baby comes, your daddy can take a picture and send it to you."

"Oh, I wanted to be here when your little brother or sister arrived."

"Well, you can visit, can't you?"

"Mm-hmm," Ruby said. She wondered if there was enough light in the room. Her father had said to go outside, the more light the better. But maybe they just needed more windows. "Let's go upstairs and take a picture in the shoe room."

"I don't want to climb in the old dumbwaiter again," Bean said. "It gives me the willies being cooped up in there."

"You don't have to," Ruby said. She ran to her father's room and came back with a key. "I found it the other day. But before we go up there, I have an idea. Now don't give me that look."

"All your ideas wind up getting me in trouble with your daddy," Bean said.

"It was one time and he never got mad at you."

"What's the idea?"

"Go in my closet and pick something out."

"What for?"

"For the picture. You put on my clothes and act like me. I'll do the same with your overalls."

"If I put one of those dresses on, I'm going to start acting uppity."

Ruby laughed as Bean tumbled through the dresses in the closet. She loved watching Bean's imitation of the people in town, and truth be told, Ruby liked to imitate Bean's mountain talk and the way she walked, her heels striking the floorboards like she was climbing to the top of the world. But what she liked most was seeing such a poor girl wear clothes she could never afford.

Bean took out a hanger that held Ruby's favorite dress. "No, not that one," Ruby said.

"You told me I could pick something out, and I pick this."

Ruby nodded and said it was okay and Bean took off her bib overalls and let them fall and pulled the dress over her head.

"Lands, this feels so soft and silky."

"My mother gave it to me," Ruby said, stepping into the threadbare denim. "Now no more *lands* and things like that. You have to pretend you're me."

Bean pressed her lips together firmly and lifted her head. "Yes. You're quite right. I have a reputation to uphold among the common people. Where's Mrs. Grigsby and my morning caviar?"

Ruby was laughing so hard she couldn't get the buttons into the bent hooks of the overalls and finally Bean helped her.

"I need to do a load of *warsh*," Ruby said. "These overalls are a mite gamy."

Bean tilted her head. "They wouldn't be that way if you would practice simple hygiene, my dear."

Ruby laughed and headed for the door. "Last one to the top is a dead polecat!"

Bean followed, stepping primly onto the stairs with her hands folded in front of her. Ruby was at the top unlocking the door when Bean said, "It's not ladylike to run like that. A refined girl is never in a hurry."

It was similar to something Mrs. Grigsby had said and Ruby doubled over laughing on the top steps, holding the camera. Bean opened the door and walked past her into the shoe room and threw open the curtains. Sunlight streamed across the wood floor.

"Now I'm ready for my picture," Bean said, pulling a chair to the wall in front of the shoes.

Ruby set the camera on a chair, then put books underneath to get it close to eye level with Bean. "Give me your most refined-girl look."

Bean tilted her head slightly and looked straight into the lens. After the click, she rose elegantly and sauntered to the camera. "Now it's time for a picture of the rabble. Go on and sit down. Let me see what I can do with this Beulah Mountain urchin."

Ruby giggled and showed her the shutter and how to push the button without moving the camera.

"I know how to do it," Bean said, breaking character only for a moment. "I mean, a lady always knows how to be gentle with such photographic equipment."

Ruby sat in the chair and pooched out her face, slouching, with one hand on her chin.

"Is that what you think I look like?" Bean said.

"Trust me," Ruby said. "Every time you look at this picture, you're going to laugh."

Bean stared at Ruby, something passing over her like a cloud. She seemed to be looking at the wall.

"What's the matter?" Ruby said.

"I hope I never get a pair of those."

"Why not?" Ruby said. "Your feet would stay warm all winter in those lace-up ones. And they'd look good on you."

"Sit still," Bean said as she reached for the shutter. After it clicked, she said, "My mother told me a story the other day. Said I couldn't tell nobody."

"Anybody," Ruby said, correcting her. "A story about what?"

"What goes on in this room. The reason you hear voices. The reason women cry sometimes."

"Bean, you're scaring me."

"I don't mean to. I should just keep it to myself." She primped her hair again. "Like a genuine lady."

"No, you can't bring it up and then stop," Ruby said.

"I don't want to scare the little mountain girl."

"I'm not scared anymore. What's the story?"

Bean looked out the window. "Do you think it's okay to break a promise to your mama? You tell her you won't do something, but it bottles you up inside like one of those soda pops downstairs? Until it feels like you're going to bust?"

"Bean, what did she say?"

Bean moved the camera and books and sat in the chair. "My mama got a pair of shoes from up here. I found where she had them hidden and she told me about them, but she swears she'll never wear them."

"Why in the world not?"

"Because of what Mr. Coleman made her do."

"I don't think I want to hear this."

"I told you," Bean said.

"No, go on. I didn't mean that."

Bean scratched her nose. "The Esau scrip ran out. My daddy didn't go back to work at the mine, so Mr. Coleman called my mother up to see him. They do awful things to some of the women, Ruby. It wasn't long after that, that my mother knew she was pregnant. My daddy hadn't been around for weeks. I don't know much about the birds and the bees, but I know enough to figure out that baby my mama's carrying isn't my daddy's."

Ruby's jaw dropped.

"I should take your picture right now because it's exactly what I thought. You can't tell nobody, you understand?"

"Your mother is going to have Mr. Coleman's baby?"

Bean nodded.

"Does he know it?"

"If he does, he ain't said nothing to her about it. And she don't want him to know. She's afraid, Ruby. If he finds out, he might hurt her. I said we should leave but she can't see a way out."

Ruby stared at the floor, trying to comprehend what she'd just been told.

Bean slapped her knees with both hands and stood. "I got to get back to Mama. The midwife is coming to check her this afternoon and I want to be there."

Ruby locked the door to the shoe room and the two retreated downstairs and changed. Ruby gave Bean a hug before she left, heading down the back steps and moving through the woods like a specter.

Ruby had dinner with her father when he returned later that day, but she couldn't think of anything but what Bean had told her. Her father must have noticed and asked what was wrong.

"Nothing," Ruby said.

"No, come on. Tell me what's bothering you."

She put down her fork and studied the pattern of the tablecloth. "Do you think it's wrong to break a promise to a friend?"

25

Ruby heard a strange sound and realized it was rain on the trailer roof. The only thing she hated to do worse than drive at night was to drive in a rainstorm.

"She looks dead," somebody said. She couldn't see him because she couldn't open her eyes.

"Get the blanket under her." That was Kelly. "She'll be easier to carry that way."

"What did Liz give her?"

"Shut up, Carl. You'll wake her."

Wake who? Ruby thought. Liz? Was Liz asleep? Or was she somewhere around the corner digging a hole? Or waiting with a shovel?

Ruby slipped back into a fog as they worked a dirty quilt underneath her. The world spun. She felt weightless and wasn't sure if she was being carried or if it was the drink. Liz had come back and given her more of the drink, hadn't she?

She heard the raindrops and felt them on her face now. She tried to speak. Tried to yell. She couldn't. She had no energy or will. She moaned a little when they set her down in the backseat of a car . . . or was it the truck? An engine fired, then another. Then they were rumbling down the hillside and Ruby was gone again.

Part 4

26

FRANCES DRIVES THE ROAD TO BEULAH MOUNTAIN
THURSDAY, SEPTEMBER 30, 2004

The rain picked up as Frances crossed the state line into West Virginia and became a downpour by the time she exited the interstate and took the first of many winding roads that led to Beulah Mountain. Her mother hated to drive in the rain—hated to even ride in a car when it was raining. What would Ruby do if she got caught in a downpour like this?

Every bend in the road, every mangled guardrail made Frances say a prayer for her mother and wonder if maybe this was the hillside where she had descended. That might be the spot where her mother left the road and this world. Frances kept driving, pulled like a magnet to a place she'd never been. The connection for her mother must have been great to make her brave these treacherous roads. But why hadn't Ruby told her about this Company Store event—or much of anything about her past?

The farther she drove, the harder the downpour came. Lightning flashed over the hills and illumined the landscape and the cascading water for a second, enough for Frances to see the beauty of the rolling hills. She would have liked fewer curves, less up and down and all around, but she knew the road had to move with the mountain instead of cutting directly through it. There was something about the drive and entering this world that made her feel like she had been transported to another place and time.

Thoughts of Wallace intruded. She felt foolish for thinking there might have been some hope of reconciliation. She felt doubly foolish for being jealous of this Carolyn. But Frances deserved someone much more than he did. She was the one who had borne the trouble of his choices. Why hadn't she found some perfect match that would patch up all the broken places of her heart? Why hadn't she been able to call Julia and say, "I've met someone"?

The truth was, after Wallace, she'd been afraid to meet someone. The wounds of the marriage had killed areas of her heart she wasn't sure would ever come alive again. But seeing Wallace and feeling hope spark, even though it died again, made her think that maybe her heart was beating in those dark places, behind the closed basement doors.

She thought of a boy from her hometown. He'd been the dream of every young woman from elementary to high school. He had it all—the smile, athleticism, a happy-go-lucky attitude. She still thought of him as eighteen, in his cap and gown, laughing and smiling, caught in time in her mind. She'd lost track of him but heard he was married and had children. All the good men were taken, she thought. And most of the bad ones, too.

Frances smiled at that and pulled over to consult her map. Each turn and curve made her woozy, but she calmed a bit when she saw a sign that said Beulah Mountain, 16 miles. She was on the right road.

Another flash of lightning and she looked out on the valley that spread like God's tablecloth on creation and it took her breath away.

She wound down, swerving to avoid fallen trees and standing water. When she pulled into the darkened town, she saw light near a hotel that looked somewhat accommodating. It was an older building with a blinking Vacancy sign, and she couldn't help but think of her own life. Was there room for anyone else?

The young woman at the front desk sat clicking through TV channels and cracking gum. Her name tag read *Summer*. Frances first asked if there was a Ruby Freeman staying at the hotel, then added the Handley just in case.

Summer punched the down arrow on a grimy keyboard and squinted at an amber computer screen and shook her head. "We got one room left tonight, but it's only for one night. Tomorrow we're booked up."

"I'll take it," Frances said.

She got the room for seventy-nine dollars and found two double beds with aged, flowery bedspreads worn thin. She wondered who else had wandered through the hills and found this town and this room. What tired bodies had chosen Beulah Mountain, West Virginia, as their resting place for the night? Did they have family in the hills? Were they here for a wedding, a funeral, a county fair?

She leaned her small suitcase against the wall and called Jerry for an update. His wife answered.

"Laurie, have you heard anything about my mother?" Frances said.

The woman didn't speak. There was just a noise on the phone like the cord was being stretched too far and then Jerry's voice came on the line.

"We haven't heard anything more, Frances. Where are you?"

She told him and asked him to call if there was any news.

"Did Wallace go home?" Jerry said.

"He left just before I did."

"Weird having him here again, wasn't it? Sort of felt like old times."

"Mm-hmm. He was a big help. It was kind of him to drive up."

"He was right about everything. You know, all the police stuff. Glad he was there."

Frances recalled her suspicion of Jerry, and though it still felt far-fetched, she entertained the possibility again. Whatever he said, he sounded glad Wallace was gone.

"Do you think you two will get back together?" Jerry said.

Frances laughed, not at the question or at Jerry's naiveté, but at the absurdity of life. "I think he's moved on."

"Well, for the record, I think you two made a good couple."

It was the kindest thing she had ever heard her brother say and it caught her by surprise.

"If you hadn't gotten together, there would never have been a Julia. I'd say she was worth the pain and heartache, don't you think?"

"I do. You're right."

He paused and instead of filling in the gaps for him, she stayed silent.

"I've been thinking of all the nights Mom waited up for me. You too, probably. She waited in the parking lot at school for football practice to end. She spent half her adult life waiting. And now we're doing the same."

"Waiting and not knowing is the hardest combination."

"You got that right, Sis."

"I'll let you know if I find out anything here," she said.

Frances slept a few hours, waking and checking her phone to see if she had missed a call. She ate breakfast in the dining area the next morning. Tepid coffee and toast and cereal and hard-boiled eggs. The rain had subsided, though droplets still fell from leaves to the ground like manna, and the birds were out and singing with the rush of creeks. There was a hint of the sun but it had yet to peek over the top of the mountain.

She checked out and dialed Charlotte Beasley's number, getting voice mail and leaving a message. At the front desk "Summer" had given way to "Fred" and she asked him about the Company Store Museum. The man pointed and said it was walking distance.

Brick buildings stood empty with plywood fastened over windows. Sidewalks heaved from encroaching tree roots. A shuttered gas station stood on the corner of two main streets with bars over the windows and empty holes in concrete, the ghosts of gas pumps. Some businesses were open, however, like the ice cream shop that advertised a banana split sale. A sign at a hair salon read Support Coal.

Railroad tracks ran through the town along a narrow corridor of old homes, a few of which had been refurbished to look like they had in the days when coal had flown from the mountains like flocks of swallows. Frances came upon a weathered metal sign that stood near the tracks.

On the second of October, 1933, the Beulah Mountain Massacre occurred. Seven people lost their lives at the company store and directly outside. Among them were the owners of the mine, Thaddeus Coleman and Jacob Handley. The perpetrator, Judson Dingess, was shot dead by Sheriff Kirby Banning on the street outside the store.

She looked past the sign, across a wide expanse of road, and saw the Company Store Museum. The structure was built on a stone foundation and concrete stairs led up to the front entrance. The wooden siding had been replaced by white aluminum, and the many gables showed the intricacy of the building's design. She counted a dozen windows from where she was standing, and she assumed there were more she couldn't see. The building looked like it had stepped off the pages of history.

Walking closer to get a different view, she stood by a railing and took in the smell of the wet earth and the rising humidity. She could close her eyes and hear the train whistle and smell the coal dust and the beasts of burden. She could see the blackened faces of the miners walking with their lunch pails. She smelled the woodsmoke burning for dinners and water heated for baths for husbands returning sweaty and grime-laden.

Her phone rang. Charlotte.

"I'm standing here at the Company Store," Frances said. "This is amazing."

"I'll be right out," Charlotte said.

The front door opened and a girl in her early twenties exited wearing jeans and a blue T-shirt with the Company Store logo. She had short brown hair that bounced as she bounded down the stairs and across a gravel walkway with ropes on either side. The store evidently expected a crowd.

"Have you heard anything from your mother?" Charlotte said, shaking hands.

"I was going to ask you the same thing," Frances said. "I was hoping I would pull up to the hotel and see her car, find her checked in, and knock on her door. I guess that's not going to happen." She filled her in on what she knew and Charlotte's face grew concerned.

"Well, we've got our eyes peeled. I feel so bad now, about bothering her. I was just looking for answers."

"Answers about what? You mentioned on the phone you've been doing research."

"Did you know this was your mother's home after your grandmother died?" Charlotte said.

"I heard that, but I don't know much more."

"Come on. Let me give you the pre–ribbon-cutting tour."

27

The rain had awakened Hollis several times in the night. Their roof had been repaired two summers ago, so he didn't worry about leaks, but when lightning struck close, it sounded like a TNT blast and he sat bolt upright. The flash came from the top of the hill and he hoped the lightning hadn't hit the big poplar by his parents' graves. That tree had grown up and out over the grassy knoll and provided shade, and Hollis loved to sit under it and think of those who had come before him. And the one who had come after.

His father had walked him through the woods when he was a child, pointing out each flower and fern and tree and where to look for ginseng and how to identify poison ivy. Most people couldn't tell the difference between a pine and an oak and he thought that was a shame. Lying back on the bed, he thought of all the pleasure that tree had brought just by growing where it had been planted. And he wondered if there wasn't a lesson there for people to do what they were made to do and leave the rest alone. There wasn't a soul on earth who would miss that tree like he would.

Hollis was usually up first, but when he pulled his head from the pillow, he saw Juniper's empty dent in the mattress and heard her stirring in the kitchen. He pushed the hair out of his eyes and threw a leg over the side of the bed. When he rose up, the bones cracked in his shoulder and somewhere in his knee. His body was a symphony, and the stomach growl was part of the percussion section.

He stood and felt a deeper ache than usual, connecting the extra humidity of the rainfall with the pain in his muscles and joints. Every time it rained, there was a new level of ache and if this was as bad as it got, he could take it. But of course, he knew this was not as bad as it got. It would get worse, especially for Juniper, and that meant it would get worse for him, too. Life had become a downhill race that no one had entered voluntarily. Everyone had a spot in line and a number pinned to their back and a finish line out of sight around the bend.

As a young man, Hollis had been terrified of death. That fear had drawn him to God. He believed there was something better on the other side, and getting there was inevitable. He could measure his days past and weigh them with those unnumbered ones in the future and be at peace with the equation. Now, death didn't scare him half as much as life. Death led to streets of gold and people he loved. Peace. Rest. But he couldn't for the life of him figure out where living led.

He found Juniper at the stove making bacon and eggs. He hadn't seen her up this early in some time and wanted to ask if she felt better but decided against it. The skillet was one his mother used, heavy and black, and he wondered how Juniper had lifted it from the drawer underneath the stove.

"Smells good," he said.

"It's supposed to."

"I guess you're right."

"Coffee's ready," she said.

He poured himself a cup and drank it black. The heat bit going down his throat.

"That was some storm last night, wasn't it?" Juniper said.

"Gully washer."

"Lightning hit close."

"You jumped when it did."

"Did not."

"Felt like it. You kind of kicked me."

"I should have kicked you a long time ago." She kept her back to him but he could sense the smile on her face.

"Probably should have. Probably should have picked up a hammer while you were at it."

"Think it hit the poplar?" she said.

"I'll check."

He put his feet in his shoes without tying them and walked out on the front step with the mug in his hand and his laces flopping and craned his neck to look at the hill above the house, preparing himself for the worst. But there it stood, keeping watch over the flock of close kin and distant relatives and friends from the town who were buried underneath. It gave him a warm feeling to see it, like an old dog that had run away loping back up the road.

He scanned the tree line down the hill but saw nothing unusual. It wasn't until he stepped into the mud at the side of the house that he saw the damage.

"Big walnut out back," he said when he returned to the kitchen and slipped off his shoes. "We'll need to cut it so the rest of it doesn't fall on the shed."

"And when will you do that?" Juniper said.

"I'll get around to it. I'm just glad it wasn't the poplar."

He sat and she scraped the eggs from the skillet onto a plate and brought it to the table. He watched her move to the refrigerator for butter and then to the toaster. It was like watching a movie where the people age before your eyes because in his mind he could see her younger, standing tall and beautiful. He blinked and there she was with gray hair and sagging breasts and wrinkles. It was all he could do not to get up and help, but she seemed to want to do it herself and he sensed he should sit still. The conflict with Coleman and the town had caused an underlying chill between Hollis and his wife, and he wondered if eggs and bacon was her way of thawing the ground between them.

Juniper sat and put her fork into the yolk of her fried egg, and yellow leaked onto her plate. Then, out of nowhere, as if it were something she had planned all along, she said, "What are you going to do when I'm gone?"

He stared at her. "Where you headed?"

"You know what I mean."

"If you leave, I'm going with you."

She smiled. "You're a rascal. Answer the question, Hollis."

He put some jam on his toast and bit into it, wiping the crumbs from his lips onto his lap. "What makes you think you're leaving first?"

"I swear, Hollis, you have to look at what is instead of what you want."

"What are you talking about?"

"You see the world through different eyes. You see it as you want it to be. You look at me and you see the woman you married, not what I've become."

"You haven't become anybody but who you always were. That's what I see."

"You don't see reality, Hollis. And you need to start."

He chewed on his breakfast, sensing he ought to be quiet instead of fight her.

"Your good intentions are getting in your way."

"What intentions are those?"

"You have a good heart. You want to do the right thing. You always have. But both of us know you're never going to cut down that walnut tree. Because you see it as it was before the lightning struck. Something will happen and you'll put it off. There'll be some other thing that's bigger and more pressing and you'll fight that battle. Until one day a strong wind will come along and that tree will smash the shed and you'll call it God's will. That's the way it happens with you. If there's not some emergency, not some crisis that gets you to move, not some tree crashing down, you'll let it go. You sprain your ankle and it swells up like a gourd and you wait. Might be broken. Might not. You act like the 'might not' always trumps the 'might.'"

He swallowed the toast and thought a minute. "I'll call Larry and get him over here with his chain saw. Is that what you want?"

She put down her fork with a clatter. "This is not about the tree or Larry coming with a chain saw. You're not getting it."

"Then help me understand. I'm listening."

"This is about you seeing the truth about the situation we got here."

"And what's the truth, Juniper? Spell it out."

"The truth is, we're on a piece of property that could set the two of us and your granddaughter up for the rest of our lives. You could sell this and we could buy something and live out the little time we have left together without listening to the dynamite and diesel trucks and bulldozers. They'll come and go like bees to a hive. I don't know how much longer I got and neither do you. I think you hanging on to this place is something you're doing for your mama and daddy. And you don't need to any longer. You need to think of yourself. And me. And the rest of the family."

The eggs and bacon didn't look as appetizing as when he sat down. Hollis put down his fork and pushed the plate away. "I wish the lightning had gotten the poplar now. It would have made it easier to leave."

Juniper picked up the medicine bottle at the middle of the table and tried to open it but couldn't. He unscrewed the cap for her like he always did and put the pill in front of her and then the three others she took each morning. She washed them down with orange juice he had bought at the Family Dollar.

"I'm asking you to do this for me," she said. "And I know it's not fair to ask."

"It doesn't matter whether it's fair or not—"

"It does to me," she said. "I know this is the end of a load you can't lift alone. And it feels like it's going to kill you to get under it. You've fought a good fight. But in my mind, this is not about winning or losing some battle with Buddy Coleman. This is about you and me. It's about our family. It's about choosing whether to live or not."

Hollis thought of the verse in the Gospel of John where Jesus said he came to bring life and life abundant. He thought he had that life, but maybe it was an illusion. Maybe the whole mountain wasn't real.

"Did you butter me up with breakfast for this speech?"

She almost smiled. "Took every ounce of strength I had to lift that skillet."

He pulled the plate closer and resumed eating. When he was done with his eggs, he broke the bread and moved it around the plate to soak up the rest. As he did, he saw his father's hand at the end of his own arm. He put his silverware on the plate he knew he would wash himself and turned in his chair, leaning forward with his elbows on his knees.

"You might be right," he finally said.

"Right about what?"

"I feel obligated to them. They treated me like their own. You have to remind me that I wasn't theirs because it always felt like I was. They gave me their name. Gave me everything they had. And they never asked a thing in return but to hang on to this mountain."

"They've been gone thirty years, Hollis."

"No, they haven't been. They're still here. Up on the hill."

"It's not fair of them to ask this."

"Maybe it's not, but you keep talking about seeing what is rather than what I want to see. Maybe you're doing the same. You want them to release me from the promise I made. But I can't change a vow."

"You've done all you could. You kept it as long as you could, and if they could step out of their graves right now, they'd walk down here and tell you to sell. Get off this mountain."

Hollis cleared his throat and coughed. He thought of their faces and their hardscrabble life. And how much joy they took in the little things. His parents could find good in sun and cloud alike.

Finally he looked at Juniper, narrowing his gaze. He tried to remove the hurt from his voice, some of the feelings of betrayal, but some of it leaked through. "I can't fight this alone. If you're not with me, I'll sell and move quick as a wink. If that's what you want me to do, I'll do it."

"Don't you see, Hollis? This is not about me getting you to do what I want. This is about us being together. It's about seeing that I'm *for* you and not against you."

He stared at the linoleum, then looked again at his work-worn hands and the creases and wrinkles life had etched. For the first time he considered what it would be like to move and what it would take to get a truck up the hill and who would help them haul their belongings away and how much it would cost to rent the truck. The feeling of going down the driveway the last time and waving good-bye in his heart. It was a moment he thought would never come, even considering such a thing. Moving and divorce weren't in his vocabulary. But now he was considering one of the two.

"You and me are always going to have Beulah Mountain in here,"

Juniper said, pointing at her chest. "We're not always going to have each other. So let me ask you again. What are you going to do when I'm gone?"

Hollis thought a minute and rubbed his hands, then scratched the back of his head and felt a little of the emotion creeping in, so he pushed it away. "I was thinking of saying something funny. Something that would make you laugh like I used to be able to. Remember?"

"I remember," she said, straight-faced. "What were you going to say?"

"Something like, when you're gone, I'll make a box out of that walnut tree and put you in it."

She smiled. "After Larry cuts it down."

"Yeah." He looked at the floor. "But that's not what I want to say now. I'm done making fun. Because it's not the truth, Juniper. And you want me to see the truth. So here it is. When you're gone, I don't know what I'm going to do. Not seeing that pretty face of yours. Your shapely behind."

She rolled her eyes and shook her head, but he could tell she liked to hear the words.

"I'll probably walk around like a zombie, just up and down the hallway. Look at our bed, stare at it, then go outside and walk up the hill and sit by the stones."

"You'll find something to do with yourself."

"You're the best thing that ever happened to me, Juniper. You know that, don't you?"

"I've been trying to get you to see that for forty years."

"I've acted like this plot of land is all I've ever cared about, but it's not true. You're worth a lot more to me than this mountain. More than a thousand acres. And I'd walk through hell itself to give you a day without the pain you carry. I wish we could trade places."

"I know you do," she said and her voice cracked. She looked at him with that weathered face, the rheumy eyes. There was an upside to seeing what you wanted to see because he was able to look past all of that to what was inside both of them.

"Hollis, I don't want you to do something just because it was my idea. Can you understand that? It would kill me to think you gave up because it was something I pushed you into or twisted your arm to do."

He nodded. "I know. It just takes a man like me a while to figure out what I really want. It takes me longer than some."

He put his hand on her shoulder. Then he put the orange juice in the refrigerator and picked up the dishes and set them in the sink and ran water over them until it became hot. "Now don't you do these. You've done enough. I'll do them when I get back."

"Where you headed?" she said.

"You know where I'm headed."

Cary Area Public Library
1606 Three Oaks Road
Cary, IL 60013

28

CHARLOTTE REVEALS TO FRANCES WHAT SHE HAS DISCOVERED
BEULAH MOUNTAIN, WEST VIRGINIA
FRIDAY, OCTOBER 1, 2004

From the moment Frances walked into the Company Store, she felt she had found a missing piece in the puzzle of her mother's life—the piece that was found in a heating vent years later, covered with cobwebs. There were old hardwood floors underfoot that shone with wax and creaked when you walked on them. Glass cases were filled with trinkets from bygone days and candy in original wrappers, miners' hats, picks, shovels, boxes of matches, and real pins with numbers on them.

On the wall by the door were framed pictures of men in suits and hats. She easily recognized the kindly face of her grandfather, but the other faces were unknown and gave her a chill she couldn't explain.

"Are these the men who died—?"

"And who do we have here, Charlotte?" an older woman said,

interrupting Frances. Her voice was welcoming but the look on her face wasn't. She came from behind the counter and approached as if they were stepping on a sacred burial ground.

"Marilyn, this is Frances Freeman. Her mother is Ruby."

"Is that right?" the woman said, her face suddenly beatific. "We've been hoping your mother would join us for the dedication. Charlotte said she's missing?"

"Yes," Frances said, shaking the woman's cold hand. "I was hoping I would find her here. My guess was she was heading this way, but so far we've heard nothing from her or the authorities."

"I'm so sorry you're going through this. I can't imagine how worried you must be. Our thoughts and prayers are with you." She said it and touched Frances's hand, but it felt as if she were checking off a to-do list. *Thoughts and prayers. Check.*

"I wanted to show Frances the store," Charlotte said. "I thought it would be of some comfort."

"Absolutely," the woman said, stepping away. "Make yourself at home. If you need anything at all, let us know. And we'd love to have you for the ceremony. Assuming everything works out well with your mother, of course."

"Of course."

Charlotte must have sensed that while Frances was interested in the memorabilia and other content in the store, this was not the time for a tour. When your heart is breaking, you can't watch a sitcom. Instead, Charlotte led Frances to the back, through a door, and up a narrow staircase. They came to another door and Charlotte opened it and ushered Frances inside, closing the door quickly.

Frances scanned the living area, which had also been decorated to reflect the decor of the 1930s. There was a fireplace and windows looking out on the mountain. A table and chairs, a couch and a reading chair with a footstool. There were books on shelves and above the fireplace were family pictures.

"Do you recognize any of this?" Charlotte said.

Frances moved toward the mantel. "I've seen old photos of my grandparents with my mother, but I've never seen this one."

"Look in here." Charlotte led Frances to a smaller room with a brass bed and dresser. "This was your grandfather's room. He designed this building and the living quarters above the store."

Frances walked to the dresser and leaned down to see the pictures scattered across it.

"After the massacre, the shop owner took the contents of the rooms and stored them. I assume they thought Ruby would come back one day and retrieve all of this. What you see has been locked away for decades."

"My mother never returned?" Frances said.

"Not that we know of."

Frances lingered by the photos until she sensed Charlotte at the door, waiting. "Let me show you your mother's room."

Ruby's room was small, with a twin-size brass bed and a window that led to the fire escape. A closet contained a few dresses from the period. A steamer trunk sat open at the foot of the bed and had folded clothes inside. A handmade quilt covered the bed and an oversize pillow with a lace pillowcase sat neatly at the head. Frances was drawn to more pictures on the narrow dresser.

"Those are the rest of the photos they found in storage," Charlotte said. "I don't know that they would have been in your mother's room, but we put them here."

"Someone's gone to great lengths to make this feel incredibly authentic," Frances said.

Charlotte nodded and bit her lip as if there was more she wanted to say.

"What?" Frances said.

Charlotte looked away. "Can you believe those steps we took, this room we're in . . . it's all where your mother lived when she was young? I grew up seeing exactly where my grandfather lived as a child. Most people never get that chance."

Frances nodded. "It does take your breath away when you put it like that. But why are you so interested in my mother?"

"As I said, I did research in school about the mine's history. My father was killed several years ago in an accident. That's how I got the scholarship."

"Was your family compensated for the loss? After the accident?"

"No, ma'am. He didn't have life insurance. And the company said the accident was my dad's fault. They offered us a settlement. My papaw was against it. He contended it was their fault. They've been known to cut corners. We tried to prove it but couldn't."

"You didn't bring a lawsuit?"

"No, ma'am. My mother took the settlement and paid off our house."

"But you took the scholarship."

"I did. I felt it honored my dad to get an education. Papaw didn't like it, but he finally gave in. And while I was there, I spent a lot of time in the library reading about the history of our area and the mines and what the people who lived here went through. They have this collection of old documents that were donated. It was fascinating."

Frances sat on the bed and looked at the slanted ceiling. Her mother had seen the same view seventy years earlier and she wondered what secrets she could reveal if only they could have one more conversation.

"Tell me what you found that made you want to talk to my mother."

"Come with me."

They took the stairwell up another floor. The staircase narrowed until they reached the third-floor landing. The ceiling was low here and gave a claustrophobic feeling. Frances entered the room where Charlotte waited, and when she set foot inside, something felt different.

She stopped just inside the door. "I don't like it in here."

Charlotte watched her expression closely. "Why not?"

"It feels . . . dark."

On the far wall were potted plants and flowers arranged on shelves. Near the window was an overstuffed cigar chair, a couch on the other side. Pictures mounted on the wall showed the same men she had seen as she entered the store.

"Is this where the massacre happened?"

"Yes, there's no question about that. There's a bit of a disagreement about this room, however."

Charlotte closed the door and walked to the window. "It was the day your mother left for boarding school. Right there is the old train station. She would have gotten on and left before her father was killed."

"What's the disagreement about this room?" Frances said.

"Marilyn, the one you met downstairs, and the rest of the historical society believe this was a meeting room for the mine owners. A place where your grandfather and his partner, Mr. Coleman, and the other men who were hired to oversee the operation met to do business. If you believe the historical society, it was to crunch numbers, decide which workers to fire, which mountain to mine next. That kind of thing."

"But you don't believe that?"

"They may have done business here, but I think the historical society has it wrong. I've heard a story from a woman who saw this room—Aidelle Mason was her name. I found her in a nursing home near Charleston. She called this the shoe room."

Frances looked around. "Why would she call it that? And why would it matter? That they sold shoes in a separate room isn't strange, is it?"

"They had shoes downstairs. And it wouldn't be controversial if there wasn't more to the story." Charlotte sat in the cigar chair. "Have you ever heard of Esau scrip?"

Frances shook her head.

"Scrip is what the miners were paid. They used it to buy at the company store—it was only good at the store. They were never paid with actual money. So they were at the mercy of the store's prices for food and clothing and the basic necessities. On top of that, they had to rent their equipment from the company, so at the end of the month, if they broke even, they were lucky.

"When a miner got hurt, which happened frequently, another member of the family sometimes took his place. But if the family had only small children, there was nothing they could do. So for thirty days, the injured miner's family was given Esau scrip. Esau was the man in the Bible—"

"I know who Esau and Jacob were and selling the birthright for a mess of pottage."

"Okay. Not everybody does. My papaw's the one who taught me about that. Anyway, the company would give scrip to the family to get them by for thirty days. And if the miner went back to work, the debt was forgiven."

"What if he couldn't go back?"

Charlotte leaned forward. "Aidelle said that if a miner went past the thirty days without working, there was a way the family could get Esau scrip. The mine owner would send someone for the wife or a teenage girl in the family. They would bring her to the store after hours. And they'd take her to the shoe room."

Frances's mouth dropped. She couldn't imagine what those women had gone through, if the story was correct.

"Aidelle said you always knew what those women went through when you saw them with new shoes."

"Why would they wear them?" Frances said. "Wouldn't the shoes be a reminder of what happened? I would think they would be ashamed."

"That might be how you and I would think. But these women

had nothing. Cold feet and hungry stomachs at home. They were trapped, in so many ways."

"My grandfather was part of that?" Frances said. She looked out the window at the old train tracks that ran through the town. The tracks that had carried her mother away from this mountain so many years earlier. "No wonder my mother never came back."

"I don't know that your grandfather was involved, but he built the store. He designed the rooms. I would think he knew what was going on."

"If it's true."

"Right."

"And he brought my mother into that world."

"You can see why the historical society wouldn't want to talk about such things. It wouldn't be good for the idyllic picture they're painting. And it would taint the image of the company. There are some who say there was never such a thing as Esau scrip. One history professor I had at school said it was a fantasy. He'd never come across anything about it in the research he'd done, and he'd written books about the mines. I think he was jealous that a student found something he'd never seen, but that's just me."

Frances stared at the mountainside and the winding roads through the town. Such a peaceful, serene setting. "If you have an eyewitness, why do you need to talk with my mother?"

"That's the thing. Aidelle is dead. And to be honest, she wasn't what people would call a reliable witness."

"What do you mean?"

"In her lucid moments, Aidelle was sharp. But her mind tended to wander. For instance, she didn't believe the moon landing was real."

"That's not uncommon for conspiracy buffs."

"No, she thought they hadn't landed on the moon because it was really Mars. And that they started a colony there. She also knew the person who killed Kennedy. She never gave me the name, but she said Jackie was in on it. Jackie had confessed to Aidelle."

"Oh, dear. But you believed her about the Esau scrip?"

Charlotte stared out the window. "Maybe I wanted to believe it. Maybe I wanted to expose some sinister plot by Coleman's lineage that would give me a measure of revenge for my dad. And what they're doing to my grandfather."

"What's happening to your grandfather?"

Charlotte pointed out the window. "That's Beulah Mountain. Our family has owned part of it for generations. But not for much longer."

"He's being forced out?"

"He and everybody else up and down the hollow. Coleman has offered a lot of money for the land so he can bring in machines and take the coal the easy way. You cut off the mountain and take what you want and leave. Everybody's selling. What choice do they have?"

"But your grandfather doesn't want to go?"

"I'm worried about him. I think maybe one day he's going to snap."

"And you want to save the mountain and tell the truth about all of this." Frances glanced at the empty wall.

"That's what I wanted to do. I thought your mother could help."

Frances stared at the pictures on the wall, then put her face in her hands. "How could people do such a thing?"

"You'd be surprised what people can do down here in the coalfields, ma'am. For good and bad."

"But the historical society isn't covering up the massacre, right?"

"No. They know it will draw people. There's just something not right here. In the sheriff's report I found information about how your grandfather was killed—"

Frances put up a hand. "I'm sorry. I don't think I can take this in right now."

"You're right. This is not the time."

"I'm interested. I'm just worried about my mother and this is not getting me any closer to her."

"We should be looking for her."

Frances shrugged. "I don't know where to look. I could drive up and down the road. But what if you're wrong? What if she was never coming here in the first place?"

Charlotte's phone buzzed. "It's my editor. I need to take this."

"By all means," Frances said. She looked out the window while Charlotte had a brief conversation.

"Is something wrong?" Frances asked when Charlotte hung up.

"I don't know. Corky said I needed to come to the office right away. I've never heard him like that."

Footsteps sounded in the stairwell and they both stared at the door until the knob turned. Marilyn stepped into the room. "I thought I might find you here. A few of us from the society are having an early lunch. We'd be honored if you would join us, Frances."

"I don't know that I'm in the frame of mind to do much of anything right now."

"It might help to get a bite to eat," Marilyn said. "To keep up your strength for when you find your mother."

"I have to get back to the office," Charlotte said.

Frances nodded and followed Marilyn downstairs.

29

Slowly, at the dinner table that night, Ruby told her father what Bean had shared about her mother and Mr. Coleman. As she spoke, her father's face grew grim. He listened to the words his daughter said, shaking his head and clenching his fists.

"This is why you're getting on that train tomorrow, away from all of this," her father said.

"I don't want to go. I want to stay with you."

Footsteps on the stairs and the voices of two men.

"I want you to stay here. Do you understand?" her father said.

Ruby nodded and folded her linen napkin beside her plate, the food barely touched. Her father walked out the door, pausing and turning toward her. He lifted a finger as if he was going to repeat himself, but he didn't speak. He closed the door and she heard his footsteps ascend.

Ruby had always been an obedient, compliant child, but her time with Bean had shown her there were certain things in life you simply couldn't miss. So she ran toward the dumbwaiter, climbed in, and was lifted to the top floor.

Around the edge of the door she could see Coleman and another man he called Saunders. The man had a flat, long face and tiny eyes. Ruby had been scared to even look at him the first time she saw him. She realized she and Bean had forgotten to close the drapes on the windows—there was still evening light coming through.

Her father was at the door, arguing that he needed to talk with Coleman, and finally the man waved Saunders off and told her father to come in.

Her father walked only a few paces inside, moving to the right so he could see both Coleman and Saunders.

Coleman tipped his head back and blew smoke from a freshly lit cigar. "And to what do we owe the pleasure of this visit, Jacob?"

Her father's voice was shaky when he finally spoke. "I want the goings-on up here to stop. I don't want you meeting in this room again."

Coleman glanced at Saunders. "And what goings-on are you talking about?"

"You know what I'm talking about. I've looked the other way far too long. It's over. I'm having the locks changed and I want you to tell your men there will be no further activity in this room."

Coleman crossed his legs. "Jacob, you know we just have a little fun up here. A man needs to blow off steam every now and then. That's not how you live your life, and that's fine. But don't tell us how to live. What's gotten a knot in your knickers? Did someone complain?"

"I will not have you treat defenseless people this way. We agreed early on this mine would be different. We'll pay the miners fairly and treat their families with respect."

"Respect? Is that what this is about?"

"Yes, respect! And not having their wives and daughters come up here to give favors to you and your men so that they can have enough to eat or shoes to wear."

"Jacob, what have you heard?"

"There's a woman pregnant because of you. And I won't be silent. You'll care for the child, you'll pay for your indiscretion—"

"Wait, wait, wait," Coleman said, standing. "What woman are you talking about?"

Her father drew closer to the man. "I'll go to the sheriff."

Coleman snickered. "I expect you won't tell him anything he doesn't already know from experience."

"I'll tell the town. I'll tell the miners themselves. Do you think they know what their women are forced to do here?"

Coleman glanced at Saunders, who was reaching inside his jacket for something. Coleman shook his head, then took a draw on his cigar. "Jacob, you take care of the business end of this mine. You take care of that little girl of yours. But you need to stay out of things that aren't your business."

"The miners and their families are my business. And I won't see them treated this way. This ends now. Right here."

"You don't like the way I do things. I understand that. Let's come to an understanding. Sell your half to me. I'll give you a fair price. Then you and your daughter can leave and begin again. Maybe find a nice miner's widow who needs a strong man like you."

"You should be ashamed. Both of you. And if there's anyone leaving this place, it'll be you, not me." Her father backed away from the two and opened the door and left.

Coleman looked hard at Saunders. "I won't have some tramp slinging my name through the mud. Who's pregnant in town?"

"Half the women in the camp are pregnant. You know that."

"What about those who have been up here?"

Ruby's heart beat wildly as she heard Saunders say, "That Dingess girl spends time with Handley's daughter. Her mother's pregnant, but I don't remember that she ever came up here."

Coleman walked to the window, just out of Ruby's sight. She heard the floorboards creak as the man swayed. "I want you to pay her a visit."

30

It felt like driving to the end of the world and pressing the accelerator when you neared the cliff. It felt like finding a high priest to collect thirty pieces of silver. It felt like the end.

Hollis rolled down the window and stuck his arm out. He reached for the radio, then thought better of it. He was partial to talk shows but those tended to raise his blood pressure with their political rancor. No music had ever been written that could calm the storm inside because he felt like he was giving up to a spineless, weaponless enemy with a lot of cash.

Is that offer still good?

He couldn't imagine getting the words past his lips. He could more easily imagine kneeling down at a tree stump and putting his neck flat so Coleman could raise an ax and let it fall.

I been talking it over with my wife and she thinks . . .

No, he couldn't do that. He couldn't pass it off as Juniper's idea. That would be cowardly. She would be okay with him blaming her, but he couldn't be that weak. This had to be his decision.

He thought of what Juniper had said about waiting for a crisis, and mulled over some of the big decisions he'd made to see if her words fit, and they did. He'd never bought a truck or any other vehicle except for when one had died by the side of the road. Any medical or dental problem had to be life-threatening for him to act. And when his favorite dog, Boone, had aged what seemed like years in a few months, Hollis wouldn't spend the money to take him to the vet. By the time the crisis came, the dog wasn't able to move. So Hollis carried him to the top of the mountain and gently laid him in a hole he had dug and put the dog's favorite quilt over him before he pulled the trigger. And he had wept, wondering if he could have made it a little easier for both of them if he'd acted sooner.

That was the thing about endings. He had never been through a good one in his life and he wasn't holding his breath for one now. He thought of his son and the bile rose. He hadn't cried at the funeral. Hadn't shed a tear in the time between then and now. Some things you don't explain, you just live through.

Though he had strayed from the church, Hollis had always believed in the sovereignty of God, even if he defined it differently than some. His version was the same as Eli, the priest, in the book of 1 Samuel. When the man heard news about the coming judgment on his family, Eli had basically said, "He's God. And God's going to do what God's going to do." Juniper called that the Hollis paraphrase. God had plans to take the bad and good and work them out however he liked. Hollis's take on Romans 8:28 said God works everything together for the good of those who follow him, but along with the good he'll leave you with a lot of questions and a whole lot of hurt and a fatherless granddaughter. That was Hollis's problem with God's sovereignty: he created a beautiful place like Beulah Mountain and then created a man like Buddy Coleman to level it.

He wound his way along the paved road that led to the CCE parking lot and stared at the building. Redbrick and tinted windows and two flags out front in the middle of a flower patch. Red, white, and blue and the state flag of West Virginia flying beside it. Why they needed two flagpoles, Hollis couldn't figure. And why not three? One for the US flag, one for the West Virginia coat of arms, and the third for the face of Buddy Coleman. And maybe that's what it would be someday. A silhouette of the man just like the POW/MIA flag.

Everything looked pristine and patriotic. Behind the building, on the side of the mountain with trees cleared, big enough to be seen from the road, stood a billboard with white letters on a black background: Proud to Be a West Virginia Coal Miner.

Hollis walked into the building and a security guard asked him to sign his name. The man was in his thirties and looked a little like Daniel. His name tag said Charles Moore.

"Who you here to see?"

"Coleman," Hollis said.

The man raised his eyebrows. "You got an appointment?"

"No. But I reckon he'll see me."

"He's a busy man, Mr. . . . ." He paused as he studied the signature on the page.

"Hollis Beasley. Tell him I'm here."

Hollis wandered to a waiting room that had coffee brewing and a big-screen TV. Some daytime talk show was on and the people on TV were yelling and hollering at each other. When the chair throwing started, he walked out the door.

"Tell him I'm outside," Hollis said to the guard on the way out.

A few minutes later the door opened and out walked the man himself in a WVU shirt and jeans and squeaky boots. When Hollis looked at him, he was just wiping the I-told-you-so smile off his face.

His hair was perfect and Hollis wondered who he'd hired to come to his office to cut it. Surely he didn't go to a salon.

Buddy stuck out a hand and smiled. "It's good to see you, Mr. Beasley. Why don't you come inside? Get some coffee. Unless you want something stronger. I can set you up with that, too." He gave a knowing wink.

"I like it out here with the flags. The TV shows make me nervous."

Buddy took a deep breath of mountain air. "All right, let's talk here."

Hollis thought of the lines he had rehearsed on the drive. None of them felt right. Finally he took a run at it and said, "I've been thinking more about your offer."

"Have you now?" Buddy said, eyebrows raised.

"I suppose you still got the papers."

Buddy winced. "Yeah, about that. You see, the statute of limitations ran out on my offer. In fact, that meeting you called actually helped get more people over here. So thank you, even though you weren't trying to help."

"You don't have to do this," Hollis said, lowering his voice. "Kick a man when he's down."

Buddy studied his fingernails, which looked pretty close-cropped, and Hollis wondered if a man with a salon haircut would also get a manicure. And if so, what was the world coming to?

Buddy crossed his arms and tilted his head toward the mountain. "I can see this was hard. I don't envy you. You're kicking yourself for waiting. So you're right, you don't need me kicking you, too. What pushed you over the edge?"

"Reality, I guess. The writing on the wall."

"Never made sense to me why you would hang on like that."

"You're from another generation. People here before us had nothing but the land. No investments. No 401(k). But if you had land, you had a chance. You could farm it. Hunt on it. The land was life. And part of me wonders if we're heading back to those times again."

"I think those days are gone," Buddy said.

"Maybe so. But once you get that in your blood, it's hard to get out."

Buddy nodded and spit on the parking lot asphalt. "I understand. It makes sense. So I can't offer the same terms, but I'll be fair."

"Fair?" Hollis said. "There's nothing fair about any of this."

"*Generous* is probably the better word." He took a radio from his belt and clicked it. "Stephanie, I need you to find the Beasley contract."

"You mean the acreage on Beulah Mountain?" a female voice responded.

"That's the one."

Hollis looked at the mountain behind him, unable to see much of the beauty for the turmoil inside his soul.

"Bring it to Charlie at the door and he'll run it outside."

"Ten-four."

They stood together with nothing but the whistling wind between them and the sound of trucks on the state route in the distance.

"You're doing a good thing for your family, Hollis. I know how hard it is to let go."

Hollis wanted to push back and fight. Instead, he focused on what was most important. "What happens to my people?"

"You mean the cemetery?"

Hollis nodded.

"We could move them. We'd even pay to have a new—"

"You're not moving them."

Buddy nodded. "All right. Well, it's not like we haven't done this before. We've got a man who can engineer it so we save the graves and the copse of trees. And there'll be a road that winds around and takes you there. It'll be peaceful. Pretty. You'll see."

"I've seen what you've done to the other mountains around here. And I wouldn't call it pretty."

"Beauty's in the eye of the beholder, isn't it, Hollis? The point is, we'll preserve things and keep them intact. We'll do the work and then put everything back like it was. Just like we're doing with the Company Store. Have you seen the inside yet?"

"You asked me that before."

The security guard walked toward them with a limp and Hollis wondered if the man had been a miner hurt on the job. Or maybe Buddy had put him here as payback to some landowner. What Hollis wouldn't give if his son had lived and taken a job like this where he could visit him instead of speaking to a stone and never getting a response. If they had moved from the mountain, Daniel wouldn't have lost his life. That made Hollis think about God again and he didn't want to. In fact, no time seemed convenient to be thinking that way.

Buddy took the papers and looked them over, then handed them to Hollis as the guard limped back to the building. "Everything should be up-to-date with what we're offering. I can go over the basics."

"I can read."

Hollis flipped the pages of *wherefores* and *henceforths* and *party of the first and second part*. It seemed like Hebrew or Greek. He studied the different clauses and came upon a monetary figure. He held the contract up, pointing to that spot. "Is that the offer?"

Buddy nodded.

It was considerably less than what he'd been offered before. He would have fought, but the amount wasn't the thing stuck in his craw. There was something else and he couldn't put a finger on it.

"How long would we have to get off the mountain?" Hollis said, the words coming out of his mouth before he had a chance to consider them.

"We'll work with you. We want to make it as easy as we can. If you want, we could write into the contract some moving help. I haven't done that for anybody else, but for you, I'd be happy to."

Moving mountains. There was a Bible passage about that. Something Jesus had said. He'd heard about mustard seeds and mountains all his life. And here he was standing beside a shrimp who moved mountains and dug the goody out from inside them and covered it over, acting like he'd done the world a favor.

"It's helpful for me to do this in stages," Hollis said. "Coming here was a big step."

"I'm sure it was. A hard one."

"Let me take this home. Maybe ask advice from Homer Sowards."

"He's been handling things for several owners. He's a good man."

That made Hollis wonder if he should go to Homer. If Buddy thought he was a good man, perhaps he wasn't. He flipped to the last page, where the signature line was empty, and he wondered what Juniper would do if he brought the contract home unsigned. What kind of crisis would it take to get him to sign?

"Is the figure holding you back?" Buddy said. "You didn't drive all the way here to take some papers to a lawyer. I can tell you want to sign."

"I had made up my mind to do exactly that," Hollis said.

"Then why don't we see if we can't agree? Everybody can win."

"There's only one person who wins from this deal and you know it."

Buddy sidled closer to Hollis and lowered his voice. "Let's go to my office. I can bump that number up. I don't want you to go away from here dissatisfied. I want you to get everything that's coming to you."

Hollis weighed the man's words and recalled a similar conversation he'd had with a used-car salesman who kept going back to his boss every time Hollis threw out a number. It was negotiation. And Hollis didn't like it.

"We don't need to go to your office for you to bump the number."

"True. I have the power to offer a fair and equitable price. Let me have that."

Hollis handed him the paper and Coleman crossed out the number and wrote a new one above it and initialed it. "Does that look better?"

Hollis looked at it and thought that it didn't matter if the number had fifty zeros behind it. It wouldn't be enough. And what he had said to the people in the meeting came back to him. *Is there anything in this life that would make you draw a line in the sand and say, 'You can come this far but you can't come no farther'?"*

"What's your cutoff?" Hollis said. "When do you need my answer?"

"I think I've moved toward you enough that you can answer right now, don't you think?"

Buddy was the kind of man who would sit in a deer stand and wait all day. He had learned the art of patience. But Hollis could tell there was a certain fear and expectation in his answer, so he just stared at him.

"But if you need more time, maybe get a second opinion on the technical parts of the sale, I understand. Let's say tomorrow by noon. I'll be over at the retreat center—you know where that is?"

"Everybody knows where that is."

"All right. I want this signed and in my hand by then. Is that agreeable?"

"I expect it'll have to be," Hollis said.

He turned and got in his truck and drove away. In the rearview mirror he saw the security guard holding the door for Buddy.

31

Frances followed Marilyn to a room off the first floor where an elegant table had been set with china, silverware, and glass. Marilyn explained this had been cold storage for foodstuffs in the mining days, but the historical society had taken the liberty of turning it into a dining area for special events. It was the only major modification they had made to the original design.

It was clear that Marilyn believed the Company Store would be the key to revitalizing the town that had lost many residents and seemed in danger of losing more with the increase of the mountain-top removal. The Company Store was the first of many improvements. When the mining was complete in the area, CCE would fill in the land with parks and open areas where people could view the wonders of God's creation, albeit wonders that had been drastically changed. More "shovel-ready" jobs were on the way and people would be attracted to the area, roads improved, schools built. Frances wasn't sure how that would happen or if the vision would become a nightmare.

One by one, the six other women on the committee entered the room and greeted Frances with polite handshakes and smiles. Most were older women, though two were about Frances's age, and all seemed to follow Marilyn in lockstep. They all wore dresses and an ample amount of jewelry and heels that clicked on the hardwood. The historical society seemed like it had lots of money, and she wondered where it came from. She also wondered how the local towns-people who were barely scraping by would react to all the changes.

"Marilyn has told us about your mother," the oldest member of the group said. She had white hair and spoke with a genteel Southern accent, not the hard Appalachian drawl of the town. She reminded Frances of what Robert E. Lee must have sounded like. "You must be terribly concerned about her."

"I am," Frances said. "I came here hoping to find her. The police are still looking and I'm waiting for a call."

"Perhaps a glimpse of her past will give you some comfort. We are praying for her to be found. Keep hoping. Don't despair. I have a good feeling about your mother." She grabbed Frances's hand and squeezed it tightly.

The other women nodded in agreement as Marilyn cleared her throat and got everyone's attention. "It's hard to believe the day is almost here. I want to personally thank you all for your hard work and dedication. Frances, what you've seen here could not have been done without a lot of sacrifice and financial backing from the women in this room. And for that I will always be grateful."

Frances wanted to excuse herself and retrieve Charlotte from the newspaper office. She wanted to call Jerry for an update. Maybe Julia had heard something. Her thoughts flitted from one person to the next and finally landed on lunch, which was served by a catering company miles from Beulah Mountain (this was something that would change, Marilyn explained—the town would bring back the bakery and several restaurants). She picked at her salad, glancing at her phone every few minutes to make sure she wasn't missing a call.

"Marilyn, the photos in the entryway," a woman said, her brow furrowed. "I like the placement, but I wonder how we're handling the interest in the darker side of the anniversary."

"Let's face it," one of the younger women said. "It's the massacre that's getting most of the press right now. As much as we might not want to play up the grisly nature of the date, it's part of the draw."

"Oh, I don't think people are coming because of that," Mrs. Robert E. Lee said. "They're coming because they want to experience a simpler time. They want to see how life was when things weren't so complicated. It's like visiting Colonial Williamsburg. No one comes because people died there long ago. They come because people lived there and flourished by determination and the sweat of their brow. They come because it gives them a vision for their own lives."

Marilyn smiled. "You're both right. People are coming for a variety of reasons. And while we will observe the rather bleak anniversary and use it to publicize the opening, we won't let that overshadow the reality of what we're celebrating."

Frances put down her fork. "And what is that, if I may ask?"

"We are lifting up the human spirit. The ability not just to survive the hard times, but to overcome. And along with that, the great impact that Coleman Coal and Energy has had on this area. The positives of the mining culture. The way hardscrabble men and women came to these hills and worked hard and got ahead. It is the American spirit we need again. The can-do attitude that said, 'No matter what happens, no matter how difficult it gets, we're going to succeed.' That's what we're honoring and celebrating."

Frances took another bite of salad so she wouldn't have to respond.

After what she'd heard from Charlotte about the shoe room, it didn't seem like they could make a Hallmark movie out of the Company Store narrative, but either they didn't know about the stories or they were avoiding the discussion.

Her phone buzzed and she jumped up and ran out of the room. She hoped to hear her mother's voice but instead it was Wallace.

"I wanted to check in and see if you've heard anything," he said. "Did you make it down there okay?"

"Yes, I'm here. No word. I haven't heard from Jerry or the police."

"Julia called and said she's worried about Ruby. About you."

"I'm a big girl, Wallace. I can take care of myself." She tried to say it without venom, but her tone was off. She wasn't prepared to hear his voice, to hear genuine caring coming through the line.

"Yeah, I know that. I've always known that, Frances." He paused a moment and his voice lowered. "And I'm sorry about us. I keep saying that, but it's true."

Frances stared at a stack of flour sacks on the floor and the old cash register on the counter in the front. A Company Store employee was filling a glass container with hard candy. Behind her, Frances noticed what looked like a small, square door in the wall. Hadn't she seen something like that upstairs too?

"I'm trying to put the past behind me, Wallace. To move on with life. You don't have to make up for what you did. Just know you're forgiven and move on."

"Thank you for that."

"I need to go. And I think I need some space. I'll call Julia. If she calls you again, tell her to talk with me. I don't want you in the middle."

"I understand," he said.

"Good-bye, Wallace."

She ended the call and closed her eyes. After a moment, she walked to the young woman putting horehound candy in the glass container. "Do you know what that is in the wall behind the counter?"

The woman turned and looked, then frowned. "I don't know, ma'am. I haven't worked here that long. It looks kind of like a window that's been covered up. But you could ask Mrs. Grigsby-Mollie. She knows everything."

Frances thanked her and slipped back inside the room. All eyes focused on her, and Mrs. Robert E. Lee was the first to speak.

"Was that about your mother? We're hoping it was."

"No, it was someone concerned about her," Frances said. "But I think I need to be going."

"You don't want to stay for dessert?"

Frances collected her purse and shook her head.

"Let me show you out," Marilyn said and she followed Frances out as the caterer brought a tray of desserts into the room.

"Before I go, can you tell me what that is behind the counter?" Frances said, pointing at the square in the wall.

"That's the dumbwaiter. It was part of your grandfather's design of the building to have that for his apartment. Food and beverages could be lifted up to them by the motorized pulley. He was quite ingenious with the design."

"Does it go to the third floor, too?"

"Yes, I believe it does."

"What was that room used for?"

"It was a meeting place for the mine owners and their colleagues. They conducted business there, met with employees, and had a drink or two."

"And there were never shoes sold up there?"

A frown and a shake of the head. "I don't know where you're getting that information, but it's been debunked time and again by historians and those who lived here. There were never any shoes for sale in that room. I can guarantee you that."

Frances's phone buzzed as she exited the building. It was Jerry and his voice sounded grim. "Her credit card was used yesterday."

"Was it in Beulah Mountain?"

"No, same state, though. Different address."

"Where?"

"A gas station in Chapmanville, then at a Walmart outside of Charleston. Then, last night, at a hotel farther down the interstate."

Frances felt her heart race. "I'm in the wrong place. I missed her."

"Now hold on," Jerry said. "I've called the sheriff and they're getting in touch with the authorities near there."

"I need to go up there."

"Frances, don't freak out. Stay put until we know more, okay? We don't know if she's up there or if it's somebody else using her card."

"If someone else is using it, what have they done with her?"

Frances stared at the mountain and tried to still her thoughts. She had to *do* something. That was why she had come here—being in motion made her at least feel like she was moving toward her mother, whether she was or not.

"Frances, stay where you are," Jerry said. "We're going to find her."

A deep breath. "Okay, I'll stay here, but call me as soon as you hear anything. And I mean anything."

"I'll do it."

32

CHARLOTTE SEES THE PICTURES
BEULAH MOUNTAIN, WEST VIRGINIA
FRIDAY, OCTOBER 1, 2004

Charlotte entered Corky's office and noticed things were quieter than usual, especially with a Saturday edition to be printed for the grand opening festivities. She called for him and he exited the darkroom. At first she thought he might need a doctor because his face was a pasty white.

"What's wrong?" she said.

"That camera you gave me," Corky said. He jerked his head toward the door. "Come in here."

She followed him into the darkroom and was met with the pungent smells of developer and fixing fluid. Corky had pictures clipped to strings over the workbench.

"One thing I've learned about old cameras," he said. "They're like guns. Always assume they're loaded. I never open one when I don't know what's inside. So I was working on the paper and I kept looking at that old thing and it bugged me so much I brought it in here and opened her up."

"And?"

"I found undeveloped film."

"Really?"

"Now, just because it's there doesn't mean you can develop it. Seventy-year-old film can crack or turn to dust. I can't explain it, but somehow the conditions were right. It went through the process and came out the other side."

"You were able to develop it?" Charlotte said.

Corky nodded. "Made prints, too. The first ones on the roll were unusable. Just spotty blotches. Four of them came out pretty well. Amazing, actually, for their age. Take a look."

Charlotte tried to breathe as she approached the prints drying on the line like wet clothing. Each picture was like taking a look in a time capsule—images caught in time and held for decades. She moved down the line, studying the faces, the buildings, the mountain. The last two pictures stopped her in her tracks.

33

HOLLIS TAKES THE LONG WAY HOME
BEULAH MOUNTAIN, WEST VIRGINIA
FRIDAY, OCTOBER 1, 2004

Hollis took the long way through the winding, rolling hills he loved. Many of the spots along the road were just like he remembered as a child, hunting with his father or taking a Sunday drive. The roads were now paved—that had changed. And at different points along the way, white scars and leveled hillsides were visible. All the seeding and planting in the world could not return the beauty only God could accomplish.

At Christmas as a boy, Hollis would grab his hatchet and his father would get his ax and the two would set out looking for an evergreen. Sometimes they walked for hours searching for the right tree. His father would usually convince Hollis that the first one they saw closest to the house was the best. Cutting a tree a mile or two away meant they'd have to drag it back, so his father had steered him toward sensibility.

Hollis's father was a man of the mines and his mother was salt of the earth, and though they were not related to him by blood, a truth they revealed when he was a teenager, he felt them in his veins as he drove. He wondered if, when he and Juniper moved, he would forget this beauty. When all their earthly belongings were packed and moved into some house with new appliances and a doorjamb that didn't admit wind, would he remember the ridges and hollows he had walked as a child?

Hollis glanced at the contract on the seat beside him and felt sick. When he looked back at the road and gripped the steering wheel, something happened that surprised him. He began to pray.

"Lord, you know it's been a long time. Part of me doesn't want to speak these words. But I'm in a tight place. I feel trapped. And the only way out is a road I don't want to take. I need your help. I haven't bothered you about Juniper. I haven't knocked on your door since you took Daniel. But here I am. And I need you to answer.

"I promised my folks I would do right. I'd hang on to their part of Beulah Mountain. As I recall, you're persnickety about people keeping their word. But I also promised Juniper I would love, honor, and cherish her, and she don't want to stay. So I'm stuck between two promises and it's like to kill me.

"I want to love my wife. I want to show her I'd do anything, leave anything for her. She's the best thing you ever gave me. I got this feeling that maybe there's another way . . . but I can't see it. And I don't have the strength to look anymore.

"So I'm going to ask you once. Speak to me. Tell me what to do. I'm out of time."

He drove along, the incline making it harder to keep his speed and the engine bogging down. Hollis thought he might hear a voice through the whining manifold or maybe the trees would spell something out like, *Sign it.* He'd read that God could speak from a donkey's mouth. He could do the same with the clouds.

As he drove, the silence overwhelmed him and he kicked himself for giving God another chance. He was alone. That's all there was to it.

Up ahead, he saw a mother deer crossing the road followed by two little ones. He slowed and then came to a full stop and watched, one fawn lagging behind at the double yellow. This was what he'd be giving up by moving away—the mix of nature and mankind so tangible he could taste it.

It was in this moment that he heard an oncoming car beyond the bend ahead and something clicked in his heart. He put the truck in park and jumped out and waved.

"Get on out of here!" he yelled at the fawn.

He thought it would scare the thing so it would run toward its mother over the edge of the road and into the gully. He also thought the crazy person driving toward him would slow down. What happened was this: when he got out, the fawn stayed, cocking its head and looking at him, even though he yelled. The sound of tires on pavement grew louder. And then it was as if some angel came down and nudged the fawn on the backside with its flaming sword. The deer moved, but in the wrong direction, back toward the other side. The car rounded the final blind corner lickety-split, and Hollis put up his hands in the universal symbol of submission and surrender.

Brakes squealed. The fawn jumped at the sound and ran right in front of the car, and Hollis closed his eyes and prepared for the thump.

But there was no thump. The little thing darted over the edge of the road toward its mother. Hollis bent and put his hands on his knees and tried to slow his heart.

The driver inched forward into the curve and lowered his window.

"You're gonna be roadkill if you don't watch out, old-timer," he mumbled.

Hollis wanted to reach out and grab him by the throat or say something snippy. He'd think of a good comeback in an hour or two. Before he could speak, the man rolled up the window and zoomed ahead.

"Slow down!" was all he could think to say.

This was the way of nature and humanity. The fawn could have been overcome by coyote, bobcat, or Toyota Tundra, but on this day it wasn't, and that made Hollis smile. He couldn't save his father's mountain, couldn't change his son's accident or control Juniper's illness, but he could save a deer. Maybe that was enough.

He walked to the edge of the pavement and scanned the woods. Birds sang and a squirrel leapt from the limb of one dead hickory to another. There was a dip by the curve and covered tire tracks, the telltale signs of an old logging road, where the mother deer had led her young. They would be all right.

Behind him a car approached and he remembered his truck was in the middle of the road. He scampered back and pulled it to the side, sitting there for a minute with his window down. Why, he couldn't tell you. Life felt better in motion, moving in some direction. But fully living sometimes meant you just sat with the window down and listened to creation's hum.

At first, the distant noise sounded like the cry of a wounded animal. He thought it might be a coyote howling. Then he realized it was a car horn that was out of place. Like it was being held underwater.

Hollis got out and looked into the woods but there was nothing. He got back in and closed the door and put his key in the ignition but waited. There it was again. It started and stopped, quickly this time. Then a pause and the horn gave a long blast that echoed through the valley. Quickly he got out and walked back down the road. It seemed to be coming from the trail the deer had taken. Gingerly he took a step off the pavement. One wrong move could turn his knee and send him tumbling. His right one had given him problems for years.

He kept walking on the berm of the road, around the bend, until he saw a silver glint in the woods. He found a sapling to hold on to and eased down the hill, one step at a time, backhanding branches from his face. Coming to a muddy place where the hills formed a V, he saw the back end of a white Town Car. Teenagers parked in out-of-the-way places up and down the road and did what teenagers did in cars, but there was something about this one that made Hollis think he was dealing with something altogether different.

The car must have plunged off the road and into the grove of dogwoods. But for the life of him he couldn't figure out how it got that far. The ground was wet and mushy and the tires had left deep impressions in the earth. No, it hadn't plunged. Someone had driven it here and wasn't concerned about getting it out. They had left it to rot, but the car was in surprisingly good shape, not old and rusted.

Hollis lifted the branches of the tree from the windshield and cupped his hands over the glass. What he saw made his heart beat faster than the fawn in the road had. The front seat was empty, but in the back was a wrinkled old woman with her head back and her eyes closed and her mouth open. A cane lay tangled in the steering wheel, the handle reaching over the headrest of the driver's seat. Hollis was as sure as he could be that he was looking at a dead woman.

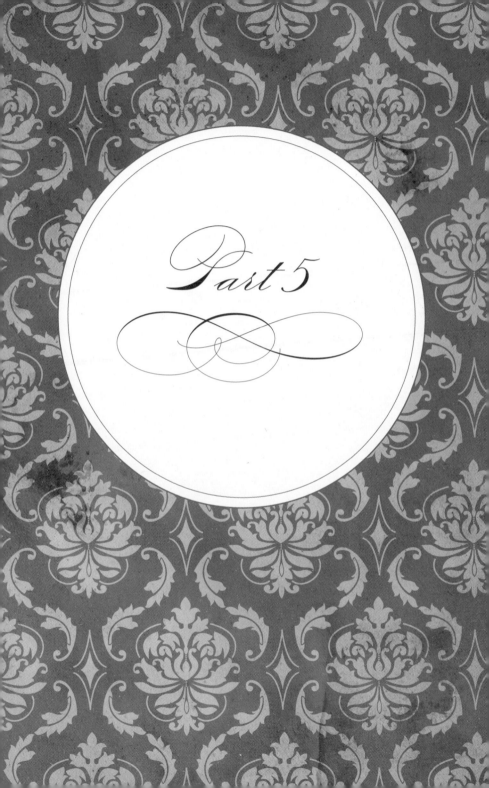

Part 5

34

RUBY GETS A LATE-NIGHT VISITOR
BEULAH MOUNTAIN, WEST VIRGINIA
OCTOBER 1, 1933

Ruby took the dumbwaiter to the first floor and hurried upstairs just as her father rushed out of their apartment. When he saw her, he hugged her tightly. He was not a man of great affection. He pulled her inside the apartment and looked into her eyes.

"I told you to stay here. Why did you disobey?"

"I thought it would be all right to go downstairs. I'm sorry."

He hugged her again and Ruby thought she felt her father trembling. Was it from the confrontation with Coleman?

She wanted to tell him what she had heard. She wanted to ask what Coleman had meant when he said to "pay her a visit." But she couldn't. It would hurt him too much to know what she had done. So she told her father she was tired and needed to sleep.

"Things are going to get better, Ruby," her father said as she stood in the door. "When you're at school, you won't have to worry about what's going on here."

"I'll worry about you," she said.

He smiled sadly. "You don't have to worry about me."

Ruby checked her small suitcase for the thousandth time and crawled into bed, but she couldn't sleep. She listened to the sounds of the night encroaching through the window, open slightly to let in the cool mountain air. That was something she would miss. She tried to imagine her room at school, a picture of her father and mother by her bed next to a picture of Bean. What would happen to her friend? If only Bean could come with her. If only Ruby could figure out a way to help.

And then she realized there was something she could do. Something tangible and real.

God, you know how much I care about Bean. And I know you do, too. You know how hard her life is. And how hard it is for her mother. I don't even know what to pray. If her dad were to change and stop his drinking, maybe that would help. Do you have enough power to make him a good dad and to work out life for her so that she finds good things? I know it says in the Bible that you raised people from the dead. Could you do that with Bean's daddy? Don't let Bean get hard in her heart because of all that's happened. Take care of her mother. Take care of the little baby.

Her thoughts drifted then, but as Ruby fell asleep, she continued to pray for her friend and to beg God to do something good for her.

She awoke with a start and a feeling something was wrong. The night was pitch-black and her room was the same. She had drifted off praying. Had God awakened her for some reason? Did he want her to pray for something else?

"Psst," someone said outside her window. Then a peck on the glass.

Ruby sat up and peered outside, trying to see. She opened the window a few inches more.

"Open up. I need to come in," Bean whispered.

"What are you doing out there?" Ruby said, pushing the window up all the way.

"I didn't know where else to go." Bean climbed inside and onto Ruby's bed, wiping the dirt she had brought with her off the blanket.

"You're shaking," Ruby said. "Come on, get under the covers."

"Ain't no amount of covers going to take away what's making me shake," Bean said.

Ruby put an arm around her friend. "What's wrong? What happened?"

"It was awful, Ruby. I got nowhere to go now. Nowhere in the world."

"Calm down. Tell me what happened. You left to go home—start there."

"I ran to see about Mama. Tilly Mae had been there and checked on her. Mama was fine. We was talking about what we'd name a girl or a boy, laughing at all the funny names you can put with 'Dingess,' and then Mama got quiet because there was somebody coming. I looked out and saw that flat-head who hangs around Coleman."

"Saunders?"

"Yeah. Mama got jumpy. I thought it was because we were being evicted. I told her they wouldn't throw us out right when she was going to have a baby, but she wouldn't listen. She told me to go find my daddy back on the ridge. I told her no, it'd be all right, but she hissed at me and told me to run for him. So I did. I never run so fast in all my life because the sun was almost down and I don't like being in the woods when it's dark."

"Did you find him?"

"I found the place he goes. Just about got shot doing it too. Those people think everybody who comes up there's a customer or a reve-nuer and I wasn't neither. They said they hadn't seen him, but I knew they had. I told them we were in a fix and that he needed to get home. Then I lit out of there. And as soon as I walked in the house, I could tell something was wrong. There was a kerosene lamp burning and I saw busted chairs in pieces on the floor. And there was a strange smell in the house."

Ruby leaned forward. "What kind of smell?"

"Like copper. The taste of a penny. I called for Mama. And I walked into her bedroom but I couldn't see, so I got the lamp . . ."

Bean stopped and put her face in her hands. She wiped her nose with her sleeve and Ruby couldn't look away.

"What happened?" Ruby said.

"She was covered with a blanket. Up over her face. I pulled it off, and there was so much blood. I shook her and tried to talk to her but she wasn't breathing. She was bruised on her face . . . and there was blood on the floor underneath the bed."

Ruby hugged her friend. It was the only thing she could think to do. "I'm so sorry, Bean."

Bean put her head on Ruby's shoulder and it muffled her sobs. She finally lifted her head enough to whisper in Ruby's ear. "Before I left, when Mama told me to go get my daddy, she called out to me. I was at the back door looking at her. She just said, 'I love you, Bean.' That was the last thing my mama ever said to me."

"We need to go to the sheriff," Ruby said.

"That ain't gonna do no good," Bean said. "Mama's dead. I don't know if Saunders killed her or if she died trying to have the baby. But the sheriff ain't gonna do nothing. There's nobody that will do anything for people like us. We got to make our own way. We got to get our own revenge."

"Stop talking like that," Ruby said.

"It's true. There ain't no way around it."

"Take your shoes off and lie down," Ruby said. "You can sleep here and we'll figure out what to do in the morning."

35

RUBY SITS IN A GULLY IN THE BACKSEAT OF HER TOWN CAR
BEULAH MOUNTAIN, WEST VIRGINIA
FRIDAY, OCTOBER 1, 2004

Somebody's trying to get in.

Ruby felt immediate danger and knew she had to tell someone. Her mother. Her father. She wasn't sure where she was, what day it was, what year it was. All she could sense was the fear of someone trying to get in, trying to hurt her. Banging on the window.

She closed her mouth and it felt like someone had stuffed a ball of cotton inside and her tongue was as big as a rutabaga. She was one of the few people on the planet who knew the difference between a turnip and a rutabaga. Funny how the mind turned at times of terror.

"Help!" Ruby said out loud. "He's trying to get in. He's going to hurt us."

She yelled into the void and tried opening her eyes but there was something wrong. Or maybe she had them open and couldn't see.

She moved a hand to touch her forehead but couldn't find it, finally touching the bridge of her nose. She heard someone yelling something a long way off.

Finally she got her hands to her eyes and rubbed. It was stuffy and the air smelled stale and she was the reason. She blinked and saw the cloth upholstery of her own car. She was in the backseat on an old quilt. And there was her cane. That's right. She had tried to honk the horn, but the pain in her wrist had knocked her out. But who was trying to get in?

She glanced out the window and saw a face, and she opened her mouth to scream. It was a man. He jiggled the handle. Ruby thought the face looked familiar in some way, but she couldn't place it.

"Ma'am, are you all right? Can you unlock the door?"

His voice was muffled by the closed window but she could still hear him. She moved but became disoriented and the car started to spin. When she reached for the handle, a pain shot through her arm and she yelped. Finally she got it unlocked and he pulled it open. She swung her legs toward him but only one of them obeyed and the sudden movement made her sick to her stomach.

"Better stand back. I'm gonna heave," she said, and heave she did. The man grabbed her arm and another pain shot through it all the way to the shoulder. She managed to plant both feet on the earth to steady herself, then gathered her wounded arm to her chest.

"I thought you were dead," the man said. "What are you doing way out here?"

When she caught her breath and the spinning slowed, Ruby said, "Tell you the truth, mister, I don't know. There were two people at a gas station. They got me a gas cap because . . . It turned out to be a scam. They took me to their trailer and I drank something that put me to sleep, I guess. They must have driven me here and left me to die."

The man knelt on one knee and his cartilage cracked. "What happened to your arm?"

"I don't . . . No, wait. One of them grabbed me and pulled. I heard it snap."

"We need to get you to a hospital."

"No, I don't want a hospital. People go there with a head cold and wind up dead. This will heal on its own."

"We'll have to disagree about that," he said.

"Can you help me get my car out of here so I can get on the road?"

"You're not serious."

She stared at him. "I was born serious."

"Ma'am, there's no way this car is moving an inch without a tow truck. Where are you headed?"

"I was headed to a place called Beulah Mountain. But I'd better get home. I'm from—"

"That's where I live, Beulah Mountain," he said, and he cocked his head slightly as if he had figured something out. "If I can get you to my truck, we can get you help. Can you stand? We'll take it a step at a time."

"That's the first good idea I've heard," Ruby said.

She struggled to stand and the man stayed away from her injured arm, but she finally sat back. "I need a couple minutes to catch my breath."

"That's all right. Take your time."

Ruby turned and looked at the road perched high above them. "How did you find me?"

"You wouldn't believe me if I told you."

"Try me."

"A deer and two of its little ones were crossing the road. I thought one was going to get hit, so I stopped. They scampered down here and I heard the horn."

"The horn?" Ruby said. That's right—she had tried the horn with her cane.

"My name is Hollis."

"Ruby," she said, and she grabbed his hand with her left and shook in an unorthodox manner. The man nodded like he was expecting her to say that.

"Why were you traveling alone way out here?"

"I lived in Beulah Mountain when I was a girl. Heard they were having a big to-do with the Company Store. I decided to drive down."

"It appears that wasn't your best idea."

"You think?" She laughed and shook her head. "You sound like my kids. They're going to kill me."

"They'll be glad to hear you're okay, I'll bet. Probably worried sick. My granddaughter said something about you going missing. There's a bunch of people worried."

Ruby turned. "I lost my purse. It had a phone in it."

"Well, I wish I could tell you I had one, but I don't. I've avoided the technology. I can get you to a phone."

"I need to stay here a minute."

"All right."

Ruby reached up to grab the handle above the door and tried to breathe. She guessed it was the effects of whatever she was given to drink and the fact that her stomach was empty. Probably low blood sugar. "You got anything to eat in that truck of yours? I'm getting the shakes."

"Stay right here."

He trudged up the bank, and she watched him grab saplings to propel himself. How was she ever going to follow him up that hill? A few minutes later he returned with peanut-butter crackers wrapped in plastic. She took them, then handed them back and he opened the package for her and she stuffed two of them in her mouth and chewed.

"I doubt you'd get reception here even if you did have a phone," he said.

"I need something to drink," she said. "I'm dry as a bone. You don't have any water, do you?"

Hollis winced. "All I've got is half a Mountain Dew."

"Sold," she said. "And if I'm going up there with you, you might as well take my suitcase this trip."

He grabbed the suitcase and climbed to the top. It took him a little longer to return. He appeared to Ruby to be in his late sixties or maybe into his seventies but still had a spring in his step. When he handed her the Mountain Dew, it reminded her of the root beer floats at the company store.

"All right, how do we get out of here?" Ruby said when she was finished.

"I don't know that you can make it up the hill with that bad arm."

"I don't walk with my arms. I use my legs. Just give me a little push and let's see what happens." She stood and gained her balance. "I think the Mountain Dew helped stop the world from spinning."

Hollis got on her left side and she hung on to him as he navigated the soft earth and up to the blacktop.

"This is awful nice of you."

"You'd do the same for me, I bet."

She nearly toppled once but he grabbed her and held on until they stepped onto the pavement. It felt like standing on top of Everest when she made it to the truck and looked back at how far they'd come. Her car was hidden from view. Surely God had opened the eyes of this man to come to her rescue.

She got in the truck and Hollis helped her buckle. He took something from the bed of his truck and put it by a tree. She guessed it was to help somebody find the car.

Ruby put her head back and felt another stirring in her stomach. When Hollis returned, she asked him to put her window down in case she needed to heave. He eased out onto the road and drove slowly and that let her know he was a kind man. Then she realized she was trusting a stranger again.

"You a lawyer?" she said.

He chuckled. "What makes you ask that?"

"That stack of papers on the seat."

"I'm taking that to a lawyer. I'm selling a piece of property. Kills me to do it, but it's got to be done."

"Why are you selling if it kills you to do it?"

"Long story. And you're kind of tied up with it."

"What do you mean?"

"It don't matter. It's none of your concern."

"Well, I asked the question, so I guess it is my concern. Now whether you answer is your business."

He kept driving, the road bending around the mountain. Ruby was glad she wasn't driving because this kind of road gave her the willies. She couldn't believe she thought she could navigate these roads by herself. Then she remembered Frances and Jerry taking her keys and the anger returned.

"I want you to take a look at something," Hollis said.

"And then you'll answer my question?"

"What you'll see is the answer to your question."

The road went straight up and leveled out and he pulled the truck to the side where Ruby could see the vista of mountains and valleys for miles. She felt like they were too close to the edge of the cliff, but Hollis assured her they were all right.

"You see that right over there? That's Beulah Mountain."

Ruby smiled. "It is, isn't it? Would you look at that."

"Now take a look that way and tell me what you see."

Ruby craned her neck. What she saw was like looking at craters on the moon. The trees and vegetation gave way to a dusty, rocky surface that flattened the hills. Even from this distance she could see the machinery lifting tons of dirt. It was like watching teenagers attack a layer cake.

"The company your father started was with a man named Coleman—do you remember him?"

Ruby nodded. "Who could forget a man like that?"

"Well, after the company was sold and everything shook out, a new one formed. CCE. And now Coleman's grandson has worked himself into the mix. Buddy's his name. He's had his eye on Beulah Mountain. Right there is as close as he's gotten."

"Until now?" Ruby said.

"The town's been losing people for years because there's no jobs. CCE has bought property up and down the ridge. Call it bad luck or pure providence, Coleman is headed our way. And he's convinced the board that he should be president. I hear they're supposed to hand him the crown at a ceremony tomorrow. And that means my land is as good as gone. Companies reward people who can get things done."

"Why don't you stand up to him if you want to keep your land?" Ruby picked up the contract. "Tell him to go take a flying leap. Just because everybody else sells doesn't mean you have to."

"You don't understand."

As they drove, Ruby looked out at the beauty of the mountains, and when the road switched back, she saw the encroaching moonscape and it turned her stomach. Hollis hadn't spoken in a few minutes.

"What's your last name?" Ruby said.

"Beasley."

Ruby searched the recesses of her mind—it was easier to locate information from seventy or eighty years earlier than it was to dig up what she'd heard that morning. "I went to church with some Beasleys. Pastor Brace was the man who was there at the time."

"He was there a long time," Hollis said.

"Talitha was her name, wasn't it?"

"Yes, it was. Talitha and Edward. I'm their son."

"Is that a fact? Do you still have the little cemetery on top of the hill?"

"It's right above the house. You've been there?"

Ruby smiled as memories flooded. "I had a friend that went with me all over those hills. I don't blame you for wanting to keep it, Hollis." She closed her eyes and breathed in the mountain air. "So why don't you say no to Coleman?"

"My wife, Juniper, isn't well. And the dust from the digging fills the air and clogs her lungs. She'll only get worse. The water's already red as Pharaoh's Nile."

"Sounds like you went to Beulah Mountain Baptist, too."

"I did for a time."

"But you don't anymore?"

"I've come to believe that God's forgot about people like me. He lets life kick you in the teeth and doesn't do much to stop it."

Ruby remembered an old hymn and hummed it quietly. She wanted to say something that would help the man snap out of his spiritual stupor, but she thought better of it. They wound down the mountain and a sign gave the number of miles to Beulah Mountain.

"I could take you to town if you want. You could call a wrecker from there and get somebody to look at your arm. How's it feel?"

"It's throbbing."

Hollis shook his head. "Juniper says I ought to have a first aid kit. If I did, I could give you some aspirin to knock out the pain."

"Juniper sounds like a smart woman."

"She is. Pretty as a speckled pup, too. Why don't I take you to our place and you can call your people?"

"Take me to your place," Ruby said.

36

HOLLIS AND JUNIPER TEND TO RUBY
BEULAH MOUNTAIN, WEST VIRGINIA
FRIDAY, OCTOBER 1, 2004

Hollis parked by the house and Cooper came barking, sniffing at the passenger side. When Ruby got out, he stopped barking and wagged his tail and wouldn't leave her alone.

Juniper came outside and grabbed the railing, watching as Hollis helped Ruby to the front steps.

"I found me a stray," Hollis said.

"Where? And what happened?"

"It's a long story," Ruby said, stopping to catch her breath. "You must be Juniper."

Juniper nodded and reached out a bony hand to help.

"Ruby Handley Freeman. Pleased to meet you."

Juniper's mouth dropped open.

"Be careful. Her arm's broke," Hollis said.

"It is not," Ruby said. "It's sprained."

"You ought to go to the hospital," Juniper said.

"That's what I told her," Hollis said.

"I'm surrounded by worrywarts." Ruby looked at the hillside like she was viewing heaven. "Help me inside and let me sit a minute."

"I'll get the door." Juniper held the screen door open while Hollis guided the old woman inside.

"Could you point me toward the little girls' room?" Ruby said.

"It's the Mountain Dew," Hollis said, smiling.

Hollis walked with her down the hallway and let go of her good arm as Ruby went into the bathroom. He wandered back to the kitchen and stood at one of the ladder-back chairs. "She was sitting in a car at the bottom of a gully just off Ten Mile. Somebody left her for dead."

"My lands. What people won't do to each other these days."

"I don't know what would have happened if . . ."

"If what?"

"There was a deer family crossing the road. I got out of the truck and heard a horn clear as a bell. It was like a message from heaven. I would never have stopped in that place in a million years."

"Do you think we should call the police?"

"Let's see what she wants to do. She's dead set against going to the hospital but that arm looks awful. She doesn't seem as concerned with justice as I would be."

"Did you see Coleman?"

"Yeah, I got the contract in the truck."

"Did you sign it?"

He stared at her. "Don't start. You don't know what it took for me to drive over there with my tail between my legs."

"Was he ugly to you?"

"Not any more than usual. I told him I wanted Homer Sowards to check it."

"I'll bet he was glad to see you."

Ruby opened the door and came walking down the hall with her left hand on the wall. "I remember this place now. And I remember your mother and father, Hollis. You weren't around when I was here." She looked out the window toward the top of the hill. "I need to call my daughter. Let her know I'm okay. And then I'd like to see the cemetery."

Juniper handed her the phone and Ruby stared at it. "I have her number written in my address book. It's in my purse. But I don't have the purse with me."

Hollis offered to call Charlotte. She could look up anything on the Internet. He dialed from the living room extension and got Charlotte's voice mail, then tracked her down at the newspaper office.

"I got somebody sitting in my kitchen you've been looking for," Hollis said.

Charlotte gasped when she heard the name. "Where did you find her? Is she all right?"

"She's banged up. I think her arm's broke."

"It's sprained!" Ruby yelled from the kitchen.

"Her hearing seems to be all right," Hollis said. "She can't remember the number to her daughter and I thought you might find it."

"She's here, Papaw. In Beulah Mountain. Got here late last night looking for her."

"Well, it sounds like a convention, doesn't it?"

"I'll bring her up there. Oh, this is wonderful. How did you find her?"

"I'll tell you when you get here."

When Hollis returned to the kitchen, Ruby and Juniper were in a conversation about cooking that he felt would last a while. He interrupted long enough to say he needed to call the sheriff.

"I don't want you to call the sheriff," Ruby said. "Leave them out of this."

"Ma'am, unless I've gotten the story wrong, you were robbed and drugged and held against your will and then left in a gully. I'd say the authorities ought to have been called a long time ago."

"You don't understand," she said. "It was my fault. I shouldn't have trusted those people. When my children find out, there will be no end to it. They're going to put me in a home!"

Hollis scratched his head. "Everybody makes mistakes. But you didn't deserve what happened. There needs to be an accounting."

Ruby frowned and waved her bruised hand. "Go ahead and call. But I don't know where those people lived."

"They'll figure it out. And don't worry about your kids—they're just going to be glad to see you."

Hollis called the sheriff's office and reported the situation and gave the location of the abandoned car. Then he sat on the front porch and leafed through the contract, trying to comprehend the legal jargon. He put it down as a cold shiver went through him. What if he hadn't stopped? What if he hadn't looked in that gully or heard the horn or seen the silver glint? What if the deer hadn't been crossing the road?

"She wants to go up on the hill," Juniper said.

Hollis jumped at her voice, he had been so lost in thought.

"Sorry to scare you. She wants to go to the cemetery."

He put the contract down and nodded. "I'll drive her."

RUBY VISITS THE GRAVES
BEULAH MOUNTAIN, WEST VIRGINIA
FRIDAY, OCTOBER 1, 2004

Ruby could tell by the way the truck tires sank that Hollis didn't normally drive up to the cemetery. He must have felt there was no way she could navigate the uneven ground and the incline in her condition. He put the truck in four-wheel drive and crawled close to the top. A half circle of boulders had been placed there since she had last been here.

Hollis helped her out of the truck and held her arm as they navigated the boulders and walked to a knoll surrounded by soaring pines. Ruby was out of breath when she reached the first stones. They were so old she couldn't read the names. She bent down and ran a hand across a moss-covered marker.

"These are the oldest," Hollis said, pointing. "My great-great-grandmother died in 1848. And that's her son, Dooley. He died at the Droop Mountain battle in 1863. I expect you don't want the history lesson."

"There's a lot of history buried here," Ruby said. "But there's more than just your family, right?"

"Oh yes, ma'am. Some people requested to be buried here. Others weren't allowed to be buried in town. It's kind of a misfit cemetery, if you will. You came to the town when you were a girl?"

"It was a long time ago," Ruby said. She kept walking, the memories stirring and the tug as strong as a largemouth bass on a line to her heart. As she walked, the weathered stones gave way to ones she could read. She studied each grave she passed and when she made it to the top, she turned, her brow furrowed.

"Is there somebody in particular you're looking for?" Hollis said.

"There was a family I knew. Dingess was their name. Judson and Cora Jean and their daughter. We called her Bean." Just saying the words felt like a dagger.

"That's a family they rejected in town. Because of what happened. They're right over here." He walked to a sunken spot at the edge of the cemetery and pointed to three graves with flat stones and no writing. "I'm not sure which one is your friend."

Ruby stared at the ground.

After a moment, Hollis said, "My parents told me that after the massacre the company didn't want anything to do with the burials. I remember my mama would come out here and bring flowers. There wasn't nobody else to do it. They didn't have family that anybody could find."

Ruby's knees gave way and she sank to the ground next to the graves, the pine needles and cones digging into her skin. She heard a sound in the distance like a wounded animal, a heart-wrenching wail that echoed through the hills. And then she realized it was coming from her.

Hollis knelt and put a hand on her shoulder. When she quieted, he said, "You must have been good friends."

"The best," Ruby said. "'Greater love has no one than this . . .'" She couldn't finish the verse. She gathered herself and wiped her face with a wrinkled hand. Hollis gave her a handkerchief.

"I haven't let myself think of them for a long time. I've tried to forget, you know?"

"Yes, ma'am, I do."

"Seeing their graves and being here . . . I didn't know it would be this hard."

Hollis rubbed his chin. Finally he said, "What kind of people were they?"

Ruby smiled. "The mother was so kind. She could love a skunk. And she did—the dad wasn't worth a plugged nickel, at least to most people. When he wasn't drinking, though, he had a soft side. The family didn't have anything. Rented a little house from the coal company. Owed more than they ever made. But Bean and her mama had the Lord and each other. I think that's all a body needs."

Her words brought back warm, rich memories. She closed her eyes and saw the kitchen and smelled the cake and heard their voices echoing through the hollow.

"The thing I liked most was going to church. The songs they sang still stick with me after all these years. Like 'Dwelling in Beulah Land.' Do you know that one?"

"I'm tone-deaf, ma'am. Couldn't carry a tune if it was strapped to my back. But I enjoy listening to others who know how to sing."

Ruby closed her eyes and called the memory to life. Her voice rose, crackling and slow at first, then gained strength as the sound wafted across the graves.

"Far away the noise of strife upon my ear is falling;
Then I know the sins of earth beset on every hand;
Doubt and fear and things of earth in vain to me are calling;
None of these shall move me from Beulah Land."

She sang the chorus all the way through, tears leaking as if she were pouring out an oblation. It was her offering on this mountain she had tried to forget.

"You all right, ma'am?" Hollis said.

Ruby nodded.

"There's some cars coming up the driveway. We should go back."

38

FRANCES EMBRACES HER MOTHER
BEULAH MOUNTAIN, WEST VIRGINIA
FRIDAY, OCTOBER 1, 2004

"Oh, Mama, Mama," Frances said as she hugged her mother tightly.
"I'm so glad you're safe. So glad we found you." She pulled back.
"What happened? Why did you leave?"

The look on her mother's face told her that Ruby wasn't ready
to talk. One look at her arm and Frances knew they needed to get
medical attention.

"We'll talk about that later," Ruby said, turning to the man and
woman on the steps of the old house. "Thank you for your kindness.
I hope we get to meet again."

Charlotte introduced Frances to her grandmother and grandfather.

"You take care of yourself, Miss Ruby," Juniper said. She was so
frail it looked like a strong wind could blow her over.

Hollis helped Ruby to Frances's car and spoke briefly about how he had found Ruby and the condition of her car.

"I don't know how we could ever repay you for what you've done," Frances said, hugging him.

Hollis was stiff but managed to return the embrace. "There wasn't nothing to it."

Ruby fell into the passenger seat like a load of bricks dropping from a great height. Charlotte hugged her grandfather and waved at her grandmother and got in her own car and backed out.

"I'm taking you to the hospital," Frances said. "Charlotte is going to show us the way. And the sheriff is going to meet us there."

Ruby pursed her lips and stared straight ahead. "Do what you're going to do."

The hospital was small and aged, but it was all they needed. Ruby sat impatiently in the waiting room in a plastic chair that squeaked, and when they took her for X-rays, she squirmed and winced as they positioned her arm on the machine. It was all Frances could do not to ply her mother with questions. The X-ray confirmed a broken bone in Ruby's wrist and Frances shook her head when she saw the pictures. The brittle bone had snapped into a jagged shape and Frances wondered if it would heal properly.

Charlotte stayed with them—a bit of a third wheel, but the girl seemed to care. Frances thought she probably wanted to ask Ruby more questions, so she suggested Charlotte stay in the waiting room. When the doctor came to cast Ruby's wrist, Frances slipped into the corridor.

She dialed Jerry to give him an update. She had called on the way to Hollis's house with the triumphal news that their mother had been found, and Jerry sounded relieved, though it was a mystery how her credit card was being used in a town two hours away. Frances cringed when she heard Jerry's voice, recalling her theory that he had been involved in the disappearance. It wasn't time to deal with that, but she would need to.

"What are we ever going to do with her now, Frances? We can't let her go back to that house. She'll take off the other way."

"One step at a time, Jerry. Let me get her home."

"What about her car?"

"From what Hollis said, I don't think we're going to have to worry about her driving it again. It's back in the woods and might be totaled. For sure it will need work."

"I can't imagine what she was thinking," Jerry said.

When Frances hung up, she dialed Julia and left a message. She stared at the phone, wondering if she should call Wallace. Frances didn't want to hear his voice. And Julia would tell him the news. But something about that felt off, felt cowardly. She hit Dial, then hit End. Wallace was part of the reason for the dull ache in her heart. But the bigger part of her wanted to do the kind thing. She was hitting Dial just as the sheriff walked in and quickly hit End again.

"This is Sheriff Rayburn," Charlotte said, introducing him to Frances.

The man took off his hat and shook her hand. "I'm glad there's good news about your mother." He asked if he could see her and Frances led him into the exam room.

Ruby was in a long conversation with the doctor about her previous maladies and the medication she had refused to take through the years, and the doctor looked dazed at the blizzard of information. When the sheriff walked in, Ruby took control.

"All right, the first question I have for you is whether or not they can fix my car," Ruby said.

"Ma'am, I'm not the best one to talk to about that," the sheriff said. "I haven't seen it. Hollis told me it was banged up. Now, the wrecker is over there and Junior's going to tow it. The local shop can take a look at it if you want and give you an estimate."

"Who is Junior?"

"He's a good old boy from town. Drives the tow truck."

"How much is it going to cost to fix?" Ruby said.

"Mama, he just said he doesn't know. And even if they fix it, you're not driving the car home."

Ruby turned a bewildered face toward her. "Why in the world not?"

Frances glanced at the sheriff as if to ask, *Do you see what I'm up against?*

"Ma'am, why don't you tell me what happened?"

"A lot's happened. Where do you want me to start?"

"I'm trying to figure out how you wound up in the gully near Ten Mile. There's a lot of people who've been looking for you."

Ruby glanced at Frances, then at the floor. "Do I get a phone call? Maybe I need a lawyer."

"You didn't do anything wrong, Mama," Frances said.

The doctor finished the cast and told Ruby to stay still, then excused himself. He seemed to sense trouble brewing and didn't need more than he already had.

"Ma'am, you don't need a lawyer," the sheriff said. "I'm just trying to figure out what happened. Hollis mentioned you ran into some people who hurt you? You want to tell me about them?"

"Hollis is the type who likes to tell stories."

"Well, that's fair. Why don't you fill in the missing pieces between when you left your house and three hours ago when he found you."

Ruby looked at Frances, her mouth pinched. "If I have to tell this, I'd rather do it in private."

"You don't have to hide anything from me," Frances said.

"Yes, I do. You'll hear this story and jump to conclusions." She looked back at the sheriff. "And the next thing you know she'll be putting me in a home. Her and her brother. They've probably been on the phone planning it."

"Maybe we should have this conversation alone," the sheriff said to Frances.

"I'm not planning anything of the sort," Frances said to Ruby. "Our only concern is you, Mama. We want you to be safe. We don't want to have to worry about you wandering off."

"You think I wandered off? You think this was something I did on a whim?" Ruby's face was red and her eyes were narrowed. "You and Jerry took my keys. That's what started this whole thing. That and the fact you sold my car out from under me."

"We didn't sell it. That was a misunder—"

"You were trying to sell it to that fellow down the road. Drew whatever-his-name-is." She looked at the sheriff. "My guess is, they've hired a Realtor and already have my house on the market. I'll get back and there'll be strangers traipsing through."

"That's preposterous!" Frances said.

The sheriff seemed vexed at the ping-ponging, looking from Ruby to Frances and back. Before he could interrupt, Ruby ramped up again.

"I've thought about coming down here for a long time. But I never made it. And I didn't want you two sticking your noses into the decision."

"Why not?"

"Because it's none of your business," Ruby snapped. "And then I thought, well, I'll ask Frances or Jerry to drive me. It's a long way to Beulah Mountain. And the more I thought, the clearer it became. I can't trust you two!"

Frances tried to hear between the lines but couldn't. "What are you talking about?"

Ruby lifted her cast and winced. "I came down here on a pilgrimage. Things have bothered me. Got stirred up like a muddy creek. I always told myself I'd never come back because of the bad memories. Then I got a letter about the Company Store and the big to-do and the dedication. The more I thought, the more it seemed like something I needed to do."

"Did Franklin Brown have something to do with this?" Frances said.

Ruby looked startled. "Do you listen to him?"

"No, but I know you do."

Ruby turned to the sheriff and told him about Franklin Brown's program and what type of music he played and how long he'd been on the radio.

"Mama, I know you called and talked with him, right?"

"How did you know that?"

"I spoke with him."

"You called Franklin?"

"I called *everybody*. I went to Eula's. Jerry drove all over town. I called Wallace. We went to the cemetery where Dad—"

Ruby interrupted. "You called Wallace?"

"We had no idea where you were. And the police have been looking. Don't look at me that way. We had to go to the authorities."

"What's that got to do with Franklin Brown?" Ruby said.

"We were frantic. I was searching for anything. I found his number on your phone and dialed it."

"So now you've gone through my phone and I suppose all my mail and my underwear drawer!" Ruby glanced at the sheriff. "Do you see what I'm talking about?"

"I think I need to step into the hall and let you two settle this," the sheriff said.

"You stay where you are, lawman," Ruby snapped. "My life has been pilfered by my children."

"Mama, we were distraught. Don't you see? This shows how much we care. How much we love you!"

"Love me?" Ruby said. "You go through my phone records and who knows what else and I'm supposed to fall down and give thanks?"

"Ma'am, let me jump in. How did you break your wrist?"

"It's just a scratch."

Frances closed her eyes and shook her head.

"Did you fall or did somebody do that to you?"

"I fell," she said, looking away sheepishly.

"Mama, tell him the truth."

"I don't want to tell the truth with you in here. You'll use it against me."

Frances locked eyes with the sheriff, then excused herself and stepped into the hall, thinking that nothing in the last few days made any sense. Maybe this was what life would be like from now on, just a slow detachment of her mother from reality.

In the waiting room Charlotte asked how things were going and Frances pulled out her phone. "She's a little hard to deal with. Excuse me. I'll be right back."

She dialed Wallace. When she heard his voice, she took a breath and began. "Wallace, we found her. I'm with her now."

"Thank God. Where was she?"

"Beulah Mountain. She was headed back here after all."

"What for?"

"She said it was a pilgrimage. I think she trusted someone and they scammed her. She's with the sheriff here at the hospital."

"Is she okay?"

"Her wrist is broken. They found her car in the woods. A man driving by saw her. If he hadn't, I don't know what would have happened."

Wallace groaned on the other end and it felt good to share this with someone who understood the backstory.

"At least she's alive and safe. I'm glad, Frances."

Frances felt the emotion coming, a release of all the tension she'd felt. She gathered herself and said, "I left a message for Julia. Maybe you could follow up with her?"

"Be glad to."

A deep breath. Possibly their last words before Wallace walked away forever. *Say something good, something positive.*

"Wallace, thank you for putting up with the way my mind twists things. I think I'm a lot like my mother, in some ways."

"No need to thank me. I'm happy you found her. Tell Ruby I said hello."

Frances hung up as Marilyn Grigsby-Mollie entered the waiting room and hugged Charlotte. When Frances moved toward her, the woman's face was aglow.

"We heard the news and we're so thankful," Marilyn said. "You must be so relieved."

Then came a flurry of questions and nonanswers because Frances didn't know much about what had happened and wouldn't have divulged it if she had. The sheriff opened the door and held it for Ruby and she shuffled out. For the first time Frances noticed that her mother was wearing the shoes from her closet, the ones she had scolded Frances for playing with long ago.

Marilyn introduced herself and gushed, "Why, the whole town has been praying for you ever since we heard you were missing."

Ruby shot Frances a glare. "I'm a bit banged up, and they gave me a prescription for pain, but I think some ibuprofen will do." She went into a description of what the doctor had told her, a little too much information about the break and how long it would take to heal.

When she took a breath, Marilyn said, "Mrs. Freeman, I want to personally invite you to the dedication tomorrow morning. I know this is not the best time and you've been through a lot, but we'll make any accommodation. We'd love to hear your recollections of Beulah Mountain."

"That's very kind of you," Frances said, stepping between the woman and Ruby, "but my mother has been through an ordeal and we need to get her home."

"Now hold on a minute," Ruby said. "I came down here for a reason. It'd be a shame to travel this far and not see the store. But Frances is right that I don't have much energy for a ceremony. Would I be able to walk through it now?"

"Mother?" Frances said.

"By all means," Marilyn said. "We will roll out the red carpet."

"Frances, could we go over there so I could look around before we head home?"

"Are you sure?"

"I'd like to see it."

39

Charlotte's hands shook as she retrieved her camera from the *Beulah Mountain Breeze* office. Corky asked what the fuss was about, and she told him Ruby had been located. *Rescued* was the word she used.

"Have you told them about what you found?" Corky said.

"Not yet. I'm waiting for the right moment."

"Well, take lots of pictures," he said. "We'll have to use them next week because the Saturday edition is done. We'll put the ones you found along with them if we get permission."

She grabbed a recharged battery and rushed out the door.

Frances was pulling in to the Company Store parking lot when

Charlotte made it to the entrance. She snapped a few photos of Ruby getting out of the car. Those looked painful.

Ruby paused, holding the door to steady herself. She glanced up at the front of the store and Charlotte snapped the photo she guessed would appear in next week's *Beulah Mountain Breeze*. Her white hair was combed back like a lion's mane and she stared as if seeing a wondrous sight or perhaps a ghost from her past.

Charlotte wanted to rush toward the woman and pummel her with questions and show her the pictures from the old camera that still hung in Corky's darkroom, but she held back, content for now to catalog the visit. Charlotte took a picture of Frances and Marilyn helping Ruby up the stairs.

When she made it to the landing, Ruby stomped on the boards. "Just like I remember it," she said.

"We've tried to make everything authentic," Marilyn said. "Wait until you see the artifacts we've uncovered."

Charlotte took a picture of the group from the bottom of the stairs, then turned on her flash and hurried inside. Ruby went straight to the glass cases in front that housed candy and toys children of the mountains could never afford.

"How did you find all of this?" Ruby said. "And in such good condition."

"It was a labor of love," Marilyn said. "Some of the candy was ordered online. There are places around the country that sell this sort of thing. Some things were donated by local families. The rest was found in storage."

Charlotte took a picture of Ruby peering into the case before she moved through the store looking at clothes and mining tools and equipment.

"What are you thinking, Mama?" Frances said.

"It feels like I went to sleep and woke up in 1933." She held out her left hand. "The only thing that's changed is my wrinkles."

"Mrs. Freeman, we have tour guides who have memorized a script written by the historical society. I would love for you to hear what we'll be telling visitors."

Ruby looked at Frances, then back at the woman. "How long will it take?"

"Charlotte, would you get Tiffany or Alice and have them come and meet our guest?"

Charlotte wanted to keep taking pictures and listening to the conversation, but she acquiesced and found the two folding flyers. Both wore jeans and T-shirts, but they would wear dresses at the dedication. Both had stellar enunciation abilities and slim figures.

Charlotte told them someone was wanted at the Company Store and the two ignored her. When she mentioned Marilyn wanted someone, they dropped their flyers and Tiffany followed her out the door.

Charlotte snapped a photo of Tiffany meeting Ruby, though Marilyn said she wanted the photo deleted because the guide wasn't in costume. Charlotte kept it.

Tiffany began the tour with an overview of the Company Store and its importance to the town. She explained it was the main hub of the community, the place where families bought their supplies. She held up a piece of paper and explained how scrip worked, but she left out anything about the inflated prices.

"Could I see that?" Ruby said.

Tiffany glanced at Marilyn, who nodded, and the girl handed it to Ruby.

"I never thought I'd see this again, but to hold it in my hands . . ." She put the scrip to her nose and smelled it.

"Do you remember anything about the scrip?" Frances said.

"I remember how precious it was. Some barely had enough to buy food. Children would gather here and look at the candy, the peppermint sticks. Horehound was my favorite. Do you have horehound candy?"

Marilyn retreated to the counter and brought Ruby a brown stick wrapped in plastic. "It's yours. I hope the taste of it brings back good memories."

Ruby tucked the candy in a pocket and Tiffany moved to the back of the store and continued her speech. "Miners rented their houses and equipment from the company."

"It was deducted from their pay," Ruby said, raising her voice. "You need to get that in there. By the time they deducted the rent each month and the cost of the picks and hats, there wasn't much left. It was an ordinary thing to see children walking to school without shoes. And in the wintertime, some children would come to school in the morning and go home and their siblings came in the afternoon, because they had to share shoes."

"That's interesting, ma'am," Tiffany said as if she wanted to stick with her script.

Ruby shuffled over and Frances followed, holding out her hands as if ready to catch her. Ruby picked up a heavy miner's hat with the lantern in the front. "This is exactly what they would wear. Every man had one of these or they didn't go into the mine. It was your lifeline, really."

"Would you like to see the apartment above us?" Marilyn said.

Frances stepped forward. "I don't think that would be a good idea. Too many stairs."

Ruby was already on the move. She waved her good hand in the air. "I'm not coming all this way without seeing the apartment. Let's go."

Charlotte took a few pictures as they entered the stairwell and she kicked herself for not getting in front of the group. She ran up the wide staircase on the other end of the building and came around to the back as Ruby made the apartment landing.

Charlotte opened the door and slipped inside, closing it and waiting. She crouched and snapped a series of pictures looking up at Ruby as she first saw the restored apartment, capturing her openmouthed gaze.

Ruby stood in the doorway, her eyes sweeping the room. Tiffany pushed through and stood in the middle, hands clasped in front of her.

"One of the owners of the mine, Jacob Handley, drew up the plans for this building and he included this apartment. This is the living room area. There's a master bedroom there and another bedroom where his daughter stayed."

Ruby shuffled to the fireplace mantel and looked at photos in ancient frames. She leaned close and tipped her head back. "Wish I had my glasses."

"What is it, Mama?" Frances said.

Ruby lingered at one picture, picking it up and holding it in better light. "He was such a kind man. Not like the others."

"You mean your father?"

Ruby set the photo down and wandered to the reading chair, glancing at the bookshelf as she sat. "Now these weren't here. The bookshelf was over by the bedroom door, and I don't remember seeing this many. Books were a hot commodity back then. There wasn't a library in town. You had to go all the way to . . ."

Her voice trailed off and Charlotte saw the first sign of concern on the old woman's face, like she had stumbled onto something she hadn't expected.

"We weren't able to find many pictures of this actual room, but the ones we did find helped us," Marilyn said.

"I understand," Ruby said. "Looks like you had to guess at most of it."

Frances grabbed a picture from the mantel and held it in front of Ruby. "Your mother was beautiful. They were such a handsome couple, don't you think?"

Ruby nodded, but something seemed off, and Charlotte wondered if the old woman had taken medication.

"Would you like to see the rest of the apartment?" Marilyn said.

"I've seen the rest of the apartment in my dreams every night of my life," Ruby said. "I can close my eyes and be here. Smell the coffee brewing down in the kitchen and the eggs and sausage and bacon. Hear Mrs. Grigsby walk up those stairs."

"Mrs. Grigsby was my grandmother," Marilyn said proudly.

Ruby stared at her. "I don't see any resemblance."

"I'm surprised you would have so many memories of this place—you weren't here that long, were you, Mama?" Frances said.

Ruby paused. "There's some places that are always with you, no matter how long you stay. Beulah Mountain was that way for me." She tried to stand but couldn't push herself up with one arm, so Frances helped.

Tiffany looked bewildered, like she'd been relieved of her job, as Ruby walked into her old bedroom. Ruby laughed. "That was not the bed in here. You folks have tried to make this a palace. It was simple. There was nothing ostentatious about the apartment. The last thing anybody wanted was to show off."

"You mean your father didn't want people to think he was rich?" Frances said.

Ruby looked out the window at the hillside and didn't answer right away. Finally she said, "People knew he was rich. But he didn't flaunt it. He was kind to people. If the miners were happy, everyone was. That's what he believed." She turned. "You tell that to the people who traipse through here. There was a difference in the way he treated people and how Coleman treated them."

"Mr. Coleman was also kind," Marilyn said.

"You didn't know him," Ruby said. "He hired thugs to manage things. To him people were cattle. Masters and slaves. That was his outlook." She went to the window and pressed her face to the glass.

"What is it, Mama?"

"My friend and I used to run down that hill—there was a fire escape leading down. We'd go through the woods and around the bend to the little church. And they would sing. Oh, it was beautiful. That's where I came to know the Lord."

"What about your father?" Frances said. "Did he go to church with you?"

"He came once, as I recall. It was complicated."

Charlotte noticed Tiffany and Marilyn exchanging glances, like they were ready to move on.

"Is there anything else you'd like to see?" Marilyn said gently.

"I think we've seen enough, right, Mama?" Frances said.

Ruby walked through the door, but instead of turning left, she turned right and headed upstairs.

40

Each step was a mountain for Ruby. The staircase narrowed and she felt closed in like she had when she was a young girl walking these steps for the first time. Her arm throbbed as she climbed. She focused on the shoes she wore and the tight laces through the eyelets. In a way, the shoes were carrying her, lifting her to a place she had never wanted to see again but had been drawn to just the same.

She reached the landing and thought she knew what Sir Edmund Hillary must have felt. Behind her came the whir of a shutter as Charlotte snapped pictures. Ruby wanted to protest, but she had only so much energy. Plus, she liked Charlotte's spunk. If the girl hadn't been so persistent, Ruby might not have made her pilgrimage.

For years, Ruby had considered the consequences of walking into this room, where her life had changed forever. Each time the

301

idea surfaced, she pushed it down and vowed to keep her secret. No one would understand and certainly no one would forgive. How could they?

She shuffled to the door as others held back as if allowing her to enter the Holy of Holies alone. By sheer willpower, she grabbed the knob, expecting it to be locked, but it turned loosely and jiggled. She pushed open the door and let go. It hit the wall with a thud and tiny bits of plaster fell to the hardwood.

There was a new-paint smell, but she caught a hint of the past in the linseed and leather. The cigar smoke that had hung heavy was gone, but she still smelled it, still was able to close her eyes and bring it back. Funny how the mind could call into being something that had vanished, like the scent of burning leaves or the inside of a dusty hymnal or a room filled with never-worn shoes.

She glanced at the pictures on the wall next to the window and something went numb. Those faces had blurred in her dreams through the years, but now they looked at her in focus, staring across the decades, accusing her. And why wouldn't they? They knew the truth about what happened on that day in 1933.

The others joined her and Frances put a hand on her arm and asked if she was all right. Ruby nodded and walked to the window, the mountain vista overwhelming.

"I think I need to sit," she said.

She fell heavily into the leather chair with her back to the men on the wall. She looked up at Tiffany. "I want to hear what you're going to tell people you bring here. I assume you will allow visitors."

"Of course," Marilyn said, stepping forward. "This is part of our history, though it's not the prettiest part."

Tiffany cleared her throat as if she were about to sing an aria. She brought her palms together dramatically, fingers touching.

"Come on, let her rip," Ruby said.

"This room was planned by Mr. Handley to be a meeting place

for the mine owners and their managers." Tiffany spoke with a prim, proper voice devoid of feeling. She opened a hand toward the window. "From here, they could see not only the town and the railroad, but also the coal being loaded and readied for transport. It was their headquarters, if you will, and a rendezvous point for the men of Coleman-Handley. This was the central hub for their decision making, as well as a place where men could freely drink an adult beverage and smoke a cigar and unwind from the hard work. They talked of their successes and failures, accidents and acts of God. There are stories of card games that went on well into the night.

"But make no mistake, there was much work accomplished here, too. Mr. Coleman calculated the tonnage of coal being brought out of the mine, deciphered their profit margins, and made plans about the next operation or how to best invest. So it makes sense that one of the most significant, though darkest, events in the town would happen here. It was in this room that the massacre you've heard about occurred. The details aren't fully known because no one survived the attack. But the sheriff who investigated the crime and kept meticulous records believes it happened this way.

"In the early evening of October 2, 1933, a miner named Judson Dingess entered the store just before closing. He was known in town as a troublemaker and had been arrested by the sheriff several times for being drunk and disorderly. Dingess had been slightly injured in a mining accident a year earlier and hadn't returned to work. His wife had died in childbirth the day before, so his mental state is in question.

"Dingess entered the store and asked to see Mr. Coleman. The manager of the store, Mr. Grigsby, told Dingess to leave. There was a protocol for meeting with management. Dingess complained but complied and left, Mr. Grigsby reported later. However, we know that

Dingess retrieved his daughter, Beatrice, who was twelve at the time, and returned to the store later that evening."

"Hold up a minute," Ruby said, raising her left hand. "How do you know that he went and got his daughter?"

"Because his daughter was among those who were killed. Dingess waited until the store had closed and gained access by another entrance—the sheriff believed he used the fire escape on the back of the building. His daughter was a friend . . . well, she was a friend of yours, wasn't she, Miss Ruby?"

Tiffany's speech slowed and stalled as she made the connection between a story she had memorized and the old woman sitting before her. "You knew her, didn't you?"

"I know everybody you're talking about. These aren't people from the history books. Grigsby gave candy to the poor kids at Christmas. I smelled the coffee on his breath. Coleman was as mean as a snake. You can't tell that from looking at his picture. All of these people you're talking about are real to me. They're not just names."

"Is how she's explained it true, Mama?" Frances said. "Is this what you were told?"

"Some of it resembles the truth. Some of it is fabrication. But I want to hear the rest. Go on."

Tiffany blinked as if trying to recall her place in the story and continued. "Dingess entered the room through that door and confronted Mr. Coleman and three of his associates who were present at the time."

"Associates?" Ruby said. "That's a polite way of describing them."

Tiffany gave a half smile. She pointed to the pictures on the wall and said the names of the men, but Ruby didn't turn.

"One can imagine an argument ensuing. Perhaps shouting. Perhaps it took several minutes to escalate, or it could have happened quickly. But at some point, Dingess pulled a gun and, at point-blank range, killed Mr. Coleman. Then he turned the gun on Mr. Handley.

The three associates also had guns and they opened fire and wounded Dingess, but not before he returned fire and killed them. Beatrice Dingess was also wounded in the melee and she died a short time later.

"It was a crime that rocked the community and the company. After the incident, stringent rules were put in place about dealing with disgruntled employees. Other mines in the area did the same. And shortly afterward every mine in the state was unionized."

Frances looked at her mother. "Where were you when this happened, Mama?"

Ruby looked at Tiffany as if she would know.

"Miss Ruby had been put on a train earlier in the day and was sent to a boarding school in Pennsylvania. She was gone when all of this took place, thankfully, and didn't find out about her father's death until two days later when word reached the school."

"Who told you?" Frances said.

Ruby put a hand on her injured wrist. "I met with the principal and the headmistress. They took me to the office and sat me down, offered tea. I knew it was bad. I can see his face now. The bushy mustache. And his mouth moving, telling me my father had been killed and that the school was my new home and they'd take care of me and I didn't have anything to worry about."

"You must have been so scared, so alone," Frances said.

"I don't think I can describe the feeling," Ruby said.

A silence fell in the room. Ruby ran her tongue around her dentures, staring at Tiffany. "The girl who was killed—we called her Bean. Tell me what happened to her father."

"As I said, he was injured in the exchange of gunfire in this room. A trail of blood ran down the stairs and out the front door. Mr. Grigsby heard the gunshots and alerted the sheriff, who rushed here and caught up with Dingess as he was exiting the store, running from the scene. Shots were fired again. The sheriff had no choice. Dingess was killed in the street."

"And that's in the report by the sheriff? His recollection was that Dingess was running? He was alone?"

"That's correct. We have the report, written in the sheriff's own hand, downstairs in the museum if you'd like to see it. Judson Dingess and his daughter and wife are buried in common graves in the Beasley cemetery." She brought her hands together again dramatically and with a smile said, "And that's why this room holds such a storied place in our history."

Ruby leaned forward and stared at the dim shadow she cast on the hardwood. No one moved. The only sound was the wind whistling around the windowpanes.

"Miss Ruby, we'd like to hear what you remember," Marilyn said. "The day you left Beulah. What do you recall about that day?"

Ruby didn't move, running the story through her mind. "The trunk was packed and sent ahead to the school. Everything I needed was in there. So I just had one suitcase with me when I got on the train."

"Your father sent the trunk ahead?"

She hesitated. "Yes. All I needed was the small suitcase I carried and the ticket."

She closed her eyes and heard the train whistle in her memory. That sound had haunted her, and every time she heard a train whistle, she thought of that lonely ride. "I'm not sure you want to hear my recollections. Especially since my version doesn't line up with what you're going to tell folks."

The women glanced at each other quizzically. Only Charlotte kept her eyes on Ruby and stepped closer.

"Well, here goes. This room was not just a meeting place for the men. It was that, of course. And you're right about the drinking and the cigar smoking and card playing. There was plenty of that, and it's something that became vexing to my father. He was on the outside of that group. At odds with them. So there was conflict between how

Coleman wanted to run things and how my father thought things should be.

"For example, there were shelves that ran the length of that wall." She pointed behind them and the women turned. "On those shelves were women's shoes. Nice ones you don't see in a coal-mining town. Some with straps and heels you'd never wear on our muddy streets. Some boots that laced up."

Marilyn smiled. "Mrs. Freeman, we put that myth to rest long ago. This was a meeting room, not a footwear display."

"Missy, judging from the lack of wrinkles you have, I'm guessing you weren't alive in 1933."

"Well, of course not. But we've been quite meticulous in our research. And the odd assertion that the store sold shoes up here—"

"I never said they sold them here. I said there were shelves full of them. This can't be the first time you're hearing that?"

"It's not the first time—but only a few have ever mentioned it, and there is no historical evidence to support what you're saying."

"I have evidence," Charlotte said.

The woman turned on her quickly.

"I found a picture that shows Miss Ruby is right. There's a wall of shoes in the photo."

Marilyn stood ramrod straight as if she were defending a castle wall. "It was probably taken on the first floor. You've seen the shoe display. It's historically accurate."

"You're right," Ruby said. "The work shoes with steel toes and the children's shoes and the regular women's shoes were down there. I'm not disputing that."

Marilyn laughed nervously. "I don't know why we're getting hung up on this. You have a memory from more than seventy years ago. Memories can be faulty."

"But Charlotte says she has a picture," Frances said. "Pictures are not faulty, are they?"

Marilyn glared at Charlotte. "We will examine what she's found, of course. It would have been more helpful if you had brought this to our attention when you found the picture, Charlotte."

"I just discovered it," Charlotte said. "And frankly I was concerned it would be pushed aside like the Esau scrip."

There was an audible sigh from both Marilyn and Tiffany as if this were an old burial ground that had been dug up and found empty.

"You don't think there was such a thing as Esau scrip?" Ruby said.

Marilyn furrowed her brow and tried to smile. "Mrs. Freeman, it's clear you've been through quite an ordeal. Maybe it's best if you got some rest?"

Ruby rose from the chair and walked around the room, looking down. "I appreciate your concern for my well-being. And my mental state. But I want to show you something before you dismiss what I'm saying." She put out her right foot as if to do the hokey pokey. "Take a look at these."

Marilyn looked down. "They look quite authentic. From the 1930s?"

"Yes, 1933. They came from this room. In a way, these shoes brought me back here. The memories they stirred are part of why I returned."

Marilyn drew close. Her voice had been clear and precise, but now she lowered it to a guttural level, barely audible. "If it's your intention to sabotage what we've worked to create, you can leave."

"What was that?" Ruby said loudly. She could hear what was said, but she wanted the woman to repeat it.

"Mama, we should go," Frances said. She took Ruby by her good arm.

Ruby pulled away. "Missy, you listen. If you want to make everything sentimental and nostalgic, go ahead. Lies will sell for a while, but eventually people will see through it. You'll get a lot more people here if you tell them the truth."

"And what is the truth?" Marilyn said. "Your version? At least what you can remember of it? I'll remind you that your children took your car keys because you're losing your faculties."

"Now hold on," Frances said.

"Those that aren't trusted to be on the road shouldn't be trusted with their stories." Marilyn glared at Frances, then walked out of the room, her heels striking the hardwood. Tiffany followed and only Frances and Charlotte were left.

"I told her she wouldn't want to hear my version," Ruby said, frowning. She looked at Charlotte. "I'd like to see that picture of yours."

"Mother, we should go," Frances said.

"I'm not ready," Ruby said.

"Why not? We agreed we would look at the store and then leave."

"I know. Something in that lady's tone makes me want to stay. The only thing worse than living through something terrible is having people not believe it happened. Or that it happened another way."

Frances sighed heavily. "I've checked out of the hotel. There are no rooms available tonight. So we'll need to get on the road—"

"You can stay with us," Charlotte said. "My mom and me. I'll get the picture for you. I'll show you everything."

41

Frances helped her mother into Charlotte's house, a three-bedroom ranch at the foot of Beulah Mountain. An upright piano sat at the far end of the living room and the television was playing *Wheel of Fortune* with the sound up loud. There were pictures on the mantel of Charlotte with her family and a special picture of her mom and dad that looked more like a shrine. Frances recalled something about Charlotte's father dying in an accident. The man looked like a younger version of Hollis, with the same tall frame and stoic face, though in one picture he smiled. Frances wondered what would keep them in this community after such a loss.

Charlotte's mother, Lillian, was a petite woman with rough hands and a kind face, though there was a sadness to her eyes. Frances guessed she and Lillian were about the same age, which was not the only thing they had in common. Both were in the same life situation—alone, without a husband. They both liked *Wheel of Fortune*, though at different sound levels. And they both had daughters they loved dearly.

Lillian welcomed them politely, then turned the TV down and retreated to the kitchen.

"I don't think I can eat anything," Ruby said. "But I'd like to get cleaned up. I smell like I've wrestled a polecat."

Frances took their suitcases into the guest room, where she found two twin beds and a dresser. She helped her mother navigate out of her blouse, being careful with her injured arm, then ran her a bath.

"I'll be all right now," Ruby said, standing in the bathroom. "There are still some things I need to do myself."

Frances argued, to no avail. "Call me when you want to get out. Last thing we need is another visit to the emergency room from a fall."

Ruby gave her a slack-jawed stare and Frances scurried to the kitchen.

"Your mother is something else," Lillian said. "She's had quite an adventure."

The toilet flushed in the bathroom. "Yes, and I have a feeling the adventure is not over."

Lillian smiled. "I know what you mean. We're going through this with Hollis and Juniper, my in-laws. They've been more like family to me than my own. I worry about them on that mountain."

"It's peaceful up there," Frances said, looking around. "Where's Charlotte?"

"She said she needed to get something from the office."

"The picture," Frances said. "She didn't have to do that."

"She seemed on a mission. I hope she doesn't mind me telling you this, but Charlotte has been obsessed with your mother's story. She was so excited to hear that your mother might be coming here for the dedication. And sad when it looked like she wouldn't be. It's been like preparing for the arrival of royalty."

Frances thought about the radio man who called her mother Queen Ruby. "How did she find out about my mother?"

"Ruby has been a mystery around here for a long time. The massacre, her inheritance—the fact that she never returned." She lowered her voice. "Hollis has spoken about her, but not too kindly. I think he considers her part of the industry that wants to take so much."

"Well, he was kind to her today. I didn't pick up any animosity."

"I think he's changing. But he's still stubborn. A trait passed down through the family, I suppose. When Charlotte was in school, just a young thing, she would stay up half the night working on some project. Had to have everything in place. Science project, writing project, didn't matter. I fought her. I told her to do it and leave it alone. Go to bed. And then her daddy died. I realized we don't have forever with the people we love, at least on this earth, so I started looking at Charlotte differently. I praised her for the grades she was making and the work she was doing. Instead of fighting her about the way she did things, I tried to give her a vision for the future and go with her. She's going to do something great someday. I can tell it."

"I wouldn't be surprised if she became very successful at whatever she decides to do."

"You and me both. When she gets it in her mind to find something, she runs at it."

Lillian offered Frances salad and stew she had made for supper, and Frances wanted to decline, but she was so hungry. From the bathroom came the sound of sloshing water and she went to the door and asked Ruby if she was all right.

"Stop your worrying, Frances. I'm fine."

"Don't get the cast wet."

Ruby groaned. Frances returned as Lillian took corn bread from the oven and cut a huge slice for her and put a pat of butter on top that melted quickly.

"If you don't mind me asking, how did your husband die?"

"I don't mind. It helps to talk about him because nobody else does. Hollis and Juniper don't say his name anymore. It's like he never existed, but I know they're still hurting like I am."

Lillian crumbled some corn bread in her stew and let it soak. "The company said it was operator error. Basically they blamed Daniel. They were making a friend of his, Johnny Maxwell, clear an area for blasting. And Johnny was scared. It was too steep. So Daniel volunteered and took a front-end loader up on this hill." She held out an arm to show how steep an incline it was. "Johnny watched the whole thing. He said Daniel saved his life by doing what he did. I take a little comfort in that. The loader tipped over and started to roll and he jumped off, but he couldn't get far enough away and it fell on him."

Frances took a deep breath. "But the company didn't take responsibility?"

"CCE settled with us for enough to buy this house and they paid Charlotte's tuition at school, basically. Called it a scholarship. The company lawyer sat at this very table and told me to my face that we could file a lawsuit and ask for whatever amount of money we wanted, but we'd never get it. He'd fight it all the way on principle."

"What principle was that?"

"The principle that says if you pay one worker's family for an accident he caused, you'll wind up paying everybody. He said I'd be a lot better off taking what the company was offering. His voice was low and gravelly, like he was all sad for us. I was in a state of shock.

"I think Hollis has held it against me that I didn't fight. Not in a mean way, just disappointed I took the money. Part of me wishes we would have fought. Part of me is glad it's over."

Frances ate as she listened and Lillian rose and refilled her bowl.

The bathroom door opened and Ruby toddled out in her nightgown, the back of her hair wet.

"I feel like a new woman," Ruby said.

"I told you to let me help you get out of the tub," Frances said.

"I'm not letting you see my old wrinkled body."

Frances shook her head. Lillian chuckled.

"Now I told you earlier that I couldn't eat anything, but my bath and the smell of that stew has changed my mind," Ruby said. "You think I could try some?"

"I'd be offended if you didn't," Lillian said, jumping up.

Frances pulled a chair out at the kitchen table for Ruby. She sat with a thump, then took a napkin from the holder in the middle and unfolded it on her lap.

"It must bring lots of memories, you being back here," Lillian said. "Or did you live here long enough to even have memories?"

"I don't think you could come to Beulah Mountain for a day and not have memories," Ruby said. "Some of them I like and some I want to forget."

"I'll bet things have changed a lot since you lived here," Lillian said.

Ruby blew on her stew. "When I was here, things were busy. People coming and going. Miners and their families trying to scratch by. The mine drew people like flies to potato salad at a church picnic. But now it seems the hills and hollows have spit a lot of them out. It's nothing like it was."

"I agree. It's shameful to see people leaving, but there's just nothing left for them here and the kids have to leave to find jobs. We've stayed because the house is paid off and I have work at the hospital, but if people keep leaving, they'll probably have to move that, too."

"Working in the hospital is job security," Ruby said, not looking up at Frances. "Everybody gets sick and needs help at some point." Ruby ate a spoonful of stew and closed her eyes, moaning with pleasure. "This is like the stew I used to eat when I was a girl. I could use a fork. Thick and tasty. What's the meat in here?"

"Venison. Hollis got him a deer last season and we've been chowing down on the last of it."

"My compliments to the chef and the hunter," Ruby said. "You send a bowl of this to Campbell's and they're likely to give you a million dollars for the recipe."

Lillian laughed and Frances shook her head. She was glad someone else could see Ruby and respond, but why couldn't Frances bring out that warmth in her own mother?

"What did you think of the Company Store?" Lillian said. "They've done a good job, haven't they?"

"The building is just like I remember. But they've gotten the story wrong. Frosts my socks. It was all I could do not to interrupt that little girl who had the spiel memorized."

"What parts are wrong?" Lillian said.

"It would take me half the night to tell. All the things about the store and the owners doing this and that because they were so nice and cared so much. I got a different view. Being upstairs was the worst. The story about the third floor and what happened in that room. It's enough to make you want to picket the place."

"You mean about the massacre?"

"That's part of it." Ruby licked her lips and mashed her corn bread into the stew. She put a generous helping of pepper on top as a light shone behind them on the wall. A car door slammed outside.

"That'll be Charlotte," Lillian said, rising to get another bowl.

The girl swept into the house like a whirlwind and tossed her things on the living room couch. She had a large envelope and a square box with her as she approached Ruby. Charlotte looked like she was about to burst with anticipation. Ruby pushed her bowl back and Charlotte placed the black box in front of her.

"Remember this?" Charlotte said.

Ruby's mouth formed an O. She picked it up with both hands, wincing a little, and examined it. "The camera I got before I went away to school."

"Do you remember the last time you used this?"

Ruby looked toward the ceiling to retrieve a memory. "We took pictures of each other. So we could remember what we looked like. Bean put on my dress and . . ." Her voice trailed off and it seemed like memories were flooding. "I always thought the camera was lost. Will you look at this?"

"It even has your initials here," Charlotte said.

"It surely does. Well, I'll be."

"I found it in the bottom of a box at CCE," Charlotte said. "And I took it to the newspaper office. My editor is a camera nut. And he got to looking inside."

Ruby squinted at Charlotte. "Was there something in there?"

Charlotte nodded and pulled two pictures from the envelope. "Film. Unexposed and undeveloped." She placed the photos in front of Ruby on the table.

Ruby was clearly stunned. "There we are. And the favorite dress. And those are the shoes. Law, I never thought I'd see these pictures." She clasped a hand over her mouth, shaking her head at the images before her. "Look at us. Look how innocent we were."

"This is amazing," Frances said. "I can't believe the film lasted that long."

"Something tells me this is not going to make it into Marilyn's wall of photos," Ruby said.

"Not with the narrative they've been floating," Charlotte said. "Do you remember the day you took these?"

A cloud seemed to come over Ruby's face. "We were playing with the camera. My friend and I."

"Bean? Beatrice Dingess?"

"Mm-hmm. I don't think two people could ever care about each other more than we did. We were two peas in a pod from the day we met. Although to say we were from different sides of the tracks would be an understatement. My father and her father couldn't have been more different."

"So this proves there were shoes in that room," Frances said.

"Honey, I don't need a picture to prove that. I lived it. I suppose this picture will make them change their story, unless they tear it up."

"Bean was the girl killed in the massacre, right?" Charlotte said, studying Ruby's face.

Ruby took a deep breath and brought her hands together. "Part of the reason I wanted to come back—" she looked at Frances—"*alone* was to make peace with all that happened. I've been running from it since I was young. I thought I could just move on with life. Put the past behind me."

"You mean run from the feelings?" Frances said.

"Run from everything," Ruby said. "The feelings. The memories. Watching people die and not being able to do a thing. There's things that happened that I never even told your father. I've never told anybody. There are consequences to telling the truth."

"What consequences?" Frances said. "Mama, you haven't survived all you've been through to clam up now."

Ruby put the pictures down and moved her jaw back and forth, repositioning her dentures in thought.

"Maybe I can help," Charlotte said, scooting closer and ignoring the food her mother had put in front of her. "Let's go back to the day of the massacre. Can you tell us what you remember?"

Ruby stared at the uneaten stew as if the venison were tea leaves. "I remember a lot of clouds. Thick as smoke, hanging over the town and blocking the sun. In Beulah Mountain, we had to order out for sunshine, and on that day God was all out. Wet leaves on the ground. The two of us were in the apartment."

"You and Bean?"

Ruby was silent for what seemed too long, then nodded. "It was before I got on the train. And the train was delayed. That girl didn't have it right that I left in the afternoon before the massacre. The two of us had talked about going to school together. Her making the trip and staying at the boarding school with me."

"Why didn't she go?" Charlotte said.

"The Dingess family wouldn't let her. Her father wouldn't take charity."

"And your father?"

"He didn't think a mining town girl leaving with the daughter of the owner was a good idea. There were a million reasons it didn't happen. But there we were with the rain coming down, spending our last hours together. Waiting for the train whistle."

When Ruby paused, Frances reached out a hand and rubbed her mother's shoulder. The muscles there were tight. "Mama, do you need the medicine the doctor gave for pain?"

"Last thing I need is something that will knock me out. I had enough of that with those two I met at the gas station."

"We don't have to talk about this now," Lillian said. "You've been through a lot."

Ruby didn't speak. She just stared at the tablecloth.

"Mama, from what I gather," Frances said, breaking the silence, "you said coming back here was about forgiving someone. Franklin Brown told me that."

"I never thought I'd be betrayed by a man on the radio."

"It's not a betrayal to tell the truth," Frances said.

"I know. It's just my pride. I want to keep this to myself and deal with it between me and the Lord, but it appears he has other plans."

"Who do you need to forgive?" Charlotte said. "Is it Bean's father? The one who killed your daddy?"

Ruby narrowed her gaze at the girl. "I suppose he's part of it, though not in the way you've heard the story. All they're saying is so mixed up."

"Forgiveness is elusive," Lillian said. "I've had to deal with that regarding my husband. I was mad for so long it nearly ate me alive. I knew I had to forgive for my own sanity."

Ruby nodded. "The man on the radio—you probably don't hear him down here—he was talking about forgiveness as releasing somebody from the hurt they've caused. It's something you do where you let go of them and give them to God. And even if that other person who hurt you never apologizes or admits their wrong, you've done your part."

"That sounds like a wise man," Lillian said.

Ruby ran her wrinkled hand across the tablecloth. "Frances, I need to ask you something important. And now is as good a time as any."

"What is it?"

"I want to know if you can forgive me."

"Of course, Mama. You don't need to ask. I understand that coming here was important. I just wish you had—"

"No, I'm not asking you to forgive me for driving down here."

"Then for what?" Frances said.

"The reason I needed to come here and see all of this was what I did that day. And every day since then."

"Mama, I don't understand. What happened?"

Ruby pushed back from the table and tried to stand. Frances reached out to help, but Ruby put her right hand down and yelped in pain and fell forward, hitting her head on the table before she fell to the floor.

Frances tried to cushion the fall and Lillian and Charlotte were by her side quickly. Lillian got a wet washcloth and handed it to Frances, and she patted her mother's forehead.

"Mama, can you hear me?" Frances said.

"Just got a little woozy," Ruby said.

"Did you hurt yourself? Is anything broken?"

"I'm fine. Just get me up and into the bedroom. I think I need to rest."

42

Ruby stayed awake all night, trying to think. When she heard her father going down the stairs, she slipped out of bed and left Bean asleep.

She found her father rustling in the kitchen. "I'm not going to school," she whispered. "I'm not going on the train."

"Why are you whispering?"

"Bean came last night. Her mother is dead. I think Saunders killed her."

Her father's face turned ashen. "What are you talking about?"

Ruby explained what she'd learned and her father's eyes fell to the table. "I'm going over there. I want you to stay here with Bean and lock the door. Don't go anywhere."

"I'm not getting on that train," Ruby said. "I'm not leaving Bean like this."

"Stay here. Do you understand?"

She watched her father from the kitchen window. He ran across the tracks and through the woods the same way Bean walked home. When he disappeared into the brush, she made breakfast for Bean and herself, but the girl didn't stir. She must have been so exhausted from her ordeal the night before that she slept the sleep of the dead.

The town awakened slowly, coming to life with miners heading for the train that would take them to the mine. Those who had worked overnight got off the train so black with coal dust Ruby couldn't see faces. The men would wash and sleep and repeat the process in a few hours.

Her father returned, walking slowly as if he were carrying a heavy load. He stopped on the street beside the store and stood as if preparing for something. Finally he disappeared under the awning.

"Is she awake yet?" he whispered when he walked into the kitchen.

Ruby shook her head.

"Sit down. I need to tell you something."

Ruby sat dutifully and stared at her father. He seemed older now and tired, the skin below his eyes sagging.

"Bean's mother did die last night. The midwife was there cleaning her body when I arrived."

"What happened?"

"She was attacked, and that sent her into labor, and she died trying to give birth. The midwife didn't know how she was injured but neither she nor the baby survived. I'm sorry."

Ruby stared through tears that rimmed her eyelids. "How awful. It was Saunders, the flat-headed man."

"You don't know that."

"Yes, I do." She wanted to tell him what she'd heard, but she couldn't.

"It could have been Bean's father. A man who drinks can become violent."

"No," Ruby said, shaking her head.

"Listen to me. We have to be strong for Bean," her father said. "And we have to move on with your life as we have planned. That's the best thing—"

"I'm not leaving my friend," Ruby said.

Her father leaned forward. "The best thing you can do for Bean is go to that school and let me care for her. Do you understand? I'm going to see she has a place to stay. Maybe in time she'll come to the school herself. I don't know. But I'm going to see that she's all right and that those responsible for her mother's death are brought to justice. But I can't do that with you here. It's too dangerous."

"I can't get on that train today."

"Yes, you can. And when you do, you'll be telling her that everything is going to work out. Confidence. Strength. That's what she needs to see in you." He sat back. "It's not easy for me to let you go. I want you to stay too. But I believe this is the best path for us now. And I need you to trust me in this, Ruby. Will you trust me?"

Ruby saw something in her father's eyes that she hadn't seen before. What was it? Was it fear that made him try to convince her to leave? Or something else? Was it the kind of faith she had come to know in the little church, that said God was in control and was working out a plan for good? She couldn't ask him these things, but she decided it was so. She nodded and wiped her face.

"We're going to be at the platform this afternoon, you and Bean and me, when the train pulls in," he said. "I want you to be ready."

"All right," Ruby said.

43

The bed creaked as Ruby turned onto her side to look at the window. It was pitch-black out and a light rain fell, ticking against the pane. She pulled her covers up and now her head hurt along with her arm. The only light on was the lamp beside her bed.

"Are you sure you don't want to take one of those pills for pain?" Frances said.

"I don't want to get hooked," Ruby said. "Too many are on pills these days."

"Mama, you're not going to get hooked. It's just so you can sleep."

Frances unzipped her suitcase and took some clothes into the bathroom. A few minutes later she returned and turned down her bed and got in. "If you need anything, let me know. I'll be right here."

"Could you turn the light out?" Ruby said. "I can't reach it."

Frances got up and turned off the light and Ruby heard the springs creak in the other bed. There was nothing between them now but the space between the beds.

"It's been a long day, hasn't it?" Frances said softly.

"Longer than I can remember," Ruby said.

"I want you to know there's not an angry bone in my body about this. I'm just glad you're safe. Glad you're all right."

"But I'm going to pay for it when we get back, right? You're going to move me into a home or assisted living or whatever they call it."

"Don't worry," Frances said. "Jerry and I want to give you what you want. And if you want to live at home, we'll help you do that. Our goal is to make you happy."

"There's nobody on earth that can make me happy, Frances. Not you. Not Jerry. Happy is something I have to choose."

Frances sounded like she was smiling when she said, "Well, I won't argue with you there. I'll just say our goal is to help you. How about that?"

"That sounds right. And I appreciate you coming down here. Don't think I don't notice that you've taken off work and put your life on hold."

Silence in the room. The rain picked up and splattered the window. A flash in the distance and a roll of thunder.

"When you said you wanted me to forgive you, what did you mean?"

Ruby thought a moment and felt her chest rising with another breath. She closed her eyes and saw the room above the company store. And her friend.

"Bean was a mimic. She had a natural gift to imitate and it would like to kill you trying not to laugh."

"People in the town?" Frances said.

"Pastor Brace. Mrs. Grigsby in the store. She could imitate different miners and the way Coleman would walk up the steps. All it took was the littlest thing to get going and we'd laugh and laugh.

"Sometimes a smell or a taste will take me back there. Just a whiff of a barn with fresh hay or the venison stew we had tonight. Or something sweet. I pass a bakery and it reminds me of those days. And to think that old camera held on to those pictures all these years, just like I have."

The other bed creaked and Ruby figured Frances had rolled onto her side.

"What happened, Mama? What consequences are there if you tell the truth?"

"If I tell you, it changes everything. I think it's enough that I know. I'm not far from my grave, and if I take this with me, it'll be all right. I've dragged this secret around my whole life. I can carry it a little further."

"But you don't have to. Let me help you carry it."

Ruby shifted and felt pain in her wrist. She got situated enough to lessen the pain and realized this was how she'd lived her whole life, trying to get in some other position to lessen the pain. But it was always there because the break was always there.

"Maybe being here and knowing I can release myself from the obligation is enough. I don't think God would make me walk through all of that again."

"Maybe what you have to say will help somebody else."

"What I've got to tell can't help anybody, Frances."

Her wrist throbbed and eventually subsided. Her breathing became more even as she drifted off to sleep. In her dream, she returned to the store and the mountain. The whistle of the train was all she needed to bring her back.

44

Ruby's father walked Ruby and Bean to the train station and it felt like the march of death. Even the skies above seemed to sense the mood, clouds forming above them dark and thick. When the man at the station informed them that the train had been delayed because of a problem with the tracks, it felt like a reprieve. The girls celebrated when Ruby's father said they could leave her suitcase with the man and wait at the company store.

"But we'll have to listen for the whistle and make it down here pronto when it comes," Ruby's father said.

"When will that be?" Bean said.

"I hope the train doesn't come until next week," Ruby said.

"It'll be later," Ruby's father said. "We just need to listen."

After Bean had awakened that morning, she'd gone back to her house and retrieved some things. It pained Ruby to see Bean walk in with a pillowcase half-full of clothes and a few pictures.

"I brought these shoes of my mother's, too," Bean had said sadly. "I don't care that they're a little big on me."

"Are those the shoes that . . . ?"

Bean nodded. "Part of me wants to burn them. But I think I need to remember what she went through." She'd wandered to the dresser and picked up the train ticket. "Hard to believe this will take you so far away from here. Just a piece of paper's all it is."

When they got back from the station, Bean sat on the bed and stared at the floor. "I don't know what I'm going to do."

"We'll figure out something," Ruby said.

"There's no 'we' to it anymore. You're still going away, and I don't blame your daddy for sending you. There's nothing but heartache here. More heartache and death than you can shake a stick at."

Ruby remembered what her father had said about remaining strong for her friend. She had told Bean what she'd learned from her father and how hopeful he was that she would be cared for here. "I prayed for your daddy last night before you came. I asked God to help change him. Maybe this whole thing will turn his life around."

"I don't think even God could do such a thing," Bean said.

There had to be some way to take Bean's mind off of all the ugly things that had happened, Ruby thought, but there were so many it felt like a full-time job. Ruby knew what it was like to lose a mother. She didn't know what it was like to lose one so close who made desserts even when there was no sugar in the house. She also didn't know what it was like to lose siblings before they had ever taken a breath of life, a brother or sister that they'd tried to name. A life snuffed out before it began.

"Maybe my father will set up a spare room downstairs. And give you a job in the store."

"What kind of job?"

"I don't know—cleaning up or the soda fountain? You'd make some money and have enough to eat."

Bean frowned. "I don't think I want anything to do with this store. Your daddy is bound to leave and you know how Coleman and the others act."

"Things are changing. My father said. The mean things are going to stop."

"I don't know how he's going to stand up to those men alone."

Bean got a far-off look and stared out the window. The rain was coming down now like tears on the pane.

The sight sent a shiver through Ruby and it was all she could do to keep from crying. Finally she said, "It's not fair."

"What's not fair?"

"You having such a hard life and me with everything I need and then some."

Bean sat and put an arm around Ruby. "It's not your fault God gave you a nice daddy. You don't have to be ashamed of it."

Ruby set her jaw, determined to do what her father had asked. She walked to the closet and opened it. "All the clothes I need are in a trunk that's already at the school. The rest are in my suitcase at the train station. These can be yours now."

Bean's mouth dropped. "You mean it?"

Ruby smiled. "Take those overalls off and put something on. Anything you want. It's all yours now."

"My lands, I might have to get another pillowcase!" Bean stood and unhooked the overalls.

While she put on a dress, Ruby grabbed Bean's overalls and put them on. "I don't want you to ever forget our game and the fun we've had. And the fun we're going to have when we see each other again."

"I don't feel like playing right now," Bean said.

"You need something good to eat. That'll help get you in the mood." Ruby grabbed a pencil and paper and the two of them thought of everything from downstairs they could eat. She put the order on the dumbwaiter and sent it down. The two watched through the shaft until the motor stopped. Then they heard Mrs. Grigsby gasp at all that was on the paper.

"It's my going-away meal, ma'am," Ruby yelled down.

Mrs. Grigsby huffed and puffed. Twenty minutes later a tray was sent up and Ruby watched Bean eat hungrily. The window was open slightly so they could hear the train whistle, but the rain was coming steady now. Daylight was nearly gone.

"Where you reckon your daddy is?" Bean said.

Ruby went to the window and looked out. What she saw nearly took her breath away. "Isn't that your father coming this way across the street?"

Bean jumped up and joined her and looked through the rain. "Yeah, that's him."

"Is he drunk?"

"Can't tell. He's not walking funny." She stared through the water-streaked window. "There's something I never told you."

"I don't think I can take another surprise, Bean."

"Do you remember that day you came to my house and my daddy showed up? I heard him talking to my mama later. He thought there was something going on between your daddy and my mama."

"That makes no sense."

"Things don't have to make sense for him to believe it."

Bean's father ran through the rain to the company store entrance. Ruby rushed to the dumbwaiter and opened it, listening through the shaft. The man bellowed like a cow bawling for hay.

"That's him," Bean said. "And it sounds like he's soused."

"Mr. Grigsby is talking to him," Ruby whispered. "He'll get him to leave."

Bean went back to the window. "Yep, there he goes. Crawling back to wherever—wait! Is that your daddy on the street?"

"Oh no," Ruby said, rushing to the window, praying nothing would happen to her father. The conversation went on for a few minutes with Bean's father pointing at the store and yelling. Ruby's father pulled him under an eave, out of the rain.

"If something was going to happen, don't you think your daddy would already have done it?" Ruby said.

Finally the two parted and Ruby sighed. She heard footsteps up the back stairs, but her father didn't stop at the apartment. They listened as he continued, then heard a banging on the door above them.

"What do you reckon he's going to do?" Bean said.

"Maybe Coleman is up there," Ruby said. She moved toward the door. "You stay here. I need to see what's going on."

"No," Bean said. "I'm going with you."

"Stay here. I'll be back in a jiffy."

45

RUBY STARTS TO TELL THE TRUTH
BEULAH MOUNTAIN, WEST VIRGINIA
SATURDAY, OCTOBER 2, 2004

Ruby awoke with a start, the crack of thunder rolling through the hills like a coal train. At first she couldn't remember where she was and movement next to her made her think she might still be in Liz and Kelly's trailer. Lightning flashed and she saw Frances's face illumined, and it scared her. Then she remembered they were at Charlotte's house.

"Are you all right?" Frances whispered, throwing back the covers and sitting up.

Frances had always been jumpy, even as a child. Leslie had called her "Linus" because she always needed a security blanket. There didn't seem to be one big enough.

"Just had a bad dream," Ruby said.

"You want to tell me about it?"

"No. I can't."

Frances began to speak, then held back. Finally she said, "I think you came down here to deal with this, whatever it is. You hid that you wanted to come here from Jerry and me."

"I didn't hide anything you didn't want me to, Frances."

"What is that supposed to mean?"

Ruby was fully awake now. "It means I gave clues to people all along. But we'd rather believe lies than uncover the truth."

"I have no earthly idea what you're talking about, Mother. Are you sure you're okay?"

"See? You'd rather believe I'm demented."

"I'm the one who's asking you to tell me what's going on," Frances said, sounding exasperated.

"Keep your voice down. You want to wake up the whole house?"

"I'm tired of playing cat and mouse. I'm ready to hear your story. Forgiveness drove you down here. Tell me what that means."

When Ruby didn't speak, Frances put her head on the pillow and covered up. "Fine. Keep it to yourself."

Ruby sat up and fiddled with the light. When she couldn't find the button, Frances rolled over and stretched to turn it on. Ruby leaned over and picked up one of the shoes, holding it in front of her.

"That Marilyn at the store says there were no shoes on the third floor. Now you know that isn't true."

"Charlotte took me there yesterday and told me what she thought happened up there."

"What did she say?"

"That some women were required to visit the room in order to keep getting Esau scrip."

Ruby looked back at the shoe and traced a finger along the laces. "Remember that day I caught you playing with these?"

"I can't believe you remember that. It was such a long time ago."

"But you remember."

"You yelled at me and it nearly scared me to death. It was uncharacteristic."

"I apologize. You weren't doing anything wrong. It's just that I didn't want you to be near them. I was mad at myself for not keeping them out of sight. Nobody was supposed to know about these shoes."

"Why didn't you get rid of them?"

"I should have. But then I'd still have the memories. These were my one link to the past."

"That and your steamer trunk. I know this will upset you, but I went through it, trying to figure out where you might have gone."

Ruby waved a hand. "It's all right. I understand. It's just that I thought I'd come here, see what I needed to see, and leave. I didn't know it would turn into all this hullabaloo."

"I believe you, Mama."

"If I tell you what happened, I can't un-tell you. Once you know, it'll change everything."

"If you say that one more time . . . ," Frances said. Then she retracted it and apologized and Ruby got quiet.

"It kills me that you lost Wallace," she said. "It kills me I wasn't able to help you keep him."

"You should have seen him the other day," Frances said. "He was really concerned. He remembered things you'd said. Ways you had been kind. Like you and him doing dishes at Thanksgiving."

"I remember a lot of things I said to Wallace but I don't remember too many of them being kind."

"He seemed to think so."

Ruby put the shoe down and closed her eyes. "We played a game when my friend and I were together."

"You mean Bean?"

"She would dress in my clothes and I would dress in hers and we'd pretend to be each other. She'd try to talk like me and I'd try to talk like her. We laughed and laughed.

"That day it got serious. We were in each other's clothes when . . . both of our fathers showed up at the store. There were men up in the shoe room, making noise."

She stopped and put her hands over her eyes. "I don't think I can do this."

"Yes, you can, Mama."

Lightning struck nearby and a crash of thunder shook the house. Ruby sat up and teetered on the edge of the bed.

"Are you okay?" Frances said.

Ruby shook her head. "No, I'm not. I'm not because I'm not who you think I am."

46

Bean stood in Ruby's dress and wished she'd never become friends with the girl. It was easier not being at the apartment or hearing about the boarding school. Ruby had stored more stuff in her steamer trunk than Bean had ever owned. Bean was glad for the food because she hadn't eaten in two days, but she would need to chart a new course for her life now that Ruby was leaving. She grabbed another half sandwich and listened as the noise upstairs quieted.

Finally she couldn't stand it any longer and hopped into the dumbwaiter. The motor whined as she rose toward the third floor. When she stopped, she heard shouting and peeked out.

She would remember this scene the rest of her life. It was something imprinted on her brain so deeply that all she had to do was close her eyes to see the men in their suits and hats, the women's shoes on the wall to the left, Ruby's father standing with his arms folded and Coleman sitting in the cigar chair with a glass full of something.

"I will bring the sheriff in on this," Ruby's father said to Coleman, his face tight.

The other three men laughed and Coleman leaned back and crossed his legs. "You're more than welcome to get Kirby right now. Seeing as he has his own key. You don't think he knows what happens here?"

"Then I'm prepared to go to the law outside the town."

"Jacob, why are we having this conversation again?" Coleman said. "It's simple. Sell me your half. Move on with your life. This is no place for that pretty little girl of yours to grow up."

The door swung open and there was Ruby being pushed inside by Bean's father. He had a gun in one hand and Ruby in the other, her overall straps wrapped tightly in his hand. Coleman's men spread out.

"Is that you, Dingess?" Coleman said. "What brings you up here? You need some shoes?"

The men chuckled nervously, each of them reaching for their guns.

Bean's father cocked the gun until it clicked. "Keep your hands where I can see them."

Ruby's father moved toward him. "Judd, let her go."

"Stay where you are, Handley."

"Judd, we talked about this. I promised. You'll see justice. This is not the way to get it."

"Lead's the only language these men understand."

Coleman took a drink. "This is where gentlemen come to deal with their disagreements. So let's be gentlemen, and you put that away and we'll talk. That thing looks so old it was probably used at Antietam."

The others laughed and seemed to relax.

"Let me take Ruby downstairs," Mr. Handley said gently.

"Stay where you are," Bean's father said, and Bean could tell he meant it. One oily string of hair hung down in his eyes and he shook it back. From the sound of his voice, he seemed more determined than drunk.

He edged a step into the room, holding Ruby tightly in front of him. "I know what you done to my wife, Coleman. I've heard what happened with the others who came here asking for help."

"I don't know what you've heard, Dingess. Only thing we did was offer a helping hand to families down on their luck. I don't know why you'd hold that against us. Just helping some pretty wives. And some that weren't so pretty. We didn't discriminate."

Coleman laughed and the others joined as well.

"Judd, please let me take Ruby downstairs."

Bean craned her neck and saw the fear on her friend's face. She was trying to stand still, but her chin quivered from fright. Bean wanted to open the dumbwaiter door and wave Ruby over, but she sat paralyzed by her own fear.

Coleman put his glass down and rose. The hardwood creaked underneath his weight. He was an unusually tall and heavyset man. "Boys, what we have here is an unparalleled opportunity." He walked forward, showing both of his hands. "We have a disgruntled worker who feels used by the company. We have an uncooperative owner who has bucked us at every turn when we've tried to make changes. When we tried to increase the bottom line."

Coleman put an arm around Ruby's father and the man tried to pull away.

"Gentlemen, it's time to thin the herd."

A single gunshot exploded in the room and Ruby screamed. Bean jerked back in shock. Ruby's father looked at Coleman, then slowly fell to the floor.

Coleman leaned down. "I tried to tell you, Jacob. I tried to get you to sell but you—"

Another shot fired and Coleman fell. Bean's father pushed Ruby out of the way and opened up on the whole room. The other men reacted quickly and fired back. Bean covered her ears in the darkened dumbwaiter.

She couldn't count all the gunshots. They exploded together and then came the smoke and sulfur smell that wafted into the shaft and choked her. She coughed—couldn't help it. Any second she expected one of Coleman's men to open the dumbwaiter and fire at her.

There came a stillness like she had never heard. A quiet so great she could hear her heartbeat and feel the blood pumping. She waited for a noise, a sign that she could move. Surely someone would move in the room. Someone would rise and collect the guns or run for help, run for the sheriff.

And then she thought of Ruby. It was that thought that moved Bean's hand to the door. She slipped into the room and saw the second sight she would never be able to forget. A room littered with men's bodies. The one nearest her was staring, openmouthed, at the ceiling, a pool of blood widening beside him. Bean crawled past Coleman, whose hand twitched. She looked at the doorway and saw her father on his back, motionless.

"Ruby!" Bean yelled.

The girl's feet were sticking out from behind a chair next to the shoe rack. Bean moved the chair and looked down at the red stain in the middle of the overalls.

"It hurts," Ruby whispered.

Bean yelled for help. She screamed as loudly as she could, her voice echoing off the walls. She knelt and wiped her own tears away.

"It's okay," Ruby whispered. "I'm going to Beulah. Don't worry about me."

"No!" Bean said. "You're going to be all right."

Ruby reached out a hand and took Bean's in her own and said something, but Bean couldn't understand.

"What?"

"The ticket," Ruby whispered. "Take my ticket. Go to school. This is your chance."

Bean shook her head. "No!"

The train whistled in the distance. Ruby tried to speak again but there was blood in her mouth.

"Move out of the way," someone said behind Bean. She didn't recognize the voice at first, but when she looked up, she saw her father, a wound in his shoulder and one in his leg. He shuffled toward Ruby.

"You go on now," he said. "You shouldn't see this."

Bean stood and watched her father pick up her friend, her hair dangling. He limped through the door and toward the stairs.

"Where are you taking her?" Bean screamed.

"To the doctor," he said, stopping. He turned and looked at her, and in that moment Bean saw something she hadn't before. It was a mixture of fear and what she could only identify as love coming from him.

"Do like she said. This is your chance, Bean. Get on that train."

Bean watched him walk to the stairs. She expected him to lose his balance and fall, but with each clap of his shoes he made his way down.

Bean glanced back at the room. Five men lay dead or dying. And she had seen the whole thing.

47

FRANCES TAKES IN THE STORY HER MOTHER HAS TOLD
BEULAH MOUNTAIN, WEST VIRGINIA
SATURDAY, OCTOBER 2, 2004

Frances sat on the bed, unable to move. Unable to form a question about what she had heard. The event her mother had described was horrific. No one knew this version of the story. No one would dare believe it. And yet the one who stood to lose most by its telling was in the bed next to her.

"So you were Bean. And you became Ruby."

A rumble of thunder shook the windowpane.

"'Greater love has no one than this: to lay down one's life for one's friends,'" her mother said. "That's what she did for me."

"And your father?"

"I hated how my daddy acted when he got drunk. But on that day, I saw something in him. He looked right at me and instead of looking past me, he saw me. He carried my friend to the doctor when he could have run."

"He got her to the doctor?"

Her mother shook her head. "Ruby didn't have a chance. He knew that. But he tried anyway. I think he felt like he had to. Like it was his fault."

Frances leaned closer. "What happened after he left?"

"I went numb, like when you cross your legs too long and everything goes tingly? I watched him walk down the first few steps and then I went down to the apartment and saw the food still on the tray and the room started spinning and I got sick to my stomach."

"That makes sense, Mama. It was so much to take in."

Her mother sat up straighter, looking back and forth as if she were right in that room again. "I didn't know what to do. I couldn't think. How does a girl my age think through all of that?"

"You were probably in shock."

"That's what it was. Shock. You have to understand, I was raised in a place where you had to fight for every scrap of food. I can't tell you how many nights I went to bed hungry and so cold right down to the bone. Looking at people eating in the store and feeling like I was on the outside. Shoes with holes in them. And to get a chance to ride away from the pain and the memories . . . I had no idea what would happen, but after I was sick, I got to my feet and ran into the bedroom and put on my mother's shoes. Then I grabbed Ruby's ticket and went down the fire escape to the train platform."

Frances watched her mother's face in the dim light. As she described the scene and told more, she grew animated.

"I walked up to the train, committed to talking and acting like Ruby. I'd never been on a train before. A man was there and I remembered Ruby had left her suitcase. So I gave him my ticket and asked if he'd get it for me. He looked at me kind of funny and asked if I was traveling with anyone and I told him no. I said my father had made all the arrangements. That was my first lie, Frances. That was the first time I told someone a lie about who I was. And it got easier from there to not tell the truth. I thought for sure he would see through me, that he would kick me off that train and notice my hair was tangled and I didn't belong in that fancy dress. Instead he treated me like a queen. Took my suitcase and walked me to a room with a bed in it. I'd never seen such a thing. I never even knew trains had beds."

Lines formed on her mother's forehead. "After he left, I looked out the window. And there he was on the street."

"Who? Your father?"

"Yes. He was limping, and I could see bloodstains on his clothes. Ruby was like a rag doll in his arms. Her hair was hanging down and her feet were dangling. He was headed toward the doctor. And I thought, maybe I should stay. Maybe I should get out and help him carry Ruby. Maybe he'd survive and Ruby would wake up and be all right. But then two men came running up the street. One was Mr. Grigsby, the store proprietor. Next to him was the sheriff. He came around the corner and saw my daddy. And the sheriff yelled something and my daddy picked up his pace. And the sheriff pulled his gun. I banged on the window, but there was no use. The sheriff shot twice and he fell with Ruby underneath him. Right there in the muddy street."

Frances forced herself to breathe. "Why would he shoot him?"

"I don't know. Maybe he thought he was getting away. Or Mr. Grigsby said he had a gun."

It seemed more plausible to Frances that the sheriff wanted the man dead. Shooting him down like a mad dog on the road would save them the time and energy of a trial.

"I crawled in the bed on that train and cried and cried," her mother said. "The steward came and asked if I had seen what happened. I told him I had and he brought me something to drink. He was a kind man. He said to stay away from the window. No girl should see that kind of thing."

"So you rode the train to the school?"

"We got there late the next morning. The headmistress was there waiting for me on the platform. Well, she was waiting for Ruby."

"And she didn't question you?"

"Why should she? She'd never set eyes on Ruby. They just knew that there was a girl coming from a wealthy family and she'd be on that train. So they treated me like I was who I was pretending to be. And I'd spent the whole night crying and combing my hair to get the knots out."

Frances put a hand to her head. "All these years. Did Dad ever know this?"

Her mother shook her head. "I never told a living soul."

"So everyone thought you had left before the shooting. When did they let you know about . . . ?"

"That was the closest I ever came to being found out. I was waiting to hear word, thinking they'd send a telegram. Two days later, Mrs. Grigsby shows up at the school and I saw her walking up the steps. I thought maybe they had figured it out. But I guess since Ruby was dressed in my clothes and my daddy was carrying her, the sheriff assumed she was me. We looked alike."

"Didn't Mrs. Grigsby recognize you?"

"I never saw her. I hid in the basement and watched out the window all day. She finally left for the train, I guess. When I knew she was gone, I went to the office and told them I'd seen her walking in and that she had been mean to me in Beulah Mountain. I was scared. Do you see how the lies keep piling up? That's when they took me to the principal's office and offered me tea. He and the headmistress told me the news and I broke down crying. It wasn't an act. I was really crying about losing Ruby and my mother and the baby she was carrying. I was sad about Mr. Handley, too, and my own daddy gunned down on the road. They believed me.

"And now you know why I said forgiveness sent me down here. I needed to forgive myself for what I did. I've lived a lie."

"Mama, no one can blame you. You were a girl."

"I could have said something. I could have gone back and told the truth. I think of Ruby every day. I don't deserve her name or the kindness she showed. I don't deserve the inheritance either."

"What about Ruby's family?" Frances said. "Did they ever reach out to you?"

"An uncle offered to take me in. And a cousin on Ruby's mother's side. I bonded with the school. The headmistress adopted me, for all intents, and took care of me until graduation. I was like a sponge, Frances. I just soaked it all up and didn't have to worry about staying warm or finding food."

"And you went into the Navy?"

"Not long after I graduated. After Pearl Harbor, people wanted to do their part. I signed up and went to the Great Lakes Naval base and from there went to California. Nobody knew my story. I felt like I could escape the cloud hanging over me."

"What about the inheritance?"

"Ruby's father's half of the company was sold and that was put in a trust. A lawyer from Pittsburgh set it all up. They gave me a stipend to pay for things."

"But you never spent the money."

"I spent some, but you're right, I kept it put away. I suppose it's because I didn't deserve it. And now that I'm headed toward the grave, I don't want to keep it from you and Jerry."

"That kept you from telling the story?"

"Jerry needs it for his debts. He's counting on it. And I suppose you and Julia have plans."

"Mama, look at me. I don't care what happens to the money. I want you to be free."

Her mother's eyebrows rose. "I thought you would be upset. I thought you would tell me we needed to keep this quiet."

"I care so much more about you than what you'll leave behind. Do you understand that?"

Tears came to her mother's eyes. "I feel like somebody has lifted a thousand pounds from my shoulders."

Frances got up and hugged her a long time, then sat on the side of her bed, looking at her face, trying to reorient herself to what she'd learned. It did change everything.

"You should get some sleep," she said. But Frances and her mother couldn't sleep. They stayed up until dawn talking and asking questions and even laughing. For the first time in her life, Frances felt like she was getting to know her mother.

48

Charlotte was awakened by a crack of thunder that shook the house. She glanced at her clock, then heard voices in the next bedroom. Frances and Ruby were talking. Why they were up at this hour, Charlotte didn't know. Ruby had to be exhausted with all she'd endured.

She put her ear to the wall but couldn't make out what they were saying because of the rain on the roof and window. Her desire for a journalistic breakthrough was trumped by not being too nosy, so she rolled over and went back to sleep.

The next morning she ate a bowl of cold cereal as her mother brought in the soggy newspaper. As a child, she had watched commercials that featured the tiger from Frosted Flakes and the elves from Rice

Krispies, but her mother had saved the thirty-five cents per box and bought the weirdly named generic cereal from lower-budget shelves. One day she hoped she could afford a name-brand cereal.

She studied what Corky had chosen for the front page of the special edition and frowned.

"I thought you took some photos of Ruby at the store," Lillian said, talking as softly as she could.

"Those will probably be in the next edition," Charlotte said. "Wish I worked for a real newspaper that comes every day."

"You're doing fine. Have you heard anything from the résumés you've sent out?"

Charlotte shook her head, then tipped the bowl and drank the rest of the milk and wiped her mouth with her sleeve. "Mom, what are you going to do if Papaw sells the mountain?"

"I don't think there's any *if* to it, sweetheart. He has the contract and Coleman wants his signature before the board meeting today. That's what Juniper said."

"I can't believe he's going to move away and leave Dad."

"I don't think he wants to, but there's some things you have to do."

"What about you? You won't leave Dad up there alone, will you?"

"You mean move from here? I don't see a need. There might come a time when the dust and the machines make it too hard. They're supposed to leave the cemetery as it is, so I can still go set with him."

Charlotte stared at the spoon on the table, a drop of milk still in the curve. "Mom, how much do you know about Papaw?"

Lillian dried a dish and put it in the cupboard. "I know everything I need to know, I guess. Why?"

"I've looked into the birth announcements for when he was born—"

"You're not bringing that up again, are you?"

Charlotte gave her mother a sheepish look and ran water into her bowl. "I'm just curious. I get it from your side of the family."

"You ought to bottle up that curiosity and use it for something productive." Lillian slapped the dish towel against her leg. "You know how Hollis felt about his mom and dad. As far as he was concerned, they were his parents, period. He's never had any desire to go digging into the past. It would be like spitting on their graves. And you ought to respect his wishes."

"Don't you think he ever got curious?"

"And tell me why it matters. He had two good people who raised him like he was their own and he doesn't need to know any more. That settles it."

Charlotte put away the cereal box in the pantry and her mother wiped the table with a rag.

"I was going to do that," Charlotte said.

"Just go on. And don't bring this up with Hollis. You hear me? You're liable to get an earful."

"There's something else," Charlotte said.

"Oh, boy. What now?"

"Bean's mother lost her baby in October of 1933."

"So?"

"Every year since I can remember, we've been celebrating Papaw's birthday in October. What year was he born?"

"I don't remember," Lillian said too quickly to be believed.

"It was 1933, wasn't it?"

"Might have been."

"And there's something else," Charlotte said.

"How did I know there'd be something else?"

"Remember the fire at the Baptist church a few years ago?" Charlotte said. "Only a few of their records survived that were stored in the pastor's office in the back. One of them was a dedication record. The record goes all the way back to 1918. In 1933, in early October, there was a dedication of baby Hollis Beasley."

"And what's so all-fired odd about that? Every baby around here got dedicated."

"The list of people standing up front at the dedication has five names. There's Hollis, then Talitha and Edward, then the pastor, H. G. Brace. In all of the other dedications, only family members stand up there with the pastor and the baby. I can't find any time when a person outside the family stood."

"I'm assuming the fifth person wasn't a member of the family?"

"That's right."

Lillian put her dishrag under the faucet and wrung it out. She turned and put a hand on her hip. "All right, who was it?"

"Does the name Tilly Mae Farrel mean anything to you?"

Frances stepped out of the bedroom and closed the door. She had a strange look on her face and it didn't appear to be from lack of sleep. "My mother has something she wants to tell you."

Charlotte glanced at her mother, then at Frances. "Is this off the record or on?"

_49_

HOLLIS TAKES THE CONTRACT TO BUDDY COLEMAN
BEULAH MOUNTAIN, WEST VIRGINIA
SATURDAY, OCTOBER 2, 2004

Despite the sick feeling in the pit of his stomach, Hollis had rec-
onciled himself to sell. The closer he got to the deadline, the more
resolve he'd felt. And when his resolve rose, Juniper drew close in
a tender way as if all the change she wanted might not satisfy in
the end.

"I just don't want you doing this only for me," she said.

Who else would it be for? he thought. But he said, "It's the best
for both of us. I couldn't see that until now." She kissed him on the
cheek before he left. It had been a month of Sundays since that had
happened.

The attorney he asked to look at the contract suggested one minor
change that Buddy could initial. There was nothing holding Hollis
back now, but he put off delivering the contract until the last minute.

When Buddy offered to stop by the house, Hollis said no. He'd meet Buddy at the retreat center, the one named after Thaddeus Coleman.

Like life, selling the land was a process. Nobody signed a contract and saw machines rolling in the next day. In a way, that made it harder because once Hollis decided, he wanted movement.

He drove down the hill and spotted a hawk in a tree about eye level. He stopped the truck and watched it survey the landscape for food. He supposed there would be hawks in the town where they would move. Juniper had mentioned a new development with cottage-like homes being built in a bigger town between them and Charleston. He supposed he'd get used to that as well as this perch he'd known all his life.

Hollis drove past the Company Store and saw a gaggle of people that would grow later in the day. He looked for Charlotte amid the throng but didn't see her. He couldn't bring himself to stop.

The venue for the board meeting was near the hospital at a retreat center CCE had constructed two years earlier. The company called it good planning and forward thinking to put a sparkling building in the middle of nothing but hills. Most people in the county were barely scraping by, so it seemed like hubris at best and maybe a little mean-spirited to build it here, but the center employed a dozen people who ran it for retreats and weddings and other special occasions.

Hollis parked his truck and glanced at his watch. He was getting in under the wire, but it made him smile when he thought of Buddy sweating. He grabbed the envelope from the front seat and made the march of death toward the building. Two men in uniform stood in front and a couple of Coleman's burly guards were inside with earpieces and sunglasses. You couldn't be too careful these days, Hollis thought.

The security guard said the meeting was invitation-only. "I know. Tell Coleman that Hollis is here with the contract. He said he'd meet me in the parking lot."

The man got on the radio and Buddy strolled outside in his boots and pressed jeans and an uncharacteristically warm smile. He reached out a hand and Hollis shook it.

"You sign it?"

Hollis nodded. "There's a little change Homer made. You'll see."

"He told me," Buddy said. He took the envelope and put an arm around Hollis. "I'd like you to come inside. I want the board to see the good people of Beulah Mountain."

Something caught in Hollis's stomach and he pulled away. "No thanks."

"Hollis, I want them to see you," Buddy said, taking his arm.

"You want to humiliate me. You got what you wanted, now let me go."

"I've got a check for you inside. The bonus I promised. If you want it, come in."

Buddy walked away and said something to the men in sunglasses. When Hollis walked to the front door, they gave him a badge that said *Visitor*. Hollis was led to a second-floor hall surrounded with windows and a view of the countryside that took his breath away. People were dressed as casually as rich people can dress. There was a long table of food that would feed a few African villages. Shrimp on ice with dipping sauce and broiled shrimp and scampi and crab legs and crab cakes. Tenderloin and roast beef along with a fellow in a white chef's hat cutting it and serving people as they went through the line. Some sat and ate while others milled around and grazed like cattle. A man behind the bar wore a tuxedo-like outfit and poured beer or wine or mixed drinks.

A tinkling of glass got Hollis's attention. Buddy called them to order and asked everybody to find a seat. Hollis wandered to the back of the room and stood with his hands in his pockets. He felt like a stranger in his own backyard, like he'd wandered into a room of people ready to play musical chairs and he was the only person without one. He thought of slipping out to his truck.

"I have someone I want you to meet," Buddy said from behind a lectern, his voice booming through the room and reflecting off the glass. He pulled a gooseneck microphone toward his mouth and it screeched. "As most of you know, I've been talking with local land-owners. Well, *negotiating* is a better word."

A smattering of polite laughter.

"There's been one main holdout in Beulah Mountain, one man who dug in his heels ever since CCE set our sights on his mountain. His family is buried up there, along with townspeople. His son is buried there—some of you remember Danny Beasley from a few years back. You can read stories his daughter, Charlotte, writes in the *Breeze*. She graduated in the spring from Marshall and we're proud of her, as I'm sure her papaw is.

"Now the knock against me is I'm young and I'm no-nonsense. I believe in the bottom line, which is digging coal and making a profit for our shareholders. I won't ever apologize for that. But my thought is: if the company wins, everybody does. If CCE makes money, share-holders are happy. And people have work. They can feed their fami-lies. All boats rise when the tide comes in.

"I don't ever want to shaft anybody. My grandfather's name is attached to this company. I've spent some time down in the earth. I know how hard miners worked long ago. It's easier today, but still tough and dangerous. And I'm proud to be part of a company that values the work and the worker.

"That's why I want you to meet Hollis Beasley. He grew up on top of Beulah Mountain. He and his wife, Juniper, live there, and I can only imagine how hard it's been to come to the decision he's made."

Buddy held up the manila envelope and put it on the lectern. He took another envelope from his jacket and placed it on top. "There's not enough money in the world for his property. Who can put a price on the memories? But I'm making you this promise, Hollis, in front of everyone here. Our goal is not just to dig out the coal, but to make sure that when you come back to visit your loved ones on that knoll, you feel like you're coming home."

Buddy cleared his throat as if he were getting emotional. "And when it comes your time or Juniper's, there's a spot for you both on that mountain. That's my promise."

Someone began to clap and the whole room followed suit in a muted but warm expression. Several women wiped away tears. Hollis could see the leadership team at the head table—mostly older, portly men who leaned toward each other and smiled as if they were happy about making Buddy top dog.

Hollis saw through the flowery words and the homespun warmth because he knew Buddy was an extension of CCE. He had dealt with the company after Daniel's death and it had been the same flowery words with no responsibility taken. Buddy was a turkey vulture circling, waiting to pick at a fresh carcass.

"Hollis, I'd like you to come up here," Buddy said. "The floor is yours."

There was applause and Hollis glanced around the room and thought it was a generous but dangerous thing to do. Hollis could unload, just back up the truck and dump all he wanted to say. But his mouth went dry. He took off his baseball cap and scratched at his head and when people stopped clapping, there was an awkward silence.

"If you don't mind, I have something to say," someone said behind him.

Hollis turned and saw a commotion at the door. Ruby Handley Freeman stood there, backed up by her daughter and Charlotte. In front of them was a guard who was trying to corral them.

Buddy waved a hand. "It's okay. Let them in."

This looks interesting, Hollis thought.

50

RUBY AND BEAN GO TO THE BOARD MEETING
BEULAH MOUNTAIN, WEST VIRGINIA
SATURDAY, OCTOBER 2, 2004

Ruby felt butterflies in her stomach, but she had come too far to let butterflies stop her. She and Frances and Charlotte had a difficult time with the men at the door until one of them recognized her from the missing person report. It was ironic that she entered the room by proving she was who she wasn't.

Franklin Brown's words returned to her and walking into the room made her feel like a queen.

"You know me as Ruby Handley Freeman, the daughter of Jacob Handley. It's been more than seventy years since I set foot on Beulah Mountain. And I've never been to this place. I heard about the festivities and thought, at my advanced age, I ought to seize the day."

"Mrs. Freeman, we are tickled to have you here," Buddy said.

"Well, with what I've got to say, I probably won't ever be invited back," Ruby said, toddling toward the microphone. She reached the lectern and Buddy pulled the gooseneck down all the way and stepped aside.

"I apologize for my general dishevelment. I tried coming down here on my own and I ran into a little trouble."

Buddy retreated to the head table and sat. He smiled politely, though there was a crease of concern in his forehead.

"My daughter and I and Charlotte just came from the museum. Everybody is excited about the ribbon cutting you all will do later. The problem is the story they're telling is on the opposite side of the road from the truth. I'm here to set the record straight."

Ruby glanced at the head table long enough to see Buddy Coleman wipe his mouth nervously with a napkin. There was only one woman on the board and the way she scowled made Ruby think she would go along with whatever the boys said. It'd been an uphill climb getting here. And the hill was about to get steeper.

"Now, to be honest, I bear some responsibility for the confusion. And I'm not talking about incidentals like what cash register was in front or the fire escape that's not there anymore. I'm talking about an eyewitness account of the massacre."

This sent the room into a general tizzy with people abuzz and looking at each other and putting down their forks. Ruby let the buzz subside.

"I'll get to that in a minute, but first I have a confession. You know I inherited Jacob Handley's half of the mine when it was sold. The man who owned the other half is your grandfather, Buddy. And I've got some hard news about him."

Buddy stood. "I think we've heard enough."

"No, I don't think you have. I want the board to hear this story before they elect a new CEO."

Buddy set his jaw and looked back. The chairman, a heavyset

man with a drastically receding hairline, lifted a hand and signaled Buddy to wait.

"I've been told Hollis tried to get his neighbors not to sell. Charlotte showed me an article she wrote. He said this: 'What's so precious to you, deep in your heart, that you can't put a price tag on it?' And his answer was the land passed down to him. Is that right, Hollis?"

Hollis nodded and she smiled at him.

"Well, I understand that. Land is precious. But my answer to his question is not land—it's truth. Truth is like an old pair of shoes you lace up and tie tight and walk around in. My faith tells me that in the end, the truth will set me free, and I'm hoping it does that today."

Buddy signaled for one of the guards and the man moved toward the front. Ruby looked at Charlotte, who scribbled in her notebook. Frances looked concerned.

"If this is about the third floor of the company store, we don't need to hear it." The female board member spoke. "Marilyn at the museum mentioned that you have bought into those apocryphal stories we've heard. If that's what you've come here to reveal, you're wasting your time. There's no evidence that—"

"She has evidence," Ruby said, pointing at Charlotte.

Charlotte stepped forward and pulled an envelope from her purse and handed it to the woman, who looked at it as if it were a dead mouse. She pulled out the photographs and the chairman craned his neck to see them.

"I think the historical society will be interested in those, but I don't see what it has to do with our meeting," the chairman said.

"If you'll give me the chance, I'll tell you what it has to do with all of you," Ruby said. "And with the legacy of your company."

"I want her out of here," Buddy said to the guard. He lowered his voice. "And I want to know who let her in."

"I have evidence, too," Ruby said. "And not just pictures. I have these." She lifted a foot in the air as far as she could. "I wear these shoes for the women who couldn't speak of what happened to them there. I wear them for the mothers who went there because they couldn't feed their children. I wear them for the daughters who walked those stairs and closed the door of their hearts to what happened."

Buddy's face was as red as a teakettle ready to whistle. The room fell silent again until the chairman cleared his throat. He looked troubled as if some tunnel of his life were about to collapse. "I'd like to hear the rest of the story."

"Thank you. I'll cut to the chase. My name is not Ruby Handley. Ruby Handley is buried in a grave on Beulah Mountain. I saw it yesterday. My name is Beatrice Dingess. Some called me Bean. My father was the man accused of starting the massacre at the company store. But that's not true."

Ruby began the story in a flurry, describing it in such detail that even those who were skeptical were drawn in. She could tell by the steady gaze of the security guard that she had the whole room's attention, though Buddy's face looked tighter than a drum.

She told everyone the secret she had promised her mother never to tell. She told about the man who was sent to her mother before she gave birth. She described how she longed to hear the cry of that little baby, but she never did.

"You have to understand what it was like. The train was about the only thing that came in and out of Beulah Mountain. There wasn't a way out for people like me. And Ruby Handley came like a ray of sunlight. She planted here and I saw the love of God go to work. I saw a sheltered and frightened girl turn into a loving, giving person. And her daddy was the same. He saw what was going on and he stood up to Coleman the best he could. He wanted to pay a fair wage—he insisted the store lower their prices. And when he discovered what they were doing to the vulnerable women through the Esau scrip, he drew a line."

"Everybody knows there was no such thing as Esau scrip," Buddy said.

Ruby turned on him. "If that's what you want to believe, go ahead. Those of us who lived it know it's true. Those women and girls who wore the shoes from the third floor knew."

"Miss Ruby—I mean, Mrs. Freeman, what are you saying about the massacre?" the chairman said. "Are you contending Judson Dingess, your real father, did not kill the men in that room?"

"I was watching from the dumbwaiter." She turned to Buddy. "And don't tell me there wasn't a dumbwaiter because Ruby and I used to ride it up and down. My daddy came to the door, and yes, he had a gun. He was upset and maybe drunk. As they were going back and forth, it was clear Coleman had wanted to buy out Mr. Handley. Ruby told me he'd never sell. Coleman shot Mr. Handley. I saw it clear as day. From there it was a melee. Shouting and shooting and men falling like dominoes. The gun smoke was thick."

Ruby surveyed the room and everyone but Buddy was with her. She described finding her friend mortally wounded and their last words. And how her father carried Ruby down the stairs and into the street.

"You can think what you want about me. You can judge me for pretending all these years. But I watched the sheriff gun down my father in the road. And for weeks I thought somebody would figure out the truth. But nobody did. Now you have to decide what to do with the truth."

Silence filled the room. Finally the female board member leaned forward. "You're saying that Mr. Coleman was the father of your mother's baby and he knew that?"

"Yes, ma'am, he found it out. And as soon as he did, he sent a thug named Saunders to beat her up so she'd miscarry, I guess. But he went too far."

"And your father discovered this . . ."

"After my mother's death."

"How did he find out?" the woman said.

Ruby paused. "I told my mother's secret to my best friend. I think she told her father. And when my daddy saw him on the day of the massacre, they exchanged words. I can't help but think that's how he knew."

She closed her eyes. Someone shifted in a chair but other than that there was no movement.

"I will not let you impugn the memory of my grandfather," Buddy said.

"There was a report written by the sheriff," Charlotte said from the middle of the room, pulling a folded piece of paper from her purse. "I have the records. Mr. Handley was killed by a gunshot wound in the back. He had no other wounds."

She handed the page to the female board member.

The chairman folded his hands in front of him. "If this story is true, it casts a shameful light on—"

"It's not true," Buddy said. "I'll sue you for defamation."

"Sue me for whatever you want, sonny," Ruby said. "I don't have a reason to lie. I have every reason to keep this a secret and I won't do it any longer."

"She's trying to stop us from moving forward," Buddy said. "She wants revenge. And these tales of Esau scrip and the third floor have been fully debunked."

The female board member pushed back her chair, a look of determination on her face. "What about the baby? The child you say was fathered by Thaddeus Coleman?"

"I always pictured having a little sister," Ruby said. "But I was scared she'd get hurt and be cold and hungry like me. So I almost felt relieved when she died before she was even born."

"The baby didn't die," Charlotte said.

All eyes turned to Charlotte.

"What are you talking about?" Ruby said.

Charlotte looked down, then back at Frances, who nodded for her to continue.

"I'm grateful to CCE for my scholarship. You helped me learn how to dig for the truth. There were things about the massacre that troubled me. I went to see Miss Ruby . . . I mean, Miss Bean."

"I've been called Ruby most of my life. I don't see a need to change now."

Charlotte smiled. "All right, Miss Ruby."

"This is ludicrous," Buddy said, standing. "I won't listen any longer—and I would urge the board to clear the room so we can get back to business."

"Let her talk," Ruby said.

Buddy pursed his lips and stared at the board members. When he didn't get a response, he spoke in hushed tones with the nearest guard.

"Go ahead," the chairman said to Charlotte.

Charlotte turned to Ruby. "The midwife—you said you remember her?"

"Tilly," Ruby said.

"Tilly Mae Farrel. She was an older woman who lived in the camp and helped pregnant women. She died in 1952. I tracked down her family for . . . for a story I was working on. They're scattered across the country. Her granddaughter, Eunice, said Tilly lived with her family until she passed. I spoke with Eunice last week. She said her grandmother had a lot of stories. She said it would have made a good book.

"There was one story Tilly Mae told over and over because she was proud. She said she saved a baby's life once. The mother had been beaten and the child's life was in danger. So she whisked it off in the night. She gave the child to a woman who couldn't have children. She said she was in church the day that baby was dedicated."

"The baby lived?" Ruby said, whispering into the microphone.

"The truth affects everything," Charlotte said, smiling. "It'll take away your inheritance, but it will also give you a family you never knew you had." She looked back at Hollis. "It was a baby boy."

Ruby stared at him and suddenly saw a flash of her mother. His height and stocky build were from someone else, but his eyes had the same kindness she had seen in her mother's.

"Hollis?" Ruby said.

Hollis stepped forward haltingly, out of place in the room. He stared at Charlotte with a confused look or maybe it was anger. Ruby couldn't take her eyes off him. He walked to the lectern and only glanced at her. Then he reached out and grabbed the big envelope and looked at Buddy Coleman. "I've changed my mind."

"You can't do that," Buddy said.

"Watch me," Hollis said, and he walked out of the room.

51

Hollis walked into the house and tossed the contract on the coffee table. He heard Juniper rustling in the kitchen.

"Is it over?" she said.

Hollis waited for her to walk into the room. When she saw his face, she said, "Hollis, what have you done now?"

"Juniper, sit down. I got something to tell you."

She closed her eyes and muttered something. Juniper had only cursed a handful of times in her life that he knew of. One was when they were driving on an icy interstate near Nitro. Another was when she gave birth to Daniel. She'd cussed a blue streak, the nurse said, and Hollis was glad he hadn't been there to hear it.

"Do you trust me?" Hollis said.

"What kind of question is that?"

"I mean it. I need to know if you trust me or not."

"Of course I do. Unless you—" She saw the envelope on the coffee table. "Hollis, don't tell me you didn't sign it."

"I did sign it, but I took it back."

"Why would you do a fool thing like that?"

"You know that thing you said to me about making decisions? That it takes a crisis? Well, you were right. It takes a lot to get me to move on something. And I've decided this is where we ought to stay. I don't want to move. And if you want to know the truth, I don't think you do, either."

Juniper's eyes wandered across his face. "They're going to dig all around us. I'm going to get sicker."

"I don't think they're going to dig."

"Why in the world not? Coleman has every deed within five miles."

"After what I just saw at the board meeting—"

"You were at the board meeting? What are you talking about, Hollis?"

He tried to explain it all to her, what he had heard from Ruby, how the midwife had saved his life, and how he'd seen the sister he never knew he had and that he wasn't sure he wanted. But he got ahead of himself and Juniper stopped him several times asking clarifying questions.

"That Ruby woman is your sister?" Juniper said. "How can that be?"

He tried again but got mixed up when he explained the part about the girls dressing in each other's clothes. It was too complicated.

"And you walked out of there without talking with her?"

He slumped into a chair. "I couldn't take it all in. It says something about me that's ugly. I've never wanted to know about my kin because I had a mom and dad who loved me and that was enough. And now this whole thing stirs up a hornet's nest inside and I don't know what to do with it."

She walked toward him and put a hand on his shoulder. "Hollis, you are who you are. This story don't make no difference about what's in your heart."

"I'm half Coleman. How can you say it makes no difference?"

"Because it don't. I don't care if you got the devil's DNA. You got a choice in how to live. And what to do with what you know."

She rubbed his shoulders with both bony hands and it felt good. He relaxed a little and let go of some of the upset feeling in his stomach.

"What I don't understand is how this is going to change things about the mining and the sale of the land around here."

"Maybe it won't," Hollis said. "Maybe it'll go on like they planned. But I think something happened in that room today. I could see it on their faces. The board and the others there. Word of this gets out and the company will have to deal with it in the press. Something tells me we got another chance here."

Juniper stopped rubbing his shoulders and sat hard in a chair beside him. "Well, I never wanted to pack all of this up anyway. It'll be easier to die in the middle of it, I reckon."

"You're not going to die. The air's going to get cleaner. No more dust floating around. You'll see. I'm going to take you to that doctor Lillian keeps talking about down at the hospital. You and I are going to live out our twilight years and grow closer than we've ever been."

Juniper blinked hard. "You been drinking?"

"I've never been more sober. And I've never had more hope for this mountain. Things are going to change, Juniper. I can feel it."

"Why do you say that?"

"I see something I've never seen before. I see a change in here." He pointed to his chest.

Juniper looked at him and instead of shaking her head like she always did and saying something smart, she got up and held out her arms like a child wanting an embrace. He hugged her and kissed the gray hair on top of her head.

52

SIX MONTHS LATER, FRANCES RETURNS FOR A REUNION
BEULAH MOUNTAIN, WEST VIRGINIA
APRIL 2005

The day of the reunion was perfect, filled with sunshine and enough breeze to call it pleasant. Frances showed the caterer where to put the food in the Beasley house. Hollis had graded a bigger area for people to park, clearing a few trees and flattening out the uneven ground.

Jerry and Laurie drove over with the kids and Hollis took them fishing. Jerry and Hollis had struck up a friendship long-distance and they talked about the acreage and how much diesel Hollis's tractor used and important things like that. Frances was surprised that Laurie actually initiated a conversation with her.

Though Frances didn't want it to, her heart fluttered when she saw Wallace's car coming up the hill. Julia was with him and she waved excitedly. She hopped out, hugged Frances, and disappeared into the house to see her grandmother and to meet Charlotte for the first time.

"How was the drive?" Frances said when Wallace made it to the house.

"Good," he said. "Had time to talk. Look at the scenery. Feels like another country up here. Another world."

"It's pretty close to it," Frances said.

"Wouldn't want to see your mother drive these roads."

Frances laughed. "She doesn't. She's voluntarily given up her keys. She's looking forward to seeing you."

Frances tried to keep things light. She asked about Wallace's job and he returned the favor, asking if she had survived the tax season. They both got quiet and stared at the hills.

"A lot of changes in the last six months, huh?" Wallace said.

"Mm-hmm. For both of us, I hear."

He kicked at the dirt. "Yeah, it didn't work out with Carolyn."

"Is she okay?"

He shook his head. "She's got more work to do. We both do."

"Well, at least you saw the truth and dealt with it."

He looked at the knoll above the house. "How's Jerry taking all this? The financial end of things?"

"He swallowed his pride and got some help with the debt. I think admitting the problem was the start."

"It always is." Wallace sat on the wooden steps. "Julia told me Ruby's not going to lose her estate?"

"There's not a lot of precedent for what happened. The board worked things out to keep her and Buddy out of court."

"He's still with the company?"

"Not as CEO, but yes. I don't think he'll ever forgive Mom for speaking up and for what the company decided about Beulah Mountain."

"They're really going to leave this whole area alone?" he said.

"For the foreseeable future," she said. "Until somebody else gets in power, probably. But for now it's safe. Some still want to sell and CCE will honor those contracts, but many are staying. The news about the Company Store, as dark as it is, has attracted a lot of interest."

"It sure is a pretty unbelievable story."

Frances smiled. "I think people see their story here. The pain and brokenness. And it helps them make sense of their own. They soak in the horror and the beauty of it."

Wallace looked away.

"What?" Frances said. "You're thinking something."

"We don't like the pain very much, do we? Feels like death. But maybe things grow better in that kind of soil."

Frances reached out a hand. "Come on, I want you to meet Hollis."

53

RUBY AND HOLLIS HEAD FOR THE CEMETERY
BEULAH MOUNTAIN, WEST VIRGINIA
APRIL 2005

Ruby had slowed a bit in the last months, but no one could tell she'd had a broken wrist. It had healed completely, except for a knot on the outside, which she said she would use to hang her purse. She'd also felt a sense of healing by attending the trial of Kelly and Liz. She testified to what had happened to her and then appeared at their sentencing hearing to ask the judge to be lenient. She had learned, she said, that people responded better to love than vengeance.

She sold her house and the land in Kentucky in record time and bought a two-bedroom bungalow in Beulah Mountain near the spot where her family had lived. Hollis picked her up and drove her to her part-time job at the Company Store three days a week. She had become a local celebrity. Everyone who visited had to see her and her shoes.

Ruby had looked forward to the reunion for months, and seeing Wallace and Frances and Julia together was an answer to prayer. Not that everything was worked out between them, but she felt a sense of hope, and that was all she needed. *That's all anyone needs,* she thought, *just a little dose of hope.*

Hollis made burgers and hot dogs, and Juniper served some of the best pulled pork anybody had tasted. Ruby noticed a difference in the woman, more color in her cheeks and a livelier step. Hollis mentioned that she had been to a new doctor and Ruby wondered if it was that or just the lack of stress over having to move that had helped her. Maybe it was both.

Everyone had to try Ruby's green bean recipe. It was the hit of the picnic and she had to tell the story again of how her life had been saved as a child by those gifts from God.

The phone rang during dessert and it was none other than Franklin Brown, the pastor on the radio. Just hearing his voice and him calling her "Queen Ruby" again was enough to make her cackle with glee.

After the food was put away and the dishes done, Hollis built a fire and people gathered to roast marshmallows and tell stories. Ruby asked Hollis if they could walk alone to the cemetery and he went inside to retrieve a flashlight. He winded up not needing it for the walk up the hill because the fire gave them light and the moon was as bright as daylight.

They stood at the graves of Hollis's adoptive parents and Ruby dropped a single rose on each grave. "They were special people."

"Salt of the earth," Hollis said.

"Do you think they knew who your daddy was?"

"I don't know. They sure never treated me like anything but a son."

"They did a good job raising you."

"Tell that to Juniper."

Ruby laughed. "You are two peas in a pod, you and Juniper."

"I wish I could have met your husband. He sounds the same."

"I wish I'd had the fortitude to tell him about all of this. But I didn't. And I guess I won't complain."

"It's okay if you want to."

"People like to complain more than they like to do anything about it."

"You're right about that. It gives them something to do."

Ruby rubbed her wrist. "How did it go with Buddy? Your meeting with him was yesterday, wasn't it?"

"Buddy doesn't come to any more meetings with me. I think he's afraid you'll show up again."

Ruby laughed. "So who'd you meet with?"

"His lawyer. I guess we reached an understanding, if you can call it that."

"What kind of understanding?" Ruby said.

"Apparently he's been scared since October I might come after the Coleman inheritance. I contacted Homer Sowards and asked some questions a few weeks back—knowing that Homer and Buddy were tight with all the property sales around here."

"You knew he'd say something to Buddy."

"I thought maybe Buddy would come back to Beulah Mountain and face me like a man. But that didn't happen."

"What did the lawyer say?"

"He said if I'd let go of any talk of the Coleman inheritance, Buddy would work with the assessor's office to lower our taxes. I told him to make it the same for everybody around here and we struck a deal."

"I don't think Buddy fell far from the tree."

"I think he might have bounced up against it."

They wandered to the edge of the cemetery and Hollis turned on the flashlight. Ruby dropped a rose at her mother's grave, then put one on her father's. At the head of the graves was a new stone with their names and the dates of birth and death.

"Tell me about our mother," Hollis said.

"I've told you about all I can remember. And I've told Charlotte the rest."

"I don't want to wait for Charlotte to write a book someday. Pick something."

Ruby sighed. "I don't like to think of the bad times. I like to think of her in the kitchen baking or just sitting in the rocking chair humming some hymn we'd sung on Sunday."

"'Dwelling in Beulah Land'?"

"Mm-hmm. That was her favorite. She would have loved to take you to that church and have you dedicated."

"I've been thinking about going back," he said.

"I was hoping you would. I've found it to be life-giving. There's some busybodies, but most are good people. We could use another bass in the choir."

"That's not going to happen. I didn't get my mother's voice like you did."

Ruby took her final rose and moved to the last grave. Another new stone stood above it. Ruby's name was there with her birth and death dates. Underneath were the words *Greater love has no one than this: to lay down one's life for one's friends.*

Far away, Ruby heard an old piano and saw two girls tripping through the woods toward doubt and fear and things of earth.

They stood together in silence, with Hollis training the light on the stone. Ruby heard something moving in the brush by the edge of the cemetery and Hollis pointed the light and there were two eyes gleaming, caught in the beam.

"Would you look at that," Hollis whispered.

"Deer know things people don't," she said. "I've believed that all my life."

The deer sniffed at the air and seemed transfixed by the light. Then it darted into the forest.

Hollis took Ruby's hand and they walked together down the mountain.

A NOTE FROM THE AUTHOR

I suppose I write to understand the world. I write to understand those who came before. Several things helped bring this story to life. The first was a photo of my father in a southern West Virginia coal camp, sitting next to his brother. I could have picked them both out of the picture because of my father's mouth and his brother's stoic gaze. Even at a young age their personalities were imprinted.

The second thing that sparked this story came from the words of my mother. Growing up in the Depression, in a place called Campbell's Creek, West Virginia, left a mark on her life she never forgot. I've asked several times if she would like to go back, to walk around the place where she grew up, and she's declined and not politely. The memories were too hard.

Several years after my father died, this story bubbled to the surface. To be honest, it was partly because she was driving and the family was concerned she was going to hurt herself, someone else, or both. (She drives a Buick, not a Town Car.) During the struggle, I saw the seed of a modern-day story that could reach through the years.

Then I came across a story about a company store museum in West Virginia and claims about the Esau scrip. Women of the era reported that sexual abuse occurred in some mining communities.

These stories of exploitation have been challenged by historians, but the stories made me wonder.

There is one more element that brought things together. I host a radio program called *Chris Fabry Live*. I've noticed, through the years, that many callers who are up in years will confide, with the right prompting, some difficult thing that happened years ago that they've never revealed to anyone. I've always believed this to be a great honor, to be entrusted with another person's past and hurts, but it is also a weight. As callers reveal themselves, I hear it in their voices. There is something taken from them in the telling, a load they have carried for decades. I can sometimes feel the removal of that thing they lay down in the phone call, and I often wonder why it took so long to put it there and if someone they know and love will help them move forward.

Then I look at my own life and the things I am carrying, things I've never told a soul, and the way those things hold me back from those I love. It is my hope that this story will remove some weight for you, that it will give you permission to allow some burden to be lifted so that there can be healing and wholeness and a lightness to your step, no matter how old or young you are.

I give thanks to my mother and father, their parents, and those whose stories have been handed down. To the people of West Virginia, who quietly go about life without fanfare or the need for it. For my wife and children, of course, who put up with me climbing the stairs humming a hymn they've never heard. For Karen Watson, Stephanie Broene, and the fabulous Sarah Rische, who take my words and help me rearrange them so they make more sense.

Turn the page for a preview of

THE PROMISE *of* JESSE WOODS

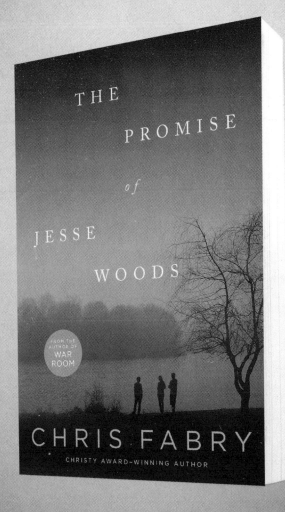

Available now in bookstores and online.

CP1083

Chapter 1

SUNDAY, OCTOBER 7, 1984

The elevated train clacked outside my apartment, meandering on its predetermined path through Chicago. Beyond the tracks loomed the Cabrini-Green housing project, where Dantrelle Garrett lived. Dantrelle sat on my couch tossing a weathered baseball into my old glove, watching the final game of the NLCS between the Cubs and Padres.

"Who's that?" Dantrelle said, pointing at a picture on my bookshelf.

"My brother and me. That was a long time ago."

He studied the photo. "You're not from around here, are you?"

It was the first time in the three months since I'd met Dantrelle that he had asked anything about my background. I took it as an invitation.

"I grew up in Pittsburgh, then moved to a little town in West Virginia."

"Where's that?"

"A long way from Cabrini," I said.

"Do you love you mama and daddy?"

"Sure."

"Then how come you don't have a picture of them?"

"I do, in an album somewhere."

"If you love somebody, they ought to be on top of the shelf."

I shrugged.

"How come you moved to Chicago?"

These were penetrating questions from an eight-year-old kid, but they grow up quickly in the projects. I told him about my schooling, how I had majored in theater and minored in counseling, but his eyes glazed.

"You want popcorn?" I said.

Dantrelle nodded and I pulled out my biggest pot and heated the oil. The smell of the popcorn and drizzled butter triggered a memory, but I pushed it aside and sat beside Dantrelle.

"When I was a kid, I loved the Pirates. The Pirates were my life. But we moved to this town where everybody rooted for the Reds. And the Pirates and Reds were rivals."

"Like the Cubs and the White Sox."

"Yeah, sort of. Except they were in the same league."

Dantrelle shoved a handful of popcorn in his mouth and butter dripped from his chin. I handed him a napkin and he put it on his lap.

"You think the Cubs are going to win?" he said, ignoring my story.

It had been a phenomenal year to be a Cubs fan. Every game on channel 9. Harry Caray and Steve Stone and "Jump" by Van Halen. Sutcliffe and Sandberg and Cey.

"Yeah, I think they will. No way the Padres win three in a row."

It was disorienting to hear Don Drysdale, a lifelong Dodger, describe the game instead of Harry Caray. The Cubs had won the first two at home and lost the next two in San Diego.

In the bottom of the seventh, my phone rang and I almost let it go, thinking it might be my mother. But I picked up the cordless handset just as a ground ball rolled through Leon Durham's legs and into right field. Dantrelle cursed. The Padres evened the score at 3–3.

"Matt?" a voice said with a familiar twang.

"Who is this?" I said.

A chuckle on the other end. "A voice from your past."

"Dickie?" I said. Keith Moreland fired the ball to the infield, the Cubs' curse alive. "How are you?"

"Lookin' for a breakthrough," he said, and his words brought back every bittersweet thing from my youth. I had lost touch with Dickie. After high school I had ripped the rearview off my life.

"You're probably going to see a breakthrough sooner than the Cubs. You watching this game?"

"I was never into baseball."

I closed my eyes and saw the hills and Dickie's bike and trips to Blake's store.

Dickie Darrel Lee Hancock was the son of a white mother and an African American father. That would have been a hardship anywhere in 1972, but it was a knapsack full of rocks on his forced march through his childhood in Dogwood. Dickie lived with his mother in a garage apartment on the outskirts of town, and it always seemed he was outside looking in. I guess that's what drew the three of us together. We were all on the outside.

"How did you get my number?" I said.

"Called your parents, PB."

PB. I hadn't been called that in years and the sound of it warmed me.

"They said you don't have much contact with the past."

"That's not true," I lied.

"Took me a while to wrangle your number from them. I suspect they didn't want me to call because of the news."

I stood and touched Dantrelle's shoulder. "I'll be right back." I stepped out of the apartment into the hall and the door closed behind me. "What news is that?"

"Jesse's news."

Her name, and Dickie saying it, sent a shiver through me. I'd been waiting for this. I'd had a foreboding feeling for years. "Is she all right? Did something happen?"

"She's engaged, Matt. The wedding is Saturday."

"This Saturday?"

"Yeah. I just heard about it or I would have tracked you down sooner. My mama told me."

I walked down the hallway to a window that allowed a clear view of the el tracks and the specter of the housing project. From my building east was a thriving, churning city. A block west, past this Mason-Dixon Line, was another world. It reminded me of Dogwood.

"Who's she marrying?"

"What's that noise?" Dickie said, avoiding the question.

I paused, not hearing anything, then realized the train was passing. The open window let in not only the heavy autumn air but the clacking sound track of my life.

I told him about the train, then asked again, "So who's the lucky guy?"

"Earl Turley."

My stomach clenched. I couldn't speak.

"Yeah, I can't believe it either," Dickie said to my silence. "I know how you felt about her."

"Wow," I said. "I appreciate you telling me."

Dickie paused like there was more. "Matt, your dad is officiating."

His words felt like a dagger. "Well, we were never on the best of terms when it came to Jesse."

"I get that. I know how they felt about her too."

"Are you going to the wedding?" I said.

"Wasn't invited."

"You didn't answer the question."

"That's not the question, Matt. The question is, what are you going to do?"

"Do?" I said. "It's a little late in the game to do anything. Jesse has a mind of her own."

"Yeah, but you were the one she turned to when life got hard. Maybe it's not too late."

"If you're talking romance, Jesse never felt the same as I did."

"That's not true."

"What are you talking about?"

"You don't know everything about her. I know she confided in you, but there are some things . . . Look, it's none of my business. I thought I'd call and let you know."

"Wait, you know something. You remember something."

Dickie sighed. "I talked with her a couple of times. After you left for college. She told me things she regretted. Decisions she made. She made me promise to keep quiet about them. But she must've figured I would be the last person to tell you anything. I guess I'm breaking a promise even making this phone call."

"Which is something Jesse would never do," I said. Though there was one promise she was breaking by marrying Earl, and I couldn't shake that fact. Dickie was privy to many of the secrets between Jesse and me, but not all of them.

There is magical thinking a child develops when he believes the world revolves around him. He begins to think he has power to control life's events. I'd always blamed myself for the 1972 Pirates. If I hadn't left Pittsburgh, things would have turned out differently. A butterfly on the other side of the world flapping its wings. A child in a suburb praying for his team. I had grown out of that mind-set by moving to Chicago and growing up, but something about the memory of Jesse and what she had done, what I had forced her to do, made me wonder if I could prevent another tragedy in her life.

Dickie broke the silence. "Do you ever think of what happened? Do you ever think of her?"

"Sometimes," I whispered, and the words began to flow. "Sometimes I smell woodsmoke or hear crickets at night and I'm back on the hill. It's all there, Dickie. All trapped inside like fireflies ready to rise."

"Riverfront?"

I smiled. "Yeah. We had fun, didn't we?"

"Remember the horse?" Dickie said.

"That was our first secret."

"What about Daisy?"

Daisy Grace. I could see her chubby face and a fistful of daisies held behind her, and the ramshackle house on the side of a hill that hung like a mole on the face of God.

"I remember it all, Dickie."

"Yeah, I do too."

"Especially the parts I try to forget."

He told me about his job and what he'd done after high school, but I couldn't hear his story for the memories he had stirred. I thanked him for calling.

"I'll say this, PB: I know it's been a long time and I don't know if you're seeing anybody, but I think you owe it to her to go back. You owe it to yourself."

"What about Earl?" I said. "You going to provide backup?"

"You're a bigger man than him, Matt. You've always been bigger than you thought you were."

His words stung my eyes. "Dickie, I'm sorry. I've never been able to tell you how sorry I am that—"

"You don't have to apologize. We were kids. I've thought about calling you and patching things up a hundred times. I was wrong to hold it against you in the first place."

"Thank you for saying that."

When I returned to the apartment, Dantrelle looked like he'd been gut-punched. The Cubs hadn't been to a World Series since 1945. Hadn't won since 1908. And with Goose Gossage throwing BBs, it wouldn't happen this year. Maybe if Jim Frey had relieved Sutcliffe, things would have turned out differently.

The old pain returned as I watched San Diego celebrate. Steve Garvey flashed his million-dollar smile and Gossage hopped around the field like a kid who had stolen candy from a general store. Bob Dernier and Jody Davis and Don Zimmer looked back in anguish. It was the end of a season and the only consolation was there would be next year.

"If they had played three in Chicago, we would have won," I said.

"Why didn't they?" Dantrelle said.

"Just the way it works. But the commissioner said if the Cubs had made the World Series, they'd have lost home-field advantage because they don't have lights."

"That's not fair."

"Yeah, well it was all about money. And life isn't fair. Especially when it comes to the Cubs."

As Dantrelle got his jacket, I took my old glove with faded words and held it to my face. The faint leather scent swirled warm, rich memories like fly balls in a summer sky. I returned the glove to a plastic bin in the apartment's only closet. Pictures lay scattered like dry leaves among the papers and playbills. The three of us, sweaty and smiling and spitting watermelon seeds.

"Who's that?" Dantrelle said, pointing at a Polaroid of Jesse sitting on a picnic table and holding a cat.

"A friend of mine from a long time ago." At the bottom of the box was a ticket. Reds vs. Pirates, July 1972.

I got out the yearbook and paged through until I found her. She stared at something beyond the camera. Her hair was too long and cut uneven and shadowed her eyes. The photo was a black-and-white, but I could see the emerald blue, her eyes like an ocean. Closing my eyes, I heard her laugh and her desperate cry for help in the year I discovered my heart.

People say you can't know love at such a young age. Maybe it wasn't love. But it was close. The longer I stared at Jesse's face, the more my heart broke for her and what had happened. I thought I had put all of that behind me, though. I had moved on with life, but one phone call had grabbed me by the throat.

"Can I watch some more TV while you look at this stuff?" Dantrelle said.

I apologized and put the bin back. "Dantrelle, I might have to take a trip. That would mean we couldn't meet this week."

His eyes looked hollow as he shrugged.

"Maybe I could ask Miss Kristin to help with your math."

He brightened. "I like Miss Kristin. You two going to get married?"

I tried to smile and shook my head. "I don't think that's going to happen."

"Why not?"

"That's a long story I'll tell another day."

A week earlier Kristin, a flaxen-haired beauty who attended a nearby Bible school and mentored young girls at Cabrini, had sat across the table from me at Houlihan's to splurge on an early dinner. I could tell there was something wrong before our salads arrived. As tears came, she said she cared deeply for me but that we couldn't go further.

"I think I just want to be friends," she said.

"What does that mean? That I'm not good enough for you?"

She shook her head. "No, you're a great guy. I see how much you care about the kids and how much you want things to change. But it feels like . . ."

"It feels like what?"

"Like you want to throw on a Superman cape and run to the rescue. I can't fix what's wrong at Cabrini. And neither can you. We can help some kids, maybe. We can make a difference. But it feels like you're doing all of this in your own power."

Her words stung because I could see Kristin and me together. I wondered who had gotten to her in her dorm and talked about me. Of course, whoever had pointed out the spiritual mismatch was right. She was a lot further down the road of faith. At times, it felt like I had taken an exit ramp miles earlier. So we agreed to part as friends and not let our relationship harm the work we were doing. It was all smiles and a polite hug while inside, the part of my heart that had come alive as I got to know her shattered.

I picked up the phone now and dialed her dorm. Someone answered and Kristin finally came to the phone.

"Hey, I have a favor to ask," I said, extending the antenna. "I need to take care of some stuff at home—but Dantrelle is counting on me this week. Do you think you could meet with him? I can't be back by Tuesday."

"Sure. I'm over there that afternoon anyway."

I gave Dantrelle a thumbs-up. "He just smiled at that news."

"He's with you?"

"We were watching the Cubs lose."

"Poor Cubs. So what's up? Is someone sick at home?"

"It's complicated. Maybe I'll have the chance to explain it someday." *If you give me another chance.*

"Well, tell Dantrelle to meet me at the ministry office."

"Thanks for doing that, Kristin."

I left a message with the coordinator at the counseling center, explaining as little as possible about the trip and leaving my parents' phone number in case someone needed to reach me. Then I walked Dantrelle home and up the urine-laced concrete stairs to his apartment. His mother came to the door, wild-eyed and unkempt. She grabbed him by the shoulder without speaking to me, and Dantrelle waved as he was hustled inside and the door shut.

I took the stairs two at a time and moved away from Cabrini, thinking of Jesse and her bad decision. If she said, "I do," that was it. She would. I had to do something to change her mind and keep her from throwing her life away. I had to help her see the truth. And though I didn't want to admit it, didn't want to open the door to even the possibility, something inside told me there might still be hope for us, even after all the years and distance.

I threw some clothes in a gym bag and set my alarm. Then I lay in bed, listening to the sounds of the city, knowing I wouldn't sleep. Dickie was right. I owed it to Jesse to make one more attempt. And before she walked the aisle that felt like a plank, I owed it to myself.

Well before midnight, I hopped in the car and headed toward the expressway, then south toward Indiana and beyond to my childhood home.

ABOUT THE AUTHOR

CHRIS FABRY is an award-winning author and radio personality who hosts the daily program *Chris Fabry Live* on Moody Radio. He is also heard on *Love Worth Finding, Building Relationships with Dr. Gary Chapman,* and other radio programs. A 1982 graduate of the W. Page Pitt School of Journalism at Marshall University and a native of West Virginia, Chris and his wife, Andrea, now live in Arizona and are the parents of nine children.

Chris's novels, which include *Dogwood, June Bug, Almost Heaven,* and *The Promise of Jesse Woods,* have won three Christy Awards, an ECPA Christian Book Award, and a 2017 Award of Merit from *Christianity Today. Under a Cloudless Sky* is his eightieth published book. His books include movie novelizations, like the recent bestseller *War Room*; nonfiction; and novels for children and young adults. He coauthored the Left Behind: The Kids series with Jerry B. Jenkins and Tim LaHaye, as well as the Red Rock Mysteries and the Wormling series with Jerry B. Jenkins. Visit his website at www.chrisfabry.com.

DISCUSSION QUESTIONS

1. Ruby and Bean are introduced as friends whose hearts beat as one. Who is the best friend you've ever had? What made—or makes—that relationship so special? What drew you together?

2. Frances and Jerry face the difficult milestone of beginning to make decisions for their mother—in particular, when to take away her car keys. Are their concerns valid? How could they have handled the situation differently?

3. Hollis feels torn between two promises: his vow to his parents to keep their land and his wedding vows to Juniper, who wants to sell and move away. Do you identify with his struggle? How would you have advised Hollis under these circumstances?

4. Frances is described as someone who "saw the glass half-empty and suspected the water in the bottom was contaminated." She always fears the worst—and part of her worst-case-scenario thinking is realized in what happens to Ruby. In what ways do you relate to Frances's tendency to worry? Does her outlook change by the conclusion of the story? How do you think she will live as she moves forward?

5. What drives Charlotte to uncover the true history of the Beulah Mountain mine, and to track down Ruby? Are her methods justified, or does she cross a line?

6. Ruby's children worry that she's too quick to trust strangers. Are their fears justified? Is Ruby's faith in people admirable or dangerous?

7. Why does Ruby takes the old shoes with her on her trip? What makes her wear them? In her place, would you have kept the shoes all those years or tossed them?

8. As she tries to figure out where Ruby has gone, Frances has to acknowledge how little she really knows about her mother. Do you think it's possible for children to truly know their parents? Was there a time when your own parents' actions surprised you? Have you ever discovered stories or secrets from their past that changed how you viewed them?

9. For most of her life, Ruby keeps the secrets of her past to herself. How might her life, and her relationships, have been different if she'd have revealed more of her story sooner?

10. Although Hollis doesn't think he's heard from God in a long time, he makes one last desperate plea. Do you think God answered? Have you ever felt that God was silent at some point in your life? If so, how do you view that experience now?

11. Young Ruby struggles to understand the inequalities of life, asking, "Why do some have it good and some have it bad?" Bean answers, "Some say it's the luck of the draw. Some call it God's will. I think it's somewhere in the middle. You got to take the good with the bad." What do you think of her perspective? When have you compared your circumstances

to others', either favorably or unfavorably? How do you make sense of life's seeming unfairness?

12. Both Jacob Handley and Hollis Beasley try to take a stand against the wrongs they witnessed from the mining company. How does each man succeed or fail? What more do you think they could have, or should have, done?

13. As the story unfolded, what came as the biggest surprise? What twists did you suspect before they were revealed?

14. At the meeting with Beulah Mountain landowners, Hollis asks, "What's so precious to you, deep in your heart, that you can't put a price tag on it? . . . Is there anything in this life that would make you draw a line in the sand and say, 'You can come this far but you can't come no farther'?" How do you respond to that question?

also by
— CHRIS FABRY —

DOGWOOD

Small towns have long memories, and the people of Dogwood will never forgive Will Hatfield for what happened. So why is he coming back?

JUNE BUG

June Bug believed everything her daddy told her until she saw her picture on a missing children poster.

Christy Award finalist

ALMOST HEAVEN

Some say Billy Allman has a heart of gold; others say he's odd. Sometimes the most surprising people change the world.

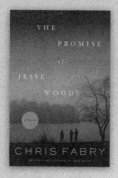

THE PROMISE OF JESSE WOODS

Years after the most pivotal summer of his adolescence, Matt Plumley returns to Dogwood and to memories of one fateful night, determined to learn the truth behind the only promise his first love, Jesse Woods, ever broke.

NOT IN THE HEART

When time is running out, how far will a father go to save the life of his son?

BORDERS OF THE HEART

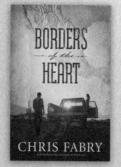

When J. D. Jessup rescues a wounded woman, he unleashes a chain of events he never imagined.

Christy Award finalist

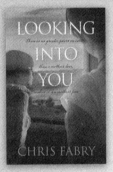

EVERY WAKING MOMENT

A struggling documentary film-maker stumbles onto the story of a lifetime while interviewing subjects at an Arizona retirement home.

LOOKING INTO YOU

As Treha Langsam sets aside the search for her birth mother, Paige summons the courage to reach out to her daughter, never dreaming her actions will transform them both as she faces a past she thought she'd laid to rest.

THE TREHA COLLECTION: EVERY WAKING MOMENT / LOOKING INTO YOU

An e-book–exclusive collection, these novels will introduce you to the unique gifts of Treha Langsam.

Reading group guides available in each book or at www.bookclubhub.net.

CP1092

TYNDALE HOUSE PUBLISHERS IS CRAZY4FICTION!

Fiction that entertains and inspires

Get to know us! Become a member of the Crazy4Fiction community. Whether you read our blog, like us on Facebook, follow us on Twitter, or receive our e-newsletter, you're sure to get the latest news on the best in Christian fiction. You might even win something along the way!

JOIN IN THE FUN TODAY.

 www.crazy4fiction.com

 Crazy4Fiction

 @Crazy4Fiction

FOR MORE GREAT TYNDALE DIGITAL PROMOTIONS, GO TO WWW.TYNDALE.COM/EBOOKEXTRA

CP0021